"*Tragic, romantic, full of heartbreak and hope,* The Plan *will sweep you off your feet. It's a tender story of love and loss and one woman's discovery of her untapped courage. Claire Matthews, the novel's infinitely relatable heroine, comes to understand that every life comes with its own set of challenges, but by trusting that she is part of a larger plan, she can find her voice and the strength to love again.*"

—MELISSA DeCARLO, *author of* The Art of Crash Landing

ALSO BY KELLY BENNETT SEILER
Shifting Time

THE
PLAN

a novel
Kelly Bennett Seiler

INFINITE WORDS

NEW YORK LONDON TORONTO SYDNEY

INFINITE WORDS
P.O. Box 6505
Largo, MD 20792
www.simonandschuster.com

© 2016 by Kelly Bennett Seiler

All rights reserved. No part of this book may be reproduced
in any form or by any means whatsoever.
For information, address Infinite Words, P.O. Box 6505, Largo, MD 20792.

ISBN 978-1-59309-670-0
ISBN 978-1-5011-1905-7 (ebook)
LCCN 2015957704

First Infinite Words trade paperback edition September 2016

Cover design: www.mariondesigns.com
Cover photograph: © Keith Saunders/Keith Saunders Photos
Book design: Red Herring Design, Inc.

10 9 8 7 6 5 4 3 2 1

Manufactured in the United States of America

For information regarding special discounts for bulk purchases,
please contact Simon & Schuster Special Sales at 1-866-506-1949
or business@simonandschuster.com

The Simon & Schuster Speakers Bureau can bring authors to your live event.
For more information or to book an event, contact the Simon & Schuster Speakers
Bureau at 1-866-248-3049 or visit our website at www.simonspeakers.com.

For my Mimi, Mary Terpak,
who loved to read, as I sat beside her,
and thought I was the funniest person she knew.
She would've gotten such a kick out of all this.

ACKNOWLEDGMENTS

Though *The Plan* is my second novel, it's actually the beginning of my writing journey. Many years ago, I wrote a screenplay and sent it to my now-agent, Sara Camilli. She signed me based on that screenplay, but suggested I turn it into a novel. Her words, "I love this story. I'm going to sell this story," were the ones to which I held tight. *The Plan* is the novel based on that original work.

I would be remiss if I didn't thank my first writing group members: Mary Summerall, Kelly Atkins, Holly Joplin, Lisa Matthews and Ramona Kelly. They were the ones (and only ones, until my agent) who read the original screenplay for *The Plan* and encouraged me to keep going—even when the task of completing an entire script seemed daunting. Without them, I would have never finished the screenplay and without the screenplay, I would have had nothing to send to an agent.

My current writing group is invaluable to me. The advice, critiques and encouragement I receive from JC Conklin and Amy Bates are nearly always spot on. There've been times when I realized I had a problem in the middle of my story and hoped no one else would notice. They, of course, did notice and pointed out the issues right away. My frustration at the situation always quickly dissipated, however, when they'd then proceed to present a solution on how I might mend what was broken. Without them, I might still be banging my head against the proverbial wall.

My gratitude goes to Kim Kremer, who has happily proofread my last two books and barely complained about their length.

A special thanks to Dr. Sally Grogono, who not only delivered all three of my children, but excitedly assisted me in plotting a character's demise.

Special appreciation must be paid to Michael Kogan, whose expertise in prosthetics got the ball rolling on Callum's disability and what would be possible or impossible tasks for a trilateral amputee, when I, initially, had no idea.

I absolutely could not have completed this novel without the irreplaceable help of Bryan and Marijo Cuerrier. In my search to find information on what it's like to be a trilateral amputee, I came across videos on YouTube of Bryan and his journey. Through his website, I contacted him and, via email, he and his wife and I became great friends. To say I sent them a hundred emails with a thousand questions may be minimizing the amount. It was a thrill when they ultimately traveled from Canada to Texas and we were able to become friends in "real life," too.

Though I've traveled to Ireland, I still needed help with the culture and language. Claire Ellenbogen was a lifesaver and it was wonderful to know that, no matter what question I had, she was a mere Facebook message away. And thank you to my Welsh penpal of over thirty years, Sonia Holmes, who, during only our second meeting in all these years, made the journey with me to Ireland and experienced the Cliffs of Moher alongside me.

I need to thank Zane and Charmaine Parker and the rest of those at Simon and Schuster for turning my books into actual novels—like fairy godmothers with magical wands.

Many thanks to Keith Saunders at Marion Designs. It never amazes me how I can explain to him what I imagine in a cover and he returns to me the precise vision in my head.

I've learned more than I ever wanted to know about building a website, a newsletter and creating a mailing list over the past few years and I wouldn't have even known where to begin if not for Nichole Renée. The patience she exhibited toward her luddite friend was remarkable.

I know many believe Facebook and social media have weakened our personal connections with people, but I'm a believer in the complete opposite theory. The life of a writer is an isolating one and yet, each day perhaps—each hour—I correspond with a different friend who shares a word of encouragement or an anecdote or a personal story of their own. Those friendships (and all of you know who you are) make my time at my laptop considerably less lonely.

I am grateful to anyone who has ever attended one of my book signings or talks, whether they knew me or not, and said a kind word—or, at least, sat in the audience and appeared to be interested.

Immense thanks to my parents, Barbara and Richard Bennett, who not only encouraged my writing, but spent a whole lot of money for me to get that English degree.

My husband, Rob, deserves recognition for coming to terms with the fact that he is married to a woman who lives almost completely inside her own head and talks to people who aren't really in our house. My children, Jordan, Bennett and Maclain, have shared me with a dozen or more characters over the past few years, and so, when they've each said to me, in their own way, "I'm so proud of you, Mom," I've had a difficult time not shedding a tear.

Not all of us are blessed to find their one true passion. I'm one of the lucky ones. It was when I encountered this unstoppable force that I knew I was where I belong.

Finally, I don't know what plan God has in store for my life, and I may not understand it until the very end, but I find peace in trusting that He does, indeed, have one.

PROLOGUE

Ireland, 1973

"Something's wrong with the baby!"

Patrick sighed and gripped the steering wheel more tightly. The rain was coming down as if all of God's angels were dumping buckets from the sky. Barely able to see the car in front of him, he was struggling to keep the vehicle on the road—to even *see* the road. Though generally a patient man, Patrick didn't have the energy to give in to Nora's dramatics.

"Nothing is wrong with the baby, me love," he said, with all the calmness he could muster. "Everything's just fine." He glanced over and offered his wife a gentle smile, then quickly turned his attention back to his driving. He should've known it would be raining on the night his child was to be born. After all, this was Ireland. Was it not always raining?

"No, I mean it," Nora said, through clenched teeth. Her knuckles were so white, they were turning blue as she squeezed the armrest on the car door and arched her back, while a labour pain ripped through her. "Something's wrong. I can feel it," she gasped.

"What you feel is labour," Patrick said, smiling slightly. "It doesn't mean there's anything wrong with the baby. It just means he's ready to make his entrance into this world."

Nora was known, to him and their whole family—and perhaps, to their entire village—to exaggerate events. It was the single thing he simultaneously loved most about her and also loathed. An odd thing to love, he recognized, but Nora's extravagant stories always made her the life of any party or gathering.

Nora had a way with words. She often said the more miserable a situation, the better a story it would make later. And, he had to admit, in her case, she was right.

So, it came as no surprise to Patrick that the birth of their baby was, in Nora's eyes, bound to be wrought with drama. He had no doubt, though, their little boy—Callum, as he was to be named—would enter this world with little to no difficulty. Nora had experienced the best medical care available in Ireland. Patrick had made certain of that. There were many perks to being a Senator, a member of Seanad Eireann, and he'd taken advantage of every connection he had. His wife and baby were going to have the best medical care in all of Ireland. Blinking hard, trying to see through the downpour of rain, Patrick was beginning to wonder why he hadn't used some of that power to ensure a driver to take them to the hospital tonight. For all of his prepping and planning, the detail of who would drive them to the hospital had never crossed his mind. Once she'd regained her composure, Nora spoke again.

"Patrick, listen to me. I am serious. This isn't one of my stories this time. Something is wrong with the baby."

"Why, me love, would you even think such a thing?" Patrick said, checking his rearview mirror. "You've had all the tests. He's perfect. Just perfect. The doctors say nothing is wrong with him."

Patrick smiled as he used the word "him." In actuality, Nora and he had not been told they were having a little boy. There was really no way to know until the lad made his appearance into this world. But, in their hearts, both of them just knew this child was a boy. They were so certain, in fact, they hadn't even discussed girls' names.

Nora sighed deeply and looked out her window into the dark, unceasing rain. "I know there's something wrong, because...I had a dream."

The words made Patrick catch his breath. *A dream?* There were four things in life that Patrick took seriously and without question. God, death, taxes—and dreams.

Years ago, on the night his baby brother died, Patrick had learned the power of dreams. Many people wrote off dreams as nothing more than figments of one's imagination. But Patrick knew better. A dream was a sign from God.

Keeping his voice calm for Nora's sake, he said, "What do you mean, you had a dream?" He quickly looked at Nora, trying to offer her a reassuring glance, before returning his eyes back to the road. "Last night," Nora said, beginning to breathe more rapidly as pain began to rise in her body, "I dreamt you and I and our baby were in the park..." The words trailed off as Nora gasped and let out another, what seemed to Patrick's ears, inhuman wail.

"The park?" said Patrick, speaking soothingly to Nora, as she panted in agony. "The park sounds lovely. I like the thought of a family day in the park. What else happened?"

Nora's breathing evened out again. "We were at the park and you were pushing our boy on a swing. I was setting up a picnic at a table, not too far away. I could see your back, and I could see the swing going up and down, but I couldn't see the baby. I called your name, to tell you and Callum to come and eat."

Patrick smiled. Despite the dread he felt over what was to come in the dream, he couldn't help but feel warmth at the sound of their son's name. Callum. A name which meant *dove*. Some might not find it a strong name, but Patrick, a politician and, above all else, an Irishman, was hopeful that a shift was finally here for Ireland. The violence and riots of the past years had taken a toll on Patrick, and, of course, his country. It was time for a new beginning. And what better way to acknowledge that he, himself, was ready for that change than by naming his first-born son after a bird that symbolized peace?

Patrick had such dreams for his child, this boy he had yet to meet. A boy who would have hair as black as Kilkenny coal and eyes as blue as the summer sky. If Patrick had thought about it long enough, he'd have recognized the child he was imagining was an identical version of the brother he'd lost so long ago. But, he never did think about it long enough. He was a man who tried to never look back. And for the past nine months, Patrick's eyes had been set on the little boy who was about to arrive. Oh, Patrick had great plans for his son. He would, of course, be beautiful. How could he be anything but gorgeous, being born from a mother as stunning as Nora? Even at the age of thirty, she was as breathtaking as she'd been when he'd met her at eighteen. No, Nora never aged. Patrick wished the same could be said of himself. The years, and his stressful career, had taken a toll on him and he looked much older than his forty-two years. It wasn't uncommon for a stranger to inquire about whether or not Nora was his daughter. But as long as Nora found him attractive and still wanted to be with him, it didn't matter to him at all how he was aging. Though he did hope a son would help keep him young. Patrick didn't know what was in store for Callum, but he somehow knew—call it intuition—his boy was to be unique.

"And, did we come for lunch when you called?" Patrick asked, breaking his thoughts long enough to focus on Nora's dream.

"I called your name and you turned and looked at me and smiled. Then you went back to pushing the baby on the swing. I looked toward Callum and I noticed a crowd of children standing near his swing. They'd all been playing before, but now they were just standing in front of him, frozen and silent. One of them pointed at Callum and said something. Then, another child started to laugh. I looked at you, but you didn't see me. You just kept pushing Callum back and forth on the swing."

Patrick put his hand on Nora's leg and gently began to rub it. He knew he shouldn't take his hand off of the steering wheel in this weather, but he had a feeling what was about to follow was not going to be good.

"Then, as if the children had seen something terribly frightening when looking at Callum, they started to scream. The girls began to cry and the boys started to yell, and they all started to run away from the playground." Nora became silent and Patrick could see, out of the corner of his eye, she had tears running down her face. "I started to run towards you and the baby, to see what was the matter. What was scaring these children? You didn't turn. You just kept pushing the swing, as all the children screamed, pointed at our child, and ran."

There was silence in the car for a moment. Patrick was almost too frightened to ask what happened next, but he did.

"And what did you see, love?" he asked softly. "When you got to the swing, what did you see?"

Nora began to sob softly. "There was nothing there. The swing was empty. You were pushing an empty swing."

Patrick hesitated. It didn't make any sense. "But, you said earlier you'd seen Callum in the swing."

Nora continued to cry as she reached into her handbag to grab a handful of tissues.

"I know," she said, tears streaming down her face. "I'd seen the back of his head as you pushed. But, when I got closer, there was no one in the swing. It was empty."

They rode in silence for a moment longer, until another labour pain grabbed hold of Nora, and she began to cry harder. Patrick was no longer sure if she was crying from the pain, or from the dream, or if the two were intermingled. To be perfectly honest, he suddenly felt like crying, too.

Get ahold of yourself, he thought. *This is ridiculous. It was a dream. Only a dream.* The words echoed in his mind. Hadn't he said that

same exact thing to himself years earlier. *Only a dream.* It hadn't
turned out to be only a dream then. Would it now?

Patrick shook his head, to regain his composure. He could not allow
himself to fall apart now. His son was about to be born, and hopefully
not on this cold, wet road. They'd almost reached the hospital. Nora's
pain slowed, and she began to speak again. "What do you think it
means, Patrick? What's going to be wrong with our baby?"

Patrick was relieved to see, through the dense fog and rain, the
sign for the hospital straight ahead.

"Look, Nora. We're here. Just a minute more and you'll be out of
this car and headed up to deliver our son."

Patrick carefully guided the car into the driveway and pulled in
front of the main entrance.

"Nora, love," he said softly, as he turned back toward her. "Listen to
me." With very deliberate, yet loving words, he said, "Our son is a
blessing from God. A blessing, me love. I don't know what we have in
store for us tonight. I don't know if he's going to be perfectly healthy
or have a bit of a problem. But what I do know is that he's ours. Yours
and mine. And he's been given to us as a gift. I am going to love Callum
from the moment he enters the world until the moment I exit it.
And whatever God puts on our plate, I'm ready to face it, with you by
my side, because there is a plan for our lives, for Callum's life. I might
not know what it is, but I know it is real and true and good."

Nora's eyes remained closed, but Patrick saw a new tear slip from
the corner of one eye.

"I love you, Nora. No child has ever had a father who loved his mother
more. Whatever lies in store for us, we're going to face it together.
Do you hear me?"

Nora nodded slowly, opened her dark eyes and looked deep into
Patrick's blue ones.

"Now, can we please go inside and have this baby?" Patrick asked.

A small giggle escaped Nora as she nodded and said, "Yes, and please, let's hurry."

Patrick rolled Nora into the front door of the hospital in the wheelchair he'd found outside. As he completed the necessary paperwork, Nora was whisked into a hospital room, and by the time he found her again, she'd changed into a gown and was being tended to by a nurse.

"It won't be long now," the woman said to Patrick. She was a large woman, with an even bigger smile. "Are you ready to become a dad?"

Patrick returned the smile. "I've been waiting for this moment all of my life."

"Then let's get the doctor in here," she said, as she left the room.

Patrick walked over to Nora's bedside and took her hand in his.

Nora smiled, then began to grimace as the pain grew.

The doctor entered the room, as the pain in Patrick's hand, from Nora's iron-tight grip, began to truly sting. Behind the doctor were two nurses.

"I hear we're going to have a baby in a wee bit," the doctor said, smiling.

"We're looking forward to it," Patrick said, as Nora's grip lessened.

The doctor examined Nora.

"Well, it looks like you're ready to begin pushing. What I want you to do, Nora, is do your best to relax, and when you feel the next pain, I want you to push as hard as you can." Nora smiled weakly. "And, if you want to call ol' Patrick, here, some terrible names, that's fine by me, too. I won't tell a soul."

As soon as the doctor said his last word, Nora's grip on his hand tightened again and she began to cry out.

"You're doing great, Nora. That was a magnificent push," the doctor said. "I can see his crown. He has hair as black as yours. You can do it. Push again."

Nora arched her back and made a sound like none Patrick had ever heard.

"That's it, Nora. One more push. I see his shoulder. One more push and he'll be out." The doctor's supportive voice was reassuring to both Patrick and Nora. The baby would soon be here.

Nora squeezed Patrick's hand one final time, cried out in agonizing pain and pushed. As Nora's scream ceased, a new one began in the room. But this was a tiny cry. A gentle wail that made both Nora and Patrick smile. It was the first sound of their child, and it was beautiful.

Patrick kissed Nora on the forehead and whispered softly, "You did it, me love." She smiled gently back at him.

Then Patrick stood up straight and looked toward the doctor, hoping to catch a glimpse of his newborn son.

The doctor and nurses were whispering softly. Patrick hadn't noticed how quiet the room had become once the delivery was over. But now that he was paying attention, he realized it was silent. Even the baby had stopped crying.

"Is everything okay?" Nora asked. She, too, had noticed the change in the room. "Is my baby okay?"

The doctor and nurses appeared not to hear her. One nurse hurried out of the room. Nervous, Patrick started to walk toward them, eager for a glimpse of their child, and as the doctor, who had Callum in his arms, turned, Patrick caught sight of the baby and the room began to spin.

Patrick grabbed hold of the instrument table, and it began to roll away from him. The other nurse, the one who'd smiled at Patrick earlier, ran toward him and grabbed his arm, just as a number of doctors and nurses rushed into the room.

"Come with me, Mr. Fitzgerald," she said gently. "Let's go out and get you some fresh air."

Patrick wanted to look at Nora, but he found he couldn't. He couldn't bear to see her face. And he couldn't bear to have her see his. *Would she see it in his eyes?* Instead, he nodded at the nurse, and followed her out of the room. He could hear Nora crying behind him.

"What's happening?" she begged. "Patrick! What's wrong? What's wrong with my baby?"

Patrick hated himself for doing it, but he let the door close behind him, and then he sank to the floor.

The nurse squatted down next to him, her hand on his back.

"Can I get you some water?" she asked.

"It's a boy, isn't it?" Patrick said dully.

The nurse nodded.

"He's missing an arm," Patrick said. He could barely get the words out. It couldn't be true. Of course, his son had two arms. They'd seen them on the scan—hadn't they? But Callum didn't have an arm. Patrick was certain of it. He'd only caught a glimpse of the baby, but he was sure he'd seen nothing more than a stub where the limb should have been.

"He was born without an arm, wasn't he?" Patrick asked the nurse, pleading with his eyes for her to correct him. Silently begging her to tell him he was mistaken.

The woman took a deep breath and sighed. It was never easy to tell a parent something was wrong with their baby and fortunately, over the span of her career, she'd only had to do it a few times. It was a heartbreaking part of her job, but it had never been like this before. Even she couldn't believe it.

"I'm sorry, Mr. Fitzgerald, your son *was* born without an arm." She lowered her eyes, as if she could no longer bear to see his pain. And he understood this. Sometimes, the pain of others was physically tangible in their eyes. He remembered the agony in his mother's eyes after his brother had died. It had hurt his chest to look at his mum from that day on. He'd thought nothing could hurt more than that sadness, but he'd been mistaken. No trouble Patrick had experienced before prepared him for the torment that was about to come.

"And, I'm sorry to tell you this, Mr. Fitzgerald, but your son was also born without either of his legs."

The sound was primal. Patrick had never heard such a low and guttural noise and for a moment, wondered how it could have risen out of him. He curled up into a ball, against the wall, and began to sob, convulsing in a burning pain more scalding than any fire. He wondered how he was going to tell Nora. And then, as he heard the agonizing scream pierce the hall, he knew he wouldn't have to.

CHAPTER
ONE

Florida, 2010

"I'd better find three little munchkins in their beds," Claire called out, as she headed up the stairs toward her kids' rooms.

She reached the top and turned into Luke's room, depositing, on top of his dresser, all the goodies she'd collected on her way up the stairs. He and his sisters could sort them by owner and put them away tomorrow.

She glanced at his bed, noticing it was empty, and bent down to straighten his *Stars Wars* sheets. The ten-year-old was a *Star Wars* fanatic. Claire blamed Jack for that. Their first date in college had been to the dollar theater to see *The Empire Strikes Back*. If that hadn't been a clear sign of things to come, she wasn't sure what was. And now that she had Luke, she even participated in it, up to a point, buying him not just *Star Wars* bedding, but Luke Skywalker, Chewbacca or Darth Vader costumes she found on clearance the day after Halloween. At last count, she'd purchased her thirteenth light saber. Who knew that something designed to be so powerful would have such difficulty withstanding the battles of a ten-year-old boy? Yes, Luke was his daddy through and through. And, with soft brown eyes, a row of freckles on his nose and legs that seemed to go on for miles, he also looked like a mini-version of Jack.

Claire paused to glance at a photo, tacked to the bulletin board, of the two men in her life. It'd been taken last summer. They were standing on a fishing dock, Luke proudly holding up his catch—the first fish he'd ever caught by himself. It was miniscule—not big enough to keep—but he had a grin from ear to ear which was almost as big as the one his daddy wore. Jack had been so proud of his boy.

"Did you see the way he reeled that baby in?" he'd asked her, for the twentieth time that night as she was dressing for bed. "He's a natural fisherman. Just like his dad. Just like his granddad."

Claire smiled, brushing her hair and inspecting her reflection in the mirror. At thirty-five, she had to admit she looked good for her age. With her thick, brown hair in a ponytail, which it often was, she was commonly mistaken for a teenager. She never tired of seeing the looks on people's faces when she told them that, not only did she have three children, but the oldest of them was ten! If the expressions of shock didn't make a woman feel good about her appearance, she didn't know what would.

"All you have to do is look at him to know he's got your DNA running through him," she said, walking over to the bed and pulling her nightgown over her head. "Sometimes I wonder if any of mine got in there."

Jack laughed and pulled her down next to him. "Oh, he's got a part of you in him, too, babe," he whispered into her neck.

"Yeah?" Claire asked. "Where is it? His feet?"

"No," Jack said, hugging her closer to him. "His heart. He's got the sweetest heart I've ever seen in a little boy. He practically cried when I took the hook out of the fish's mouth, asking if I was hurting him. He's got a heart as pure and gentle as his mama's."

Claire smiled now, remembering the comment. It'd been just the right thing to say. Jack always seemed to know the right thing to say to make her feel special.

"Hmmm," Claire said loudly, remembering she was supposed to be playing an impromptu game of hide-and-seek with her kids. "I don't see Luke in his bed. Where is he? Maybe he's in the closet?"

Claire grabbed two of the clean shirts that were stacked on Luke's desk chair, folded them and put them away in his drawer.

"I still can't find Luke anywhere! Where on earth could he be?" She smiled at the giggling she heard coming from somewhere down the hall as she hung up three pairs of pants in his closet.

"Maybe he's under the bed," Claire said, with mock loudness, as she placed some underwear and socks in their appropriate drawers. The giggling was getting louder, and Claire wondered if the kids might just burst if she didn't put a stop to it soon.

Sitting down on the vacant bed, she paused to catch her breath before walking into the chaos she was sure was ahead of her. She'd never realized having three children would be such an exhausting task. When she was a little girl, and even as a teenager, she used to tell her mom she wanted to have eight kids when she grew up.

"Eight?" her mom would ask, her face a mixture of shock and humor. "Are you sure about that? Eight is a lot."

"Eight is enough," Claire would say, chuckling as she remembered the Dick Van Patten television series she'd enjoyed so much growing up.

"Okay, well then," her mom would say, "you have one child and get back to me on whether or not you still feel that way after a few months of sleepless nights and endless diapers."

Claire had always rolled her eyes at her mom. After all, what did her mom know about having a big family? She'd only had Claire and oftentimes, seemed overwhelmed by just her. Her mom wasn't cut out for a lot of kids, but somehow, Claire had always thought she, herself, was.

Of course, her mom had been right—up to a point. Eight kids had no longer seemed like such a brilliant idea after Claire had had three. Three children, in fact, had almost done her in. She remembered how, after the twins were born, Jack would come home from work, look at her, still in her pajamas from the night before, her hair a wild mess and food and booger stains on her clothes, and say to her, "Are we drowning?"

"Oh, we are *so* drowning," she'd say to him. And mean it. There were days when she wondered what she'd been thinking getting pregnant again after Luke. One child had been so manageable. In retrospect, so *easy*. But three? Forget it. She was just doing her best to make it through each day.

When people would ask her, "Do you think you'll have any more kids?" she'd always laugh and say, "Oh, no, the twins were our grand finale."

She understood now the amusement of her mother when Claire had said she wanted to have eight children. Though she'd had only one child, her mom had realized that, along with the immense joy of being a parent, came incredible struggles, frustration, and exhaustion. Claire sighed as she once again felt a pang of regret that she'd never been able to tell her mom how she now understood what she'd meant.

Neither her mom nor her dad had had the chance to see Claire as a mom to even one child. Both of her parents had died while she was in college—her mom of cancer her freshman year and her dad of a heart attack three years later. Though Claire always tended to believe he died less from an attack of his heart than from a break in it. The happy-go-lucky father she remembered from her childhood couldn't be reconciled with the man he became after they lost her mom. He hadn't known what to do without the wife he'd loved faithfully and so completely for twenty-eight years. And, though Claire missed them both terribly, she also tended to believe it was best they were together. She'd been able to forge a life of her own after they were gone, but she never truly believed her dad, even if he'd lived until the age of eighty, would've been able to do that without her mom. Some people were meant to be together, whether it be in this life or the next.

Claire sighed and called out again, her voice thick with exaggerated sorrow. "I guess Luke must've run away. That's too bad. I'll miss him. He was such a nice boy. I think I'll go kiss Ella and Lily goodnight now."

She stood, gave the room a quick once-over and then turned out Luke's light, making her way down the hall into her girls' room.

A mound of covers, apparently hiding three little bodies, awaited her as she walked into her twins' pink and yellow room. Claire might have thought the girls had piled all of their stuffed animals underneath if she couldn't visually see the mound shaking and shuddering with each little giggle.

"Oh, no! The girls are gone, too!" Claire said, trying to muster as much agony as was possible in her voice, as she made her way to the bed. "Boy, am I tired, and this bed looks so comfy! I think I'll just lie down for a little nap."

Claire plopped her body right on top of the enormous pile, careful to not injure anyone underneath.

"Mommy! Get off!" a muffled voice cried from beneath her.

"Ow! That hurts!" a boy's voice complained.

"Mom! We're under here!" another little voice cried out.

Claire jumped up, her hand to her chest.

"Oh! There's something under there!" Claire exclaimed. "Whatever could it be?"

With a single motion, Claire grabbed the comforter and yanked it to the floor. Three small faces peeked up at her.

"What are you doing under there?" Claire asked, with such surprise in her voice that she, herself, almost believed she was startled by their appearance. "I thought you'd run away!"

"We wouldn't run away, Mommy," little Ella said. "We like living here."

"Well, that's a good thing," Claire replied, tweaking her daughter's nose. "Because I like you living here, too."

Claire picked the comforter up and straightened the covers over the three children. They each got comfortable, snuggling deep into the pillows as she sat down on the edge of the bed.

"Now, what are you all doing in here?" she asked her babies. Despite the fact that Luke was ten and the twins had just turned six, she still viewed them as just that—her babies—and had a feeling she always would. "If I remember correctly, Daddy and I bought each of you your own bed."

Lily yawned. "We like to sleep together."

"I'm not scared at night if Luke and Lily are with me," Ella replied.

Claire glanced at Luke. "And what about you, mister? What are *you* doing in here?"

"I'm not scared like the girls," he said defensively. "I just stay here to protect them."

Claire tousled his hair. It was hard to not smile at this child, part little boy, part little man.

"Well," she said gently. "That's what big brothers are for. Do you know how lucky you all are to have each other? When I was a kid, I'd have done anything to have brothers and sisters."

With a look of disgust directed at his sisters, Luke said, "You were lucky. You didn't have little kids to drive you crazy!"

"No, I didn't," Claire replied softly. "But I also didn't have anyone to play with or talk to when my parents were busy with grown-up stuff. You three will always have each other."

The girls smiled at her words, but Luke rolled his eyes at Claire, in much the same way she used to roll her eyes at her own mom. Claire smiled at him. She knew he loved his sisters dearly, even if it was no longer cool in fifth grade to admit it.

"Now then," she said. "It's bedtime. No one in my room before seven a.m. You hear me?"

"Okay," they all said in unison.

"And, if you go downstairs to watch TV, it had better not be loud enough to wake me and Daddy."

"Yes, Ma'am."

"Whose turn is it to pray?" she prompted.

"Yours," Luke said.

"Are you sure?" Claire questioned, as the kids all nodded.

"Okay, then. Dear God. We thank you for our blessings and that we had a great day as a family. Please take care of those we love. Amen."

"Amen," the children said in unison.

"Mommy," Lily said sleepily. "Can you sing to us?"

"Sure," Claire whispered, with a smile. This was one of her favorite parts of the bedtime ritual, though, as the kids had gotten older, she found she didn't do it as often. It wasn't that she didn't still like to sing to them, or that they didn't still love to hear her. It was that once all three kids started school, bedtime had become more hectic. There were teeth to be brushed, hands to be washed, homework that was left to the very last minute. Sometimes, bedtime consisted of nothing more than a quick goodnight peck on the cheek and an "I'll see you in the morning."

But on weekend nights, such as tonight, when there was no rush to make sure those little eyes closed quickly, Claire enjoyed taking a few extra moments with the kids as she put them down for the night. She paused for a moment as she thought of what to sing, and then decided on their favorite. It was an old, classic Irish lullaby she'd been singing to the children since they were each in her belly. The twins closed their eyes as she began, but Luke stared straight at her.

"Over in Killarney, many years ago, me mother sang a song to me, in tones so sweet and low. Just a simple little ditty, in her good old Irish way. And I'd give the world if she could sing, that song to me this day."

Claire's voice drifted softly through the room, beautiful and pure. There was a time when people had paid money to hear her sing, but these days, she sang solely for her children.

"Too-ra-loo-ra-loo-ral, too-ra-loo-ra-li, too-ra-loo-ra-loo-ral, hush now, don't you cry!

Too-ra-loo-ra-loo-ral, too-ra-loo-ra-li, too-ra-loo-ra-loo-ral, that's an Irish lullaby."

Claire was fairly certain the girls had fallen asleep by the second line, but Luke's eyes had stayed open, til nearly the very end, when, despite his best efforts, his lids dropped, and he turned to get more comfortable next to his sisters.

Claire stared down at her children. Somehow, no matter how much love she felt for them during the day, it always seemed to intensify as she watched them sleep. She rose and walked to the door. Pausing, she glanced back at her sleeping babies, turning off the light to the girls' room. She was blessed, and she knew it. Life with three kids wasn't ever easy, but she also couldn't help but wonder how a girl like her had gotten so lucky.

"I love you," Claire said softly into the darkness, as she turned and walked away.

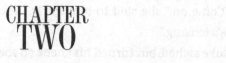

CHAPTER
TWO

"Hurry up, Luke!" Claire called up the stairs as she slapped peanut butter and jelly on two pieces of bread, shoving them into a small plastic baggie. "The girls are already in the car."

Luke ran down the stairs, jumping over the last three as he reached the bottom.

Claire slit her eyes as she glared in his direction. "I've asked you to not do that. One of these days you're going to break a leg." Luke shrugged.

"Did you grab your jacket? It's gonna be cold at Grandma and Grandpa's." Claire threw the pile of sandwiches she'd just made into a small cooler, alongside six juice boxes and a baggie full of sliced apples. If she'd learned anything about traveling with kids over the years, it was they were always hungry.

"I already put it in the car," Luke said, as he opened the refrigerator and examined its contents.

"Hey, get out of there," Claire said, softly slapping his hand away from the door and closing it. "You already had breakfast and I'm packing food for the car. You don't need anything else to eat."

She handed him the cooler and a bag of pretzels.

"Here, you can carry this to the car for me," Claire said. "Don't eat anything out of it! And make sure to bring some games and books. It's a long drive."

She laughed as she leaned in to kiss him on the cheek and he attempted to free himself of her embrace.

"Come on," she said to him softly. "You can kiss your mama. No one's looking."

Luke sighed, but turned his cheek so she could peck it.

"See, that wasn't so bad, was it?" Claire asked him.

Luke shrugged.

The two of them made their way out the front door, just as Jack was heading back in.

"Do you need anything else from inside?" he asked her. "I'm about to lock up."

"I think I have it all," Claire said, as Luke ran to the minivan, throwing the cooler onto the front seat before jumping into the back. "Anything we forget, we can buy once we get to your mom's."

She walked over to the car and peeked her head in the side door. Though they hadn't even left the driveway, all three of her kids had their headsets on and were immersed in the music on their iPods. The MP3 players had been the kids' big gifts for Christmas this year. Claire was fastening her seatbelt as the driver's side door opened, and Jack slid into his seat.

"All locked up," he said, calling into the backseat, "Everyone ready?"

"Yes!"

Smiling at Claire, Jack put the car into reverse and said, "Are *you* ready?"

"Yes," she said, smiling back at him. It was hard not to smile when looking at Jack. He was just so...handsome. That's the only word that came to mind whenever she thought of her husband. At six feet four inches, and built of nothing but lean muscle, Jack was better-looking than most of her friends' husbands. Okay, he was better-looking than *all* of her friends' husbands. And their gardeners. And their plumbers. And their local firemen. Jack was unbelievable looking. The first time Claire had laid eyes on him in college, she'd wondered if he was for real.

"Who *looks* like that?" she had whispered to her college roommate,

Gia. "I mean, in real life—not in a movie. Who actually looks that incredible?"

The answer, of course, was Jack. And, in the fifteen years since college, he'd never become one bit less attractive.

But it wasn't just his external features Claire found so appealing. No, it was who Claire discovered he was inside that had made her fall deeply in love with him.

It'd seemed to take forever for Jack to ask her out, but in reality, it was only a few weeks from the first time she and Gia had spotted him across the crowded college cafeteria. It didn't take long for them to strike up a conversation in the library one night. (She *just happened* to be working in the study carrel next to Jack's and *just happened* to need to borrow a pen, because hers *just happened* to run out of ink.) After an evening spent chatting over their respective molecular biology and educational psychology textbooks, he finally asked her out. And she was thrilled.

Of course, a *Star Wars* movie at the campus discount theater wasn't exactly her idea of a romantic evening, but the dinner that followed had been nearly perfect. The two of them found they had so much to talk about—school, families, politics, music—even their faiths and future dreams seemed to be on similar tracks. The conversation flowed easily and Claire began to wonder if she'd actually known him her entire life. Before they were served dessert, she was smitten.

She was so completely engaged in conversation with Jack, she never even saw Gia enter the restaurant.

"What are you doing here?" she asked her roommate, slightly irritated, as Gia sat down next to her.

And that's when she saw Gia's face. There'd be no dessert. Claire's hometown police department had called her dorm room and, in Claire's absence, relayed the message to Gia.

Claire's dad was dead. An apparent heart attack while driving his car. Fortunately, he'd been going so slowly. *Hadn't Claire always told him he drove like an old man?* He hadn't hurt anyone else, but himself. And, like her mom three years earlier, he was gone.

If Claire had given it any thought, she would've assumed Jack would have quietly excused himself. After all, despite a fun movie and tasty dinner, she barely knew the man. But it was in those initial moments that Claire caught her first glimpse of the man Jack truly was. As she collapsed into Gia's arms, he began to take charge, booking not just her flight home, but flights for himself and Gia, too. He contacted the school, notifying them of Claire's loss and informing the university that he and Claire and Gia would be missing classes for the next few days. As Gia and she went to pack, Jack contacted the police who'd handled the accident, finding out where her dad's body had been taken and the next steps Claire needed to take.

For Claire, the next week was a blur, but the one thing she remembered clearly was how Jack had been by her side every moment of it, walking her through the terrible process of planning her father's funeral. He handled nearly all of the arrangements, deferring to her for her opinion, but lifting the burden from her shoulders in such a way that all she had to do was grieve. And grieve she did. She could not believe that here she was, twenty years old, and an orphan. What was she going to do? How was she going to go on without either her mom or her dad to help guide her? It was unbearable.

But every time she felt she couldn't take one more moment of the pain, she'd look up and see sweet Jack standing right by her side. This man she hadn't even known eight days ago was her rock during that week and in the weeks and months to come. He'd never disappointed her. And, just as in the days following her dad's death, in the past fifteen years, whenever she'd had a bad day or was irritated with her job or frustrated with their kids, all she had to do was look beside her, and she knew Jack would be right there, supporting her, loving her, and giving her the strength to keep moving.

"Now tell me again why you always seem to think it's a good idea to drive into the night?" Jack asked her, shaking her out of her memories. "Wouldn't it make more sense if we left early in the morning?"

"You know, as well as I do, if we leave now, in a few hours, the kids will be asleep and we won't have to hear any more whining or fighting," Claire said.

"Don't forget the 'Are we there yets?'" Jack joked.

"Ugh," Claire groaned. "I hate those the most! This way, they'll watch their movies until dinner and then, if we're lucky, it'll just be peace and quiet from that point on."

"From your lips to God's ears," Jack said, taking her hand and squeezing it.

God must have been listening, because everything went exactly as Claire had planned. *Truly, this must be a first,* she thought, as they pulled into the strip mall parking lot of the Chinese restaurant where they ate every time they took a road trip to West Virginia. Never could she remember having such a peaceful drive to her in-laws' home, or anywhere else for that matter.

It was one more sign that her babies were growing up. Claire remembered the first time she and Jack had taken a car trip with Luke. He couldn't have been more than a month old and had screamed the entire drive.

The family piled out of the car and into the restaurant.

"Welcome," a little Asian man called from a table at the back of the empty restaurant, as he rolled silverware into napkins. "Sit anywhere you'd like."

The kids hurried over to a large table near the wall, and Claire and Jack followed them.

"Okay," Jack said, taking off his coat and putting it on the back of his chair. "What does everyone want to eat?"

As the kids called out their orders, Jack and Claire exchanged glances over the menus and smiled at one another. She knew exactly what he was thinking. These were the moments they both loved the best. These crazy, chaotic, boisterous moments that screamed, "We're together as a family."

"Mommy," Lily said meekly, once the orders were placed. "Can I sit on your lap?"

"Of course," Claire said, gently smiling at her little girl and pushing her chair back from the table to make room for her daughter. "Come here."

Lily climbed up onto Claire and snuggled into her mother's chest. Even though already six, Lily was tiny for her age, barely the size of most four-year-olds. Claire had heard that was often common with twins. Ella wasn't quite as small and, at about a half a head taller than Lily, appeared to tower over her sister. Rarely did people realize the girls were twins. With their identical blonde hair and blue eyes, it was easy to see they were sisters. But, twins? No. Ella easily looked two years older than Lily.

And, as different as their height were their personalities. Ella was a spitfire. Feisty and funny and always up for a new adventure. She was the child who loved to go snowboarding and waterskiing with Jack and was constantly in search of a new challenge. She was already the star of her soccer team and relished all of the attention playing so well brought her. Never without a smile, you just couldn't help but marvel at her confidence. Claire rarely worried about Ella. Whether it was a new school or a birthday party where she didn't know any of the other kids, Ella would jump in, feet first, and thrive.

But Lily? Lily was different. She was quiet and shy and prone to tears if she became too uncomfortable in a situation. Though on the soccer team with her sister, she tended to avoid the ball and, if it happened to come her way, was likely to duck. Never wanting to be too far away from Claire, Lily was the child who, while the others were off skiing with Jack, would stay back at the lodge with her mom, enjoying every moment of snuggling in front of the fire as much as

Claire did. She still slept with her favorite blankie, and Claire had fears that someday she'd take that ratty old thing on her honeymoon with her. Yet, despite her timid nature, Claire'd been pleasantly surprised when Lily had started kindergarten last year and had done exceptionally well. She might not be as bold as her sister, but she was certainly every bit as smart. Both girls had been incredibly successful in kindergarten and now, halfway through first grade, were some of the brightest kids in the class.

"I love you," Claire whispered in Lily's ear as the girl snuggled closer. "Are you having a fun trip?"

"Yes," Lily said softly. "But I want to sit with you in the car."

"Oh, baby," Claire said, resting her head on Lily's crown and rocking her gently. "You know you have to sit in your booster seat in the back and I have to sit up front with Daddy so I can help him with the driving. But how about this? When we get to Grandma's house, you can fall asleep in bed with me. Does that sound like a plan?"

Lily nodded. She loved to sleep with Claire. And, though her daughter was getting a bit too old to do it regularly, Claire tended to overlook the fact that, most mornings when she'd wake, Lily was pressed up against her in bed. Claire was never sure when the child snuck into the room, and always told her when she woke that, from that point on, she needed to sleep in her own bed all night. But, truth be told, Claire secretly enjoyed the few quiet moments, each morning, when she held onto her baby girl and listened to her breathe deeply in her sleep. She knew, someday, none of her kids would want to get in bed and cuddle with her and so she'd better cherish each one of these moments before they were gone.

When their food came, Claire told Lily to get back into her chair and eat dinner.

"I don't want to hear anyone tell me they're hungry from this point on!" she said firmly. "Eat!"

And eat they did. And laugh. And enjoy time as a family, something that, with all of the kids' activities and sports and practices, was getting harder and harder to find time for these days. Before children, Claire hadn't understood why people would say it was so hard to sit down for a family dinner. "Make time for it," she'd think. But now she realized how judgmental she'd been. With Jack's work schedule, Luke's baseball practice and guitar lessons, and the girls' soccer team and dance lessons, it was hard to find time when everyone was home together. More often than Claire liked to admit, dinner was spent in the car, before they piled out of the vehicle for their next activity, or else, she found herself standing at the kitchen counter, eating her own meal while she prepared everyone else's food. No, having three kids with active schedules wasn't easy and it was a constant juggling act. She just hoped she kept the balls in the air more often than she dropped them.

An hour later, with full bellies and a large box of leftovers Claire would need to put in her mother-in-law's fridge when they arrived, they were all back in the car. As predicted, the kids immediately put the headsets back on their ears and were immersed in their music before they left the parking lot.

"Why do we always stop at this place?" Jack asked Claire, as he backed out the car. "We don't even like the food, and it never fails to give me heartburn."

Claire laughed at the truth in Jack's statement.

"Tradition. Habit. We'll try something new next time."

"Hey," Jack said, turning to Claire for a moment, "I heard you singing to the kids last night. It sounded nice."

"Thanks."

"I miss your singing. And, you used to play the piano all the time."

"That was before we had three kids," Claire said wistfully. Though she appreciated that Jack always said nice things about her music, she had to admit that when he brought it up, the topic made her uncomfortable. It'd been years since she'd felt she had the time and energy to devote to her singing. It wasn't that she no longer enjoyed her music. It was just there were so many other, seemingly more important, areas of her life that took precedence these days. There were PTA meetings and carpool and Boy Scouts and dance classes. Yet, every time Jack brought up her music, she felt a pang of guilt. And perhaps regret. She'd put her life and career on hold to have a family, and she'd never been disappointed in her decision. Her husband and kids filled her life with such joy and purpose. But—and she hated to admit there was a "but"—wasn't there a part of her that wondered where in her music career she'd be now if she hadn't given it all up to stay home and raise a family?

She'd never expressed those feelings to Jack. She never wanted him to think she wasn't happy on the path she'd chosen for her life, because truly, she was. She knew when Jack brought up her music, he wasn't doing it to pressure her or try to imply she wasn't doing enough with her life. He wasn't that kind of husband. He just wanted her to be happy and he knew music had always given her pleasure in the years before they'd had children.

A year before she found herself pregnant with Luke, Claire had begun to experience quite a bit of success with her music, something she'd dreamed of since she was a child. But when she learned she was pregnant, she made the decision to put that part of her life on hold to stay home with her baby.

"I know life's crazy," Jack said, "but maybe you could start performing again."

"Oh, yeah," Claire said, sarcasm thick in her voice. "In my spare time."

"The twins are in school now and you have a little bit more time than you did when they were small. Maybe you could go to an open mic night sometime at the café downtown."

"I don't know..." Claire hesitated.

"Come on," Jack said, giving her a soft smile. "I'd be there in the front row, cheering you on. At least say you'll think about it."

Claire sighed. Even if she didn't mean it, what harm would come of telling Jack she'd consider it?

"Okay. I'll think about it."

"Did I mention how sexy I find your eyes?" Jack interrupted her reverie.

Claire laughed and slugged his arm. They continued on with their fun-loving banter until Claire realized she was having a hard time keeping those sexy eyes open.

"Hey, how are you doing?" she asked Jack. "Do you need me to help keep you awake or can I fall asleep for a bit?"

"Weren't you the one who said we'd be able to stay up all night driving?" Jack asked teasingly.

"It did sound better in theory, I must admit..." Claire's voice trailed off as her eyes closed and she fought to reopen them.

"It's fine, babe. I'm fine. I've had a lot of caffeine," Jack said reassuringly. "Go to sleep and if I find I'm getting too tired to drive, I'll pull over, okay?"

Claire nodded. At least, she thought she nodded. She was too tired to be sure, though. Already, her thoughts were beginning to make little sense, a sure sign she was quickly falling asleep. Within minutes, she was softly snoring.

Ever since Claire's parents had died, she had, on occasion, dreamt about them. It wasn't often. And, not nearly as frequently as Claire would've liked. The dreams always seemed so real, as if her parents were truly there with her again. In most of them, she usually found herself in her childhood home, with her mom cooking dinner in the kitchen. Claire would sit at the table, her dad coming in to sit across from her. Both her parents would ask about Jack and her children.

She was always surprised they knew she was married and had kids. But, she'd happily tell them all about Luke's latest science fair project and how adorable the girls had looked in their dance costumes at their recital.

This time, she was sleeping in her old bedroom—the one that had the pink-flowered wallpaper and the big canopy bed. It had been the perfect room for a little girl to grow up in and when she'd had the twins, she'd made sure to create one that was just as inviting and frilly for the two of them.

It felt so good to be back in her old bed, and she wanted to sleep there for days.

"Wake up, baby." Someone shook her gently.

"Uh...." Claire moaned. "Go away. I'm tired."

"Wake up, Claire." The voice was more urgent now, and Claire opened one eye.

Standing next to her was her dad. She closed the eye again.

"I'm tired, Daddy. I'm not ready to wake up."

"Baby, I'm not kidding. You need to wake up." Her dad was full-out shaking her now. "Jack needs you to wake up."

Jack? Did he say Jack? What was her dad talking about? She was in her bed at home. Jack wasn't there.

"Claire Elizaebeth Matthews. You need to wake up this very moment." Her dad was using his angry tone with her. She rarely ever heard that one. "Your husband needs you."

This time, Claire's eyes flew open. She was no longer in her childhood bedroom, surrounded by stuffed bunnies and panda bears. She was in the car with Jack and the kids. Jack was driving. He appeared to be wide awake. The kids were asleep in the back. What had her dad been talking about?

Rubbing her eyes, and realizing it had all been a dream, she began to close them again when she heard Jack's voice.

"What the...?"

Claire's eyes flew open again. In the distance, a bright light was in front of them.

A flashlight? No. Too bright. A motorcycle? Why did it seem like it was coming toward them?

And just as Jack gripped the steering wheel and began to swerve to the right, Claire realized what it was. A car. With one headlight. On the wrong side of the road.

Instinctively, as Jack jerked the wheel, Claire turned her head away and reached into the back of the car, trying to shield her babies.

The impact was massive and stunning. Claire had never felt anything like it before. Even with her seatbelt on, Claire was thrown forward with alarming force.

She tried to brace herself as the car began to roll, flipping from top to bottom as if it were one of Luke's toy cars he'd kicked down the hill in their backyard.

Claire could hear the kids, who'd clearly been awakened by the crash, begin to cry out in fear. She wanted to tell them it was okay, that they'd all be okay, but somehow all she could do was scream, too.

And then, as suddenly as it began, the tumbling, and all the cries, ended with extreme force.

"Uh...uh..." Claire moaned.

Slowly, with deliberate effort, Claire opened her eyes. Where was she and why did she feel like she was upside down?

The car. Claire suddenly remembered and her body tensed. Looking around her, she could see very little in the dark. Reaching out, she felt for her window. There was nothing there.

"Jack," Claire called out. "Are you okay?"

She heard nothing. No noise at all.

"Luke... Ella...Lily?!" Claire cried, louder. "Can you hear me? Are you all right?"

The silence pounded in her ears.

She quickly turned to her left, trying to catch a glimpse of Jack, but something was in between them? A piece of metal? She wasn't really sure. She tried to push it away, but it wouldn't move. Twisting her head as far as she could, she attempted to look behind her. Where were her kids? She couldn't see anyone or anything. It was as if the car had caved in around her.

She struggled to undo her seatbelt with one hand, while using her other hand to stabilize herself on the roof the car. She was fairly certain she was hanging upside down and didn't want to fall on her head when she undid the buckle. The belt caught on something as she clicked the button and it began to retract. She twisted her body, feeling a pressure in her abdomen as she worked the belt loose. When she was finally free, she pulled herself through a hole where the car window used to be and onto the ground. She sat there for a moment, gasping for breath. Every inhale took effort.

"Jack!" Claire called. "Where are you? Can you hear me?"

The car's headlights shone on the trees in front of it, but other than that, it was pitch-black. Claire stepped back a few feet, trying to get a better view of the car and where everyone might be.

Her stomach flew into knots as vomit raced into her throat. *The car.* If that's even what it was, and it must be, because she'd just crawled out of it. But it no longer looked like the minivan they'd all piled into for their journey. It was now a twisted piece of metal, turned upside down and bent around a large oak tree.

Where were her babies in that mess?

"Oh, God. Jack! Luke! Answer me! Are you okay?" Claire began to scream as she moved around the van, trying to find an entry inside. Why couldn't she find them?

"Help! Somebody help!" Claire's voice was becoming hysterical. "Ella! Lily! Are you okay? Answer Mommy!"

Claire was so focused on locating her family she didn't hear the sirens or see the people as they rushed down the embankment toward her. As she clawed at the hot metal—*why was it so hot?*—she felt a hand on her arm. *Thank God,* she thought.

"Help me! Please, help! My family's in that car. Please! Get them out!"

"Ma'am," a deep voice said. "You need to get back. We'll take over from here."

Get back? What was he talking about? She couldn't leave this spot until her family was out of the car.

"No!" Claire spat at him. "I need my family."

"Ma'am, you need to back up. The car's on fire. Let us do our job."

On fire? What? How could it be on fire? Her kids were in that car.

"Come on, sweetheart," a soft, soothing voice said to her, as two hands gently grasped her shoulders. "Why don't we back up and let the firemen do their job? We don't want to be in their way now, do we?"

Claire looked up and saw an older woman, with a kind face, smiling down at her. In a daze, Claire nodded. The woman was right. She needed to get out of the way.

Getting off her knees, Claire stood and allowed the woman to wrap her arms around her, slowly leading her away from the wreckage.

"My babies..." Claire moaned.

"Who's in the car?" the woman said, softly and full of concern.

"My whole family...my husband...my three kids..." Claire's voice drifted off as she watched the scene unfolding in front of her. Suddenly, it seemed there were dozens of police and firemen and passengers from other cars, all trying to break apart the minivan and find her family inside. For a moment, Claire felt a sense of relief. Surely, with all these people to help, Jack and the kids would be out of the car soon, wouldn't they?

"They'll get them out," the woman said calmly, though if Claire had been looking at her, she would've seen the absolute fear in the stranger's eyes. It didn't look good. The car was demolished. And, it seemed like the fire department was having a hard time getting their equipment down the steep embankment. From where the woman stood, she didn't know how anyone could have survived such an accident. But the fact that Claire was standing in front of her was evidence miracles do happen, though she could tell Claire hadn't escaped injury free. The woman imagined adrenaline had kicked in and Claire wasn't feeling any of the pain.

"Dear, I think you need to lie down and not move. We need to get you some help." She rested her hand on Claire's stomach, but was scared to push too hard for fear of making the injury worse. "Help!" the woman called out. "She needs help!"

Claire didn't hear a word the woman said. "Jack!" Claire screamed again, struggling against the woman's arms. "Get the kids out! Jack!"

"Get back! Everyone get back!"

Claire didn't know who yelled those words, but in horror, she watched as all the rescuers turned and fled from the car.

"Where are you going?" she wanted to scream. *"My babies are in there! Go back! Go back!"*

She tried to break free of the woman's grasp, and even in her desperate state, was surprised at how tight this old woman could hold onto her.

"I need to get my babies! I need my babies!" Claire screamed, writhing and pushing away from the woman.

She'd just broken free when something hit her so hard, she was knocked to the ground. For a moment, Claire couldn't lift her head. And then, slowly, she forced herself to look up.

The car was completely immersed in flames from the explosion.

"No," Claire whispered. "No."

This couldn't be happening. Not to her. Not to Jack. Not to their babies.

"No!" Claire screamed. "No! No! No! God, please! No! Please, God. Please! Please! Please!"

And, as the reality hit her that, in just a moment, she'd lost everything, Claire laid her head on the ground and began to sob.

CHAPTER THREE

Claire walked through the front door of her home as Gia held it open for her. She hadn't been back since the accident. Gia had been the one to select clothes for her family to wear to be buried. It seemed like a ridiculous task to Claire. No one had said it to her, but she knew their bodies had been severely burned. There would be no open caskets. What was the point of putting the girls in frilly pink dresses when their beautiful faces were no longer distinguishable? But, the funeral home had asked her for the clothes and she'd asked Gia, from her hospital bed, to go to her house and do it. Gia had asked if she had any idea of what she'd like everyone to wear, but Claire had told Gia she didn't care.

Everything was empty now. The future. Her house. Her heart. There was nothing left. Nothing at all.

Without speaking or even looking around her, Claire headed toward the stairs and made her way up them—slowly. The funeral had been postponed for over a week so Claire could recover from surgery. Though she'd taken her pain medication that morning, Claire's abdomen ached as she navigated each step. Upon finally reaching the top landing, she avoided the doors that led to her children's rooms and, instead, headed straight for her own. The room was dark, though it wasn't quite dusk yet. She and Jack had closed the blinds the night they left, because they'd be away for the next week. The bed was unkempt. She hadn't made it. Making beds had never been her forté.

As a child, her mom had insisted she make it every morning when she got up. She'd continued to make her bed regularly in college, not wanting her friends to see a messy dorm room when they visited. But, once she and Jack had their own home, the ritual seemed so silly to her. Jack certainly didn't care if the bed was made each day. And neither did she. After all, they were both just going to get back in it that night. On occasion, she did feel like she was setting a bad example for her kids by not making her bed—and not insisting they make their own. But there were so many other things to worry about as a mom—like did they know their spelling words for Friday's test, had they brushed their teeth, could they tie their shoes? And now, Claire realized, what did making beds matter? Or brushing teeth or memorizing spelling words for that matter? Nothing mattered. Her babies hadn't needed any of her well-intentioned lessons. It'd all been for nothing.

Claire crawled onto the bed and under the comforter and then, curling her tired body into a fetal position, pulled the covers over her head.

"Do you want me to open the blinds?" Gia asked. Claire hadn't even realized, until now, that her best friend had followed her up the stairs and into her room. She didn't reply as Gia went over to the nightstand and turned on the light.

"You didn't eat anything at the reception. I brought home a lot of leftovers. How about I heat up some soup and make you a cup of tea?"

Claire closed her eyes and squeezed them tightly.

Gia paused, seeming to wait for a reply from Claire.

"I'll be right back, sweetie."

Claire could hear the soft footsteps fade away as Gia left the room and headed back down the stairs. She pulled the pillow, from Jack's side of the bed and buried her face in it. It still smelled like him—a mixture of his Kenneth Cole Vintage Black cologne and the outdoors.

She wrapped her arm around the outside of the pillow and pulled it closer to her body. If she let her mind go, she could make herself believe she'd wrapped herself around her husband and that soon, she'd hear the soft whistle of his breathing as he fell into a deep slumber.

Jack had never been a snorer. But he did breathe loudly when he slept. Sometimes, she'd have to nudge him to turn over. How funny that the noise, which had kept her awake over the years, was the one sound she needed to fall asleep now.

"Here, sweetie," Gia's voice lilted through the room. "I brought you some food." When Claire didn't reply, Gia spoke again. "Claire, honey, you need to eat something."

Why?

"I'll tell you what," Gia continued. "How about I leave the food and when you're hungry, you can have a bite, okay?"

Claire pulled Jack's pillow closer.

"I'm going to get ready for bed. If you need me, I'll just be down the hall in the guest room. I'll come back in a few hours to give you your pain medicine." Claire could hear Gia sigh before walking out the door again.

"Gia," Claire whispered, so softly, she wondered if Gia would even hear her.

"Yes?"

"Do you think you could sleep with me tonight?"

The thought of sleeping alone, in this house, was more than she could bear.

"Of course," Gia replied. Claire heard Gia turn off the light on the nightstand next to Claire's side of the bed and then walk around to the other. Claire felt the pressure shift in the mattress as Gia lowered her body onto the bed and adjusted the sheet and blanket, before grabbing Claire's hand and gently squeezing it.

The pressure of that squeeze was all the force she needed to let go.

As she held Jack's pillow close to her face, breathing in what was left of her husband, she took a deep breath and began to weep.

"I think today would be a good day to take a shower," Gia said.

Claire glanced at her friend and then back at the television screen. An all-day marathon of *Project Runway* was on. The designers had been tasked with creating an outfit out of a burlap potato sack. Seriously. Claire picked up the remote and turned the volume up.

"Oh, no you don't," Gia said firmly. "You can't tune me out." She snatched the remote from Claire's hand and clicked the TV off as Claire sat up in protest.

"Hey!" Claire said, bolting up in bed. "I want to see what Pamela and Jesus come up with. They're not doing very well."

"Wow. She speaks," Gia said sarcastically. "Come on. Get out of that bed. You're going to hop into the shower and I'm going to change the sheets and do some laundry. Throw your clothes out of the bathroom door when you take them off."

"I'm perfectly comfortable, thank you very much," Claire said, falling back down into the mound of pillows.

"Well, I'm not comfortable. You stink. My nose will never be the same again. The doctor said you could take a real shower when we got you home over two weeks ago, so that's what you're finally going to do. And we're going to open some windows in here," she said, crossing the room and yanking the cord to raise the blinds. The clatter they made going up hurt Claire's ears.

"No, don't," she said, shielding her eyes from the bright light. "Put them back down."

"I will not put them back down," Gia said, unlatching the locks and reaching to the bottom of the window to tug it up. Claire felt a breeze float across her nightgown. She pulled the covers up to her chin.

"I mean it, Gia. Close the window. Put the blinds back down and give me that damn remote!" She didn't mean to sound so harsh with Gia, but seriously, the woman was getting on her nerves.

"No," Gia said again. "I will not. Get up."

"No."

Gia and Claire glared at each other across the foot of the bed. Gia folded her arms in front of her, a look of dispassionate irritation on her face.

"I can stand here all day."

"I can lie here all day," Claire countered.

"Then I guess we're at an impasse. I wonder who can outlast the other."

Claire gave Gia one more glare and then flung her legs—with as much force as she could muster these days—out of the bed. If she knew one thing about Gia, it was that the woman would not give up. When they were in college, she'd won the MS dance-a-thon, wiggling her body for twenty-six straight hours until every other co-ed had dropped off and she was the only one left boogying. Claire would never win in a stand-off.

"Fine," she said and gave an exaggerated huff so Gia knew she wasn't happy.

"You can huff all you want. Just get in the shower. And grab some new clothes on the way in. I hope the ones you're wearing haven't molded themselves to your skin."

Claire opened the top drawer of her dresser and pulled out a pair of old cotton panties. Not pretty, but functional. Reaching into the drawer below, she grabbed an equally old tee.

"Don't forget shorts or pants of some sort. You're not going to walk around in nothing but a T-shirt all day. You need to put on some semblance of an outfit."

"I won't be walking. As soon as I'm bathed and you've made yourself happy by changing the sheets, I'll be getting right back in bed," she said, though she did reach into another drawer to grab a pair of Jack's boxer shorts. They said "Farticus" on the butt. Luke had begged Claire to let him use his allowance money to buy them for Jack one Father's Day. Her son had thought they were the funniest thing he'd ever seen and nearly laughed himself off the kitchen stool as Jack opened the wrapping.

"It's going to take more than changing the sheets to make me happy. But, I might smile once you're clean. And make sure you wash your hair, too. Unless, of course, you're beginning dreads."

If this had been any other time in her life, Claire would've had a quick comeback regarding the dreads remark. Out of the two of them, Gia was the much-more likely woman to sport such a look. When describing Gia, Claire usually used the term "Bohemian Chic." Gia was a stunning woman, with long, blonde hair that fell all the way to her waist. Whereas Claire was most comfortable in jeans and a T-shirt, Gia's style was all about flowing lines. Her long, gypsy skirts were almost always fastened with a drawstring and she usually donned a bell-sleeved peasant top, if she wasn't just wearing a plain white tank top. Gia's hair nearly always had a band in it, and if not a band, then a braid of her own hair wrapped around her crown.

Gia's individuality was clear by the way she dressed. She was a stubborn woman who'd never had the desire to conform to the fashion styles of those around her. Most days Claire loved Gia's tenacity.

Today was not one of those days.

Claire turned with her clothes in hand. Gia was stripping the bed.

Claire had to admit, the sheets *were* beginning to have a certain funk. She always did enjoy what she and Jack referred to as "Hotel Day"—the bed made up with fresh, crisp sheets. She and Jack had celebrated it as sort of a holiday in their bedroom. It was the closest they'd come, in years, to anything resembling a romantic getaway.

"Hotel Day!" she'd shriek as she'd jump on the bed and roll around, the smell of Tide wafting up as Jack would laugh at her.

"It's the small things in life that make life worth living," he'd say, as he'd crawl in next to her. More times than not, they'd then participate in an activity which would leave the sheets no longer clean.

Claire smiled to herself. Most of the time, the memories of Jack were too painful to remember. She'd push them aside as if swatting a fly interrupting her picnic lunch. But sometimes, one would creep in that would make her heart a little bit lighter. For a split-second, she'd forget the way the story ended and just focus on a piece of the tale.

Her smile faded, though, as she realized Gia was tugging the pillowcase off Jack's pillow.

Claire's clothes dropped to the floor and she lunged at Gia, wild as a lion attacking a wildebeest.

"No!" Claire screamed, yanking the pillow from Gia with such force, Gia cried out. She'd been so focused on the laundry, lost in her own thoughts, she hadn't seen Claire coming. Frankly, she was surprised Claire could move that quickly after the beating her body had taken.

"Geez, Claire!"

"Not this one. You can't change this one." The tears began to flow again. She was ashamed of the smile from a second earlier. She couldn't forget—ever. Not even for a millisecond. It was a betrayal. Disloyal. Disgusting. She collapsed back on the sheet-less bed and pulled the pillow close to her as her body resumed its fetal position. She buried her nose in the soft fabric. Jack's scent was becoming fainter, but it was still there.

"This is ridiculous," Gia spat at her, losing her characteristic cool. "You can't *not* wash that pillowcase forever. It probably smells more like you than it does him by now."

"Shut up," Claire hissed.

"No. I will not shut up. Get up. I mean it, Claire. *Get up!*" She tugged at Claire's arm. "I can't make the bed if you're in it and you reek!"

"I do not!"

"You do! Have you smelled yourself?!"

Claire remained silent. Truth was, she had kind of smelled herself and it was a little gross. She did need a shower.

"Listen, sweetie," Gia said, calming down a bit as she sat next to Claire. "I won't wash the pillowcase. And, if it makes you happy, I noticed Jack's laundry basket is full. There are probably a dozen shirts that smell like him in there. You can get one of those when we do, eventually, wash his pillow, okay?"

Claire nodded slowly.

"Now, get up." Gia stood up. Her voice was stern again. "Now!"

Claire wanted to tell Gia she was being a bitch. A big one. But she kept her mouth shut. She was afraid Gia would get so mad at Claire, she'd leave. Claire couldn't let that happen. It'd been nearly three weeks since the funeral and Gia had spent every single night at Claire's house. Claire knew what a sacrifice that must be. Gia was single. She had a single person's life. But, the only time she was away from Claire was when she went to work each day. And within thirty minutes of getting off her job as an elementary school teacher, she was back at Claire's house—except for the days when she stopped at the grocery store on her way home. If it wasn't for Gia, Claire would've certainly starved to death by now. Not only would there be no one to buy food for her, there'd be no one to feed her. Claire had only ventured downstairs one time since they'd been home. Gia had been at work and Claire had suddenly gotten a craving for apples and peanut butter. She'd slowly made her way down the stairs and into the kitchen. She'd gone so far as opening the fridge door and grabbing an apple out of the crisper drawer. But then, the thought of cutting the apple and getting the peanut butter out of the pantry had seemed too daunting a task, so she'd left the apple on the counter and shuffled back up the stairs again, getting back in bed. And that's where Gia had found her four hours later.

"Okay," Claire said softly and got off the bed again. Gia was holding the clothes Claire had dropped to the floor. She shoved them into Claire's arms.

"Don't get out until you smell like a rose in June."

Claire nodded and went into the bathroom. Gia closed the door behind her, with a little bit too much force, reminding Claire she was supposed to stay in there.

Claire placed her clothes on the bathroom vanity and looked into the mirror. What she saw would have been horrifying if she hadn't just seen it yesterday when she'd come in here and accidentally caught a glimpse of herself as she washed her hands.

She looked like a shell of her former self. Gaunt and gray—the gray being both her skin and her hair, as she hadn't dyed her roots since before the accident. She'd been horrified when she started going gray in her late twenties, though it made sense. Her mom had been completely white by the time Claire was in high school.

Claire lifted her finger, which was skinnier than it used to be, and rubbed at the skin below her eyes. It looked as if she had purple eye shadow there, but it didn't come off. Her eyes, which once sparkled so much Ella had said they looked like fairy eyes, now had a dull sheen to them.

The bruises on her face from the accident had nearly faded and all that remained was an icky yellow tone on her forehead and her left cheek. Claire hadn't escaped the accident injury-free, but the agony in her heart had been so much worse than the actual physical pain from her injuries, the bodily wounds had never even registered on the scale. She had a head laceration, which had required twenty stitches, in addition to her two broken ribs, a collapsed lung, numerous bruises and contusions and a fractured collarbone. The worst injury, though, had been to her abdomen. She'd been impaled by a piece of metal from the car. It wasn't until the surgery was complete, and she was in recovery, that she'd felt any pain. Claire hadn't even noticed the dagger-like shard in her stomach and knew nothing until Gia told her about it after the surgery.

"It punctured your uterus. They thought they'd have to do a hysterectomy, but luckily, the doctor was able to repair the injury."

Luckily.

Claire had nearly snorted over the word. If she was anything, it wasn't lucky.

And what could be more symbolic than the impaling of her uterus?

After the initial hospital stay, she'd never gone back to the doctor. When Gia realized there was no way she was going to get Claire out of the house, she'd somehow convinced the doctor to do a few house calls. It probably hadn't been that difficult. Bell Springs was a small town and most everyone who lived there was doing everything they could think of to help Claire during this difficult time.

Claire turned away from the mirror and twisted the faucet on in the shower. She held her hand under the stream until the water got warmer. Then, slipping out of her clothes, she stepped into the hot cascade. It felt good against her thin, cold frame. Gia had been right. Claire did need to shower.

But she still couldn't avoid the question of why? *Why* did she need to be clean? *Why* did she need to change her clothes? For what purpose? To what end? There was no one to see. No one to talk to. Nowhere to go. Nothing. There was just *nothing.*

And, as that realization once again washed over Claire, more scalding than the water, she rested her head against the shower and began to cry.

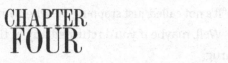

CHAPTER
FOUR

"There's someone here to see you," Gia said, standing in the doorway to Claire's bedroom.

"I don't want to see anyone."

"I know."

Claire turned the volume up, just a few notches, on her TV show. Today, the marathon was of women who kill their in-laws. The channel she normally watched had an *Everybody Loves Raymond* marathon playing, a show Claire and Jack had always enjoyed—especially because of the twins in the show—but these days, she couldn't bear to watch any show that involved a family.

Murder was a much safer bet.

"Why are you still standing there?" She could see Gia in her peripheral vision. The woman hadn't moved an inch.

"You're getting very bossy," Gia said, not smiling. She'd been much more curt with Claire in the past few days—or was it weeks? It all blended together.

"Sorry," Claire said, but she didn't sound like she meant it. The breaking point for the current murderer had been when her mother-in-law had said her chicken pot pie tasted like pig slop. *The nerve.*

"I can't tell them to go away. It's Bill and Nancy."

Speaking of in-laws you'd want to kill...

Claire clicked off the television and let out a deep, frustrated sigh.

"I know. I can't believe they just stopped by, either," Gia said.

"It's not called 'just stopping by' when you live fourteen hours away."

"Well, maybe if you'd returned any of their calls..." Gia said with a shrug.

"And say what? I'm sorry your son and your grandchildren are all dead and I'm still alive? Lucky me!" Claire rubbed her eyes with the bottom of her palms. She was exhausted. This whole doing-nothing-thing was really tiring.

"You have to come downstairs."

"And what if I don't?" Claire asked. It sounded more like a challenge than she'd intended.

"Then I'm going to tell them to come up here."

"You wouldn't."

"Just watch me," Gia said defiantly. Her patience with Claire was running thin these days and it showed.

Claire pushed down the covers and got out of bed. "Fine," she said as she tried to walk past Gia.

"I think you should put on some clothes."

Claire looked down at herself. She was wearing one of Jack's college T-shirts and another pair of his boxer shorts. These were a Christmas theme and said "I've Been Naughty" on the butt.

Without saying a word, Claire went back into the room and into her own closet. She pulled on a pair of jeans, but left Jack's T-shirt in place.

"Better?" she said, as she walked back into the bedroom.

"Much. Be nice," Gia hissed.

Claire acted like she didn't hear Gia and went downstairs. She'd been down more regularly over the past week, ever since her forced shower, but not as often as she probably should. She noticed things looked a little dusty down here, and there was a stack of dirty dishes in the sink. Gia was a loving, wonderful and nurturing friend, but not much of a housekeeper. Claire remembered that from their days of rooming together in college.

Bill and Nancy were sitting side-by-side on the couch, as stiff as pokers. They were an attractive couple. Bill, like his son, was tall and, though not as muscular as in his youth, still stayed fit by swimming at the gym every day and refusing to ride in a golf cart when he played on Thursdays. "The day I need to ride is the day I need to quit," he often said. Nancy gave off the image of being the stereotypical Southern lady. She still wore the beehive hairdo she'd sported in her youth and was never, ever seen in anything but a dress. Claire had always found that to be so weird. They weren't the casual and comfortable sundresses Gia often wore. Nancy wore prim, church-style dresses. All the time. Who wore a church dress just to hang out at home or do the dishes or pull weeds in her garden? Nancy did, that's who. If you were to first meet Nancy, you'd think she was as fragile and gentle as a bird. But, as time went by, Claire had come to realize the bird she'd first thought to be a robin was really a crow. Her voice was as annoying to Claire as incessant cawing. Nancy constantly had something to say and she always made sure you heard it.

Bill stood the moment he saw Claire enter the room. Nancy remained seated, which didn't surprise Claire in the least. She was the type of person who felt others should come to her, not the reverse. The only time Claire had seen her in-laws since the accident was at the funeral. Nancy had fallen to the ground and wept uncontrollably. Claire, in such a state of shock, had found it impossible to cry. But she'd wanted to kick her mother-in-law. The funeral was about Jack and the kids. Not Nancy. The fact that Claire had lost her husband and children made no difference to Nancy. Nancy had lost her one and only child. That was much, much worse. Claire wasn't sure how—since Claire had lost three children—but somehow it was. At least, in Nancy's eyes and, to Nancy, her eyes were the only ones that mattered.

"Claire, Claire, dear. How are you? We've been so worried about you." Bill rushed over to Claire and pulled her into a bear hug. Claire did her best to hug him back, though her body was weak from all of her recent inactivity. She'd always had a soft spot for Bill. He wasn't much of a man, in her opinion. He never stood up to his wife, even to defend his own son when she would, on the rare occasion, get on Jack's case. And, it was rare. Jack had walked on water and air and everything in between as far as Nancy was concerned. Bill was a mild-mannered man who, if Claire were to psychoanalyze him, she'd say he was a first-class enabler. He allowed Nancy to get away with all kinds of inappropriate behavior, toward her daughter-in-law and other people in their inner circle. Nancy was as sweet as cherry pie to perfect strangers, but as tart as a lime to her family members and a few old friends Claire felt kept Nancy around out of habit.

"I'm okay," Claire said as Bill let her go. He smelled like Jack. The same mixture of cologne and pine. She wanted to both push him away and hug him tighter.

Claire's eyes went to Nancy. The woman still sat perched at the edge of the couch, her legs tightly together, her hands folded in her lap, her lips pursed. Clearly, there would be no hug from her.

"Hi, Nancy," Claire said, dutifully walking over to Jack's mom and leaning down to peck her on her cheek. Despite the overabundance of flowery perfume she always wore, she smelled musty to Claire. Like the damp, stale smell that wafted into your nostrils the moment you opened the door to an antique store. Bill resumed his seat next to Nancy while Claire sat down in the big armchair next to the couch. Gia, who'd followed Claire down the stairs, pulled out a chair from the kitchen table, which was still in view, but far enough away to not be an active part of the conversation. Claire appreciated this. Gia knew all the sordid details of Claire's relationship with her mother-in-law and, being the good friend she was, wasn't about to leave Claire alone with her. Not yet, anyway. It was too soon.

They all sat in silence for a few moments. Awkwardness permeated the room.

"How've you been?" Bill asked, even though he'd already asked her the same question when she came down the stairs. Despite the fact she really liked Bill, it was truly the most stupid question he could ever ask her once, let alone twice.

"Okay," she said again.

"Listen, Claire," Nancy piped up. "We're sorry to just stop over like this, but you know, you haven't returned any of our calls."

Claire nodded. She didn't have anything to say to that. She knew Gia had spoken to them a few times, because Gia told her so, but she'd never asked Gia what was said during those conversations.

"The funeral home called us because they couldn't get hold of you."

Gia interrupted now. "They haven't called the house."

"Well, I imagine they called Claire's cell phone. Have you been answering that, too?" Nancy snapped. She didn't wait for Gia to respond. "Anyhow, they couldn't reach you and so they called us to say someone needed to come in to select the headstones."

Headstones? Claire hadn't even thought about the fact someone had to select those—decide what was to be written on each one.

"We have an appointment in an hour," Bill said gently. "We tried to call to tell you, in case you'd like to come, but ...well, as we've said."

Claire nodded. *Headstones.* Headstone made it seem so final. So real. So cold and hard.

When she pictured the heads of her babies, deep in slumber, she saw them surrounded by stuffed pandas and Winnie-the-Poohs and pillows that said, "Sweet Dreams." Not a rigid piece of rock.

"I'm assuming you'll want to go with us," Nancy continued. "We'll wait while you get dressed." Her tone was matter-of-fact. No nonsense. *Of course* Claire would go with them. Why would she decline? After all, it was her family, was it not? Families pick out their loved ones' headstones. They put things on them like "Loving Husband" and "Our Little Angel."

But Claire hadn't even completed the kids' baby books yet. She couldn't write "Sleep, my little ones, sleep" on a hard slab when she hadn't yet handwritten "Luke's first pair of shoes" next to the photo.

"Um...I can't," Claire said. "I'm sorry. I can't."

"What do you mean you can't?" Nancy said, the last word rising like a whining child's *"But why can't I go outside?"*

"I..." Claire was at a loss for words. "I..." She looked over at Gia in desperation. Gia picked up on Claire's cues and came to the rescue. Jumping up from her seat, she walked into the living room.

"I think Claire might not be ready for that."

"We understand," Bill said, his voice kind.

"We do *not* understand," Nancy barked. "She *must* select the headstones."

"I'm sure you can do it," Claire said softly. "You'll do a lovely job. I wouldn't know what to put on them."

"And you think I *do?*" Nancy snapped.

"I..." Claire knew she was stammering, but she didn't know how to reply. She couldn't go pick out her babies' headstones. *Could not.* It wasn't even an option. Her palms were clammy at the thought. Her heart was racing. A repetitive pounding began in her ears. She felt her limbs detach from her body as the panic began to rise.

"I lost a child, too, Claire. Not to mention my grandchildren. Sometimes I wonder if you remember that."

"Of course she does," Gia said soothingly.

"Claire hasn't forgotten that," Bill said to his wife, placing a hand gently on her knee. She promptly removed it.

"I don't think she has. Has she once called to see how *we're* doing?" This woman was unbelievable.

"Are you kidding me?" Gia nearly screeched. A calm soul, Gia rarely lost her composure, but when she did...Claire didn't like to be around.

Where were her meds? Claire had been trying to wean herself off the tranquilizers and painkillers the doctor had prescribed right after the accident. She'd always been the type of person who was extremely conscious of not getting hooked on any kind of medication. She didn't even like to take too much Tylenol. But, heaven help her, she needed something right now.

The pounding grew louder and louder.

"Claire needs some time..."

"You have no right to..."

"I know better than you..."

"You're not even family..."

The arguing grew distant until Claire could no longer make out the words. The world around her became a blur of slow-moving figures. Mouths opening and closing with exaggerated sluggishness. She thought she could hear *Chariots of Fire* playing as she watched her mother-in-law's mouth move while her finger wagged at Gia.

Only this wasn't a movie. And she couldn't sit and watch any longer.

"Enough!" Claire yelled, jumping to her feet. She must've screamed it even louder than she thought because, instantly, the other three froze. All eyes were upon her.

"I'm sorry, Nancy, that you and Bill came all the way here today. I know it's a long trip. But I will not be going with you to pick out headstones. If you feel you're up to the task, then by all means, go over there and select them. I don't care one bit what they say. Or, if you don't want to do it, but instead, feel it's my job, then you can just drive all the way home and one day, *maybe,* if and when I'm ready, I'll go and select the stones for my husband and children. But I will *not* be bullied into doing something I'm not ready to do one second before I'm ready to do it."

Nancy's mouth was agape. Claire wanted to tell her to pick her jaw up off the ground. A ding of happiness sounded inside Claire's head. She'd always wanted to make her mother-in-law speechless. She wished Jack was around to see the look on her face. He'd always wanted Claire to stand up to his mother. He'd be so proud of her now.

"So, if you don't mind," Claire said, regaining her composure. "I'm going back upstairs. I'm sure Gia will see you out."

Claire turned and strode to the stairs. She hadn't planned on looking back, but then, quickly, glanced over her shoulder. "It was good to see you, Bill."

"You, too, Claire," her father-in-law said sincerely.

She knew she'd receive an email from him later today, apologizing for his wife's behavior. Claire had received too many of those emails to count over the years. Though she didn't respect the way the man never stood up to his wife—at least, not in front of her and Jack—she did appreciate the fact he tried to smooth things over later. He loved Claire. She knew that. And he never wanted her to be hurt. It was just unfortunate he couldn't prevent the hurt from happening in the first place. But, as Jack used to say, "What cha gonna do?"

Claire hurried up the stairs. She could hear Gia making it clear to Nancy and Bill it would be best if they'd leave—immediately. She wanted to jump back into bed and flip on her murder show. Or any other program that would take her mind off her current reality. But as she reached the top landing, her eyes wandered to the closed doors of her children's rooms.

She hadn't been in those rooms since the day she'd hurried her kids out of them and into the car. She knew Gia had gone in them when she'd come to pick out the kids' clothes for the funeral but, except for that one time, the rooms had remained untouched and silent.

Since she and Gia had arrived home the day of the funeral, Claire had made a point of not even glancing at their doors. They contained such a multitude of memories. Claire wasn't ready to open that Pandora's box. At least, she hadn't been.

But maybe today, she could. Hadn't she just stood up to her mother-in-law? Maybe today was a day for other firsts.

Claire slowly made her way down the hallway and stopped at Luke's door. *"Do Not Enter,"* the handwritten sign, secured with Scotch tape to the wood, screamed at her. Luke had carefully printed those words, with bursts of fire coming out of them, when he'd found his sisters chewing an entire pack of gum he'd bought with his own money.

Claire almost heeded the warning and then changed her mind. She turned the knob, which was still sticky from dirty hands, and opened the door. It was dark inside. Luke's room was always dark. Unlike his sisters' room, with its whole wall of windows, Luke's room had only one tiny glass opening in the back corner and his ceiling lamp never seemed bright enough. Claire had been meaning to get him a floor lamp to add some light, but had never gotten around to it.

She flicked the switch to her left and the ceiling bulbs hummed as they lit. The room was as unkempt as she remembered. Legos all over the floor. The bed unmade. *Star Wars* posters, drawings, and souvenirs Luke had collected from every school event he'd ever attended hung from thumbtacks on the wall. She walked over to the hamper and removed the lid. Like Jack's, it was full. She picked up the shirt that was crumpled on top. It smelled like Tide. That little bugger. Instead of putting away his clean clothes, as she'd no doubt asked of him, he'd put them all back in the hamper to be rewashed.

That's one way to avoid putting your clothes away.

Such a trick would have irritated Claire to no end a few months ago. Now she had to smile at his ingenuity.

Still, she was sad the clothes smelled so clean and not like her little boy. She wanted to breathe Luke in again.

She laid the shirt back in the hamper and replaced the lid. She didn't want to change anything in the room. She wanted it to remain exactly as it had been the last time her son was in it. She walked quietly to the bed and sat down on the end. She could feel the springs through her bottom. Why hadn't she gotten Luke a better mattress? He'd never complained, but each time she'd lie with him, she'd think,

This kid has the most uncomfortable bed in the whole house. Why had she waited to give him something better? Why did she put off so many things for tomorrow?

Why hadn't she known tomorrow might never come?

She picked up his favorite stuffed bear, Lester, and held it to her chest. When Luke was little, Lester used to travel everywhere with them—to the grocery store, the bank, church, sleepovers at Gia's house. Eventually, he'd graduated to simply a friend for bedtime.

Claire kissed the top of Lester's head and placed him gently against the pillow. Then, thinking better of it, she laid him down and pulled the covers up to his chin, as she'd done to Luke two thousand times before.

She found herself wandering, next, into the twins' room. As she pressed the door open, she was greeted by a burst of sunshine. The star mobile hanging from the ceiling glittered in the light. The matching vanities, at the end of each bed, were covered in lipstick and eye shadow stains—items the girls were not supposed to have, but somehow seemed to get their hands on anyway. The beds, as expected, were unkempt and their clean clothes, unlike Luke's, were in piles at the ends of the beds.

At least these kids hadn't tried to pull one over on her.

But what did it matter? *Disobedient children?* What she wouldn't do to have them back—the scowls, the tempers and the stomping of feet as she told them to clean their rooms. In fact, if she had them back, she'd help them all clean their rooms. Why hadn't she done that more often?

Keeping your rooms clean isn't my responsibility.

She's said that a hundred times. But, what had been her responsibility? Keeping them safe? She'd failed at that. Miserably. The least she could've done would've been to hang up Nike sweatshirts and tuck Elmo T-shirts into drawers.

Claire wanted to go lie down on one of the girls' beds. She wanted to pick up their stuffed animals and hold them and cry for all the things she wished she'd done better as a mom and all the things she'd now never get to do with her girls. She used to joke with Jack that, like on *The Brady Bunch*, the girls would have a double wedding. Now she'd never get to see either one of them in a wedding gown. Never watch them grow into young women and see them float down the stairs in their prom dresses. She'd never buy another baseball bat or ballet slipper or school notebook. No more piano lessons or Girl Scout meetings or Sunday School musicals.

She hadn't just lost her children. She'd lost her life.

And, without a life, what was the point of living? How was she going to spend the next sixty years without her family?

She didn't think she could survive the next sixty minutes.

It was all too much for one person to handle. Too heavy a load to bear. She couldn't possibly be expected to continue.

She was living in a hell worse than anything she'd ever imagined. Every mother fears the loss of a child to a miscarriage, an accident or an illness. Sometimes, when her babies were tiny, Claire would watch them sleep and feel such pain for the parents who'd lost a child to SIDS. She hadn't been able to imagine anything worse than waking up to find your baby was gone.

That would be a complete nightmare.

Torture.

A man who loses his wife is a called a widower and a woman who loses her husband is now a widow. But what is someone who loses a child called?

There was no name for that.

And if there was no name for that, there was certainly no word for someone who'd lost everyone.

She no longer had an identity. She wasn't a wife. She was no longer a mom. She'd stopped being a daughter years earlier. There wasn't anything to call her. She wasn't anything to anybody.

Claire had always found her identity in those she loved. She loved being Jack's wife. *Mrs. Matthews.* She used to beam when the other kids at her children's school would call out, "Hi, Ella's mom!" Or Luke's or Lily's.

She used to be proud to be her parents' daughter.

But now she belonged to no one.

That was insufferable. She wouldn't live like that.

She couldn't.

Her babies needed her. Jack was missing her.

She needed to be with them again.

Claire turned and left the room, pulling the door closed behind her. There'd be no more nights alone. She wanted to be with her family. *Needed* to be with them. *Why couldn't other people see that?*

She should've gotten back in that car, allowed herself to burn with it. Why had she let someone pull her away?

She hated herself for leaving them alone.

But no more. They wouldn't be alone anymore. Mommy was coming. Mommy would be holding them soon. They'd be a family again. The way they were meant to be.

Forever.

Gia rolled over in bed for what seemed like the hundredth time. She couldn't sleep. The visit with Bill and Nancy had set her nerves on edge and they weren't even her in-laws.

She'd never cared for them. Claire hadn't, either. But being the kind person Claire was, she'd rarely complained about them over the years. In fact, she'd barely spoken about them, which was a sure sign Claire disliked them. If Claire liked someone, as she did most people she met, Gia couldn't get her to shut up about the interesting tidbits of their lives she'd uncovered.

But Nancy and Bill? Claire was practically mute on the couple. Gia always felt Claire believed complaining about the Matthews would be disrespectful to Jack. They were his parents and had raised him to be a wonderful man and husband. There must be something redeeming about them, right?

But Gia had never been so sure.

Nancy had pulled a lot of crap over the years, making Claire's life much more difficult than it needed to be. Nancy would change their plans to visit at the last moment, always right after Claire had spent two days cleaning the entire house. Or, like today, they'd just "pop in" for a visit, when Claire was knee deep in Play-Doh and poop. For years, that had been Claire's favorite expression. Whenever Gia would call, Claire would inevitably say she was "knee deep in Play-Doh and poop." When Nancy would show up on such a day, unannounced, she'd inevitably have some snide comment to make about the condition of Claire's house or the state of the children.

Nancy felt the world revolved around her. Instead of coming to help Claire after she gave birth to Luke, Nancy insisted she had a stomach bug or a broken toe—Gia couldn't remember which. Maybe it was both. And, she actually asked if Jack could come stay with *them* so his dad could get a break from helping her. Jack, of course, saw through the charade and refused to leave Claire's side. Claire had been grateful for this, but she'd felt as if she'd somehow caused Jack to choose between her and his parents.

Gia couldn't stand Nancy and the fact she'd had the nerve to show up today and act as if her life was worse than Claire's. It had taken all Gia had to not punch the woman.

Claire hadn't said a word since her in-laws had left and Gia had given Claire space. When Gia eventually made it upstairs, Claire was back in bed, a new murder show on the TV. She'd barely acknowledged Gia, even though Gia had lain down on the bed next to her to watch an episode. The show had been so depressing Gia didn't know how Claire could watch such horror while in the middle of her own nightmare.

Grief was a funny thing. After the accident, Gia had begun reading a number of books on it, searching for ways to help Claire. It wasn't as if Gia and Claire hadn't been down this road of sorrow before. Gia had been Claire's roommate when both of Claire's parents had passed away. When her mom died, it had almost been a relief for Claire. She'd watched her mom suffer, for such a long time. Claire had felt some emotional release with the knowledge there'd be no more pain. But when her dad died? That had been a completely unexpected tragedy. Gia had done her best to help Claire through that time. She was Claire's closest friend and confidante. Gia had to admit, though, she'd been so thankful Jack had come into the picture right then, when

Claire needed him most. Truth be told, Gia needed him, too. She never seemed to know what to say or do to help Claire. Because of Jack, she didn't need to worry quite as much about not doing the right thing because he seemed to always be doing it. He took a lot of the pressure off Gia and she knew she'd be eternally grateful. She owed Jack.

Now, it was just her. There was no one else to help Claire through these dark days. No family. Very few friends. Everyone loved Claire, but Claire didn't have many people to whom she felt close. Though always pleasant, she was a quiet soul who'd invested most of her time and life into her family. Jack. Her kids. Her parents before that. Gia was all she had left. And it was a weight Gia felt heavily. Gia wanted to help Claire through her grief. She truly did. But boy, did Gia miss Jack. He'd always been the one who knew what to say in a difficult time.

Now there was no one. And Gia worried about that constantly. She was *it*. Claire's only lifeline to the world of the living and Gia was scared to death she wasn't up to the task.

She'd been living with Claire ever since the accident. Eventually, she'd need to move out. She had a life to get back to and Claire, as sad as it was, would need to find a way to live a life without her family. But Claire wasn't at that point yet and Gia didn't see it showing up in the near future. It stressed her out.

Jack had made sure Claire and the kids would be provided for in the event of his untimely death, so there was a large life insurance policy. There were, though, no children who needed to be supported. The policy was for more money than Claire, alone, would ever need. She could easily pay off the house and live quite well for the rest of her life. Or, she could lie in bed for the next fifty years.

At the rate they were going, the latter was a distinct possibility.

Some days, Gia felt successful. She and Claire would have an enjoyable weekend. They'd go out to lunch or a movie. Or for a walk around the park downtown. Claire would never exactly smile. And she certainly would never laugh. But her cheeks would show some color and Gia would notice the emptiness, which had taken up residence in Claire's eyes, wouldn't be quite as consuming.

Then they'd come home, and Claire would crawl right back into bed, despite Gia's pleas to stay downstairs and watch TV from the couch in the living room.

When Gia was at work, she wasn't sure what Claire did. She doubted Claire moved much. When Gia left in the morning, Claire was in bed. When she came home, Claire was in bed. There would sometimes be a dish or two in the sink, but other than that, there was no sign of life.

Gia rolled over again. She needed to fall asleep. The past month had begun to take its toll on her, too. She'd lost weight. Constantly felt exhausted. Couldn't remember the last time she'd hung out with any of her other friends. She knew they were beginning to worry about her. And dating? Forget it. Gia hadn't been out with a man in way too long. She always held out hope that one day, she'd find him. *Her Jack.* She'd never been envious of Claire for finding such an incredible man. If anything, it had given her hope such men existed, but she could never figure out why it was taking her guy so long to show up.

Gia could feel herself beginning to drift off to sleep. Her thoughts were becoming muddled and, before she knew it, she was gone, deep into slumber.

She wasn't sure what woke her. A bad dream? A crash? She was certain she'd only been asleep for a few minutes. Though, to her surprise, when she looked at the clock on the nightstand, she saw it was after one in the morning. She'd been sleeping for close to two hours. Sitting up, she peered through the darkness.

"Claire," she whispered. Some nights, when Claire couldn't sleep, she'd come wake Gia or get in bed with her. But the room was silent.

She fell back onto her elbows. Sleep would come easily this time. She was so tired.

Then she heard it again. The sound was loud and violent, as if someone was taking a sledgehammer to the dining room hutch. Glass breaking. Wood crashing. And screaming. Lots of screaming.

Gia jumped out of bed as her brain snapped from a dream state to consciousness. Without stopping to put on a pair of pants, she yanked open the door and ran into the hallway in nothing but a tank top and panties.

"Claire!" Gia called. "Claire!" She rushed to Claire's bedroom and swung open the door. The bed was empty.

Gia heard another crash. This one sounded like a window being smashed in.

The screaming was getting louder. More desperate. More intense. Gia couldn't make out the words being hurled, but she had a feeling she knew the pain they contained.

Gia dashed down the stairs and into the kitchen, toward the sounds. As she turned the corner, her head barely dodged a flying butter dish. It shattered into hundreds of little pieces as it hit the wooden door frame and splattered to the ground.

"How could you do this to me?!" Claire screamed. "I didn't deserve this! You had no right! I hate you!"

A Corning Ware baking dish was launched at the refrigerator, not breaking until it hit the floor, but Gina noticed it left a large dent in the stainless steel door.

"I hate you!"

Wineglass to spice cabinet. Crash.

"I hate you!"

Dinner plate to kitchen island. Smack.

"I hate you!"

Glass measuring cup to tile floor. Bam.

Claire looked around the room, searching for something else to break. From Gia's perspective, there didn't seem to be much left. The cabinet doors all hung open, their contents strewn in tiny pieces over the floor and countertops, as if Claire had stood on the counter and wiped them all out, violently, in one fell swoop.

Then, suddenly, Claire fell to the ground. A marionette with sliced strings.

If Gia had thought she'd heard Claire cry before, she'd been wrong. The crying of the days after the car accident had been sad and grief-filled. Appropriate. Expected. Neat. Yes. That was the word Gia was looking for—*neat*. Claire's weeping had been neat and tidy and could fit snugly in the box labeled *Grief.*

The sounds that came from Claire now were ones Gia had never heard in her entire life. They were the wild cries of an animal. Gutteral. They were dark and black. Catastrophic. Ugly. Macabre.

Gia was embarrassed to be witnessing this very private moment of such raw anguish. It was personal. She had no right to intrude.

Except, Gia knew, she had to intrude. There was no one else to intervene.

She stood, leaning against the wall, watching her very best friend in the whole world purge her sorrow and heartbreak. And then, as quickly as the horror had begun, Claire calmed. The tears continued to flow, but the sounds ceased.

The silence was almost as unnerving as the screams.

Claire lifted herself by the palms of her hands and pushed her torso off the ground. She crawled two feet over to the stove, the way her twins used to when they were getting underfoot in the kitchen. She turned so her bottom was on the ground and leaned her back against the door. Drawing her knees to her chest, she laid her head down and continued to cry.

Gingerly, Gia navigated the minefield of shattered glass—doing her best to not step on any with her bare feet—and sat down next to her. For a moment, she was unsure whether Claire even knew she was there.

"I'm having a bad night," Claire said, breaking the silence, her head still on her knees, face to the floor.

Gia surveyed the mess. "Yeah. The mosaic kind of gave you away."

Claire choked back a sob. "It's just...how can my whole family be dead and I'm *not*? How am I supposed to live in a world where there's no Jack or Luke or Emma or Lily?"

"I don't know." The response was truthful, though tragically inadequate.

The two friends sat in silence. The weight of the question more than either of them could bear.

Claire lifted her head and looked at Gia, for the first time that night. Her face was red and splotchy. "Do you think there's a God?"

If there was anything Gia hated, it was the topic of religion. If she went on a date and the man instigated such a discussion, their evening would be over before the second course.

But religion and God were two different things in Gia's mind. She had no interest in formal religion, but a belief in a higher power? That was a concept she could get behind.

She sighed and, looking directly at Claire, nodded.

"If there is, why would He take three little children?" Claire asked. "They hadn't even begun to really live. And, if He was going to take them, why did He give them to me in the first place?"

Her eyes bored into Gia, as if she thought, deep down inside of her, Gia might actually have an answer to such a question. There was, of course, no answer, nothing that would make sense of the senseless.

"That's going to be the first thing I ask when I meet Him someday," Gia said.

"Yeah...me, too." Claire's voice drifted off, as if her body was present, but her mind was elsewhere. She shifted her eyes from Gia to somewhere in the distance. Gia glanced over, almost wondering if there was someone outside the back patio door, someone she couldn't see because of the darkness.

"I thought that might be tonight." Her voice was so tiny, Gia had to lean in to make sure she didn't miss a word.

"What would be tonight?" Gia whispered.

"Meeting God."

Gia sighed.

"Oh, Claire..."

"I just want the pain to end. I want to be with my family again. I want to *die*."

Gia wanted to scream. To slap Claire. To yell at her and say, "Are you crazy!?" But, she did none of those things; frankly, she couldn't blame Claire. There wasn't anyone on this planet who could fault Claire for those thoughts. There was no worse a loss than the one Claire had experienced. It wasn't only one loss. She'd lost everyone. Everything. What Claire had experienced was worse than death. Passing away, in comparison, would seem like a respite from the world.

And that was exactly what Claire was thinking. Death would be a relief.

"Claire..."

"I came down here looking for a knife. I'd thought about swallowing pills, but I couldn't find any of them."

Gia was thankful she'd taken proactive steps a few weeks back. She hadn't really thought Claire would try to harm herself. If nothing else, Claire seemed too catatonic to go off in search of pills or a weapon. But then Lucy, the woman who was subbing for the third-grade teacher on maternity leave, had made a comment in the teachers' lounge that had rattled around in Gia's brain until she couldn't stand it any longer.

"If someone killed my entire family, I'd blow my brains out!"

All the teachers had frozen, their sandwiches immobilized in mid-air. Upon realizing what she'd said and how callous it was, Lucy had tried to recant it, but the words were out there and Gia hadn't been able to forget them.

Luckily, Claire and Jack didn't own any guns, but there were other ways to commit suicide. Gia did some research and found the most typical way for a woman to take her life was to ingest pills. Thus, Gia had cleaned out the medicine cabinet and removed every bottle from Claire's nightstand. She'd shoved the prescriptions under her mattress, knowing if Claire were to attempt to concoct a lethal cocktail, she'd have to move Gia's sleeping body to do it.

"That's because I hid them."

"Oh." Claire didn't seem surprised or annoyed or even thankful. The "oh" just lingered in the air of the messy kitchen, like the fog over the Golden Gate Bridge.

"I don't see any blood," Gia finally said.

"I couldn't do it," Claire said, her voice bland, as if reading one of her kid's math word problems aloud. "And, the thing is, I don't even know why I couldn't. It's not like I'd be leaving anyone behind."

Gia's shoulders slumped.

"I know," Claire continued. "I didn't want to do that to you. I knew it would be a shitty thing to do, especially to have you find me. But..."

Where was Jack? He'd know what to say. But then, if Jack were here, there'd be no need for this conversation.

"I had a friend once tell me the most powerful prayer he ever read was, 'Let me not die while I'm still alive.'"

"I don't even know what that means," Claire said.

"Don't you?" Gia asked pointedly. "Claire, I have no idea what it feels like to be you. But, if you ask me, I think the only way to get to the other side of the pain is to walk right through it. You can't just give up on life. Jack and the kids aren't here, but you *are*. And yes, you're the only one here to feel the pain, but maybe once you force yourself to walk through it, you'll feel like you can begin to live again."

"I don't want to live again."

Gia put her arm around Claire and pulled her friend close. Claire rested her head on Gia's shoulder. "I know, sweetie. I know. But, if I were going through this kind of hell, I know you'd remind me there's some sort of plan for all this, a bigger picture. I don't know what it is. I certainly can't see it from where we're sitting on this trashed kitchen floor. But there's a plan for your life. That much I do know."

Claire sat up quickly, a snicker slipping from her lips. "A plan?" she asked, choking over the words. "What kind of plan includes killing my *entire family?*"

Gia could see rage blazing in Claire's eyes. She was grateful there wasn't much left to break in the kitchen.

Gia shimmied her body around the floor, so she was in front of Claire on the tile. She grabbed Claire's hands.

"You know how they say, 'God only knows'? Well, I think that's true. You didn't die that night. You just *didn't*. You may wish you had, *but you didn't*. There's got to be a reason you're still here."

Claire shook her head.

"Hold on, sweetie," Gia said, squeezing Claire's hands.

"I don't think I can." The tears were streaming down Claire's blotchy cheeks.

"Yes, you can," Gia said, with a certainty that surprised even her. "I have faith in you. You can. And, when you can't, I'll hold on for you."

Out of the corner of her eye, Gia spied a spider crawling through the broken glass on the floor, making its way over and under the slivers. How did it avoid getting hurt with all the jagged pieces surrounding it? How did *anyone* avoid getting hurt in this world? If Gia had learned anything, it was that no one escaped the painful shards of life unscathed. Some pain was small and some was monumental like Claire's, but it existed for everyone.

If there wasn't a reason for it, she didn't think she could bear to go on, either. She knew for certain, Claire couldn't.

"I love you, Gia," Claire finally whispered.

"I love you, too," Gia said, moving back to Claire's side and wrapping her friend in her arms.

Claire wiped at the tears, surveying the room. She'd done some serious damage. "This place is a mess."

Gia gave her a half-smile. Talk about understatements.

"I'll help you clean it up."

Claire nodded. Gia waited for her to make some movement to indicate she was ready to get up off the floor, but Claire remained still.

The silence was excruciating, like the torture of Zen meditation.

A sob escaped from Claire. "I just want my babies back." She laid her head on Gia's lap as she wept. Gia stroked her hair, the way she'd seen Claire do to the soft hair of her babies so many times before.

Babies who would never need their hair caressed again.

For the first time, since she'd heard the news on that terrible night, Gia let the tears cascade down her own cheeks. She owed it to those children—the ones she'd loved as if they were her own—to take care of their mama. She couldn't let anything happen to Claire. But if there was a plan for this whole hideous situation, she definitely hoped it included a Gia-assistance program. How could she handle this weight alone?

And then, with the idea that perhaps she wouldn't have to, Gia closed her eyes and began to pray.

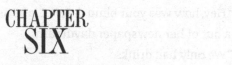

CHAPTER
SIX

Florida, 2012

"Hold on! Hold on!" Claire called out. She straightened the family photos she'd been dusting on the top of the piano. Heading to the front door, which was shaking from the heavy banging on it, she wiped the sweat from her forehead with the hand that held the feather duster.

Unlocking the top bolt, she opened the door. A sweaty and irritated-looking Gia stood on the doorstep.

"What's all the pounding about?" Claire asked.

"I was starting to melt on your doorstep. It must be close to a hundred and ten degrees out here." Gia strode through the door, making her way past Claire and into the air-conditioned house.

"I think they said it was ninety-four."

"Whatever." Gia shrugged, walking into the kitchen as Claire followed behind. "Please tell me you have something to drink."

"I have ice water."

"I was hoping for lemonade, but water will do."

Gia grabbed a glass from the cabinet and filled it from the spout on the refrigerator door.

"Did you lose your key?" Claire asked, beginning to wash the few dirty dishes in the sink.

"No," Gia replied, giving no other explanation as she sat down at the kitchen table and began to flip through the newspaper that was placed on top of it.

"Hey, how was your blind date?" Claire asked, the question shaking Gia out of her newspaper daydream.

"We only had drinks."

"He didn't make it to the dinner round?"

"Definitely not," Gia said, turning to the "Life and Culture" section.

"What's wrong with this one?" Claire said, loading the last plate into the dishwasher and turning it on.

"I didn't like his job."

"What does he do?"

"He's a mortician."

"And..."

Gia looked up from the paper. "I can't date a man who touches dead people all day. It'd creep me out to have him lay his hands on me."

Claire chuckled. "Weren't you weirded out by the last guy's job, too?"

"Yep. He was an odor tester," Gia said, kicking off her flip-flops and resting her legs on the chair across from her.

"A what?"

"He tested deodorants to make sure they were free of funk."

Claire giggled again. "I must've still been in my zombie zone to have missed that one. Whatever happened to being a plumber or a banker?"

"Exactly," Gia said, with an exaggerated, exasperated moan. "I will never meet a man."

"No, you'll meet a man," Claire said, wiping down the counter tops. "I'm just not sure he'll make a living doing something that pleases you."

"A girl's gotta have standards," she retorted to Claire.

Claire opened the door to her fridge and stood motionless, staring inside. "I have no milk."

"Nope."

"And there's no food."

"Nope," Gia replied, her nose still in the article she'd begun to read.

"Why is that?"

"Why is what?" Gia looked up, trying to pay attention to what Claire was moaning about.

"Why do I have no food in my fridge?"

"Oh," Gia said, returning her gaze to the paper. "Because shopping would entail you leaving the house."

"Good point," Claire said, closing the fridge door and finding a seat at the table, next to Gia. "Don't they have those services where you can order your groceries and they deliver them to your door?"

"If they do, I'm not giving you their number."

"Why not?"

"Because *you*," Gia said, pointing her finger at Claire, "need to go out. Even if it's just to the grocery store."

"Listen," Claire said, as if she hadn't just heard Gia. "I know you do this for me all the time, but next time you go out, can you pick up a few things for me? I don't need much." She stood up and took down the magnetic grocery list pad off the side of the refrigerator. She grabbed a pen from the junk drawer and began to jot down a few items.

"Nope."

"Come on," Claire said, opening the fridge door and digging around inside, trying to determine what it was she needed. "Nothing much. Milk, eggs, bread, soup."

She wrote down a few more things.

"No." The word was firm. There was no mistaking the meaning.

Claire looked up at Gia, her face full of surprise. Gia could see some hurt there, too. Damn. She hated that. She hated to hurt Claire. A part of her wanted to take it back—to say, sure, she could run to the grocery store for Claire. What was the big deal, really?

But it was a big deal. Everything was a big deal nowadays. Getting Claire to leave the house, even for thirty minutes, was a big, big deal. The times when Gia had convinced Claire to actually attend a movie or go eat in a restaurant, Gia had felt like throwing a parade in her own honor. It was so difficult to get Claire to do anything. Sometimes, Gia thought the only place Claire ever went during the week was to her therapist, and Gia was pretty certain that if she, herself, didn't drive Claire there and wait for her in the lobby, Claire wouldn't do that, either.

Still, Claire was doing so much better, it was difficult to complain. Gia had been able to move out just a month after Claire destroyed the kitchen. The weekend before she left, she and Claire had gone to Bed, Bath & Beyond and purchased some of the necessary items Claire had destroyed. A few days later, Gia had moved back into her own apartment. Though only six miles away, Gia had worried so much that first night over leaving Claire alone, she'd almost rushed right back over. But she didn't. Claire needed to learn how to live on her own again. And Gia needed to stop being such a mother hen.

Gia wished she could say the transition had been an easy one for Claire, but her friend had struggled. Every night, around bedtime, Claire would call Gia, apologizing for bothering her, but saying she just needed to hear someone's voice. And then, more often than not, Claire would burst into tears. A few times, she'd even shown up on Gia's doorstep around ten o'clock at night.

"Please tell me you don't have a man in here!" she'd say, the second Gia opened the front door.

Gia's reply, each time was, "I should be so lucky," and she'd let Claire in.

Gia had worried she was enabling Claire, not forcing her to handle life on her own. But whenever she decided to be more firm with the woman, Gia had been overcome with a landslide of guilt. After all, who was she to tell Claire how quickly she should move on? Gia didn't know a single person who'd come through something so tragic. She was in no position to judge.

At times, Gia's other friends would get on her case. "You can't be her nursemaid forever," the teacher, in the room next door, would say. "It's really rude of her to ask that of you."

Gia knew the comment wasn't intended to be harsh, but she still wanted to slap the woman. Claire wasn't asking anything of Gia. If Gia was ever too busy to hang out, she told Claire. And, she'd been telling Claire that more and more these days, as she, herself, began to regain the life she'd put on hold the night of the accident. Claire was always extremely understanding and apologetic.

Gia had finally gotten Claire to agree to a little field trip to a quaint town about two hours away. They'd done some shopping and gone out to lunch. Claire had seemed so relaxed that day. The weather had been perfect and they'd eaten outside on the front sidewalk of a cute French bistro. They'd even laughed together. Gia hadn't heard Claire laugh since before the accident. She was reminded of what a joyful sound it was. There was no laughter in the air today, though.

"No," she said clearly. "I will not go to the grocery store for you."

"I'm sorry. I shouldn't have asked," Claire said. Her cheeks flushed bright red, a look of absolute embarrassment on her face. "I depend on you way too much."

"Claire..."

"Of course you don't have time to go grocery shopping for me. You have a life. Or, you did. Before I hijacked it. I am so sorry! I know you think I take you for granted..."

"Claire..."

"...but I really don't. I promise. I am so grateful for you. So, so grateful. I could never have survived without you. You must be so angry with me."

"Claire!" Gia hadn't meant to yell. Claire jerked back in shock. "I'm not mad at you. Not in the least. You asking me to go to the grocery store was not an inconvenience to me. I totally have time to go. That's *not* the problem."

"It's not?" Gia could see the relief rippling across Claire's face.

"No! Not at all. The problem is that *you* need to go on your own."

"I hate going to the grocery store," Claire said, leaning her elbows on the kitchen island so she was facing Gia.

"Everyone hates going to the grocery store."

"No. I really hate it. I mean, I always hated it. You know, bringing three kids grocery shopping totally sucks. The whole process takes twenty times longer than it should."

Gia smiled. She remembered the funny stories Claire used to tell her about trying to purchase all the ingredients for a huge holiday dinner while having the kids in tow. More often than not, Gia or Jack would have to run out right before the rest of the guests arrived to go grab cranberry sauce or dessert napkins because, in the chaos of shopping with the little ones, Claire had forgotten what she'd gone shopping for in the first place.

"But as much as it sucked to grocery shop with them, and I remember it clearly," Claire continued, "the thought of shopping without them now—well, that sucks so much more."

Claire didn't start to cry. She was able to keep her composure better now that the first year had passed. Not everything brought her to tears. But her eyes were still full of a deep sadness.

Gia wanted to give in to her. Why should Claire have to face the cereal aisle without a kid in tow? It'd be so easy for Gia to go herself.

But she couldn't. Coddling Claire wasn't helping her. It was enabling her. Claire needed to find her own strength and not be allowed to crumble and die.

"All of that makes sense. It really does, but...listen, sweetie," Gia began. "You spend too much time alone now. You need to get out. Meet new people."

"At the grocery store?"

"Bag boys need friends, too."

The sadness that had tempered Claire's blue eyes was gone. Instead, she rolled them at Gia.

"Claire," Gia continued. "It's been over a year now. You—we—have lived through all the firsts without everyone. I know they weren't easy, but we survived them. Maybe, it's time to start living again."

"I don't know what that is anymore."

"And you won't until you get back out there in the world. Take baby steps. Go somewhere besides your therapist's office, and go there *alone*. Have lunch with friends—besides me. Everyone misses you. Grocery shop. If you don't, you're gonna be awfully hungry for the next seventy or so years."

"'Cause you're not going for me?" Claire asked apprehensively.

"I'm not going for you," Gia stated, winking at Claire.

"I don't know..."

"Well, I do," Gia said, grabbing the keys from the table and throwing them to Claire.

CHAPTER SEVEN

Claire turned her car away from the highway and veered onto a side road. She couldn't manage the large supermarket just yet. Not with its car-shaped shopping cars and parent-with-small-child parking spaces. If she saw one cashier hand a little boy or girl a sticker at the checkout, she might just crumble into a puddle on the floor.

It was better to stay close to home and McGord's, a small grocer, wasn't far from the house. She'd shopped there regularly, for years, when she needed a few items and didn't want to run into town.

Claire pulled into the small lot and turned off the engine. Her hands were sweaty on the steering wheel. It seemed ridiculous to be so nervous about grocery shopping. *Grocery shopping.* An activity she'd done a million times before. Taking three deep breaths and wiping the palms of her hands on her khaki shorts, Claire opened the car door and stepped outside.

The heat was sweltering. Gia hadn't been kidding.

Claire hurried across the parking lot, anxious to reach the air-conditioned store. The blast of cold air was a welcome relief.

She grabbed a small hand basket and rested it over her forearm. She surveyed the store. It looked exactly the same as the last time she'd been in here. Claire and the twins had run in for a few snack items to take on their road trip. Time seemed to have stood still for the tiny shop. The same chip displays. The same rack of flip-flops to the right of the door. The same misspelled "Donught" sign over the bakery counter. Nothing had changed.

Except, everything had changed.

Claire decided not to think about any of that and instead, hurried to complete her shopping. She looked down at her list: milk, eggs, butter, bread, Coke—she couldn't navigate her life, especially now, without her Coke—apples, bananas and ice cream.

No self-respecting, grieving individual could survive if they didn't drown themselves in ice cream. Especially if she scooped it into some of that Coke.

She found Rocky Road ice cream to be the most therapeutic. But, if McGord's didn't carry that, she could get by on plain chocolate. Or chocolate chip. Mint would be even better.

She'd never been the type of person who used food for comfort. But then, she'd never before needed so much comfort. She'd lost so much weight over the past eighteen months, even she couldn't help but notice how gaunt she looked. She hadn't had any appetite. However, it seemed in a single day, something had changed and, instead of feeling nauseous at the thought of food, she now found it to be a tremendous way to cope with the sadness. A lot of pain could be pushed down by smothering it in chocolate sauce and Cool Whip.

She assumed the weight would begin to pile on any day now. With the crap she was eating, how could it not?

Lost in thought, Claire didn't see the cart until she walked directly into it.

"Oh! I'm so sorry!" Claire said instinctively. "I didn't see you there." She rubbed her leg where the metal had stung her thigh.

"Claire?" a slow Southern drawl purred.

Claire glanced up into the heavily mascaraed eyes of Loni Thompson. *Of all people...*

"Hey, Loni," Claire said, with all the sweetness she could muster.

"Oh, my heavens, Claire! I wasn't really sure that was you when I saw you walk into the store. I said to myself, 'No, it couldn't possibly be Claire Matthews. No one has seen her since her family'...well, you know. No one has seen you..." Loni's voice trailed off.

"Well, here I am," Claire said, with a lift of her hands. "I'm alive."

As soon as the words were out of her mouth, she regretted them.

"You look so skinny!" Loni said, ignoring the awkward comment. "We need to fatten you up!"

She pinched the skin on Claire's upper arm. Literally, pinched it. Claire couldn't believe it.

On second thought, yes, she could.

Loni was all about looks, which made sense, since she was all about makeup. Loni was their resident cosmetic salesperson. She was now a director in the Lottie Mae makeup organization. Claire knew this because Loni never failed to mention it whenever she saw Claire. Or any of the other mothers in their school. Or anyone she ran into at the post office or at the shopping mall or at a soccer game. She mentioned it a lot, right before she tried to recruit you to sell makeup, too.

Claire couldn't believe she hadn't realized Loni would be inside McGord's. How could she have possibly missed the lavender Cadillac outside, the symbol of "making it big" in the Lottie Mae organization, in the small McGord's parking lot?

"And you look so pale..."

"I'm fine," said Claire. "I just need a little more sun."

"Yes, you do. Oh, I know!" Loni said, an idea popping into her mind. "Barry and I are having a pool party this afternoon. Around four o'clock. Why don't you come? Everyone would love to see you."

"I ..." Claire wondered how she could get out of this one. Loni wasn't one to take the answer "no" easily.

"Really, dear," she crooned, her bright blood-red lipstick glaring at Claire like the flashing red lights of a police cruiser. The movement of Loni's mouth was making Claire dizzy. She reached out to grab hold of the grocery shelf to steady herself.

"I'm not so sure..."

"Now, I won't take no for an answer. You remember where I live, right?"

Claire did. It was the very, very large house on Rollingwood Way. At the top of the hill. You could see the extravagant home from the distant highway. Every time they used to drive in that area of the city, the twins always cried out, "There's Polly and Nathan's house!"

Polly and Nathan were the only other twins in the girls' grade. Thus, the four children had bonded. And, by default, Claire had been thrust into the glitzy — or maybe it was gawdy — world of Loni Thompson.

When the kids began school, parents, teachers and kids, alike, all realized referring to "the twins" would cause confusion, since no one was ever sure which set of twins were being referenced. Thus, someone had coined the terms BG twins (for boy-girl) and GG twins (for Claire's girl-girl set). Oftentimes, her kids would be referred to as the GG's, and Loni's kids were the BG's, which always made Claire think the Thompson twins should break out singing "Stayin' Alive."

The GG's. Claire hadn't thought about that in a while. She'd been the GG mom.

She wondered if Loni's kids were still called the BG's or if they were now merely called "the twins."

She didn't want to know.

"Yes, I remember where you live."

To Claire's relief, Loni's cell phone went off at that moment. "I Feel Pretty" was the ringtone.

Of course it was.

"Oh! Oh! I need to get this! I'm waiting on a big sale to come through." Loni reached into the side pocket of her rhinestone-studded handbag and pulled out her equally bedazzled iPhone. She pushed the "answer" button and put the phone to her ear.

"Loni Thompson, your very own Lottie Mae sales director! How can I make your face shine?"

Loni answered the phone like that every single time. Even if she knew who was calling. Even if it was the school nurse calling to say one of her kids was sick.

Putting her hand over the mouth of the phone, Loni leaned over to Claire. "Don't forget, four o'clock. My house. Bring your swimsuit. No need to bring anything else. We'll have all the food and drinks ready. I am s-ooooo excited to have run into you, Claire," she said, breaking the word "so" into two imaginary syllables.

Claire nodded. She hadn't actually said she'd go to the barbecue, but she realized she hadn't actually refused the invitation, either.

"Ta ta!" Loni whispered with a wave of her perfectly manicured hand, before raising her voice again. "Hello, darling! I was just thinking about your gorgeous skin and how your cheeks would positively shine with the Citrus Blossom." Loni was back to her call, pushing her cart down the aisle and Claire was left standing alone, wondering if she was now obligated to attend that dang barbecue.

If she showed up, Claire knew it would stun everyone there. Other than Gia, Claire hadn't socialized with a single friend since the accident. There would be a lot of whispers. All eyes would be on her. Everyone would be analyzing how she looked. The thought of walking into such an event, where there would, no doubt, be all the parents of her kids' closest friends, made Claire begin to dry heave. She bent over and put her hands on her knees.

Deep breaths. Deep breaths.

She hoped no one in the small store could hear her as she gagged on the panic that crept up her esophagus.

She couldn't do it. She couldn't bear to see everyone, all the people who'd been a part of her Mommy Life. She couldn't bear to have them see *her.*

But, if she didn't go, they'd still talk. Her absence wouldn't stop that. Claire couldn't avoid the gossip simply by not showing up.

Loni would be sure to announce to everyone who'd gathered that she'd run into Claire at McGord's that morning.

"You will not believe who I saw this morning!" she'd say, delight leaping from her eyes as the keeper of fabulous news.

Once everyone around her had asked, "Who?" Loni would say, as dramatically as if she were performing at The Globe Theater, "Claire Matthews!"

"NO!" all the other parents would cry out.

"Yes!" Loni would say with glee, busting with pride that she was the one with the first scoop on the widowed woman who'd lost all her children.

That did it. Claire couldn't take it. Her parents hadn't raised a wimp. She was not one to back down from a fight. And, though she knew this wasn't actually a battle, she wasn't about to let herself be the center of gossip and speculation for one more day. She could imagine what everyone had been saying for the past year, and that was bad enough.

It was time for them to stop talking.

Or, if they were going to talk about her, it was going to be on her terms.

Regaining her composure, Claire stood tall and hurried down the aisle. She was relieved to see Loni exiting the store as she peeked around the endcap display. Claire hurried to the dairy section and grabbed the milk, eggs and butter and then quickly made her way to the checkout counter. If she was going to get to the party by four-thirty, she was going to need to do some self-maintenance. Claire couldn't remember the last time she'd shaved her legs, or her armpits, for that matter. The state of her eyebrows was even worse. And her hair! Claire quickly rushed back over to the beauty aisle to grab some dye. She couldn't show up with the roots that had now grown down half her head.

If she was going to show up, she was going to show up looking her best.

At least, her best these days. She knew it wouldn't come close to her "old" best, but she could try.

Returning to the front of the store, Claire placed her basket down on the checkout counter and her arm squealed with relief.

"Miss Claire! It's so good to see you in here!"

Claire looked up into the sweet eyes of Irma Jean. Irma and her husband had owned McGord's for close to thirty years. Claire could remember the days when she'd come in there and find Monty Beasley behind the counter. He'd been a man with a smile as big as Texas and a hug so tight, it could squeeze your intestines into your rib cage. The kids had loved seeing Mr. Monty, as they called him. He was never without a lollipop for each of her children, never forgetting the kids' names or their favorite flavors. He made her children feel special, though she believed he made all the children in town feel special, as he knew their names and favorite flavors, too. He was just that kind of man.

It had broken Claire's heart, during his last year, before the cancer finally took him, to see him sitting slumped in his wheelchair, outside the front door of the shop. He was out there every day, greeting the patrons. "Have a good day!" he'd say, smiling that big smile, the one that eventually seemed too large for his shrunken face. "Smile! It's a beautiful day!!" he'd say, as the people would head back to their car. Claire had often wondered, during those days, how he'd found the strength to smile, both physically and emotionally. It didn't seem as if he'd had much to smile about. The twins had been young, but Claire vividly remembered using Mr. Monty and his contagious grin as a teachable moment for Luke.

"Mr. Monty is always smiling!" Luke would say.

"And how does that make you feel?" Claire would ask her son.

"Happy!"

"Do you think he has a lot to smile about?" Claire would prod.

"No," Luke would answer. "He's really, really sick."

"And yet, he keeps smiling. And his smile brightens your day. And mine. And everyone who sees him. He must have a good *what?*" Claire would ask.

"Attitude!" Luke would exclaim, happy he knew the correct answer.

"You bet. Mr. Monty has a good attitude. Even when things aren't good in his life, he's doing his best to make lives a little better. Don't you wish we could be like that, too?"

She would always see Luke nod, in the rearview mirror, as he sucked on his lollipop. She'd been thankful for Mr. Monty and the example he'd set for her children. She'd been heartbroken when she heard he'd passed away, about eighteen months before her own family's tragedy. And then, she felt even worse when she'd learned, about six months later, his wife, Irma Jean, had been diagnosed with breast cancer.

"Life really isn't fair," she'd thought at the time, not realizing how true that could be.

"Thanks, Irma. It's been awhile." Claire lifted the bread and the rest of her items out of the basket.

"Looks like you needed a cart!" Irma said, eyeing the way Claire rubbed her sore arm.

"I guess I did."

Irma began to ring up Claire's items. "Listen, love," Irma said, in that sensitive tone of hers. "I'm so sorry for all your losses. Your babies were like bright rays of sunshine. I miss 'em runnin' around, gettin' underfoot."

"Yeah. Me, too." Claire shifted her weight. She never knew what to say when someone offered their condolences.

"Oh, dang it! I forgot to grab ice cream!" Claire said, scanning the items on the counter. She'd been so flustered by running into Loni, and then been thrown off guard at the thought of going to the barbecue, she'd forgotten one of the most important items on her grocery list and there'd only been six original things on there.

"Go! Go!" Irma shooed her away from the counter. "I'll hold your things up here. You go pick out what you still need and I'll ring you up when you're done."

"Thanks so much, Irma," Claire said, mouthing a silent apology to the man behind her in line who didn't look thrilled with how long she was taking. "You go ahead of me," she said. He nodded grimly and stepped forward.

At the freezer section, Claire was grateful to see Irma had stocked both Rocky Road *and* Mint Chocolate Chip. This must be her lucky day. She grabbed one carton of each and stopped at the soda counter and got herself a small fountain drink.

She let the fizz die down and then placed the lid on top. Sticking the ice cream containers in the crook of one arm, she picked up the soda with the opposite hand. The freezing cold temperature felt soothing against her bruised forearm.

As she'd expected, the checkout line was now long and she'd have to wait to finally purchase her items. There was no such thing as a fast checkout at McGord's. Irma knew everyone in town and would, without a doubt, have a conversation with each customer as they reached the counter. Once again, Claire was wishing she had a shopping cart.

Claire couldn't help but marvel at how well Irma looked. The last time Claire had seen the woman, she'd been hiding her bald head under a bright red-and-pink scarf. That had been almost two years ago. Claire hadn't seen or heard anything about Irma since then, but it was clear to see she was doing much, much better. Claire wasn't sure if the woman was in remission, but her hair had grown back. Irma looked good, healthy, happy and content.

Claire wondered how that was possible. The woman had lost her husband and then nearly her own life. But she seemed to be doing okay these days and that thought made Claire happy.

When she was only one customer away, Claire glanced up at the bulletin board to the side of the counter. The board had been there for years. It was where Claire had found Luke's first babysitter and where Jack had located a company to come out and fix their leaking sprinkler system. When the twins were three months old, Claire had found a Moms-of-Multiples support group on there, too. There was always something of interest on that board.

Claire scanned the papers up there now. Someone was selling a trampoline. A woman named Frances was in search of a caregiver for her aging mother with dementia. A man named Greggory was looking for someone to carpool with to work.

It was the color poster in the top-left corner, though, that caught Claire's eye, just as it became her turn to check out. She stepped forward and placed her items on the counter, still staring at the board.

Callum Fitzgerald: A Message of Hope for a Hopeless World

It wasn't the title that caught her attention. It was the photo of the man above the words.

His eyes were mesmerizing—bluer than any summer sky Claire had ever seen. She couldn't help but feel as if he were staring directly at her from his beautiful face. And, his face was definitely beautiful. Claire knew this wasn't a word men generally preferred to hear when used in reference to them, but she could come up with no better description. He was just *beautiful*.

That was why her eyes jolted so when she focused on the entire poster and the rest of him.

"You should go if you ain't ever heard him," Irma said, pulling Claire's earlier grocery items from under the counter where she'd stored them.

"Really?" Claire said, doing her best to tear her eyes away from the poster.

"Remember when I had cancer a few years back?" Irma asked, scanning the barcode of the Rocky Road.

"Right after you lost Monty," Claire said. "I remember. That was an awful time for you."

"I thought that cancer was gonna get the best of me. And, honestly, I didn't really care. My Monty was gone. We'd been married forty-three years when he passed on."

"I remember."

"I decided I was just gonna give up. If Monty had been here, I woulda fought that cancer; no two-ways about it. But without him, the whole thing seemed so pointless. What would I be fightin' for, I kept asking myself."

She scanned the milk and placed it in a plastic sack.

"Then someone took me to hear that man, Mr. Fitzgerald. Changed the way I saw everything in my life."

"How so?" Claire tried to keep the skepticism out of her voice, but she was curious.

"I'd been so busy thinking about what I didn't have, I'd forgotten to be grateful for what I did have. After listening to him, I made up my mind. As long as the cancer hadn't taken away my breath, I was gonna keep fightin'. I've been cancer-free for a year now."

"Must've been one powerful speech." Claire had to force her eyes away from the man, in order to make eye contact with Irma. She was having a difficult time wrapping her mind around how someone with such a perfect a face could have a body that didn't match.

"That man has a gift, I tell ya. Look at him." As if Claire had been able to do anything but look at him.

"He's got one arm. *That's all.* An arm. No legs. Just one arm," Irma continued. "Now you know he's faced more than his share of tough times, but he has an outlook on life like no one I've ever met. His happiness is contagious. Go hear him. You'll see what I mean."

Claire hesitated. "I don't go out much."

"Not since the accident?" Irma asked. She asked it straightforward. There was no pity in her voice and Claire appreciated that. Claire shook her head.

"Are you going?"

"You bet I am!" A huge smile spread across Irma's face, reminding Claire of the one she always used to see on Monty's. "I'm takin' my whole family. There's nobody who's got it so easy they can't use a little encouragement, right?"

"Yeah, I guess you're right."

She took money out of her wallet and handed Irma the cash for her groceries. Irma gave Claire her change.

"You think about going. It's tomorrow night. You won't be sorry. I promise you that."

She handed Claire her two bags of groceries.

"Okay. I'll think about it."

"Wait one second," Irma said, as if she'd just remembered something. She reached under the counter and pulled out an envelope. Sticking her hand inside, she pulled out a paper ticket. "I heard on the radio the event's sold out. It's a two-day thing, you know."

"*Two days?*" Claire said in disbelief. "What on earth could he say that would take *two days?*"

"Well, the first night is really him speaking to everyone—telling his story and all about how he overcame his troubles. The second day is more of a seminar, a workshop, where he gives everyone practical steps to move forward with their own life. The ticket will get you into both events."

"Oh, Irma, I couldn't take that from you."

"No, really. My daughter-in-law can't make it. She just found out she has to work. I have an extra one now."

Claire sighed. She didn't know what to say.

"Here. Take it with you," Irma said, shoving the paper into Claire's hand. "It was going to go to waste anyway. You can think about it and decide later."

Claire looked down at the ticket. "Let me pay you for it," she said. Though the ticket price, printed on the paper, wasn't outrageous, Claire also realized the event wasn't free.

"Absolutely not. You go and you get something from it. Besides," Irma said, "I always did mean to bring you a meal and never got around to it. Consider this my way of clearing my guilty conscience."

Claire nodded and folded the ticket, sticking it in one of her bags. "Okay."

"See you tomorrow night," Irma said, cheerfully, as if Claire's attendance was a sure thing.

Claire smiled softly at the dear, older woman, as she walked out the door.

"Maybe."

Once outside, Claire placed the groceries in the back of her car and turned on the air conditioning the second she sat down in the driver's seat. It was unlikely she'd go to hear that man speak. She'd already psyched herself up to attend the barbecue. That would take all the energy she had. Going out two nights in a row seemed impossible and unrealistic, especially when she hadn't left the house for anything social for close to two years.

But she hoped Irma and her family got a lot out of Callum's speech. Irma was a sweet woman and she'd been right. Everyone needed a bit of encouragement every now and again.

She bet that Callum man was good at it. He must help a lot of people, if the way Irma spoke about him was any indication of his potential influence. In all Claire's years of shopping there, she'd never heard Imra rave about another human being the way she'd praised him.

Yes, Claire hoped many people were touched and encouraged by Mr. Callum Fitzgerald's talk.

She just wouldn't be one of them.

CHAPTER EIGHT

Claire stood at the door to Loni's house, poised to knock. She hesitated and lowered her arm again. What was she doing? Was she really up for this? A party with all her kids' friends and their parents? Maybe she should have started small, lunch with a couple of the moms.

But she wanted to get this over with. She knew she must be the center of a lot of gossip and chatter around town and she wanted to put an end to it, or at least help it diminish. And, if she were to be completely honest with herself, she was beginning to miss these people. She'd never been extremely close to any of the other parents, but she wouldn't exactly call them merely "acquaintances," either. She'd enjoyed seeing them at school functions and going out for couples' nights where they'd hire a babysitter to watch all of the kids at one family's home and then all pray the kids wouldn't trash the place or scare off the babysitter so they'd still be able to use her again next month. In three years, they'd gone through seven different sitters.

She also realized she was missing all the children, too, and not just her own. She loved her kids' friends. She'd always encouraged Luke and the twins to have their classmates over to the house for play dates. She'd treasured hearing the little voices and watching them run around together. She adored all their little faces and hands and pigtails and chubby cheeks. She hadn't seen the other kids in so long. They all must've gotten so big.

Claire lifted her hand, once again to knock, when the door unexpectedly flew open.

"Claire!" Loni crooned, her Southern drawl in full swing. "I thought I saw your car pull up. I was beginning to wonder if you were ever going to come inside!"

"I, um, was just putting on a little lipstick."

"And it looks grand!" Loni stepped aside and made a wide, swinging gesture to motion Claire through the door. "Welcome to our humble abode."

Claire wondered how Loni could say those words without giggling. The house was anything but humble, with a long sweeping staircase in the center of the foyer that reminded Claire of *Gone with the Wind*. Dark mahogany railings carried you past a portrait gallery wall Claire bet rivalled the Met. An enormous crystal chandelier hung from the ceiling and Claire couldn't help but wonder if it had cost more than Claire and Jack's entire home. A fresh display of flowers, as tall as Claire, sat on a table in the crook of the stairway, and was flanked by Bastille armchairs, covered in pale lavender linen. Loni *loved* the color purple and it was present in various ways throughout the home.

"Here," Claire said, handing Loni a bottle of wine. "This is for you."

"Oh, silly girl! You didn't have to bring us anything. We're just so happy you're here! When I told everyone you were coming...well, no one could believe it."

Claire could imagine how *that* announcement had gone.

"Am I late?"

"Nope, you're right on time. Everyone's out back. Follow me."

Claire cautiously trailed behind Loni as she made her way through the elegant foyer and into the extravagant living room, to the back patio. Loni slid the door open and stepped outside, ahead of Claire.

"Attention, everyone! Guess who's here!" Loni's voice trilled.

"Claire!" a dozen voices rang out in unison. Within seconds, everyone was out of their chairs and on their feet.

Claire hadn't been hugged this much since the funerals and probably never before then.

"We've missed you *so* much!" the moms cooed.

"It's good to see you looking so well," the dads boomed, squeezing Claire so tight, she lost her breath.

Claire's eyes filled with tears. She'd missed these people so much. She hadn't even realized how much until this very moment.

"Come on; sit down," Valerie, a mom Claire had always particularly liked, encouraged her. "Sit next to me. Joe, you go sit somewhere else," she barked at a pudgy man with a receding hairline. Her husband shrugged and found a seat closer to the pool. Valerie was a stunning woman, with exotic features and black, luscious hair. Jack and Claire had held many a conversation wondering about how Joe, with his mediocre looks and unimaginative personality, had managed to score a wife that hot.

Claire placed her bottom in the seat next to Valerie and crossed her legs nervously. Suddenly, she didn't know what to do with her hands. Should she fold them? Sit on them? She was thankful when Loni came over and handed Claire a glass of wine.

"I hope you like red."

Claire peered down into the glass. She actually didn't know if she liked red. She didn't even know if she liked white. Claire didn't drink. Never had. It just didn't appeal to her. Claire was about to hand the glass back to Loni, reminding her she didn't drink alcohol. After all, Loni already knew that. All the parents knew it. Claire had been teased, good-naturedly, of course, more times than she could count during their big nights out.

"Hey, Jack! Did you marry Claire so you'd always have a designated driver?" the men would chortle.

"Ha, ha. Very funny," Claire would retort. Jack would always come to her rescue by saying, "I married her because she was the most beautiful girl I'd ever seen." And then he'd place a kiss on Claire's lips that would make all the other women envious.

"Um...Loni," Claire said, holding up the glass. "I don't..."

"Oh, sweetheart, you aren't going to tell me, after all you've been through, that you still don't drink, are you?"

"Um..."

"Let me tell you something; if anyone on this earth deserves a drink, it's you."

Valerie nodded in agreement as she and Loni and two of the other women, nearby, lifted their glasses.

"Cheers," Valerie said.

Claire lifted her glass, knowing it was expected of her.

"Cheers," she said meekly.

"So, Claire..." Valerie leaned closer, as if she was about to tell her a dirty little secret. She placed her hand on Claire's knee. "How are you? Truly, I mean."

"I'm...well, I'm fine." Claire laughed nervously and took a sip of the wine. It tasted good. Sweeter than she'd expected. And she found it to be quite refreshing on such a hot day.

Claire took another sip as she added, "It's been really, really hard."

Valerie nodded as if she truly did know. Which, of course, she didn't.

"I have my good days and bad days. Sometime, it's just hard to get out of bed. But, other days, like today, I feel I'm making some progress."

Claire took another nervous sip of her drink. She could already feel her face flush the way it did whenever she'd had more than two sips of alcohol. Jack used to tell her he thought she might be allergic to the sulfites in the wine. She wasn't sure, but she did know a few sips were often too much for her. Yet, here she was, holding an entire glass. She wasn't sure how much of it she could actually get through. She knew she should probably put it down and go off in search of a soft drink, but she was so nervous, she wasn't sure her legs would hold her as she walked across the yard. She hadn't been around so many people in ages. In her entire life, she'd never gotten past the first few sips. She'd never drunk an entire glass of wine in one sitting. She wasn't sure if she'd consumed a whole glass of wine over the entire course of her life. Maybe if she plowed through, she'd find she enjoyed it. She'd always wondered what other people found so pleasurable about a glass of wine.

"We're so thrilled you decided to come today. I've missed you so much," Valerie said, leaning over to give Claire another hug.

Claire noticed tears brimming in Valerie's eyes and Claire was touched. The two women had never been exceptionally close, but Claire had enjoyed her company. She'd missed Valerie. She'd missed all of them.

"Okay, okay," Claire said, fanning her face, partly from the heat and partly because she didn't want her own tears to begin to flow. "No crying. No crying. We're here to have a good time. It's been a long time since I had a good time."

Valerie dabbed at her eyes with the corner of a napkin that had the word *Party* splashed across it in bright purple.

"You're right. You're absolutely right."

Claire smiled. "Tell me about you. What have you been up to?"

"Life is exhausting. We're go-go-go all the time. The kids are all in new sports this year. No more soccer."

Valerie had two children. A girl the same age as Claire's twins and a boy who was only three days younger than Luke. All the kids had played on a neighborhood soccer league together. Valerie and Claire had held their best conversations at those games.

"Oh, no?" Claire said, taking another sip. A wave of uneasiness began to rock in her belly.

"No! Both kids decided they'd had enough. Liam's now on the baseball team and Ava's playing volleyball."

"Wow. How are they enjoying it?"

Sip.

"Oh, they love it," Valerie said with a wave of her hand. "It's *me* who's exhausted. When they played the same sport, I just had to cart both of them to the one location and wait till they were done, but now," she paused for emphasis, "Liam practices at Meadow Elementary on Tuesdays and Thursdays and has games at Linden Middle School on Saturdays and Ava has practice on Tuesday and Wednesdays at Polamer Middle School, but her games are back at Meadow Elementary on Saturdays. Joe and I have to split up the games on Saturdays. We can't be two places at once."

Claire nodded.

Sip.

"How's the schoolwork this year?"

"Well, Ava's doing really well. You know, at that age, it's really about learning to read and color. But Liam! He's struggling. The work has become too much. We spend over an hour on homework each night and most of the time he's crying and I'm literally yanking out my hair by the roots."

"Wow."

Sip.

"And the teacher, Ms. Mandell, I'm pretty certain she doesn't have any children of her own. She has no patience with Liam. I realize he's a handful." She winked at Claire. "You and I *both* know he's a handful."

Claire couldn't resist smiling. Valerie wasn't kidding. Liam was a handful. Though Luke had loved having Liam over for play dates, Claire had always braced herself for the trouble those two were bound to get into together. When they were about four, the boys had gotten into the twins' Desitin. After not hearing them for some time, and realizing that silence most likely meant nothing good, Claire had found them covered, head to toe, in white cream. It was everywhere—

their hands, feet, hair, noses, bellies—all over their clothes. They told her they were snowmen. At first, Claire had resisted the urge to giggle and grab for the camera, but after she saw how the cream was wiped all over the carpet in Luke's room and his walls, his bed and books, she'd had to stifle the urge to scream at the top of her lungs.

"Valerie," she'd said as calmly as she could when she'd called her friend. "Do you think you could come over here and help me out?"

Valerie had gotten there in less than ten minutes and the two moms had spent well over an hour scrubbing the boys in the tub. It took a bottle and a half of shampoo, with a little Dawn dish soap thrown in, to get all the oily residue off their boys' skin and hair and out from under their fingernails.

They hadn't even touched the carpet that day. Claire had announced she was going to leave that for Jack.

Claire hadn't thought about that memory in ages.

"Remember the time, at my house, when I had eight-pound bags of popcorn kernels stacked in my hallway for the school carnival," Valerie said.

"And the boys decided they were hungry..."

"And they pulled out the air popper..."

"By the time I got to your house to pick up Luke," Claire said, "you had seven pounds of kernels on your kitchen floor."

"And one pound of popped popcorn."

"They had no idea what they'd done wrong," Claire said.

"We were just having a party, Mommy!" Valerie mimicked the boys.

Both Claire and Valerie burst into giggles.

Claire took another sip of her wine. She was definitely feeling more relaxed. She'd forgotten about the boys' hysterical antics.

"What are you ladies laughing at?" Joe pulled his chair closer to his wife and Claire. Claire noticed many of the other parents were now looking at them and smiling.

"Oh, we're just remembering how much trouble Luke and Liam used to get into together."

Joe began to laugh, too.

"Remember the time they both climbed up in the big tree in our yard?" he asked.

"And none of us could find them?" Valerie went on.

"You called me and Jack to help in the search." Claire took another sip of her wine, smiling as the warm liquid slid down her throat.

"We searched the whole neighborhood," Joe said, beginning to laugh.

"Jack was dialing nine-one-one on his cell phone," Valerie added, tied up in laughter.

"And the boys jumped out of the tree behind us, yelling, *Boo!*"

"I don't think any of us had ever screamed that loud before!" Joe snorted. His face was now bright red. He was having a tough time catching his breath as his body contorted from the laughter.

Claire was laughing, too. She was slapping her legs, her body rocking back and forth, tears streaming down her face. For the first time since the accident, she had tears of laughter and not grief. It felt so good to laugh, like a thousand-pound weight had been lifted off her body and she was suddenly floating midair. It felt wonderful to sit back and listen to the other parents reminisce and drink her wine.

Out of the corner of her eye, she saw Loni approaching with a bottle of wine. Without saying a word, Claire calmed herself enough to lift her glass to their hostess, silently requesting it to be filled. She deserved some wine, didn't she? She'd *earned* this laughter. No one had been through such a difficult time *ever in the history of mankind.* It felt good to drink. Her face was now as cool as the ocean. Her heart was light. She felt like dancing.

Dancing. What a wonderful idea. She hadn't been dancing in such a long time. Jack had never been much of a dancer. Actually, neither had she. But sometimes, if the music was right, she was known to hit the dance floor. There was music playing at the party, but she noticed no one was dancing. She couldn't just stand up and begin to dance. Or could she?

"Claire..." Someone was calling her name.

"Yes?" She was torn away from her thoughts as she looked up.

"I just wanted to come over to say hi."

The voice was coming from a tall, thin women who clearly had a better body than any of the moms here. She was wearing the smallest bikini top Claire had ever seen, in a bright red. A Mexican-inspired sarong was draped low on her hips, which fell below the flattest stomach Claire had ever seen, other than in a Victoria's Secret catalog.

She's never given birth. Claire couldn't help but sigh at the thought that she, too, had once had a body like that. Maybe not as tall, but definitely as thin. She missed that body. She hated her muffin top. She used to tell herself the muffin top was the price she'd paid for her three beautiful children. But now, without those children, the muffin top seemed to have been for naught.

My muffin top sucks.

Sip.

"Yes?" Claire said, feeling a bit dizzy. The woman's voice seemed a bit familiar, but the setting sun was in Claire's eyes so she could only see as high as the woman's boobs. Her perky, round, braless boobs.

Yep. No baby had nursed on those. Claire looked down at her own saggy breasts, glad she'd put on her best push-up bra.

Sip.

"I want to tell you how sorry I am. I loved your kids."

"I loved them, too," Claire said and then giggled, not sure why she was giggling. *Was her comment funny?* It felt funny.

The woman shifted from her left foot to her right and then back again.

"I know you did. I hope you're doing okay."

Sip.

"I'm doing just fine. Great, acthally." Why did that word sound a little bit off. Acally? Actilly? Something wasn't quite right about it.

Who cares?

Sip.

"Um...that's great," the woman said.

"You know what?" Claire said, suddenly jumping out of her seat. "I'm so good, I'd like to dance."

"Dance?" The woman sounded startled.

"Yep. Dance. Come dance with me!" She grabbed the woman's hand and began to pull her toward the dance floor. "Oh! Ms. Harper!" Claire exclaimed, suddenly realizing who the woman was. It was the twins' preschool teacher. She'd been Luke's teacher, too, many years ago. All the parents had liked her so much, they'd begun to invite her to all of their dinners once their kids were no longer in her class. Ms. Harper looked so young to Claire. Had she always looked this young? She'd always seemed like a blah preschool teacher to Claire before. But tonight, she looked great. Her hair was down. Her glasses were MIA. She looked *hip*, in her teeny-tiny bikini top and multicolored sarong. She looked like a party. She looked *fun*.

Claire needed some fun. No more talking to the other old people, like herself, at this party. She wanted to feel young again.

Free!

Claire pulled Ms. Harper to the dance floor. Did she still need to call her Ms. Harper? That seemed so weird.

"What's your name?" Claire asked, as she began to sway to the music.

Ms. Harper seemed a bit uncomfortable. She looked around her, but they were the only two on the laminate flooring.

"Um...what?"

"Your name!" Claire yelled out, over the music, holding onto Ms. Harper's left hand with her right, as she attempted to spin the woman around. Ms. Harper was much too stiff on the dance floor. Maybe she needed some wine.

Wine was awesome. Why hadn't she known this before? She lifted the glass to her lips with her free hand.

Sip.

"Oh...um...Abigail."

"Abigail! Abby! Gailey! What do they call you?"

Claire twisted her body under their linked hands.

"Abigail. Just Abigail."

"Well, that's okay, Just Abigail. Not everyone can have a cool nickname."

Abigail was looking everywhere but at Claire. Claire didn't like that. They were dancing. Together. Abigail should be paying attention. She should be having *fun*.

"Come on, Just Abigail. Loosen up! Let's dance!"

Claire let go of Abigail's hand and spun around the dance floor, her arms outspread.

"Oh, dang it," she said, as she stopped spinning, eyeing a puddle beneath her. "Some of my wine splashed out onto their dance floor. *I bet Loni's not gonna like that.*"

Abigail shook her head. She looked even more uneasy.

Claire leaned in and said, in a whisper, or, at least what she thought was a whisper, "Loni's a little bit too into her stuff, you know. She's gonna act like I spilled this wine on her white carpet or on top of her itsy-bitsy, teeny-weeny dog. Have you seen that dog?"

Abigail nodded, a bit uncertainly.

"That dog is the size of a *mouse.* Or a *rat.*" Claire laughed aloud. It felt so good to laugh. And she was so funny. She'd never before known she was so funny! "It is totally the size of a rat. It's a white rat!"

She looked over at the other parents, where she had been sitting moments ago. All eyes were on her.

I bet they never knew I could dance like this!

"Come on, everyone!" Claire said, raising her now-empty wine-glass. "Dance with me! It's getting dark. Let's dance! This is a party, isn't it? Let's party like we're twenty-one!"

She could see Valerie stand and begin to walk toward her.

"Valerie, could you bring me another glass of wine?"

Valerie paused for a brief second and then continued on her way across the patio.

"The wine, Valerie!" Claire called, waving for her friend to go back to the table. "Don't forget the wine!"

Claire turned back to Abigail, who was standing still, her arms crossed in front of her.

"You're not dancing!" Claire waved her finger accusingly at the teacher. "Don't be a spoil sport. I'll have to give you detention!"

That cracked Claire up. She was a hoot.

A hand rested on Claire's shoulder.

"Hey, dear," a sweet voice said in her ear. "Why don't we go sit down for a little bit?"

"Sit?" Claire swung her body around to face Valerie. "Why would we do that? I've done enough sitting. Do you know how much you sit when you're in mourning? *A lot*. You do a *whole* lot of sitting."

Valerie nodded in understanding. "I know, dear, but let's go sit for a little bit longer. Dinner's out now. Let's go get something to eat, okay? Maybe you a need a little food." She tugged at Claire's arm, but Claire shook off her hand.

She leaned in, a little wobbly on her feet, and whispered into Valerie's ear. "You know how much food you eat when you're in mourning? *A lot*. People bring you cake and casseroles and donuts and cookies. What do they say in *To Kill a Mockingbird?* Something about 'with death comes food'? That is soooo true! I got soooo much food!"

"That's great, dear."

"Why are you calling me dear? Do you like me?"

"Of course I like you."

"I like me, too." Claire winked at Valerie.

"That's great. Come on; let's get something to eat."

"We should dance." Claire began to spin around again.

"I'm not really a good dancer..."

"You know what? I didn't think I was, either. But I was wrong!"

The music felt so good. Her body felt so good. Life was so good. She could barely remember how it felt to be sad.

"Mommy?"

A little voice popped up above the beat of the tune.

Instinctively, Claire turned. "What, baby?"

"It's okay," Valerie said, to a small girl beside her. "You can have a piece of cake. Tell Daddy I said it was okay."

Claire stopped spinning and stared at the little girl. It was Ava, but it wasn't. She was taller. Thinner. Her hair was longer than Claire remembered.

She was older.

How had she gotten older?

The little girl looked up at Claire. "Hi, Ella and Lily's mom." She waved at Claire and then ran back toward the house.

Ella and Lily's mom. She'd forgotten the kids had called her that. Ella and Lily's mom. She used to think it was so weird the kids had never called her Mrs. Matthews or Ms. Claire. Just "Ella and Lily's mom" or "Luke's mom."

That was her identity.

She stumbled a bit and grabbed onto Valerie's arm, trying to balance herself.

"Are you hungry?" Valerie said. "You must be. I think it would be good to get some food into that stomach. It's getting a bit chilly. Did you bring a jacket?"

A jacket? It was getting chilly. She hoped she'd packed jackets for the kids. They always got so cold after swimming.

"Where are the kids?" she asked Valerie.

"Oh, I think they're all eating their dinners around the pool. Loni had little picnic tables set up for them there."

"I should go see if they've gotten enough to eat. Lily doesn't always eat enough."

"Um, Claire, let's go sit down." Claire noticed Valerie's tone was now quite serious.

"I'll sit later. Let me go check on the kids. Luke tends to eat nothing but dessert. If he's left to fix his own plate, he'll fill it with cake and cookies and no dinner."

Valerie's grip on her arm tightened.

"Ow. What are you doing?"

"Claire," Valerie said, her voice now gentle. "Your kids aren't here."

"What do you mean they aren't here? I wouldn't come without them. They *love* playing with your kids. They'd be so mad at me if I left them at home!"

Her face was feeling hot again. She could feel the sweat forming on her lip. She pressed the palm of her hand against her cheek, in an attempt to cool her skin.

"Claire, dear, I really think maybe we should go inside. How about I take you into a guest room where you can lie down for a bit?"

"Lie down?" Claire could hear her own voice rising. "Why would I want to lie down? Who's going to watch my kids if I lie down? You know Jack never keeps a close enough eye on them."

A crowd had somehow formed around her. Other moms and dads. They were all looking at her. *What was their problem?*

She yanked her arm free from Valerie's grasp and pushed past the couple in front of her, two lesbian moms who had a son in Luke's grade. *Mindy and Cindy.* Something stupid like that.

"Excuse me," Claire said. "I need to get through."

She tripped over something. She wasn't sure what. Maybe her own flip-flops. She caught hold of Joe's arm, just as he got close to her, and steadied herself.

"Where you headed, Claire?" The voice was gentle, but firm. It was posed as a question, but it somehow sounded like a command.

"Oh hey, Joe," Claire said. "I'm heading over to the pool. Valerie said the kids were eating there." She looked around his chunky frame. She could see a number of children running in the distance and could hear their laughter and screams. She hoped the girls were wearing their swimming vests. They weren't good swimmers yet. She'd been meaning to put them in lessons, but somehow, had never gotten around to it.

"Yep, I think they are. But why don't we go inside and get you some food, too?" He stepped in front of her, blocking her view.

"What is *with* you people?" Claire said, irritation filling her voice. "I said I want to go see my kids."

"Claire! Claire! *What* is going on?" Suddenly, Loni was in front of Claire. "Did I give you a little bit too much wine?"

Loni's voice was light and teasing, but Claire could sense a tension under it.

"No, you didn't give me too much wine. I'm tired from dancing and want to check on my kids before I eat dinner. Is there a problem with that?"

The color sapped out of Loni's face. Claire could see it literally drain down from her forehead to her chin, a smooth cascade of peach that left nothing but chalky white in its wake.

"But, Claire," Loni said, her voice shaking. "Your kids aren't here."

"What do you mean?" Claire was getting fed up with Loni and all the other parents at this party. "I wouldn't come to a pool party without my kids. They love to swim."

Claire could feel Valerie's hand back on her arm and she fiercely shook it off.

"Hands to yourself, Val!" When did people become so touchy-feely?

"Claire, your children are gone."

"What do you mean *they're gone?*" Claire stepped closer to Loni so their noses were nearly touching. Claire wasn't one to get into a fight, especially not a physical one, but damn it, these people were pissing her off. "I didn't give my kids permission to go anywhere."

What had they done with her kids?

No one messed with Claire's kids.

"Claire, they passed away." The words were so soft. A whisper on the wind. But the sting was so intense, Claire felt the knife enter her heart.

They *what?*

That had been a dream, hadn't it? Her babies weren't really gone. They couldn't be gone. She was here at this pool party. She was with all the other parents. She could see their kids running around the yard, diving off the board into the deep end of the pool. Her kids must be in the midst of it all. They were always at the center of the fun.

They *were* the center of the fun.

They were *her* fun.

Shaking free of all the hands that were suddenly upon her, she shoved past Loni and began to run toward the pool. Her heart pounded to the beat of her feet racing on the soft ground. Loni was wrong. All those people were *wrong*. She'd show them. Her kids were here. They were eating pasta and pickles and ice cream and brownies. Just like all the other kids. They would have messy faces and chocolate dripped on their bathing suits.

"Lily! Ella!" Claire called as she reached the gaggle of children. "Where are you, girls? It's time to go."

The children were running around her in circles, playing some sort of game of tag. Or maybe hide-and-go-seek. Her girls must be hiding.

Claire spotted Luke at the picnic table at the far end of the yard. His blond hair was tousled from playing in the pool for so long. She imagined his fingertips were prunes and his lips must be blue from the cold. He never could handle the cold very well. She could see him talking and laughing with a bunch of boys. His body quaked with glee at something the boy in front of him said. His back was tan and smooth. She wanted to wrap her arms around that smooth skin and hold it to her.

"Luke!" she called out. "Where are your sisters? Have you seen them? I can't find them."

Luke didn't turn around, but kept giggling with his friends.

He never pays attention.

"Luke!" she called louder. "Luke!"

She reached the table as the group of boys let out of whoop of laughter. She grabbed his shoulder to spin him around.

"Luke! You need to listen to me when I call you! *Where* are your sisters?"

Luke turned his head and looked into her eyes. Only it wasn't Luke. It was Timmy Cox, one of Luke's Boy Scout buddies. He stared at her as if he'd seen a ghost.

"Timmy! I'm sorry. I thought you were Luke. Do you know where he is? I can't find him or the girls."

Timmy's eyes filled with tears and fright. He looked around her.

"Mom?" he said, calling out into the distance.

"Timmy, I asked you a question." Claire put her hands on his shoulders. "Do you know where Luke is? I said I can't find him."

Timmy wouldn't make eye contact with Claire again. Frozen in place, he called out again. "Mom!"

Rachel Cox came running from behind. "It's okay, honey." She sat down on the bench and put her arms around her son, pulling him from Claire's grasp.

"Oh, Rachel. I'm so glad you're here. I was just asking Timmy if he's seen Luke."

Rachel's eyes were also brimming with tears. Timmy buried his head in his mom's lap and she rubbed his head.

"You're scaring him," Rachel whispered to Claire.

"What do you mean I'm scaring *him?* You're all scaring *me!* I just want to know where my kids are. Why won't anyone tell me?"

She felt another hand on her forearm. Valerie was back again. Claire tried to shrug her off, but this time Valerie's grasp was tight.

"Okay, Claire. Enough. Let's get away from the kids. We'll go talk inside."

"I will not talk inside. I will not go anywhere until I find my kids."

She saw Loni running in their direction. If she hadn't been so distraught, Claire would have laughed. Loni and running did not go together. She held her skirt up on both sides. A nineteenth-century shop woman chasing hooligans out of her store.

Claire twisted her body around in anger. "You!" She pointed an accusing finger at her host. "*You* did something to my kids! It was *your* idea for us to come here."

A panic-stricken look rose on Loni's face. "Will someone please get her inside before the neighbors call the cops? She's becoming hysterical."

"*Call* the cops!" Claire screamed. She felt more hands on her forearms and she shook to get free of them. "I'll tell them you've kidnapped my children!"

All eyes were upon her now. She could feel them. The music had stopped. No one was talking. A few kids, oblivious to the ruckus, were giggling off in the distance, but the ones standing close to Claire were silent and still.

With one strong yank, she pulled herself loose from the people gripping her and ran toward the pool. She felt dizzy and lightheaded and very, very tired. But she needed to find her kids. They'd all go home together and get in her bed and she could finally sleep—when they were safe under her sheets and in her arms.

Reaching the pool, she saw three girls in the deep end. The twins? It was hard to tell.

"Ella! Lily! Is that you?"

It was dark and the pool wasn't well lit. It didn't seem very safe. It was getting too late to be in the pool.

"Girls! Time to get out! It's time to go home."

The girls continued to swim, diving down to the bottom to collect quarters someone had thrown there. One girl would whack each of the other girls on the head with a pool noodle as they emerged. They giggled uncontrollably.

"Girls!" Claire leaned in closer. "I already gave you five minutes. It's time to go!"

All three girls dove down to the bottom again. She was going to have a word with them when they came up again. It wasn't like her kids to be this disobedient.

"Claire!" She could hear Valerie and Loni and Joe and maybe some of the other parents closing in behind her. She'd had enough. She needed to grab her kids and get out of here—away from these insane people. How had she ever thought they were her *friends?*

"Girls!" The girls were up again. "It's time to go!"

She leaned in some more. They were still giggling.

"Girls!" Claire shrieked. And, just as the swoosh of the last syllable left her mouth, Claire lost her balance. Her flip-flop slipped into the pool, her right foot following. She tumbled, headfirst, the cool, dark water enveloping her.

Out of the corner of her eye, she saw the girls turn her way—their eyes a mixture of surprise and alarm. Dark brown eyes, all of them. Eyes that didn't belong to her girls.

Claire felt herself falling. Dropping deep and hard and far from the life she always knew.

It was a steep fall. A painful one.

One from which she knew she wouldn't rise anytime soon.

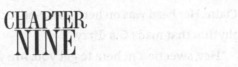

CHAPTER NINE

Gia drove her car up the long, winding driveway and pulled over next to the figure huddled on the curb. The woman was covered, from head to toe, with a large, violet, fleece blanket. She was barely recognizable and if Gia hadn't seen that defeated posture a thousand times before, she might not have known it was Claire.

She put the car in park, opened the driver-side door and got out. Valerie, who was seated next to Claire, her arm wrapped around the woman, stood up to greet Gia.

"Hi, Valerie," Gia said softly, as the woman approached her. She'd met the woman a dozen times at parties Claire and Jack had hosted at their home. "How is she?"

Valerie shrugged. "She's sobering up. We made her down a whole pot of coffee. She didn't need a cold shower. She got that in the deep end of the pool."

Gia shook her head and ran her hand through her hair.

"Geez."

Valerie put her hand on Gia's shoulder. "I'm sorry. We didn't know who to call and then someone mentioned you were living with her right after the accident. I found your number in her phone after I convinced her to give me the passcode."

"You did the right thing. It's just..." Gia exhaled loudly. "Can you help me get her into the car?"

Valerie nodded and the two of them squatted down in front of

Claire. Her head was on her knees. She rocked back and forth, an even rhythm that made Gia dizzy.

"Hey, sweetie. I'm here to get you. Are you ready to go home?"

Gia took Claire's ceased rocking to mean yes.

"Okay, then," Valerie said. "Why don't we help you up and we'll get you into Gia's car."

"I can get up myself," Claire said, startling both her friends with her sudden, decisive words.

"Great," Gia said. "I wasn't looking forward to carrying you."

"Do you want to take the blanket with you in the car, since you're still pretty wet?" Valerie asked.

"No," Claire said, so emphatically both Valerie and Gia exchanged a look. "I don't want to have to come back here to return it."

"Got it," Gia said, removing the blanket from Claire's shoulders and handing it to Valerie. "No blanket." She could imagine how wet the seat of her car was going to get.

"Bye, Claire. It was good to see you. We'll have to get together another time..." Her voice trailed off into the night. Claire ignored Valerie and opened the passenger door to Gia's car.

When she was safely inside, Gia closed the door and turned back to Valerie.

"What happened?"

"I don't know. Honestly, I don't really know. She showed up at the barbecue, which really surprised me."

"You and me, both." To Gia's knowledge, Claire hadn't seen any of these friends since the funeral. She hadn't even mentioned them.

"When Loni said she'd run into Claire and invited her, well...none of us thought she'd actually *come*. I mean, we all hoped she would. We've missed her and everyone feels so awful about what happened."

Gia nodded. When she'd gotten the call from Valerie, she'd almost been tempted to ask if they were talking about the same Claire. The

Claire she knew didn't venture out to get a haircut, let alone attend a large social gathering at the town's largest mansion.

Valerie continued. "She walked in and she looked great. I mean, *great*. A little too thin and rather pale, but just so pretty and the fact that's she's lost a little weight and was wearing such little makeup, she actually looked ten years younger. I would've thought the tragedy would have aged her twenty years, but...she looked really well and it was nice to have her here."

"And then she got wasted?" Gia asked, shaking her head in disbelief. "You know, I've never even seen her take more than a few sips."

"Well, Loni handed her a glass of wine and at first, Claire declined, but then everyone reminded her if anyone deserved to drink, it was her. She began to sip away at it."

"And, apparently, kept sipping."

"Yeah, I guess. I wasn't really paying attention. She seemed to be having a great time. We were reminiscing and laughing so much. Everything seemed great, until it wasn't anymore."

"Okay. Thanks again for calling me. I'll see to it she gets home safe and sound."

"I took Claire's car keys out of her purse, but I left her house key in the inside pocket. Joe and I will return the car on our way home and put her keys under her mat. I'm sure she won't want to come back here to get the car in the morning."

"Thanks. Since I'd be the one to drive her back, you're saving me the trip, too."

Gia turned back to the car. Claire had her head resting against the passenger window. Gia wondered if she was sleeping and hoped she hadn't passed out. It would be so difficult to get her out of the car and into the house if she had.

"Listen, Gia," Valerie said, her voice sincere with worry and sadness. "I'm really sorry we had to call you. This can't be easy for you, either.

I should've been around more to help you out. To help Claire. I guess I didn't know what to do or say after...well, after everything. I'm kind of ashamed to have been such a bad friend. I hope Karma finds you and rewards you with wonderful things for all you've done."

Gia smiled at Valerie. "Thanks, Valerie. That means a lot."

"Please call me and let me know how she's doing in the next day or so. I'll try to stop by to check on her. It's not fair this weight has fallen so much on you."

Gia gave Valerie a spontaneous hug. She really didn't know Claire's friend very well, but her words were touching and very much appreciated.

"I will. I'll call you."

With a final wave, Gia went around the car to the driver's side and got in.

When she started the car, Bon Jovi blared out of the speakers. Gia reached over and turned it off. The car filled with silence as she put the car in drive and headed down the long, circular driveway.

When they reached the road, Claire broke the silence.

"I'm sorry."

"Uh-huh." Gia turned on her blinker and carefully made a left turn, against traffic.

"No, really. I'm sorry." Claire lifted her head and surveyed Gia's attire. Her friend was wearing a short skirt and a blue ruffled top. Claire glanced down and saw Gia's shoes were strappy heels, not her usual barefoot sandals.

"I interrupted a date, didn't I?"

Gia drove in silence for a beat. "Yep."

"Was it a good one?"

"Best one I've had in years."

"Oh, Gia. I'm so sorry."

Gia said nothing.

"I'll make it up to you. I'm really sorry. I didn't mean for you to have to come all the way out here to get me."

"Who did you think was going to come get you when you got wasted and decided to take a swim in the deep end of their pool in your clothes?" Gia snapped. She cringed at the harshness in her own voice. It wasn't that she wasn't concerned, but her patience was running thin with Claire these days. In the past year and a half, Gia couldn't even begin to count the number of times she'd had to change plans because of Claire.

Claire's head hit the headrest as if she'd been literally slapped. She'd never seen Gia so mad.

"I made a poor choice."

"Ya think?"

"You have every right to be mad at me."

"I know." Gia pushed her foot down on the gas as she merged onto the highway.

"Just drop me off at home. Don't come in. Is it too late to finish your date?"

"Of course, it's too late. I was almost an hour away when Valerie called me. The poor guy had to drive me home so I could get my car. He'd splurged on a beautiful, expensive meal on the coast. I'm sure he wasn't thrilled when we had to ask for it to go."

"Oh, Gia. I'm so sorry."

"So you've said."

Claire thought it best not to say more. It seemed the more she apologized, the more agitated Gia became. This was so unlike Gia. The two of them had never really argued. She couldn't remember them ever having any sort of fight. But Claire knew she'd pushed Gia to her limit and she hated herself for it. It was just one more thing that made Claire want to cry.

Ten minutes later, Gia pulled up in front of Claire's house. She put the car in park but remained silent.

"I guess you don't want to come in."

"Nope." Gia stared straight ahead into the stream of light the headlights made on the street.

"Claire," Gia said, finally turning toward her friend. "You need to get it together. I'm sorry to have to tell you this, but you do. I don't know how you're going to do it, but it's time you began to figure it out. You and I both have lives we need to get back to. We've been stuck on this Ferris wheel long enough. We're just going round and round. Jack would be horrified and you know it."

Claire nodded. She felt terrible she'd caused Gia to be so angry with her. But she knew Gia had every right to be. Every person's patience has its breaking point and it was perfectly clear to Claire that Gia had reached hers tonight.

"Thanks again for coming to get me."

"I'll call you tomorrow to see how your hangover is. I guess you're about to experience your first one."

Claire smiled, grateful for the kind words, even though she knew Gia wasn't feeling them.

"Okay. I'll talk to you tomorrow."

She opened the door and eased her way out of the car, closing the door gently. Gia didn't even wait to make sure Claire made it inside. She was down the street and around the corner before Claire had reached her front door.

Claire found her house key inside her purse and let herself in. The house seemed so quiet and empty. And cold. She'd left the air on too high and, in her wet clothes, Claire was now freezing. She debated making herself another cup of hot coffee, but then decided her bladder couldn't take any more and, instead, headed straight upstairs. Stripping her clothes off and letting them drop onto the bedroom floor, she went to the shower and turned it to as hot as she could tolerate. Standing under the scorching heat, she thought about what Gia had said in the car.

Jack would be horrified.

He *would* be horrified. Not upset. Not hurt. Not annoyed. *Horrified.* Had she ever, in their entire marriage, done anything to horrify her husband? She didn't think so.

But now, maybe now, she had.

She turned off the water and dried herself with a fluffy blue towel. Claire tousle-dried her hair and wrapped the soft terrycloth around her. Walking into the bedroom, she momentarily debated putting some pajamas on, but decided she was too exhausted and instead, laid her body on the bed, her skin still damp.

She was asleep the moment her head hit the pillow and, for once, dreamt of nothing.

Claire wasn't sure she'd ever felt such a pain in her life. She was pretty sure a wrecking ball had smashed in the side of her head, and then, just for kicks, kept smashing.

She stumbled down the stairs and into the kitchen. Last she remembered, there was some Tylenol in one of the cabinets. She began to open them, finding she had too little energy to close them behind her. She was rewarded when, in the fifth cabinet, she located the bottle.

Struggling to get it open, and cursing the whole time, Claire finally dropped two, then three, and finally four tablets in her hand. Popping them into her mouth, she swallowed the pills without water and then regretted it as she felt them lodge in her throat. She scrambled to the sink and grabbed the nearest dirty glass, quickly filling it with water and downing it. She bent over and rested her head on the counter, wondering how long it would take for the tablets to begin the repair inside her head.

How did people do this every Friday night? How did they function the next day? She couldn't imagine ever doing this again. Gia had been right. She'd had her first hangover and Claire was certain it would be her last.

The phone rang, but she ignored it. At least, she tried to ignore it. The ringing was a discotheque pulsing through her brain. Whoever it was would have to go away—and quickly. A moment after the ringing stopped, she took the phone off the hook. She couldn't risk its resounding clangs again.

Claire staggered to the couch and eased her body down. Plopping would have hurt too much. She needed to move slowly. *Very, very slowly.* One wrong move and her head might fall off her body and shatter into a million pieces on the floor.

The thought almost made her smile. If it shattered, would it stop throbbing?

She placed her head on one of the decorative pillows and closed her eyes. She was determined not to move until the pain ceased.

Claire wasn't sure how long she slept. When she opened her eyes, the room was dim. Had the sun already shifted to the west? She couldn't have possibly been here that long.

But, when she rolled over to peek at the clock, she saw it was close to four in the afternoon. Today had definitely not been a productive day. She hadn't gotten out of her bed until nearly noon and then she'd done nothing by lie on this couch ever since.

She thought she should feel guilty but realized it had been a long time since she'd had *any* sort of productive day. Today was no different, other than she was paying the price for getting plastered last night.

Claire sat up and was pleased to realize she felt much better. Not great. Not a hundred percent. But the excruciating pain was gone. It'd been replaced with a dull ache. Her head felt tender, but not unbearable.

She wandered into the kitchen. Her stomach rumbled and she remembered there were Chinese leftovers that sounded appealing. Opening the fridge, she removed the container and scooped its contents onto a plate. While it was heating in the microwave, she scanned the kitchen counter. It was amazing how clean the kitchen stayed now that she was the only one living here. The microwave beeped its announcement that the food was done. She carefully removed the hot plate, grabbed a fork and headed to the table. Taking her first bite, and then spitting it back on her plate because it was too hot, her eyes fell on the event ticket she'd left on the table the day before. The one Irma had given her at McGord's. She'd forgotten all about it.

The paper said the event started at six o'clock. She glanced at the clock again. It was ten past four. The auditorium was nearly an hour away. She could make it if she really hustled, though her brain still begged her to move slowly.

Maybe she should skip it. She'd be very content turning on a chick flick tonight and crawling back into bed.

But she'd spent way too many days in her pajamas in the past year and a half. And she'd already seen nearly every chick flick on Netflix. Gia's words from last night rang in her ears.

You need to get it together.

Jack would be horrified.

She was right. Jack *would* be horrified. He, like she, had enjoyed the occasional day in bed, a bowl of popcorn in between them and an old black-and-white movie on the TV. But one day of that was all he could take. Even if Claire begged him to do it again the next day, he'd inform her he could only be lazy for so long.

Claire hadn't exactly been lazy for the past eighteen months. She'd had a reason to stay in bed. But perhaps it was time to get out of bed. At least for tonight.

And last night, too. Though, she wasn't going to think about that. She was never, ever going to think about that again, if she could help it.

Claire remembered the man's eyes from the flier. They were mesmerizing. A shocking blue that contrasted with his jet-black hair.

His eyes had seemed to speak to her, as if he had something to say and, for some reason, she needed to hear it.

Deciding to let her food cool for a moment, she bolted up the stairs, ignoring her head as it screamed for her to creep along.

If she was going to make it to his talk by six o'clock, she needed to get moving.

CHAPTER TEN

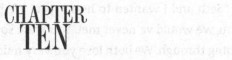

"Hold that baby closer to the camera," Callum said into his tablet. "I can't see him well enough."

"He's heavy!" the woman on the other end of Skype said. "I can barely lift him already!"

Callum laughed, a big, hearty laugh, much larger than one would expect from someone of his body mass. "Just wait until he's fifteen. He'll be lifting you."

"Hush, you," the woman scolded. "Don't wish away the years just yet. I'm enjoying every second of him being a baby. Seth and I waited a very long time for him to come into our lives."

"And I'll bet he was worth the wait and all the struggles." They were referring to the many years of infertility Seth and Terri had experienced. Callum and the other team members had held front-row seats to their friends' pain and sorrow. After many years of not being able to conceive, they'd then been dealt even more years of miscarriages. It had been heartbreaking for everyone, but no one more so than Terri.

"Every second of them. Good things come to those who wait, right?" Terri kissed the baby's head. "Would you like to know his name?"

"Frank told me it's Noah. A good strong name for a good, strong boy."

"Noah Callum."

"No way! That's fabulous! I am honored beyond belief." He would've slapped his knee in delight if he had one.

"Seth and I wanted to honor you. We both know if it wasn't for you, we would've never met. You were so supportive of all we were going through. We both love you very much. We don't know a better man than you, Callum. We wanted our son to represent some of that strength."

"Well, I'm touched. Truly. You nearly made this grown man cry. And, as you know, Irish bucks don't cry." Callum made sure to strengthen his brogue at the end of the sentence, for emphasis.

The door of Callum's hotel room opened and a man anyone would refer to as a cowboy, sauntered in. Wearing faded jeans and his usual pearl-snap shirt, he plopped down in the seat across from the desk where Callum was seated. Kicking up his never-absent cowboy boots onto the desk, he leaned back in the chair.

"Guess who's dropping pieces of dirt on my desk?" Callum asked the screen in front of him.

"Tell Wyatt to take his feet down. That is disgusting. You don't know what he's stepped in."

"Knowing Wyatt, nothing good." Callum laughed.

"Laugh away, you Yankees. You wouldn't know a solid day's work if it kicked you in the arse," Wyatt said, raising his voice so the woman on the tablet could hear.

"Oh, arse is the new term?" Terri laughed. "Are we cleaning up his language a bit?"

"There's a British woman he's hot on," Callum said and then turned his attention onto Wyatt. "People from Ireland aren't Yankees."

"Anyone not from Texas is a Yankee."

"Well, there you have it," Callum said back to the screen. "Clear as mud."

A loud scream pierced the room and Callum's eardrum.

"Oh, no. I'd better go," Terri said, lifting the baby to her shoulder and patting him on the back. "It's feeding time."

"You go take care of that baby, *Mom.*" Callum stressed the last word, making Terri smile, just as he knew it would. "My namesake shouldn't be uncomfortable in any way."

"Bye! It was great to talk to you! Let's do this again soon."

"Whenever you get the chance," Callum said with a smile. "I sense you're going to be very busy for the next eighteen or so years. Sing him some of your beautiful lullabies. We're all jealous he's the only one who gets to hear your voice from this point on."

"Oh, you'll find my replacement soon. Bye, Wyatt!"

"See ya later, Terri! Good to catch you!"

The screen went black and Terri was gone.

"Now that Noah Callum is one handsome boy. As, of course, he'd have to be seeing as he bears my name."

"I knew when Seth told me what they named him, it would go to your head. We're going to hear about it for the next month, aren't we?"

"At least. I do love a chubby baby."

"You love any baby. You're such a girl."

"Now there, don't go picking fights you can't win, Wyatt. I'd hate to have to take you out with my wicked left hook."

Wyatt smirked. "Your phantom arm can't be any worse than the one you've actually got." He shifted in his seat and tapped his shirt pocket.

"No cigarettes there, buddy," Callum said.

"I know. I know. But I keep looking."

"How long has it been now?"

"Three long months."

"I'm proud of you."

"Yeah, yeah." Wyatt grumbled, but Callum knew Wyatt was proud of himself, too. It was a habit he'd been trying to break for years now.

"Women don't like to kiss men who smell like nicotine."

"Why do you think I'm going through this misery?" Wyatt muttered. "Not for my smooth skin."

Callum laughed again. Wyatt had that effect on him. It was difficult not to wind up laughing in Wyatt's presence. He wasn't a jokester, by any means. But he was funny. Perhaps because he was so outrageous, so out of the box. At least no one in Callum's native Ireland had ever come in a box like the one Wyatt must have inhabited.

"So, what's the latest?" Callum asked. "Everything set up at the convention center?"

"Yep. They have a big crew getting the stage and everything else in place. It's busier over there than a funeral home fan in July."

Callum gave Wyatt a quizzical look, but didn't say a word. He'd long ago learned it was pointless to question the colorful Texas sayings that flew out of Wyatt's mouth.

"Has Frank found us a new singer for the seminars?"

"Not that I've heard. He was holding auditions yesterday, but from his mood when he arrived at dinner, I'm thinking he didn't find anyone."

"Anyone who could meet his unachievable standards?" Callum asked.

"You got it."

"Did you remind him it won't be long before we're heading to Europe?" Callum asked.

"I waved my plane ticket at him."

"And what did he say?"

"Wyatt Roy, why don't you go load some wheelchairs into the truck and keep your nose out of my musical business."

"That sounds like Frank."

"It wouldn't hurt for him to carry a few wheelchairs."

Callum pondered on Frank's diminutive and slight build. The man couldn't be more than five feet six inches, but he held himself with such an elegant stature, Callum often felt Frank gained another inch or two by holding his chin so high. The man possessed self-confidence by the bucket load, yet never came across as arrogant or pompous.

Well, maybe he did seem a little pompous, Callum had to admit with a chuckle. But, that was okay. Each of them had their own issues and hangups. For Frank, it was his suits. The man had never found a three-piece suit he didn't adore. Callum often wondered what percentage of Frank's salary was spent on trips to the tailor.

Frank was constantly in his signature ensemble. Other than on very rare occasions, when Callum had unexpectedly shown up at Frank's hotel room door unannounced, Callum had never actually seen him in anything other than his wool threads.

"It's a little bit too hot for that in Uganda," Callum would remind Frank, pointing at his suit, when they traveled to warmer climates.

"I can take off my jacket and roll up my sleeves," Frank would say, and that would be that. Callum knew better than to argue with the man.

"He carries his music stand. What more do you want?" Callum said, winking at Wyatt.

Callum shifted his attention back to the screen of his tablet and began to type.

"I need to learn to type as quickly as you do," Wyatt said. "I just peck away."

"Which is pathetic, since you actually have two hands."

Callum's five fingers flew across the screen as he completed his message and hit send.

"You know, they've invented computer voice recognition. You could say what you need to type directly into the computer and it'll type it for ya."

"And waste all that time I spent, as a teenager, learning how to soar across the keyboard? No thanks. I needed to send an email to my folks. They get worried if they don't hear from me every few days. Not sure what they think is going to happen to me. It's not like I'm gonna lose a leg in a car crash or something."

There was a knock at the door right before the key was inserted and it swung open.

"Ready, Callum?"

Callum glanced up at Mitch, just as he saw the words, "Message Sent," pop up on his screen.

"You bet." Pulling the joystick on the arm of his chair toward him, he backed away from the desk and then rolled toward Mitch. "You gonna stick around for the peep show, Wyatt, or are you gonna go clean yourself up?"

"I've seen you strip down more times than I care to think about," Wyatt mumbled, dropping his feet to the ground and standing up. He was a big man, not only in height, but in sheer body mass. Wyatt said everything was bigger in Texas, and if his size was any indication, he was one hundred percent correct. "I'm gonna go see if there are any lovely ladies in the hotel bar."

"Just don't forget we're heading back over to the convention center at five on the dot."

"Wouldn't miss it."

He strode out the door as Callum began to expertly unbutton his shirt with his one hand.

"One day, I'll have this shirt off and be completely dressed before you even get in the room."

"That'll be the day. And, what are you trying to do? Put me out of a job?" Mitch said, a good-natured grin on his face as he walked to the closet, selecting Callum's clothes for that evening.

"No worries there. I have plenty more for you to do." He hoisted himself out of his chair and onto the bed, lying back so he could begin to wiggle out of his cut-off jeans.

Mitch returned with a short-sleeved, button-up blue shirt and khaki shorts.

Callum slid into the shorts Mitch handed him. He buttoned and zipped them himself. There were some things he couldn't do, but putting on his own pants was a task he'd mastered as a little kid. And though it would be easier to let Mitch help him—the pants' button could be tricky—he had a good deal of pride and maintained it whenever possible. When he finished, he put out his right, and only hand, so Mitch could help pull him back up into a sitting position.

Callum buttoned his shirt, his fingers working quickly to slide each one into its hole. Glancing up, he noticed Mitch staring at him.

"Didn't feel like brushing your hair at all today?"

"What are you talking about?"

"It looks like a wild mess."

"If it makes you unhappy, feel free to fix it."

"Want me to wipe your ass for you, too?"

"Nope. I got that covered," Callum deadpanned.

"Come on then," Mitch said. "Let's make you presentable."

Callum rolled into the hotel bathroom. Most days, Callum let his curls have their own way. He always felt he looked a lot better when they won the battle. His team, however, did not seem to feel the same way.

"If you want to look like Mowgli from *The Jungle Book* on your days off, that's up to you. In the meantime, if you don't comb your hair, Mitch will be doing it for you," his assistant, Alison, had said.

Mitch was such a lapdog, Callum thought, but never said aloud. If Alison said jump, Mitch said, "How high?" If she said brush, he said, "How hard?"

Callum had never been such an arse-kisser. Not with any woman. Not that there had been all that many in his past, but there had been a significant few. Despite his disabilities, he could always get a date, if he wanted one. But oftentimes, he didn't want one. The women he met seemed to fall into two categories: nursemaid or activist. They either felt it was their duty to take care of Callum—though he was fully capable of taking care of himself—or else, they were out to change the world and Callum was just a part of that overall plan.

"Hey!" Callum said, as water trickled down his face and onto his dry and pressed shirt.

"If you'd just brush it after you shower, we wouldn't have to wet it to get it to lie down."

"I have thick Irish hair, just like my mam."

"Great. Remind me to have her style it next time she comes. When are your parents coming next?"

"In about two months."

"Awesome. We love when your mom comes."

"'Cause she always stays in a hotel room with a full kitchen and bakes you biscuits?" Callum remembered his surprise, when coming to America as a college student, he'd learned the biscuits here were actually small round buns of baked dough. In his mind, they would always be the delicious cookies of his youth.

"Yep. Those little lace things rock."

Callum lifted the toothpaste, which was already missing its cap, off the counter and raised it to his lips. With a gentle squeeze, he squirted a dollop into his mouth and then placed the tube back down on the counter. He grabbed his toothbrush and began to brush.

"There's a full crowd this weekend."

Callum nodded, his mouth full of toothpaste. Leaning over the sink, he spat into it. Then, after turning on the water, he picked up his cup and filled it. Once he'd rinsed his mouth out and replaced the cup on the sink, he turned the faucet off. Even after all these years of never being able to do it any other way, Callum still found it a bit annoying that simple things took twice as long as they did for other people.

"Alison said she closed registration early because it filled up so quickly."

"That's great."

"She was talking about convincing you to add a few more cities to the tour."

"Nope."

"They'd all fill up."

"I know. But we're busy enough as it is. I need some down time. So do all of you. I'm not into working my staff to the bone. We have nothing to give to others if we don't take care of ourselves."

"Good. I thought it was a lousy idea when she brought it up, but you know..."

"You didn't want to be the one to tell her." Mitch smiled at Callum's reflection in the mirror and shrugged. "Man, you are so whipped."

"Who's shaving today?"

"You can," Callum said. "But only because..."

"You are a terrible shaver and cut yourself all the time. If we left it up to you, you'd have hair as wild as a smoke bush and pieces of toilet paper stuck to your face."

"A smoke bush? That had to have been Wyatt's term."

Mitch shrugged. "It's accurate. That's all that matters."

Mitch picked up the can of shaving cream. Callum opened the palm of his hand and Mitch sprayed the foam into it.

"Lather up."

Callum wiped the cream all over his cheeks and chin, smoothing a little bit above his top lip.

"Okay, sit still now. You don't want me to cut you."

"You don't want to cut me *again*," Callum said, smiling at his reflection in the mirror. "You're really no better at this than I am."

"Oh, so you're now a comedian, too, huh?" Mitch said, raising his eyes at Callum's expression. "Make sure to use some of your jokes in your talk tonight."

Callum sat in silence, watching Mitch shave his face. He could absolutely shave his face on his own. He could do nearly everything on his own—or with minimal help. But, sometimes, he let people help him. The days he agreed to accept the most help were the ones where he had a whole weekend event ahead of him. Talking to a crowd for two days straight was exhausting. He poured everything he had into these seminars. He was often hungry and thirsty and exhausted, and his back ached. By the end of the weekend, all he'd want to do was sleep for three days, straight, which, of course, he couldn't because the next morning, he and his team would get in the van and head off to the next city for another seminar.

"There you go," Mitch said at last.

"Pretty as a picture," Callum replied, inspecting his reflection.

Mitch grabbed the folders from the desk, along with Callum's personal items, and tucked them inside the satchel permanently attached to the side of Callum's chair. "You ready to head out?" he said, grabbing Callum's and his own coat from the back of the desk chair.

"Yep. Except..."

"Except what?" Mitch said, turning back to Callum.

Callum gave Mitch a big grin, the one even he knew could make the ladies melt. The one that had gotten him in and out of a number of sticky situations throughout his youth. The one that said, "Oops. I made a mistake, but we both know you're going to forgive me for it."

"I'm thinking I probably should have used the loo before I zipped up my pants."

And then, with a shake of the head from Mitch, Callum rolled his chair into the restroom and closed the door behind him.

CHAPTER
ELEVEN

Claire hurried into the auditorium. She was running late. The traffic had been a killer and halfway here, as she sat in the bumper-to-bumper parking lot on the thruway, she'd been pretty certain she wouldn't make it at all. Then the traffic jam had unexpectedly cleared and, with a bit of a lead foot, she'd arrived at the auditorium just in time. Parking had been another issue. Claire couldn't believe how full the lot was. She'd finally found a spot a few streets over and walked at lightning speed to get back to the building.

She was thankful that Irma had given her the ticket in advance. She wasn't sure how she would've found the woman in this crowd. She'd also noticed signs on the doors to the building which stated the event was completely sold out and there were no on-site tickets available. When she'd accepted the ticket from Irma, she'd had no idea it was such a hot commodity.

Claire was sweaty and tired as she found a seat, a little further back than she would've liked. Collapsing into it, jammed between an oversized woman and a man who clearly had not put on enough deodorant this morning, she took a few deep breaths. She was here. She wasn't sure why, but she was here. There had to be a few thousand people here, so she was surprised when her eyes actually landed on Irma. Claire waved her hand as the two of them made eye contact and Irma waved in return. Irma was surrounded by a number of younger men and women and Claire assumed they were her children.

Claire began to relax as she heard the music start. She sat back and closed her eyes. The piano playing was lovely. Soft and gentle. Soothing to Claire's soul. She'd always loved the piano. She played it herself, but not very well. She'd constantly wished she was better at it. But, perfection came with practice, and Claire had never been good at the practicing part. She enjoyed singing so much more. She'd never minded practicing that. When she was young, she'd made a point of finding time for it. Once the kids arrived, though, time to practice had been hard to come by. She sang less as well, unless you counted the lullabies at bedtime and all the singing along to Justin Bieber, with the kids, in the car.

The music picked up in tempo and volume. The crowd, which had been noisy and talkative until this point, began to quiet down. The lights dimmed a bit. Claire noticed a small man seated at the piano to the side of center stage. His hands soared over the keyboard, barely landing on one note before they flew to another. And another. And another. He was an incredible musician. Claire didn't need to hear any more to know that. What he was doing to those keys was amazingly difficult and complex. Claire might not be able to do it herself, but she could appreciate such talent in others.

When the man finished, with gusto, the crowd broke into loud applause and cheers. The little man, who was dressed as if he'd just stepped from the page of a Charles Dickens novel—*dapper* was the word that popped into Claire's mind—stood up and bowed at the waist, before quickly making his way off the stage.

"Good evening, everyone." A man, much taller than the pianist, was standing in the center of the stage, a microphone in hand. "Thank you for coming this evening. If you have never heard Callum Fitzgerald speak before, you're in for a treat. This is a man who, by all accounts, would have every right to feel sorry for himself. But instead, he's inspiring millions, all around the world, to achieve their dreams, no matter what their limitations. Over the next two days, you will not only be inspired to change your life and turn your pain into power, but you'll be driven to help others do the same. Will you please give a warm welcome to Mr. Callum Fitzgerald?"

The people around Claire stood and began to applaud loudly. Claire rose to her feet, too. She wasn't really sure why she was standing—it wasn't like this guy was a rock star—but she felt it was rude to not join in.

The man in front of Claire was unusually wide, but luckily, not so tall that Claire couldn't see above his head. She had a good view of the stage and noticed a man riding his electric wheelchair toward a long, wooden table in the center of the stage. As he reached the front of the table, he stopped his chair and, using the one arm he had, hoisted himself on top. He turned to face the crowd.

"Thank you. Thank you very much," he said to the audience, as they continued to clap.

Another man, who looked to be in his early twenties and in incredible shape, hurried out to the stage. He flipped a switch on the arm of the chair, rested his hand on the back and guided the wheelchair off the stage.

"Thanks, Mitch!" Callum called out before gesturing to the crowd. "Please, have a seat. Evenin', everyone. How are you? Before I begin, I'd like to first take a moment to thank you. There are many ways you could be spending your time, especially here in sunny Florida! I know you could be tanning yourselves on the beach or drinking a piña colada. It means a lot to me that you've chosen to spend some of it with me."

He turned to face the piano. "Frank," he called out. "Come back out here."

The little piano man rushed back out on the stage.

"I'd also like to thank our pianist, Frank Rossen, for the beautiful music he provided this evening."

The crowd applauded politely as Claire, once again, marveled at this man's talent. Even if she got nothing out of Callum's speech, hearing that beautiful music had made the trip and all the traffic worthwhile. She hoped he'd be playing again during the event.

Frank took a deep bow and left the stage once again.

"I have to apologize to you," Callum continued. "For the past five years, we've had a wonderful vocalist who's traveled with us all over the world. If you'd come to hear me speak two weeks ago, you'd have had the privilege of listening to her incredible voice before I rolled out. Unfortunately, for us, not her, she left to have a baby. I'm thrilled to announce she gave birth to a beautiful little boy she named Noah Callum."

There was a slight "aah" from the crowd as Callum's face broke into an enormous grin.

"I *know!* How awesome is *that?*" He laughed. "But, as a result, we're now a little short in the music department. So, the only person you'll get to hear tonight is me."

His face dropped in mock sadness as the crowd chuckled.

"No worries, though. I won't be singing for you. You've been spared." He wiped his hand across his forehead and smiled again. He had an amazing smile. Even from this distance, Claire was taken in by it. He didn't just smile with his mouth. His whole face lit up and Claire found it difficult not to smile with him.

"I will do my best to make tonight and tomorrow worth your while. And, hopefully, next time we meet, there will be vocal music to go along with your evening."

Callum adjusted himself on the table with his arm.

"For those of you who don't know my story, I was born this way."

Claire's eyes fell to Callum's body, *what there was of it.* Immediately, she felt guilt at thinking such a thought. But, well, it was hard to think otherwise. Where his legs should have been were two small stumps.

And, where his left arm would have been, was an empty shirt sleeve. The contrast between his exceptionally beautiful face—and it was *beautiful*, there was no denying that—and the rest of his body was startling. His cheeks were chiseled like a finely carved Michelangelo. His nose was perfectly symmetrical. His lips were full, the kind of lips that ended in a little smirk at the corners, as if he knew something no one else did. How could one part of a man's body be so incredible, the image of tall, dark and handsome, minus the tall, and the rest of him be so lacking? It was an oxymoron if Claire ever knew one.

"In the Bible, in the book of Psalms, it says 'children are a heritage from the Lord. They are a blessing.' Thirty-five years ago, my parents were expecting their first blessing, a son. My mam had the best doctors and medical care in Ireland and took no medication. Nothing was expected to go wrong."

Callum shrugged and, with his hand, waved down at his body. "And then I was born. The doctor held me away from my mam so she wouldn't see me. My dad caught a glimpse of me and had to hold on to a table so as to not pass out. 'What's wrong?' my mam kept asking. 'Tell me what's wrong with my baby.'

"Quietly, a nurse sat down next to my mam and told her the terrible news. Her baby, the one she had waited for for nine months, would never be able to fulfill the dreams she had for him. He would never be able to walk or take care of himself or have his own career and life."

Claire could sense that even now, Callum could feel the pain his mom must've felt that day. "Her son," Callum continued, "had been born with only one arm and no legs."

His tone was soothing, hypnotic. Claire not only got lost in his words, but in the sound of his voice. The crowd of thousands vanished and it was as if Claire and Callum were the only ones left in the room. He was speaking directly to her.

"I could've given up. I wanted to give up. Do you know how cruel kids can be? There were many days, especially during my teen years, when I'd wake up and think, 'I can't get out of this bed,' and not just because I had no legs on which to stand." Even from so far away, Claire could see him wink and slightly lighten the mood. "I'd think, 'I can't face this life I've been given. Who's going to hire me? What women is *ever* going to love me looking this way? How will people see me as normal?'"

Callum smiled at this point, a smile that said he held an amazing secret and was about to let you in on it.

"You know what I've learned? Normal isn't so great. Why would you want to be normal? The people we remember aren't the ordinary ones in life. They're the *extra*-ordinary ones who've faced incredible, unimaginable struggles and yet, overcome them. There's a reason people like to root for the underdog. A reason why we go to the movies and cheer for the long shot to win the race, or the wimpy kid to beat up the bully. Because, at some point in our lives, we've all felt like the underdog. You don't have to be lacking legs or an arm to feel that way. It's not the circumstances you're given in life that make you who you are. It's what you *do* with those circumstances that defines you."

Callum held up his right arm and again gestured to his small body.

"I clearly know about struggles. What are the struggles you're facing today? If you're breathing, I know you've got them. Do they feel so heavy you think you can't stand to bear them one more day? Do you want to quit? Run away? Give up? I understand."

Tears rimmed Claire's eyes. She blinked rapidly to keep them from falling.

"Hold on," Callum continued, speaking directly into Claire's soul. "There are better days ahead. If you feel you can barely move forward, take baby steps." He chuckled. "And just by doing that, you'll be doing more than I can do!"

Callum paused, his face growing serious again. "Listen to me. If you don't know how to help yourself, help someone else. Look around you. There's no shortage of pain in this world. Find power in your pain. Find a purpose *for* your pain." He let his gaze scan the crowd. "Feel like your life is lacking in blessings? How about becoming one of those blessings for someone else?"

Claire watched as the line to speak to Callum grew. She'd love to have some time to meet with him, herself, but by the looks of that line, her chances were slim, even if she waited for hours. Callum had been right. There was a lot of pain in this world and people, it seemed, wanted to share some of theirs with him.

Perhaps, tomorrow, after the longer training session he was conducting, there'd be time to meet him. Though she hadn't initially been certain she'd attend the second day, it had only taken five minutes of listening to Callum to change her mind. She was drawn to him and what he had to say.

Claire hoped she'd have the chance to thank him. He hadn't done anything remarkable on that stage. He hadn't done a juggling act with his one arm. There'd been no one-handed handstand. All he'd done was speak the truth and remind the crowd that everyone can hold on to hope. In a world full of lies, deception and selfish endeavors, his brand of selflessness and optimism was refreshing. He had no time to feel sorry for himself and he'd made an incredible case on why those in the audience shouldn't, either, no matter what their life circumstances. Life was short, something Claire knew all too well. He'd asked the crowd to ponder how they were going to spend it. Were they going to wallow in their misery? Or were they going to grow and become the best version of themselves? Someone who would make those they loved, especially those who might've been lost, proud of them. It was something Claire had absolutely, positively, needed to hear.

She looked toward the piano and saw that the small man had returned and was beginning to play softly.

I should go home, Claire thought. *I have things I have to do there.*

But then, she realized, she really didn't. There was nothing she had to do. *At all.* No one waiting on her. No one who needed her.

Claire suddenly knew she wanted to be needed. She *needed* to be needed.

Maybe, as Callum had said, she *was* needed. Maybe not at her house. Maybe no longer by her husband and her children. But maybe *somewhere.*

Mustering all the courage she could find in her slender body, Claire stood, picked up her purse and marched down the aisle toward the piano. She walked quickly so as not to lose her nerve before she even made it halfway down the stairs.

She tiptoed up the four steps to the stage. Gently, she tapped the pianist on his shoulder. He turned gracefully, his hands continuing to glide across the keys.

He smiled at her. A wide grin under a full, brown, neatly trimmed beard. A smile that said to Claire, "I know you and I know why you're here."

Though, of course, he didn't. But Claire did. She knew why she was standing behind this man. What she needed to do. What she needed to say.

"Hi," Claire said, as clearly as she could. She would not let herself cry. She took a deep breath. "I'm Claire." She took another deep breath. "I'm Claire and I sing."

CHAPTER
TWELVE

The line was growing shorter and, for that, Callum was grateful. He loved to greet the people after a speech, loved to listen to how his talk had motivated them to make changes in their lives. He empathized with their stories of sadness and hardship. They hugged him. He hugged them back. And he hugged. And he hugged. He sat on a table so he could be closer to their height, but still his back ached from the leaning that was involved in all that hugging, especially when balancing on his stumps was already an issue.

"Hey, boss." Callum felt a tap on his shoulder and knew it was Wyatt coming to rescue him. There were only a few people left in line and Callum was ready to go back to his room at the hotel and call it a night. No matter how enjoyable these talks were, they were exhausting. Callum imagined anyone would be tired after speaking to a crowd of a couple thousand for almost an hour and then, spending another hour or two meeting with those people individually. And this was only the beginning. He still had all of tomorrow's workshop to go. His events were especially exhausting on a body like his and that was precisely why Callum employed Mitch. If not for his assistant, Callum would be physically depleted before he even got on the stage. In his mind, that wouldn't be fair to the crowd who'd come to see him. He knew they'd spent their hard-earned money to do so.

If Callum could afford to run these events for free, he would. He wasn't in it for the money. He already had enough of that to live comfortably. He'd written two books over the years and both of them had been quite successful. He could easily live off those royalties for quite a while, until he needed to write another book. But he wasn't just supporting himself. He had a staff that needed to be paid. And travel expenses. And venues that needed to be rented. Not to mention the money that was used to help those with disabilities similar to his own. The money people paid to attend his events went to cover all of those costs.

"I'm just about done here," Callum whispered back to him. "Can you pull the van around? I'm pooped. Ready to watch some mindless TV tonight."

"Yeah, well," Wyatt drawled in the way he often did. "That TV might have to wait a bit."

"You're kidding," Callum said, gesturing to the young woman next in line that he'd be right with her.

"Nope. But, it's for a good cause. Frank has someone he'd like you to meet. Let's finish up here and then I'll take you to them. They're in one of the back rooms."

Wyatt stood in silence as Callum patiently spoke and hugged the woman. After her, there was one small boy, who only wanted to have his photo taken with Callum and then they were done.

Wyatt had Callum's wheelchair poised and ready to go when Callum turned around.

"You read my mind."

"Anything for you, boss," Wyatt said, steadying himself for Callum to hold onto as he jumped down into the seat of his chair. "Vamonos."

The first thing Callum noticed about Claire wasn't something he saw, but rather, something he heard. As he rolled beside Wyatt, down one of the back halls of the auditorium, the sweet sounds of "Amazing Grace" floated toward him, filling his body with joy.

"Wow!" Callum said to Wyatt.

Wyatt nodded as they reached the room at the far end. There was a window along the side of the door, fortunately low enough so Callum could see inside. All they could see was Frank's back, as he played, and the back of the woman standing beside him. She was slender and slight, with long, brown hair flowing halfway down her back. She also had a nice bum. Callum couldn't help but notice the bum.

"*When we've been there ten thousand years, Bright shining as the sun. We've no less days to sing God's praise, than when we've first begun...*"

The voice faded away as Frank tinkled the last few notes of the song, which had always been a favorite of Callum's. He saw Frank look up at the woman and say something. He wasn't sure of the words Frank used, but by the look on his face, Callum knew what they contained.

Wyatt turned the handle on the door and held it open for Callum so he could roll in. At the hum of the wheelchair, the woman turned around, her eyes meeting Callum's.

They were brown. And warm. And perhaps a bit sad.

Callum had never seen anything more beautiful in his entire life.

"Callum," Frank said, an enormous smile on his lips that reached from one side of his beard to the other. "I'm glad you're here. This is Claire Matthews. Ms. Matthews, this is Callum Fitzgerald."

The woman smiled shyly at Callum as he rolled toward her, extending his hand. She reached out to shake it. Her touch was gentle, while his was firm.

"Ms. Matthews," Callum began.

"Claire," she interrupted. "Please call me Claire."

"Okay, Claire. You have an amazing voice. And I'm not just saying that because we're in search of a vocalist. I mean, that was...well, *amazing.*"

"You said that already," Wyatt joked from behind him.

"Wasn't it amazing, though?" Callum asked, glancing back at Wyatt. Wyatt, a smirk on his face, nodded. *"Amazing."*

"Yes, amazing....so...Frank?" Callum stuttered as he looked at his pianist for guidance. "I mean, I know this is really up to you, but..."

"Are you asking me if I offered the position to Ms. Matthews?"

"Claire," Claire repeated.

"Yes. Did you offer the position to Claire?"

"I certainly did."

"And?" Callum and Wyatt said at the exact same moment, their eyes boring into the attractive woman.

Claire looked from one man to the other. There was such a contrast in their appearances. One so tall and big, in cowboy boots, and the other, more handsome than the first, seated in that wheelchair. She liked them both, instantly.

"Well...I don't really know what to say." Claire didn't mean to sound so shy and indecisive. But truly, she *didn't* know what to say. She hadn't arrived here looking for a job. And this appeared to be much more than a regular job. Was she really about to change her entire life in such a drastic way?

"Yes," Callum said. "Or, as we'd say in Ireland, 'Aye.' Not to be presumptuous, but you should say 'aye.'"

"Okay, then," she said, shrugging as lazily as if he'd simply suggested she try the new flavor of ice cream at Baskin-Robbins, instead of asking her to step off a metaphorical cliff. "Aye."

"Hot *damn,*" Wyatt said, slapping his hands together in celebration. "We've got us a new singer."

"Welcome to the team, Ms. Matthews." Callum put his hand out, again, to Claire and she shook it, a sign of their verbal contract.

"Claire," she corrected softly.

"Claire," Callum said again, as he stared into her eyes. Eyes that reminded him of sunlight shining through Irish whiskey. He felt something. He didn't know what it was. It was like nothing he'd ever felt before. But he knew, in that instant, it was a feeling he never, ever wanted to lose.

"Please tell me this is a joke!" Gia said as soon as Claire opened the door to her house to let her best friend in. Gia kicked her flip-flops off at the front door and stormed past Claire, glancing at the suitcases parked in the hall.

"It's not a joke," Claire said. "Do you want something to drink?"

"Go on. Tell me you're kidding," Gia said, ignoring Claire's question. "You can't be serious about this."

"I can and I am."

"Were you drinking the night you went to hear this guy?"

"Of course not."

Gia gave Claire a look that indicated her question was not so out of the realm of possibility.

"What about Kool-Aid? Did they give you some sort of fruit punch as you walked in the door?"

"Gia, be real. I was not drunk and they didn't brainwash me. Come upstairs. I still have a few things I need to pack." She began to walk up the stairs and Gia hurried to catch up with her.

"You don't even know these people! They could be convicted criminals. They could be whisking you away to the far ends of the earth where they'll sell you as a sex slave."

Claire paused her packing to give Gia a disbelieving look.

"You need to stop watching so many crime dramas. Didn't you Google them after I called you?"

"Yes."

"So, what's the problem?" Claire asked, opening the top drawer of her dresser and pulling out a stack full of panties and bras.

"It's crazy. This idea is so nuts! Is this because I got so mad at you the other night? I shouldn't have done that. I'm really sorry."

"Of course it has nothing to do with that. You had every right to be mad at me. I'm a complete drain on you. And you're the one who told me I needed to get out more!" Claire said, shoving the underwear into the top pocket of the suitcase.

"You are *not* a drain on me. And I meant shop at the mall. Get your hair done. Go to the dentist! Why would you go away with a bunch of strangers to foreign countries with no plan on when you'll be coming back? You have friends here who love you. You have a life here."

Claire stopped packing and looked straight into Gia's eyes, which were now crazed with hysteria.

"No, I don't. I lost my entire life when I lost my family."

"You didn't lose yourself," Gia shot back.

"That's exactly what I lost. I lost me. Who I was, who I hoped to be. I lost everything. There's nothing here for me anymore."

Gia's tone dropped from one of panic to sadness. "Don't say that."

Claire sat down on the bed, next to her full suitcase. "It's true. There's nothing but memories of a life I can never have again. You were right. I don't *do* anything. I don't *go* anywhere."

"I was being too harsh. You went out to that barbecue the other night."

As she turned toward Gia, the expression on Claire's face made Gia squirm.

"Okay, okay. Bad example. But we've gone out to dinner. And last month I convinced you to go to that cute new shop that opened downtown."

"Gia, field trips don't make a life. Besides, you can't babysit me and keep me entertained every minute of every day."

Gia sighed loudly and sat down on the bed, across from Claire. The women faced each other, an entire lifetime between them.

"You know what I do when I'm alone here?"

Gia shook her head.

"I wait for my kids to come home."

Claire raised her hand to stop Gia from saying anything and Gia, who'd just opened her mouth, closed it again.

"I know it's crazy, but if I try hard enough, I can just about convince myself they're at school and will be home any minute. I even open the front door at three o'clock because I know the school bus will be dropping all the neighborhood kids off at the end of the block. I sit at my kitchen table and hear the kids running down the street, yelling and laughing, and I close my eyes and pray that, for once, for just one more time, I'll hear my screen door slam open and three little voices will yell out, 'Hi, Mommy! We're home! Can we have a snack?'"

Tears were silently running down both Claire's and Gia's faces, but neither of them wiped them away. Tears were a part of life now. Not something to push away, but something they'd learned to accept and live with.

"But the door never opens and no one ever comes running in. No one is ever going to come running in again to tell me about their day or about the mean kid on the playground or how they got an 'A' on a spelling test."

Claire stood up and began to fold a shirt that was sitting on the bed. "That was my life. And it's gone. No matter how long I sit at that table, no matter how many batches of cookies I have cooling on the counter, they're not coming back."

"Claire, I'm so sorry."

"You know what?" Claire said, laying the shirt in the suitcase and picking up another one to fold. "I'm sorry, too. I'm sorry because I miss my husband and my kids. I'm sorry because I know it hurts you to see me like this. I'm sorry for the mess all of this has made of your life, as well as of mine. I can't do this anymore. I need a fresh start."

"And you have to get that fresh start halfway around the world with a bunch of strangers?"

"I think I do," Claire said, closing the suitcase and pressing down to get it to latch. "For the first time in a long time, no one will look at me with pity in their eyes. I won't be Claire, the woman who lost her whole family in an awful tragedy. I won't be the one in need. Instead, I can be the person who's helping. I realized last weekend that God can use you, no matter what your situation."

She lugged the suitcase off the bed and walked around to sit next to Gia.

"Deep down, even you know I need to leave."

"But I don't want you to leave me."

Claire, full of love for her friend, this woman who'd given up so much of her own life to care for Claire, gently rested her hand on Gia's arm.

"I know. That's the hard part. I'm gonna miss you so much. I don't know how I would've survived this nightmare without you. I know I *wouldn't* have survived this nightmare without you. You've been a much better friend to me than I've been to you over the past year and a half and I'm sorry for that, too."

"That's not true."

Claire laughed. "Can you actually say that with a straight face?"

Gia grinned.

"Of course it's true. I couldn't give you what I didn't have to give. I'll be a better friend when I come back. And, I will come back."

"Promise?" Gia asked, her eyes revealing the fear of losing Claire forever.

"I promise," Claire said, pulling Gia toward her, embracing the woman who loved Claire more than Claire deserved. And Claire knew it.

She was going to make sure she became the type of woman who deserved Gia's love. Even if it killed her.

Though she doubted it would. If losing her family hadn't done her in, it would take something completely catastrophic and otherworldly to destroy Claire now.

And she wasn't going to let that happen.

CHAPTER
THIRTEEN

"About how many wheelchairs will this donation cover?" Callum asked Alison, as she sat across from him at his desk, a stack of files on her lap and another dozen or so on the desk.

"Seventy-five."

Callum let out a long whistle. That number was music to his ears.

"Wow. That's just grand. Make sure I personally thank Mr. Maxwell when we see him next. I don't want him to just get a letter from us."

Alison pulled a clipboard out from under the stack on her lap and jotted down a note to herself.

"Got it."

"Anything else?"

"That about covers it," Alison said, always the professional. When they were talking business, she barely cracked a smile. But Callum had seen her let loose after a few drinks, and she could be quite a hoot, as Wyatt called her. She was especially entertaining if you got her on the back of a mechanical bucking bronco, which they'd done at a tiny hole-in-the-wall bar in New Mexico. He understood what Mitch saw in her. She was smart, sophisticated and quick as a whip when it came to verbally sparring with Wyatt. They all enjoyed watching that happen, and it happened often. The two of them just couldn't help themselves. Callum smiled at the memory.

As if on cue, Wyatt walked into Callum's office as Alison was exiting. He plopped down in the seat Alison had just vacated and, as was his habit, kicked his cowboy boot-clad feet onto Callum's desk.

"Hey, boss."

"Hey," Callum replied distractedly, as he sorted through papers on his desk. "I hate when you call me that."

"I know, boss." He grinned. "So, what'd cha think of that new singer lady?"

"She was incredible." He stopped going through the papers and looked directly at Wyatt. "Okay, you always know what's going on around here. What's her story? I mean, she comes to hear me one night and then gives up her whole life to travel with us, just like that?"

Wyatt picked up the paperweight on Callum's desk and began to turn it around in his enormous hand. An ice cube in the hand of the Abominable Snowman.

"My guess? She's running."

"Running? From what?"

"Oh, I don't know." Wyatt placed the paperweight back on the desk. "Pain. Isn't that what most people run from?"

"That and the law."

Wyatt chuckled. "Oh, no. She's clean as a brand-new Ford pickup. Frank did a thorough background check on her. No, what she's runnin' from is deep inside."

"Didn't Frank find out anything in his research?"

"If he did, he ain't sharin' it. And, frankly, it's not any of my damn business. I'm not about to go Googling her. Don't matter to me as long as we get to hear her sing every night."

"You can say that again." Callum focused his attention back to the paper in front of him. "Did Alison tell you that Steve Maxwell donated enough money for us to get seventy-five wheelchairs?"

Wyatt let out a long, low whistle. "That's more chairs than I can shake a stick at."

Callum glanced up at him. "If you say so."

"Okay, Mr. Leprechaun. What better Irish expression do you have?"

Callum paused for a moment and then his eyes lit up. "We're sucking diesel now."

"And you think Texans are weird."

"Isn't that what they say in Austin? Keep Austin weird?"

"It sure is." Wyatt grinned, patting his pocket.

"There still aren't any smokes in there, paddy."

"I know, but I keep hoping." Wyatt stood up and stretched his long legs. "By the way, I saw the way you were looking at her."

"Who?" Callum said, surprise registering on his face. "Alison?"

"No way, padre. Claire."

"Claire? Ms. Matthews? What are you talking about? I wasn't looking at her in any way."

"Oh. I see. That's how we're gonna play this."

"Play this? We're not playing anything. I don't know what you're talking about."

Wyatt laughed and grabbed hold of the door handle. "Boss, you had the hots for her."

"The *what?* I did not." Callum gave Wyatt an indignant frown.

"Actually, I should have used the present tense. You *have* the hots for her."

"I don't have the hots for anyone."

"You're so hot for her the hens are laying hard-boiled eggs."

"There is no heat. There are no hens. And definitely no eggs." Callum could feel the volume of his voice rising. Why was he getting so worked up over this? Who cared what Wyatt thought? He knew Wyatt enjoyed getting under his skin and Callum was giving Wyatt what he wanted.

Callum could hear Wyatt's laughter long after he closed the door behind the big cowboy. Suddenly, he didn't feel like getting back to work. He stared at his computer screen.

He wanted to Google her.

"It's not any of my damn business," Wyatt had said.

He'd been right. Callum had never felt the need to Google any of the other members of his staff before. As long as they had clean records and nothing incriminating in their past, and Frank had assured them she was good to go, then her personal business was just that. *Personal.* She had a right to enter their team with no assumptions being made about her. No preconceived ideas.

Still, the urge to learn more about her nagged at Callum. So much so, he wheeled his chair away from the desk to avoid the temptation.

He needed to go for a walk. Or, as it was, a roll. Some fresh air was necessary for him to gather his thoughts.

Callum wouldn't go so far as to say Wyatt was correct about him having the "hots" for Claire. But, he was intrigued by her. He had to admit there was something about her that had sparked his interest. He was happy she was joining the team. If Mitch, Frank or any of the others had been around, he would've said he was merely excited to hear her sing. And he was.

But, he was also eager to get to know her. And not by researching her online. Callum wanted to have an old-fashioned, get-acquainted conversation with Claire. He'd make sure to put that as a top priority on his agenda as soon as she joined the group in a few days.

Callum always had introductory conversations with new team members, not that there were many. They were a small, tight-knit group and the turn-over rate, other than Terri leaving to give birth, was pretty much zero. He often spent quality time with the others, and he knew them very well. Just as they knew him.

Speaking with Claire and getting to know her wouldn't be any different. She was the new vocalist and he needed to know her so they could work well together. Callum and his crew traveled all over the world, sometimes to some unsafe and rather undesirable locations. They all needed to feel comfortable with one another. Trust was an intricate and vital element to all of their relationships.

The bond he was going to build with Claire would be no different than the connections he had with Frank, Wyatt, Mitch and Alison.

Then why, Callum wondered, did getting to know Claire not feel like another professional responsibility? Why did the thought of speaking to her, the idea of looking into those espresso eyes, make his stomach tumble in ways that weren't familiar to him?

Callum rolled his wheelchair down the hall and into the elevator as it opened. He definitely needed to get some fresh air. He spoke in front of hundreds of thousands of people each year. He did *not* get nervous.

So why was it, he had to ask himself as he pressed the Lobby button on the elevator panel, did he have visions of yellow and blue and orange and purple and pink butterflies fluttering all around in his intestines?

And why did those butterflies only seem to be in there when he thought about Claire?

CHAPTER
FOURTEEN

Claire heard a soft knock on her hotel door just as she finished applying her mascara in front of the bathroom mirror.

"Coming!" she called out, brushing over her lashes one last time. She returned the mascara brush to its tube and inspected her reflection carefully.

Not too bad.

She'd flown into Savannah, Georgia earlier that morning. Frank had picked her and her two suitcases up at the airport. She couldn't believe she was going to live out of two suitcases for the next two months. Once she was in the car, they'd headed straight to the event center where they'd rehearsed for about two hours. She was rusty and she knew it. And, though Frank didn't give her anything but positive compliments and constructive criticism, which she welcomed, she knew he knew it, too.

Oh, well. Singing was like riding a bike, right? Or, maybe it was more like running a marathon. She could only run a mile or two now, but give it time and a whole lot more practice and strengthening of her voice and she'd be doing that metaphorical twenty-six-point-two miles in no time.

That's the pep talk she gave herself, anyway.

She'd been so glad to finally reach her room and lie down for a bit. She hadn't slept much over the past month, what with all the packing and preparation required for her to be gone for months at a time.

There was the mail that needed to be forwarded to Gia's house, bills that needed to be set up for automatic payment, landscapers that needed to be hired to mow the lawn, a fridge that needed to be purged of all its food; the list seemed endless. On top of all that, she'd needed to pack. She hadn't taken much with her, but the process of whittling down her closet to what she would definitely need was not an easy task.

The nap at the hotel had come as a welcome relief. Claire had fallen asleep within seconds of her head hitting the pillow. She'd set an alarm to make sure she didn't oversleep. She'd wanted to ensure she didn't miss her first dinner with the team.

Hurrying out of the bathroom, she looked out the keyhole. A young woman, with a short blonde bob, stood outside Claire's hotel room. *Alison.* Claire remembered seeing her the night she went to hear Callum speak and Frank had mentioned her during a number of their conversations.

Claire undid the chain lock and opened the door.

"Hey, Claire. I'm Alison. I hope you don't mind me stopping by like this. Frank told me you'd arrived earlier today."

"Oh, yes. I mean, no." Claire blushed and wondered why she sounded so nervous. "I mean, no, I don't mind, and yes, I arrived earlier today. Frank and I had a good rehearsal right after I got here." She stepped aside to invite Alison into her room. The young woman entered, wearing an adorable sundress and what Claire thought must be at least four-inch heels. Her height, which was already much taller than Claire's, was dizzying.

"That's what Frank said. Anyway, I thought I'd come by before dinner. I figured we could talk a bit and then walk over to the restaurant together, if that's okay. It's two doors down from the hotel."

"Sure. That'd be great. Have a seat while I finish getting ready. I'll only be a minute."

"Oh, no hurry. Most of the group is usually late anyway. We aren't exactly punctual people. Well, Frank is, but not the rest of us."

"Oh, yeah?" Claire called out from the bathroom where she was digging in her toiletry bag for her favorite pair of earrings. She was sure she'd thrown them in here. "How does he handle all of you being late?"

"He's usually had two martinis by the time we get to him. If he was annoyed before, he isn't by the time we show up."

Claire laughed. "Good to know. Frank. Martinis. I'll remember that tip." She walked out of the bedroom, fastening the earrings she'd finally located. Alison was seated in the chair next to the window. "Anything else I need to know? Why don't you give me the lowdown on everyone?"

"Girl talk! Perfect. Music to my ears. Ever since Terri left, I've been thirsting for another woman! Mitch is wonderful and all, but..."

"Okay, so is Mitch your boyfriend?"

Alison nodded. "Did Frank tell you that?"

"Not exactly, though maybe he alluded to it. I saw the two of you close together on the first night, the one where I auditioned for Frank. You weren't holding hands, but you looked like you wanted to," Claire teased.

"You're very astute."

Claire smiled. "How long have the two of you been dating?"

"About a year now. We kept it a secret for a while. The team works so well together, we didn't want to make anything awkward amongst any of us. We were also worried about what would happen if we broke up. We didn't want others to worry about that, too."

"Now you're not so worried?" Claire said with a smile.

Alison smiled along with Claire. "Nope. Life is short. We don't know what the future holds, but for now, Mitch and I are happy together."

"Well then, I'm happy for you." Claire went to the closet and bent down, digging through the duffle bag on the bottom, in search of her black, strappy sandals.

"What about you?" Alison asked.

"What about me?"

"Any man at home? A boyfriend?"

Claire paused, thankful her face was hidden by the door of the closet. She took a deep breath before replying. "Nope. There's no one."

She'd wondered if Frank would tell them. She knew he was aware of her situation. He hadn't said much to her about it, but had indicated in conversation he'd researched her and learned about the accident. He'd left the conversation open so Claire could have continued on with the topic and, when she didn't, he didn't pursue it, much to Claire's relief.

She was grateful, too, when she'd realized he hadn't said anything about her past to the others. In the short amount of time she'd spent with Frank, he'd come across as an ethical, no-nonsense type of man, so his discretion didn't surprise her. She didn't plan to keep her story a secret forever. Eventually, she imagined, the others would all need to know. She'd want them to know. They just didn't need to know right away. She didn't want the first thought on their minds, when she walked into the room, to be of tragedy and loss.

Poor Claire. There's that woman who lost her whole family. How does she get up each morning?

No. Claire wanted to walk into the room tonight and have them merely think, "Oh, there's Claire, the new member of the team."

Thanks to Frank, it looked like she'd be able to do just that.

"That's probably good," Alison said. For a moment, Claire couldn't remember what Alison was referring to. "It's difficult to have a long-distance relationship with a job like we have. I know. Before Mitch, I was dating a guy from my hometown."

"You didn't get to see him much, huh?"

"Barely at all. Callum is in high demand. We travel around forty weeks a year."

"So, I should plan to live in a perpetual state of exhaustion?"

"That would be a good idea. You'll be more tired than you ever thought possible. You'll sleep in places that, before joining us, you'd never, in your worst nightmare, have even thought you'd lay down a pencil."

"Gee. This is sounding better and better by the moment."

Alison laughed. "I know. I'm awful. Mitch and Callum would kill me if they heard the pep talk I'm giving you. They're both so excited you're here, especially Callum. He'd be furious with me if he thought there was any risk of me scaring you off."

"Callum's excited I'm here?" Claire asked, sitting down on the edge of the bed.

"Very. He'd been getting fed up with Frank."

"Oh?" Claire asked. "Why?"

"Frank had known we'd need a new vocalist for months, at least since Terri was about five months along, when we were all pretty sure she wasn't going to lose this baby." Alison's voice softened. "She'd lost three in the past."

"Oh. I'm sorry to hear that."

"Yeah. It was rough on her and Seth. He worked with the team, too, helping Wyatt."

"Has someone been found to fill his job?"

"No. Callum and Wyatt think we can get by, at least for now, without bringing someone else on."

"But Terri needed to be replaced?"

"Oh, definitely. For one thing, music is vital to what we do."

"How so?"

"Music is a universal language. A lot of people Callum speaks in front of don't speak English, and so he has to have a translator. He doesn't love it. It would be so much better if he spoke their language or if they spoke ours, but...well, that's not realistic. However, when it comes to music, no matter what the language, it seems it can touch everyone's soul. It speaks deeper than words." She shrugged her shoulders. "At least, that's what Frank says."

"I think he's right."

"Callum thinks so, too. That's why he was so anxious to find another singer—that and the fact that we needed another woman to join the team."

"You didn't like being the only one?" Claire sat down on the bed.

"Not really. All the guys are extremely nice and I have Mitch. But it's always more fun to have another woman around."

Claire nodded in understanding. Alison was a pretty girl. It was easy to see why Mitch was attracted to her. Even at her young age, which Claire took to be late twenties, Alison had an air of sophistica- tion about her. It was in the way she sat and held herself, the way she crossed her legs and the way she tilted her head. She was bubbly. Claire could already see Alison was going to be fun to hang around with, but she was no dumb blonde. It was clear Alison was a smart cookie, smart enough to hold her own around four men in places all over the globe.

"Plus," Alison continued. "We go to a lot of countries that are...well, kind of backwards. They aren't big fans of women and one woman traveling with four men, especially when she's not married to any of them, that's a big no-no. I need another female to travel with and room with in those countries."

"I see," Claire said. She hadn't traveled extensively during the course of her life, but she was an avid reader and always prided herself on keeping up with world news. She knew the issues that existed in many countries around the globe. "So, tell me what your job is. I'm not really clear on that."

"Okay, let me explain it this way. Callum speaks. Wyatt carries stuff. Frank plays the piano. Mitch helps Callum."

"And you?"

"I do everything else." A wicked little smile rose from Alison's mouth to her eyes and Claire couldn't help but completely love the girl.

"A woman after my own heart!" Claire knew all about the concept of "doing everything else." After all, wasn't that the role of a mom? Nurse, cook, chauffeur, tutor, maid. Maintaining the lives of her family members had been like running a small company.

She could envision Alison's job being very similar with nothing but four men around.

"I am the organizer. The booking assistant. The accountant. The donation consultant. The funds' raiser. The travel agent. The thank-you-note writer."

"I'm beginning to be very thankful all I have to do is sing a few songs."

Alison sighed. "I wouldn't have minded if Callum had said he was also going to hire someone to take on part of my job, but alas, that has not yet been the case."

"You sound overwhelmed."

"Oh, I am. Completely. But I also love my job. I mean, love, love, *love* it, so I can't complain too much. Though I sure do moan about it often enough, as you'll see." She glanced over at the nightstand next to the bed. "Dang it! We need to go!" She hopped off the chair.

"Frank will be on his second martini by now?"

"At least!"

The woman could move quickly when she wanted to. Claire was impressed with the speed she gathered in those heels. Claire took three steps for each of Alison's one.

They made it to the restaurant in record time. The hostess took them to a small room in the back, which held just one long table and at a quick glance, Claire could see she and Alison were the last ones to arrive.

"Claire, I saved a seat for you," Frank called out and indicated the chair next to him. Alison slid into a seat next to Mitch. Claire gave Mitch the once-over as she took her own place at the table. He was the quintessential All-American male, with his fraternity-boy smile, square jawbone and dirty-blond hair that spiked a bit, no doubt with the help of some gel. Claire remembered how she used to style Luke's hair that way and her heart dropped, but momentarily. She still loved her babies, fiercely, but she was beginning a new life. She couldn't let memories of her old life ruin it. So much had already been ruined.

Claire looked across the table and directly into the piercing blue eyes of Callum. It was clear he'd been staring at her and Claire had to wonder for how long. If he was embarrassed she'd caught him in the act, he showed no signs of it.

Frank stood and clinked his glass with his spoon to get everyone's attention, though it wasn't really necessary. There were only six of them. Claire got the feeling Frank was a showman, even when not on stage.

"Good evening, everyone, and welcome to Savannah. I hope you all had a wonderful two weeks with your families and got a lot of sleep! We won't be getting very much of that for a while, unless we can manage to stay in one time zone for more than two days."

Everyone around Claire chuckled. She did, too, though she wasn't sure it sounded all that funny. It sounded extremely tiring. But also exhilarating. Claire was in need of an adventure and this was going to be one heck of one.

"I'd also like to introduce the new addition to our team. Claire, would you mind standing?"

She looked up at Frank like he must be kidding. There were only a half-dozen of them here. Was it really necessary to be so formal? He was acting like they were in front of a hundred people.

"Nothing like making her feel uncomfortable," Alison piped up.

"Don't feel bad, Claire," Wyatt said. "Frank here could spook a stick horse."

Claire stood hesitantly. "I'm not sure I know what that means," she said to Wyatt.

"Don't worry," Mitch said. "None of us do, either."

Frank continued as if the others had been carrying on a dialogue that didn't concern him. "Claire is going to be our new vocalist. If you haven't heard her practice, you're missing out."

Claire couldn't help but blush. She wasn't that good. If he talked her up too much, she was worried she'd end up disappointing.

"Claire," Frank turned to her. "Why don't you tell us a little bit about yourself?"

He gave her a warm smile. She knew he didn't mean for her to tell them about the most significant part of her life. Even in the short amount of time she'd spent with him, she knew he wasn't that type of person. But, she would've appreciated a warning he was going to put her on the spot tonight so she could have come up with something witty and entertaining to say.

"Um..."

"Come on, Claire," Mitch said. "What should we know about you?"

"Well, I live in Florida, or at least, I did until two days ago when I packed up and came here. I have a degree in Vocal Music, but haven't done much singing lately."

"You'd never know it," Wyatt said.

"Thank you," Claire said, smiling timidly. "I've actually been working as a writer for the past ten years."

"What kind of writing?" Alison asked.

"Mostly magazine articles. A few online things."

"Do you have family?" Mitch asked, casually wrapping his arm around Alison with an ease that reminded Claire of how Jack used to pull her close.

She paused and could sense the silence becoming awkward. How was she supposed to answer that?

"Doesn't everyone have a family?" she finally asked.

She looked across the table. Callum was still staring intently at her. That shouldn't have come as a surprise. She was, after all standing up in front of them. But there was something about the way he was looking at her that made her believe he'd be staring at her even if she was one of a thousand people standing.

"Yes," said Alison. "And many of us would like to forget we do."

Everyone laughed and the tension Claire had felt, as thick as gravy, dissipated.

"Can I sit now?" She posed the question to Frank.

"Of course," he said, putting his hand on the back of her chair.

"Well," Wyatt called out. "I, for one, am pleased as punch you'll be travelin' with us. If you ever need anythin', you just let ol' Wyatt, here, know about it."

"Why," Mitch said, "I think Wyatt has a little schoolgirl crush."

The team laughed.

"Mitch, I wouldn't be goin' and cornerin' anything bigger than you."

Mitch raised his hands as if he was putting them up to fight. Wyatt took his right arm and swooped it through the air as if he'd knocked Mitch across the side of his head.

Alison, seeming oblivious to the men's antics, turned her attention back to Claire and asked her what television shows she enjoyed.

"Most of the places have horrible television shows. At least, *I* think they're horrible. I do, though, enjoy the British ones when we go to the U.K. Thank heavens for Netflix, Hulu and the ability to download movies and TV series to our tablets!"

"Alison is addicted to *Scandal*," said Mitch. "I refuse to watch it so she's feeling you out to see if you'll be her new TV buddy."

"I've never seen it before."

"It's awesome," Alison said, the same exact second Mitch moaned, "It's dreadful."

"It's nothing but corruption, lies, sex and murder," Mitch said, his voice oozing disgust.

"*I know.* It's incredible," Alison said dreamily.

Claire couldn't help but smile at the couple, so similar to Jack and her when they were young and newly married. They'd never agreed on the same television programs, either. But Claire hadn't really minded. She'd been so happy to lie next to Jack during his tedious History Channel marathons. When she'd reach her ultimate boredom limit, she'd find contentment by throwing herself into a good book.

"Well, I can check it out," Claire said. "But I'm not sure I'll know what's going on."

'That's okay. The entire series is on Netflix. I'll totally get you caught up."

The rest of the meal was like the *Scandal* conversation, full of laughter and smiles and teasing and witty banter. Claire couldn't remember the last time she'd so enjoyed spending time with a group of people. She didn't contribute much to the conversation, but she was happy to sit back, listen and observe the interaction between the others. She found it to be a good way of getting to know each of them, seeing how they related to one another.

Every once in a while, she'd look up and see Callum still staring at her. He hadn't said much, either, during the entire meal. He'd simply sat at the end of the table, eating his meal slowly, keeping his eyes fixed on her. If she met his gaze, he smiled, but didn't attempt to begin conversation.

She noticed Mitch had cut Callum's food when it arrived and Callum hadn't seemed embarrassed by this in the least. Once the meat was cut, however, Callum fed himself and seemed completely self-sufficient from that point on.

"Hey, Claire, you can get back to the hotel on your own, right? Mitch and I are going to go for a walk," Alison asked as they stood after dinner.

"Of course! Have fun."

Alison waved to Claire as she took Mitch's hand and they left the restaurant.

Claire reached to the back of her chair to lift her purse.

"Are you ready for this new adventure?"

"Oh, you startled me. I didn't see you there," Claire said to Callum, who suddenly appeared behind her. "I think so. Frank's been really great. Very patient with me. I haven't sung in front of anyone in years, but I think I'll be okay."

"You'll be more than okay. If you're nervous, just look my way. I'll be right off stage and I'll wink. There's magic in my wink."

"Oh, is there?" Claire said, a bit of teasing in her voice.

"That's what the ladies tell me."

"I'll bet they do. Okay, I'll remember that," Claire said, running her fingers up and down the strap of her bag. "I'd better get to bed. Long day ahead of us tomorrow. It was nice to see you again."

"Me, too. I'm looking forward to spending more time together."

Claire stopped fiddling with the strap of her bag and rested it on her shoulder. "Bye, everyone," she said to Frank and Wyatt, still at the table finishing their nightcaps. "Good night, Callum."

As Claire walked out of the restaurant, she felt her face flush. She wasn't sure what had happened during that brief encounter with Callum, but if the sudden racing of her heart was any indication, something surely had.

Callum intrigued her, though she knew very little about him. She'd meant to read more about him online before she left Florida, but had been so busy with preparing to leave, she'd run out of time. His disability was obvious. It was too "in-your-face" to ignore. He'd written a few books, and though she'd hope to pick up copies to read on the plane, she'd never managed to get around to doing that, either.

But other than those things, and the information he'd provided about himself during the seminar she'd attended, his life was a mystery to her. She was curious to find out how he got by in a world designed for people with four limbs. How did he navigate foreign countries? And planes? And subway stations with no elevators? He had such a contagious smile. How did he keep it on his lips, despite *everything?* Did he have a family of his own? She didn't think so or it would have probably come up by now.

She wondered if he had a girlfriend.

Her steps picked up nervously. *Where had that thought come from?*

Wouldn't any woman wonder about Callum's love life? He had a stunning face. Many women would be attracted to those eyes. But then there was the rest of him. How would the whole process of loving a man like him work?

Ashamed of herself for invading his personal life, even if it was only in her own head, Claire walked faster.

Callum's love life was none of her business, but much of the rest of his life was. The two of them, along with four others, would be working closely together from this point on. She'd get to know them and the intricate details of all their lives.

If any of the romantic details of Callum's life popped up, then great.

Or if they never came up, that was fine, too.

It was really none of her business.

That was what she kept telling herself as she unlocked the door to her hotel room and undressed for the night. Callum was her new boss. She had no business thinking about his personal life. It was wrong on so many levels.

And yet, as she closed her eyes and began to fall asleep, she couldn't seem to push away the image of him staring at her. He hadn't looked at her the way a boss looks at his new employee. He hadn't observed her out of curiosity, the way you watch someone you've never met before.

His stare hadn't been like that. It had been something completely different.

As Claire drifted off to sleep, she realized what had been nagging at her all night.

Callum had stared at her the way a man stares at a woman.

And, more than that, she recognized she'd wanted to stare back.

CHAPTER
FIFTEEN

Claire stood completely still as she scrutinized herself in the mirror. She looked nice. Professional. The new haircut she'd gotten right before she left Florida was flattering to her face, the face that was so much thinner than it had been two years ago. But, it wasn't gaunt anymore. She no longer had circles under her eyes. Whereas a short six months or so ago, she'd looked as if she might be on the verge of visiting her maker, she looked a little more alive now. She wasn't doing any jigs yet. Her face wasn't flushed with excitement and enthusiasm and life. But, she did look like she was alive, and that was something.

Baby Steps. Isn't that what Callum had said when she first heard him speak? That's what she was taking today.

She and Frank had spent the morning rehearsing again. It felt so good to sing. Before Luke's birth, Claire had been on the cusp of a respectable music career. Upon graduating with a degree in voice, she'd gone on a number of auditions and been successful enough to earn some pretty great music gigs. She regularly performed in up-scale clubs and restaurants. She'd even opened for Striker Lewis, a well-known musician from Miami. It wasn't the big leagues yet, but she'd felt as if she were headed that way. Her one big dream in life had been to have a singing career. Singing was the thing she could really do, ever since she was a little girl when her parents would have dinner parties and say, "Come on, Claire, sing everyone a song." Her parents' friends would clap and cheer and Claire, even at age eight, knew this is what she was meant to do. This was where she belonged.

A relatively well-known music producer, who happened to be in Miami when Claire was opening for Striker, heard Claire sing and offered her a music contract. Claire and Jack had been beside themselves with excitement. They'd gone out to celebrate the night Claire signed, certain this was going to be Claire's big break. She'd spent the next year working on that album, convinced it was going to project her up to the stars. Sadly, she never got much further than the trees.

The album was met with a lukewarm response. She received some respectable reviews but, mostly, the Tuesday it launched was not all that different from any other Tuesday in Claire's life. The sales were minimal. It was a tremendous disappointment which Claire took to heart.

"There will be other opportunities. Other albums. Concerts where you can perform," Jack had said, two weeks later, while they were in the kitchen cooking dinner. "Very few people make it on their first try."

Claire had shrugged and continued to mash the potatoes, adding extra butter and sour cream because, if she wasn't going to become a famous singer on a world stage, she might as well get fat.

"You're not a quitter, Claire."

Claire, though, wasn't so sure about that. She'd set her hopes so high, she hadn't even let herself consider the possibility she might fail. She'd thought she had the golden touch.

Jack had hounded Claire to pursue other opportunities, to go on more auditions. For a bit, it seemed as if she might accept a role in the traveling tour of *Les Misérables*. She'd done a little bit of musical theater in college and Jack believed it was the perfect fit for her.

"We'll be apart so much this year, though," she'd whined to him.

"We can survive a year. I'll fly out to see you whenever I can. It'll be worth it in the long run."

Claire had begun to think maybe Jack was right. One year of touring. She'd learn so much. Make so many new contacts. Gain so many new skills. Her spirit began to lighten again.

Then, right before she signed her contract, Claire found out she was pregnant.

She couldn't believe it. They hadn't been trying. Though, if she were to be honest with herself, they hadn't exactly been *not* trying, either. She and Jack were lazy. Some nights they used protection and some nights...well, they were so consumed with each other, they'd said, "Screw it."

And now that's exactly what they were. Screwed. Or at least, Claire's musical career was.

She'd hated to turn down the role, but she'd had no choice. Jack, sensing her disappointment, did his best to console her.

"Next year. You can do it next year."

But Claire knew next year would never happen. Even though this baby hadn't been planned, he was loved. She might not have been pleased the moment she saw that little plus sign pop up, but once the shock wore off, she knew she wanted this baby, this combination of her and Jack.

She wouldn't be leaving their child so she could tour with a Broadway show. Not next year. Not any year until that baby was grown and out of the house.

Claire's musical career was officially put on the back burner, despite Jack's protests. "You can still do local theater," he'd say. Or, "Why don't you get a job singing at one of those fancy restaurants downtown?"

She'd smiled and hugged him, appreciating his faith in her, but as the years went by, especially when they added the girls to their family, Claire realized music was no longer her path. Yet, she still longed for some sort of creative channel.

"Play-Doh and popsicle stick art just aren't cutting it for me," she'd told Jack, one evening, over a glass of iced tea on their back patio. "I need some other outlet—something I can do around the kids' schedules."

The two of them had spent the entire weekend brainstorming ideas. On Sunday morning, an opportunity arrived on their doorstep.

"Hey, look at this," Jack had said, his hands holding the Sunday paper. *The Miami Arts and Times Magazine* is looking for freelance writers to interview local musicians and artists."

Claire had stopped beating the eggs she was preparing for omelets and looked over Jack's shoulder to read the advertisement.

"I could do that," she said. "I could *totally* do that."

And she was right. She could.

That job had proven to be a godsend. It had allowed her to utilize the creativity burning within her and given Claire some independence in the form of a paycheck. Not that she needed financial independence from Jack, but there was something about knowing she was contributing monetarily to the family that added a little bounce to her step. She felt better about herself and she knew if she felt good, her children would feel good, too.

She'd completed her last article, a story on how local jazz musicians were paying homage to Miles Davis, the morning of the accident. She hadn't written another one since.

There was a knock at the door right as she applied the last of the lip gloss.

"Coming!" she called out. She knew it would be Alison. They'd become fast friends.

"Wow!" Alison said as Claire threw open the door. "You look hot!"

"You think?" Claire said, looking down at her body. "I don't look too dressed up, do I? I'm worried I'll look out of place. I know Callum dresses casually."

"You're not dressed up as much as Frank, if that's what you're worried about."

"No one is ever dressed up as much as Frank!"

"You look great. It's the perfect outfit."

Claire was relieved. She'd tried on no less than five different options. Jeans were too casual. A dress was definitely too formal. She'd finally settled on a pair of black slacks that fit a bit more like skinny jeans, a light-blue chambray shirt, and champagne-toned heels. She thought the short, tan blazer she wore over it all completed the look.

She grabbed her purse, a brown leather hobo one she and Alison had found when they went on a girls' shopping trip earlier in the week.

"Okay. Let's go."

"Nervous?"

"Of course," Claire said as they walked down the hall.

"You have no reason to be."

"Whether I do or not, I still am! But that's okay. Sometimes I think nerves are good. They don't let us get too complacent."

"That's the spirit!"

There was a cab waiting for them by the curb.

"I called in advance," Alison explained. Wyatt and the guys had all gone over earlier, taking the van. Claire was grateful for the waiting car. Her heels were high and she wasn't sure she could stand in them for longer than necessary. She really should've worn them a bit more before going out in them today.

Oh, well. Live and learn.

Seated in the back of the cab, Claire twirled the wedding band she now wore on a chain around her neck. Alison had asked her about it on their shopping trip, as they took a break to eat BLTs and drink sweet tea.

"I used to be married, but now I'm not." She'd offered no more in terms of an explanation and though she was certain Alison had wanted to know more, the woman hadn't followed up with any further digging.

"Here we are!" Alison said enthusiastically, no more than ten minutes later. Claire looked up at the auditorium. Though she'd rehearsed here this morning, it seemed larger than she remembered.

"Come on. Get out," Alison said as she hopped out of the car. "Or Wyatt will come out here to drag you inside."

"I'm coming!" Claire said, as she carefully balanced her weight onto her shoes. She didn't want to break her ankle on the way in.

She walked carefully into the building, behind Alison, who was practically running.

She's anxious to see Mitch, Claire thought and smiled. Young love was so sweet. So innocent. All you could see ahead of you were your dreams, not the hardships and sadness that would, inevitably, come. She and Jack had been like that once, bright with possibility. She'd missed those days, later in their marriage, even before he died. Their marriage had been wonderful in so many ways, but no relationship can maintain that initial spark and passion. Frank was waiting for her by the back door of the auditorium.

"Ready?" he asked.

"That seems to be the question of the day."

"You'll be great."

Claire nodded in thanks. Everyone had such confidence in her. She hoped she didn't let them down.

Claire walked backstage and peeked around the corner so she could see the inside of the auditorium. To say it was packed would be an understatement. She couldn't remember the last time she'd seen so many people in one location. A professional sporting event, maybe. A rock concert?

But these people weren't here to see their favorite team play or listen to their favorite band. This was a room full of people who'd come to hear a man best known in the world of inspirational speakers for missing three-quarters of his limbs. Why did *that* draw a crowd?

Because these people were hurting, too. They weren't all physically disabled, though Claire could see some of them were. They hadn't all been in accidents or had serious illnesses. Yet they were hurting nonetheless. They'd lost family members or jobs or friends. They'd made mistakes. They'd drunk too many beers. They'd spent too much time with the wrong people. They'd been abused. They'd abused. They didn't know how to fit in. They were from every walk of life. Every race. But they were all the same. Every person in this room needed hope. They needed to know how this one man, who'd clearly suffered so much, could have the strength to carry on day by day, and they wanted some of that strength, too.

Claire had been one of those people just a very short time ago. She wasn't "cured," by any means and doubted she ever would be. Every day was still a struggle. But Callum had provided her with something no one else had yet been able to give her. Hope. Hope that life could go on, *would* go on. Hope she'd survive. And the faith that nothing she'd experienced was in vain.

At least, that was the philosophy she was going with these days.

Looking at these people, she knew they all needed that philosophy, too. *Fake it till you make it.*

Claire wasn't exactly faking it, but sometimes she felt like she was putting one foot in front of the other, not exactly sure where she was going, but wherever it was would be better than remaining stagnant. And sad.

"It's time," Frank said, heading out onto the stage.

Claire was startled. She didn't realize she'd been staring at the crowd, lost in thought, for so long. She saw him sit down at the baby grand. He held his fingers above the keys, for the briefest of moments, and then quietly began to play.

The crowd, slowly, upon hearing the soft music, began to settle down. People found their seats. Conversations lessened. The audience began to cast their eyes on the stage.

Claire could feel her palms begin to sweat and she nervously wiped them on her new pants. In a moment, Frank would look her way and nod. He'd expect her to step out, from behind that curtain, and head toward him. He was going to expect her to sing.

Sing? She looked at the crowd, which somehow seemed to have grown even larger in the past minute.

This had been a terrible idea. *An awful one.* Why had she ever agreed to this? She wanted to throw up. She looked down at her heels and prayed she didn't tumble off them in a moment of nausea. A train was steaming its way through her ear canal, gaining speed and volume with each passing second.

How did Callum do this on a regular basis?

Callum.

Claire lifted her eyes from the floor and looked across the stage. He was just where he'd said he'd be and his eyes were boring into her. She knew, instantly, he'd been staring at her for a very long time.

She wanted to smile at him. She wanted to give him a "thumbs-up," but she couldn't. She wanted to cry. She wanted to leave the auditorium, get in a cab and cry as it drove her home.

But to what home? She no longer had a home. At least, nothing more than mortar and bricks.

She wanted more than mortar and bricks.

This was the first step to building that home.

If she could just take the first step.

"Just by doing that, you'll be doing more than I can do," Callum had said.

Callum's eyes smiled at her. Not his whole face, just his eyes, as if he was reading her mind. Claire and Callum stared silently at each other. Frank's playing faded into the distance as if there was no one in the entire auditorium but the two of them.

Frank!

Claire's head jerked back at the pianist. He, too, was staring at her and there was no smile in his eyes. He nodded and she realized he must've been nodding for a while.

She glanced back at Callum. This time his mouth was smiling as brightly as his eyes.

And then, just as he'd promised, he winked.

Claire's heart leapt and then calmed. She took one more deep breath, releasing it slowly as she stepped out onto the stage.

The roaring in her ears ceased as the crowd quieted. She walked across the stage calmly, as if she weren't teetering on stilts, but rather, gliding barefoot through sand. She smiled at Frank. He smiled back.

Taking her place in the center of the stage, Claire put her mouth close to the microphone. Then, resting her hands delicately on the base, and smiling to the crowd as if she did this every night, she opened her mouth and began to sing.

CHAPTER SIXTEEN

"Hey, guys."

Wyatt and Mitch looked toward the door as Callum rolled inside the bed and breakfast's sitting room. His chair cleared the door, but barely. It was Alison's job to locate and book sleeping accommodations. She did an excellent job, considering all the restrictions and requirements placed upon her by everyone involved. The hotel needed to be close to the venue, come with a good group rate, have enough rooms, but not too many, so there weren't a lot of other guests. Handicap-accessible. A dining room, on premises, that provided home-cooked meals when possible. Free Wifi. The list went on and on.

But, most important to Callum and the team, it needed to feel like home.

Maybe not their own homes, which none of them seemed to see very often these days, but they all hated having to spend too many nights in typical hotel rooms. They begged Alison to find them the cutest, quaintest, friendliest place in town.

Most towns had these gems—bed and breakfasts, cottages, old castles and plantations that had been renovated over time. The whole team loved finding new buildings and homes to explore.

The handicap-accessible part, though, was the pricker in the bush. Many of these locations existed, in every city, town and country, but not all were wheelchair accessible. Castles rarely had elevators, ramps, wide doors and handicap showers.

Callum knew Alison struggled with each event, trying to find a place that suited the team, but would also be manageable for Callum and, ultimately, Mitch, who would be doing the legwork. She pulled rabbits out of hats.

The current rabbit was an old Victorian home with a huge wraparound porch, situated on a private lake. It had a large handicapped suite on the main floor. Not only was the building wheelchair-friendly, but so were the grounds. The porch had ramps on all four sides of the house and the paths that led around the gardens and the lake were not only extra-wide, but level enough that Callum could glide his chair along easily.

Alison said the owner's mother had been in a wheelchair and so he'd done the remodel with her needs in mind.

It all suited Callum perfectly. The door frames might have been a bit tight, but considering the old-fashioned frame of the house, it was amazing the builders had been able to make the house work as well as it did.

As they were all saying good night, Callum said, "So, I think things went well with Claire tonight, don't you?"

"She's amazing," Alison said.

"We really lucked out getting her," Wyatt added. "Almost like it was meant to be."

"I think it was," Callum said. "Hey, Mitch, I'm gonna stay up for a bit more. When I'm ready to hit the hay, if I need help navigating anything in the room, I'll call you; okay?"

"Sure," Mitch called out as Callum rolled out the door.

The pebble skipped three times. Not bad, but she could do better.

Claire leaned back on the log and slid her hand along the ground until her fingers found the perfect-sized one. With a lift of her arm and a swipe through the air, the pebble flew across the water.

One. Two. Three. Four.

Dang it. She used to be able to do six.

"Not bad."

Claire jumped off the log in surprise.

"Beautiful night, isn't it?" Callum asked from behind her.

"Oh! You startled me! I didn't hear you coming."

"My chair and I are like a stealth bomber," Callum said, chuckling. "I'm good at sneaking up on poor, unsuspecting souls."

"Well," Claire said, taking her seat on the log once again. "You took me by surprise."

She threw another pebble into the water. Three skips. She was getting worse.

"Were you okay with how tonight went?" Claire asked. She hoped he hadn't come all the way down to the lake to give her a critique. She knew she probably needed one, and no doubt Frank would give it to her, tomorrow, but for tonight, she just wanted to revel in the fact she'd done it. She'd gotten up in front of all those people, sung, and survived. "My singing, I mean. I know I'm a bit rusty."

"I was coming down to tell you how much I enjoyed it. You have a great voice."

"Really?" Claire looked away from the lake and up at him.

"Of course, really." He seemed startled by her question. "It's pure and calming. I'm going to be very happy to have you precede me the next time we fill a football stadium."

Claire picked up another pebble and rolled it around between her fingers. "The crowds you draw are amazing. You've gotta feel like a rock star."

"Oh, they're not coming because of me. They're coming to hear about hope. I'm just the messenger." Callum shrugged. "Perhaps a funny-looking messenger, but the messenger nonetheless."

"Funny-looking?" Claire's eyes filled with surprise. "I'd hardly say that."

"Well, that's very kind of you."

"No, I mean it. Your eyes are striking."

Callum laughed and shook his head. "Is that like saying a girl has a good personality?"

"No!" Claire was mortified. She hadn't meant for her comment to come across that way. "It's nothing like that! I'm serious. You have the kind of eyes a girl could get lost in."

Callum cocked his head, his striking eyes looking at her curiously.

"At least..." Claire could feel her face reddening. "I imagine some girls have gotten lost in them...I...um...Can I ask you a question?" Claire needed to change the topic and quickly.

"Shoot." The day was losing its light, but Claire could still see a smile on his face.

"I heard Alison and Wyatt talking about a bunch of wheelchairs and walkers being shipped to one of our upcoming events and...well, how many could you possibly need?"

Callum let out a loud, hearty laugh. Claire could feel the blush rising up her cheeks again.

"They're not all for me. Boy, you really took a leap of faith, didn't you? I would've thought you'd know a little bit more about our mission before signing up."

"There wasn't much time to do a whole lot of research."

"Apparently not. Yes, a big part of what we do is travel the world to speak to large crowds. But the part that excites me the most is the equipment we're able to provide to disabled people all over the world. When we go to impoverished places, we bring wheelchairs, canes and walkers. You have no idea the freedom mobility can add to some-one's life. Not being able to walk or get off your bed and then, suddenly, having a chair that will take you anywhere? It's life-changing."

"That's incredible."

"In a lot of Third World countries, people have never even seen a wheelchair."

"You're kidding."

"I'm not," Callum said.

"You're a very giving person, Callum Fitzgerald."

"To whom much is given, much is expected."

As she listened, Claire tossed the pebble she'd been playing with into the lake.

Four.

"You really believe that, don't you?" she asked.

"Don't you?" Callum asked her with such intensity, she was worried she might actually give a wrong answer.

"Well, sure. But, what I mean is, you really seem to feel like you've been given a lot, despite..." She motioned at him and his chair with her hand. "Everything."

"Despite my only limb being an arm, you mean?"

Claire hesitated, fearing she was offending him, but wanting to be truthful. She nodded.

"You wait, Claire," he said. "Just wait until we go to India or some African countries and you'll see I have been given a lot. I have immense fortune. Maybe not the monetary type, and certainly not the physical kind, but the blessings I've received are enormous compared to the suffering that's out there."

She picked up another rock and tossed it.

Three. Damn.

"Are you not going to let me try?"

"Try what?" Claire looked up at him, startled.

"Tossing pebbles. You're sitting here, having all the fun while we're talking and not once have you offered me my own pebble."

"Oh! I'm sorry." She reached behind her and grabbed a handful of gravel. She put her hand out to Callum, who dug through it for a bit and then selected his stone.

"Now, Claire, watch carefully as I show you how it's done."

Callum swung his arm to the side and then, with one easy motion, tossed the pebble into the pond.

Seven. He'd gotten *seven.*

"Well, now I'm embarrassed."

"As you should be," Callum said, chuckling. "You might be able to outrun me, but very few people can out-skip my pebbles on a lake."

"The world record is eighty-eight skips."

"Is it?" Callum looked surprised at her knowledge.

"Yep. It was set in Pennsylvania."

"You have to wonder at the amount of free-time that man must have had to get that good at skipping pebbles."

"We all have our gifts."

"That we do." Callum smiled. "And, it seems yours might be random facts."

Claire laughed. "Can I ask you another question?"

"You just did."

Claire smiled and took his teasing as an invitation to proceed. "What's Mitch's job?"

"He's my caregiver."

"Your what? Don't caregivers work on estates with gardens that need to be weeded?"

"First of all, m'lass," Callum said slowly, his Irish brogue getting thicker, as he intentionally spoke to her like a small child. "That's caretaker, not caregiver."

Claire blushed again. Of course. She knew that.

"And, I am much more work than *any* estate. He assists me in my everyday tasks, the ones most bucks take for granted. You know, dressing, showering, cooking."

Claire stared at him, a look of confusion on her face.

"Have I lost you?"

"By bucks, you don't mean deer, do you?"

A loud "ha" escaped his lips.

"A buck, in Ireland, is a boy. A man." Callum smiled.

"Gotcha." Her eyes twinkled to indicate she'd been teasing him.

She hadn't known the term, but hadn't needed it clarified, either. "I have to say," Claire continued. "I didn't realize you needed that much help. I mean, of course, you would. But...well...you seem so self-sufficient."

She felt a little uncomfortable and was suddenly wishing she hadn't brought up the topic. She'd been curious. After all, who *wouldn't* be curious? She'd never met anyone with no legs and one arm before. In fact, before Callum, she'd never really even heard of anyone like that.

She found Callum so fascinating. Claire had this great curiosity and wanted to figure him out. Everything about him seemed so foreign, and not just his accent. His disability. His limitations. The way he overcame them. His outlook on life.

Even his chair. Claire had seen many a wheelchair in her life, both in person or on television, but she'd never seen one like this. It was black and electric, with four small wheels, instead of the traditional two larger ones in back. And, instead of having handles where someone might push him, there was a large black box. On that box was a lift which could lift his seat up and down. The first time Callum had hit the control and he'd risen up, not quite to her eye level, but to a considerably higher height than a typical chair, she'd jumped back.

"Weren't expecting that, huh, love?" he'd said with a laugh and a wink.

No, she certainly hadn't been expecting that.

"I am self-sufficient." Callum's voice took Claire by surprise. She'd been lost in thought, once again staring at his chair and wondering how it worked. She hoped he hadn't thought she was gawking at him. "In fact, it would probably be more politically correct to call Mitch my assistant. Though, I did enjoy your reaction to the word *caregiver*." Claire could see his grin. "Don't get me wrong, Claire, I'm perfectly capable of living on my own. In fact, when we're back in

Atlanta, I do. I have my own house and live all by my lonesome. But when you're working with less than half your parts, all those daily activities take up a lot of energy. And, though I hate to admit it, traveling is full of challenges for someone like me. I have a routine and a system at home. On the road, I never know what roadblocks I'm going to encounter, hour by hour. I've learned my strength is better spent preparing my speeches and meeting with people who come to hear me. You get the idea."

Claire nodded. It all made sense. If she were to lose most of her limbs, she'd need more than one guy named Mitch to help her out. She'd need a full-time staff.

"It's not ideal," Callum continued. "I'd love to be able to travel and not worry about all the logistics. But, that's not my reality. Thus, it's more convenient to have someone help me out."

Claire nodded.

"Listen," Callum said, "it's getting late and I know we both have a full day ahead of us tomorrow. But I also felt like we spent a whole lot of time tonight, talking about me. I'd like to get to know you better."

"I'm sure there's plenty of time for that. No rush."

"Well, that's where you and I disagree, Ms. Matthews. I would like to rush it along a bit, if you don't mind. The Irish are not known for their patience." He winked at her.

"Oh, by the way, I appreciated your wink today. I meant to tell you that."

"Ah, did you? That's wonderful. Did you feel the magic?" He grinned at her, and even with only the moon to light the lake, Claire could tell his eyes were sparkling with mischief.

"I felt something ," Claire said. "But I think it was the hotdog I ate for lunch."

Callum laughed again. Claire liked his laugh. It made her smile, even if she didn't always let her lips show it.

"As I was saying, I was wondering if you'd like to have dinner with me tomorrow night. I know we'll both be tired after tomorrow's seminar, but we'll be done by mid-afternoon. I thought dinner after that might be nice."

"Dinner?"

"Yes. You know, that meal you eat a few hours after lunch?"

"Just you and me?"

"Yep."

"Um." Claire didn't know what to say. She suddenly felt very awkward sitting here with Callum. They'd been having such an enjoyable time talking this evening. For the first time, in years, she'd actually gotten lost in the moment. She hadn't forgotten her family or the sadness of the past couple of years, but she'd felt like Claire again. The Claire who used to feel a good conversation was one of the greatest joys in life.

But he'd asked her to dinner. Alone. It was one thing to sit outside at night, talking to her boss, while the rest of the team was twenty-feet away, but... *Dinner. Alone.* She couldn't get her mind past those two words.

"Did that sound like I was asking you on a date?"

Claire felt her face blush for what must be the twentieth time that night.

"Oh...no...I..." Now she was completely mortified. She must be coming across as pathetic and desperate to him.

"Well, then, I must not have asked correctly."

"Oh." Claire was speechless. Now she really didn't know what to say.

"So?" Callum looked at her, expectantly.

"So...what?" Claire asked.

"You're leaving me hanging here, love, and I don't have very good balance. Should I take your non-answer to be a no?"

"No...it's just...I don't..."

"Eat? Now, I know that's not true because I've seen you. Just this evening, in fact."

"No, I mean...I don't...date."

"Well, then, I guess it's time we changed that. We can come back, rest and change and then how about I pick you up, at your room, around six o'clock? Does that work?"

"Um...I guess. Okay."

"Great, then. It's a date!" Callum pulled the joystick on his armrest, backing his chair up. Claire stood from the log and wiped any attached bark pieces off her bottom. "I've enjoyed spending time with you this evening, Ms. Matthews."

"Me, too," Claire said, her voice barely above a whisper. Ten minutes ago, she'd been laughing and playfully teasing Callum and now, she felt so nervous around him, she was bordering on embarrassed.

"Ready to head back?"

She nodded and followed him up the path.

Just as they reached the porch, Claire heard Mitch call out, "Hey, Callum. You want to make sure all your stuff is laid out for tomorrow?"

"You bet," he said. "Night, Claire. I'll see you in the morning."

Claire nodded and hurried off in the direction of her room, thankful Mitch had appeared when he did.

She had a date for tomorrow night. *A date.*

How had this happened? How had she *let* this happen? Her first date since becoming a widow. And it was with her boss.

She wanted to slap herself for getting into such a situation.

She wasn't ready to date. She had no desire for any of that. She was here to sing. To see the world. To make new friends.

Not to meet a man.

Yet, she had.

And, to her surprise, she didn't feel nearly as nervous or uncomfortable, or *guilty* about it as she'd thought she would.

CHAPTER
SEVENTEEN

Claire spent most of the night looking at Callum.

Not the actual man. He'd left her to head back to his room and she'd made her way back to her own.

Instead, Claire stared at his photo. She'd found a number of them on the Internet when she'd Googled his name. Some of them were from his own website, but many were snapshots people had taken when they'd met him after an event, and then posted online.

Claire knew it was silly, but she felt the need to fixate on his image, very carefully, for hours before their date. Many women would want to look at a photo or two of the guy they were about to go out with. That was only normal. But Claire's reasoning was anything but normal.

She was staring at his photo, at his body, from every angle, so she didn't embarrass herself by doing it tomorrow night.

Claire hated herself. She felt small and petty and superficial. Callum was a handsome man. His upper body was fit and trim. His face looked like it belonged on a billboard in Times Square. When they were together, she had a difficult time tearing herself away from his piercing eyes.

But that was part of the problem. She'd been spending so much time lost in those baby blues, she hadn't really spent much time looking elsewhere. And she knew she'd have to. In fact, she'd want to, if for no other reason than morbid curiosity. She just didn't want him catching her doing it.

Callum's physique was so odd. That was the only word she could come up with while she scrolled through the photos on her laptop screen. From the shoulders up, he was, perhaps, the most stunning man she'd ever seen. His blue eyes contrasted spectacularly with his jet-black hair. He had a dimple on his right cheek that popped out with delightful regularity. Callum smiled a lot and it was downright impossible for Claire not to smile back.

Yet she had a feeling there were many kids in school, when he was growing up, who didn't smile back at Callum. She had a hunch he'd been the brunt of many a joke, many a cruel word or taunt. How could he have avoided such things? Kids are mean. They can pick up on even the littlest difference and exploit it to such an extent that the one being bullied begins to feel as if he's a walking ball of disgust.

And that could be over nothing more than a pimple.

But no legs? One arm? She could only imagine the things Callum had heard on the playground.

He might have cheekbones any woman would kill for, but no one would be fighting to acquire the rest of his body.

Claire peered closely, her nose to the screen, at Callum's left arm, or rather, what there was of it. It wasn't completely gone. There was a small stump right below the shoulder. She felt guilty even thinking that word—*stump*. Somehow, it seemed so derogatory. So offensive. Was it even politically correct? But that was what it was, wasn't it?

A stump where an arm should've been.

His legs were pretty much the same as the missing arm, gone, but not completely. She imagined, if he'd had full limbs, his knees would have appeared about six inches further down his leg. It seemed he'd "lucked out," that he had a piece of leg at all. With what part he did have, he could sit relatively normally, his stumps sticking forward. Claire had seem images, online, of other amputees missing their legs, who seemed as if they needed to prop themselves up on their butts. It didn't look comfortable.

Of course, having no limbs, in and of itself, didn't look comfortable.

The fact she'd just distinguished between levels of comfort, when missing your legs, seemed ludicrous to Claire.

She needed to make sure she didn't say something so obtuse at dinner. She didn't want to offend Callum.

Claire glanced at the clock. It was after midnight already. She needed to get to bed. The team had a long day ahead of them tomorrow. It would be the second day of Callum's seminar and Claire knew it would be much more exhausting than the first night. Though she had yet to attend one as a member of the team, she'd been to the one in Florida as an attendee and it had been an emotionally draining day for her. She could only imagine how much more tiring these days were for Callum and those who worked with him.

Snapping the top of her laptop shut, Claire jumped up and headed into the shower. She needed to relax and clear her head before even attempting to sleep. She hadn't been on a date in close to twenty years. And she'd never been on one with someone who had any sort of disability.

There was so much to process. The date. The man. The disability. The new friends. The seminar. The singing. So much had changed in Claire's life in a matter of weeks.

Then again, less than two years ago, so much had changed in Claire's life in a matter of seconds.

The changes this time, though scary in their own way, were so much better. They were changes that promised hope and a future. Not complete and utter despair. She would take these changes over the other ones any day of the week. Claire had thought she'd never again have a single reason to look forward and, tonight, she realized she had many.

As she let the warm water cascade down her face and body, she closed her eyes and began to count her blessings. They weren't the ones she used to have. They didn't completely fill her soul like her family had, but they were blessings all the same.

And for that, she was grateful.

"So far, it's going really well," Claire said into her cell phone. She'd propped it up between her shoulder and her head, so she could attempt to get the little post of her earring through the tiny hole in her ear.

When did these things get so small?

"Uh-huh," Claire continued. "I'm making some good friends and I'm enjoying singing again."

The earring slipped into the hole. *Success!* Now if she could buckle the straps on her sandals.

"You can stop worrying about me," Claire said, sitting down on the bed and sliding her feet into her shoes. She wasn't making the same mistake as last night. These weren't flats, but they weren't killer stilettos, either. "No, Gia, I have not run away forever. This is temporary. I promise."

She'd just finished the last buckle when there was a knock at the door. She glanced at the clock. It was exactly six. Callum was prompt. Claire liked that. She appreciated promptness.

Leaving the phone in the crook of her neck, she picked up a tube of lip gloss and quickly applied it. She glanced in the mirror.

Not bad.

"It'd better be temporary," Gia said on the other end. "I'm so happy for you. I really am. I miss you. We don't need to live together again, but I'd love to go out to dinner once in a while."

Claire unbolted the lock on the door and pulled it open.

And then she dropped the phone.

Callum laughed from his place across the threshold.

"Are you going to get that?" he asked.

Claire could faintly hear Gia still talking from the hotel room carpet.

"Oh...um...yeah," Claire stammered. "Give me a second."

Claire bent down and grabbed the phone. She interrupted Gia, mid-sentence.

"Hey, listen, I've gotta go. Can I call you tomorrow?" Claire straightened and stared directly at Callum, holding the phone to her mouth. She couldn't have pried her eyes from him even if she'd tried. "Thanks. Love you, too."

She pressed the "End Call" button before Gia could say goodbye.

The two of them stood in silence for the next moment. Claire's eyes met his, rolled down his body and then back up again.

"You look surprised to see me." When Claire didn't respond, Callum continued. "Did you forget we're having dinner?"

"No. I'm not surprised to see you. I'm well, surprised to see so *much* of you."

The Callum standing in front of her was, well...standing. She'd expected to look down at his chair when she'd opened the door and instead, had to raise her eyes to reach his.

Callum chuckled. "Ah, yes. I guess there have been a few changes since we last parted ways. You don't approve?"

"Um...no...I mean, yes...it's great...it's so different. I...um..." Claire giggled nervously. "I wasn't expecting you to look this way. But, it's great. Though the other way is fine, too."

Callum took her hand in his, clearly in an attempt to calm her.

"Oh, boy," Claire said. "I sound like an idiot."

"No, you sound normal," Callum said calmly. "People are usually very startled to see me standing like this. When I add the arm, well, that really throws them."

The arm. Claire hadn't even noticed the arm. She'd been so blown away by the legs.

But, he had an arm. In fact, he had two of them.

Claire felt like she'd walked onto the set of *The Twilight Zone.*

"I rarely dress like this," Callum said, gently letting go of her hand and motioning to his prosthetics. "Only for special occasions."

"Oh, and this is a special occasion?" Claire asked, beginning to regain her composure.

"It sure is. It's not every day I get to take such a lovely woman out to dinner. It doesn't get much more special than that."

"I'm flattered. Truly, I am." Walking back into the room, she grabbed the sweater she'd left on the chair. "Where to, boss?"

"You're beginning to sound like Wyatt."

Claire smiled. "Do you like 'Sir' better?"

"Since we're on a date, I'd really prefer the term 'Handsome.'"

"You got it, Handsome," Claire said. "So, where are you taking me?"

"Oh, the best place in town. At least, according to the little, old man I met at the Seven-Eleven today. I hope you're up for Italian."

"I love Italian! Lead the way."

Callum extended the crook of his arm—the real one—to Claire. She hesitated for a moment and then linked her arm in his.

"You did not!" Claire said, laughing.

"We did! My brother carried me out of the ocean yelling, 'A shark! My brother's been eaten by a shark!'"

"No way. You were an awful child."

"Oh, the worst. People started screaming and running. They didn't know what to do. Parents were yelling for their little kids to get out of the water."

Claire was laughing so hard, tears were literally rolling down her cheeks.

"Did you get in trouble?" She could barely get the words out through her chortles.

"A boatload! The police showed up."

"No!"

"Yep. They wanted to arrest me for causing a public disturbance. And I think they would have, but what were they going to do? Handcuff my arms together? Put me in shackles?"

"You're terrible."

Callum shrugged, but the grin never left his face. "I learned early on that if I didn't laugh at my troubles, I was going to spend a whole lot of time crying."

"Good point," Claire said. "Do you get to see your brother much?"

"Not as often as I'd like. He still lives in Ireland, as do my mam and dad. They try to visit once a year, though. I'm sure you'll meet them soon enough," Callum said. "Okay, my turn."

"What do you want to know?"

"Where do your parents live?"

"They both passed away when I was younger. My mom died of cancer when I was a freshman in college and my dad had a heart attack three years later."

"I'm sorry to hear that."

"It's okay," Claire said. "It's been a long time. What else?"

"Why'd you give up singing?"

"Oh, you know," Claire said, trying to plaster her best, most sincere, smile on her face, though she was pretty sure she was fooling no one with it. "Life. Things just got in the way."

"Like what type of things?"

Claire sighed. She was learning one of the things she was most fond of about Callum was he wasn't surface deep. He never took a story at face value. He was inquisitive. He wanted to know more, and not in a nosey, obtrusive way. He genuinely cared about people. She'd seen it at his events. When people came up to him and told him about their problems, he listened. He didn't pretend to listen. He really and truly *listened*.

And then he asked questions, because he cared.

She admired that about him.

She just wished he wasn't asking so many questions of her.

"Well, wanting to pay the bills, for one," Claire said. "I found I made a lot more money writing than I ever did singing."

That was only a partial lie. She had made more money writing than she'd ever made with her music. The lie part was that she hadn't given up the music for that reason.

"And writing was such a good job for working around my..." Claire caught herself and stopped.

"Around your what?" Callum asked gently.

"Oh, you know," Claire said, ripping a piece off the bread that was still sitting on the table, though their meals had long ago been devoured. "Around my life. Okay, enough about me. Back to you. Do you like to write?"

"I do. In fact, I just finished my third book!"

"I guess that was a stupid question, since I already knew you'd written two other books."

"Not stupid at all. I'll bet a lot of people who write books don't actually like to write."

"You think?"

"I don't know. Maybe. I speak about how to find power through your pain, and a lot of publishers thought that concept would translate well into print. But though it seemed like a smart enough plan, and, thankfully, it turned out to be a financially fruitful one, it didn't necessarily mean I would enjoy the process of writing it all down. Lucky for me, since I had to spend a lot of time working on it, I did, indeed, find it to quite pleasurable."

"That's fabulous. What's the new book about?"

"Me."

"Oh." Claire chuckled.

Callum's big grin appeared on his handsome face.

"It's about my life," Callum continued. "The other books have touched on my struggles, in relation to how others can move forward with their own lives, but this one goes more into depth regarding the struggles I've had. I hope it helps others overcome the adversities they face, especially those suffering from physical disabilities."

"Well, I'll bet it's incredible," Claire said. "When can I read it?"

"It should be out sometime next year, though if you're really, really nice to me, I might let you have an advance copy. We might have to alter next year's travel schedule a bit so I can do a bunch of book signings."

"I hope you're right-handed."

Callum laughed so loudly, the people at the table next to them turned.

"You're *good*," he said, wagging his index finger in her direction. "Thanks for having dinner with me."

"It's been my pleasure," Claire said, and realized she meant it.

"Well, I know I didn't give you much of a choice, but still, I appreciate you giving me a chance."

"A chance at what?"

"Wooing you."

"Wooing me? Is that what this is?"

"Yes," Callum said. "Is it working?"

"Hmmm...I don't know," Claire said, raising the corner of her mouth, as if this issue deserved deep pondering. "Split a very fattening dessert with me and I'll think it over."

"You're on," Callum said, lifting his hand to signal the waitress.

"That was fun," Claire said, as they walked up the path, back to the house. It still felt so odd to have Callum walking beside her. He definitely had a limp when he walked, but walked well nonetheless. For much of the evening, Claire had completely forgotten about his disability. Part of that, no doubt, could be attributed to the prosthetics. It was likely no one else in the restaurant had even noticed he was missing any limbs. He'd looked like any other man enjoying a meal on the town. But, more than the fact that his body had looked complete, Claire had found herself so lost in who he was, and not what he looked like, that within moments, the physical aspect no longer mattered.

Except for the ones she found exceptionally attractive.

"It was," Callum said, bringing her back to the present moment. "I had a wonderful time."

"I haven't been on a date in years."

"That seems hard to believe."

"It's true," Claire said, not making eye contact with him.

"I'm sure it's not from a lack of requests."

"Actually, no one else has asked me."

"Well, now I know you're lying," Callum said.

"I promise," Claire said, glancing sideways at him. "I'm not!"

"Okay," Callum said, disbelief in his voice. "If you say so..."

He gestured toward the porch swing, a request for her to sit. Claire sat and then steadied the swing so he could sit down easily next to her.

"Ah. It feels so good to sit!"

"Oh! I forgot about your legs. Do they hurt?"

"They get sore if I wear them for too long," Callum said, rubbing his right thigh. "Kind of like wearing those high-heels you had on yesterday."

"Yeah, I'm sure it's just like that," Claire said, then turned to look at him. "You noticed my shoes?"

"I notice everything about you."

Claire took that in, but said nothing about it.

"You know," she said, instead. "You didn't have to wear them—the legs, I mean. It would've been fine if you'd been in your chair."

Callum smiled at her, with a softness that made Claire's heart melt. "Thanks, love, but I never miss a chance to walk beside a beautiful woman. Listen," he said, suddenly changing the subject. "Do you mind if I take off my arm?"

Claire burst into laughter.

"Now that is something no man has ever asked me. You get two points for originality."

"Only two? Oh, come on. That had to be worth at least ten."

"Okay, then. Ten. Go ahead," she said, waving her own arm at him.

"Do you think you might be willing to help me?" Callum asked. "Or, is that an inappropriate thing to ask on a first date?"

"Of course, I'll help you. What do I need to do?"

"If you could unbutton my shirt, that'd be a good start."

Claire turned her body toward him and began to undo the buttons. "I've never undressed a man on the first date."

"Well, then, I'm glad I'm your first."

"What's next?" Claire asked, once she'd completed the buttons.

Callum hestitated. "You know what, give me a second. I can do it myself."

"Honestly, Callum. I don't mind helping you. Tell me what to do next."

"Well, if you could help me take my shirt off..."

"Sure."

Claire yanked at the sleeve and it slid off his real arm and then he used that hand to slide it off the other.

"I truly can do this myself," Callum said, again. "It's just a bit of a struggle for me. I'd need to stand to do it, or move away from this swing and it would take me a bit longer than it took you."

Claire shook her head. "Really, it's no big deal."

She glanced up at him and realized he was looking at her, as if to see if her words were sincere.

"Really," she said again, softly. "I don't care."

He nodded and then his face broke into a grin. "Okay, I have to be perfectly honest with you. I made a bunch of that up so I'd have a reason to get you close to me."

Claire whacked him, good-naturedly, with the sweater she'd rested on her lap.

"You're terrible."

Callum winked at her. "Aye. That I am."

"Wow," Claire said, looking at the prosthetic arm system closely, now that his shirt was off. "It looks like you're wearing a backpack."

"A backpack with no pack, but does come with an arm."

Callum slid the straps, from around each of his shoulders and then slid off the prosthetic arm, which was attached to the bands.

Claire tried not to stare, but it was difficult, and not because his left arm was once again missing. If she'd spent any time thinking about it, she would've expected Callum to be wearing an undershirt. Without his shirt and his arm attachment, he was completely bare-chested. The sight caused an inadvertent intake of Claire's breath.

What was most shocking, even more so than the missing left limb, was Callum's right arm. From the elbow up, it was covered in one large, expansive tattoo. Claire had never been a fan of ink. Jack had once joked about getting a small tattoo during a weekend trip with his buddies to Cancun, and Claire had put her metaphorical foot down immediately. No tattoo. No way.

She thought she hated all tattoos. That is, until this very moment.

Callum's tattoo wasn't of any particular image. It wasn't an eagle or a flag or a skull, and, thankfully, not a woman's face. It was tribal. Deep brown and gray. Flames of ink intertwining with his fair skin. Claire wasn't sure if the design would be called a sleeve, because it only went as far as his elbow. *But maybe a short sleeve?* Claire doubted that was the hip term.

She wasn't even sure the word "hip" was hip.

As her eyes followed the intricate design, she realized its path was taking her eyes to Callum's chest. The tendrils of the design draped and unraveled across the right side of his body and down onto his abdomen. His body was shockingly masculine and muscular. He had a six-pack, an actual six-pack, like the ones Claire had seen in movies where the man rips off his shirt, buttons flying and women swooning. Callum's chest was smooth and hard—not that she touched it—though she had to admit, she did think about it for the briefest of seconds. And he had pecs. Really, *really* good ones. How was that even possible? She could see how he might achieve those abs from doing sit-ups, but how does a person even begin to bench press when they only have one arm? Was there a prosthetic for that? She had no idea.

It didn't really seem like the time to ask, either.

I notice your incredible muscles are of an even mass on both sides of your chest—not that I should be looking, but, how did you get them so symmetrical?

Claire felt herself blush and hoped Callum didn't notice. She would definitely sound like an idiot if she said anything like that.

So, instead, she focused on the more practical aspects of his appearance. His stump wasn't bare, as she'd expected it to be.

"Is that a Nike basketball sock?" she asked.

Callum smiled, mischievously. "There are socks you can buy that are designed especially for prosthetics, but if I can't happen to find one of mine, which is often the case since I live out of a suitcase, I grab the nearest tube sock and slip it on."

"I guess it makes the arm fit better?"

"Yep. And helps it not rub so much."

Callum pulled the sock off with ease and set it down next to him, on the opposite side of the swing. And then, with no assistance from Claire, he slipped on his shirt.

"Funny," Claire said. "You had no problem getting that shirt back on again."

"Nope. Though you can offer to help me with my buttons whenever you like." He hadn't redone them, thus leaving bits of the tattoo, and his chest, visible through the front opening.

"Ha!" Claire said, keeping her eyes on his face and not any lower. "Now that I know you're fully capable, I'll keep my hands to myself."

"Well, that plan sure did backfire on me." Callum grinned at Claire. "Would you like to hold my hand?" he asked, extending the prosthetic arm.

"Why, of course."

Claire reached out and took the fake arm in hers. She placed it so it rested on both their laps. She made a point, though, to hold onto the hand.

"Wow. It's lighter than I would've thought."

"Welcome to the world of prosthetics," Callum said. For a moment, neither of them spoke, both staring out into the darkness. "You're a fascinating woman, Ms. Matthews."

"Am I?"

"Yes. I don't always know what to make of you."

"Are you implying you've spent time trying to make something of me?"

"Perhaps I should be embarrassed to admit it, but I have."

"Oh. And what have you come up with?" Claire asked.

Callum leaned back, deeper into the swing. "I think you used to be very happy. And then, suddenly, one day, you weren't. How am I doing?"

"You're good. And what am I now?"

"Now? You're doing your best to be happy again, but there's a big part of you that's still very, very sad."

Claire didn't say a word. She pushed the swing backward with her legs and gently let it rock. She didn't allow herself to make eye contact with Callum because, she knew, the moment she did, the tears would begin to flow.

"Claire," Callum said. "I don't want to pry. Your personal life is just that. Personal. But, if you ever want to talk about anything, I have to say I'm a pretty good listener. So, whenever you're ready to tell me, I'm ready to listen. And, if you're not, then it's more than enough for me to sit here on this swing, next to you, enjoying the night."

Claire continued to stare out into the night. It wasn't that she didn't want to tell him. If anything, she was drawn to him. He felt safe to her. He was a soft place to fall. She'd known that from the first moment their eyes had locked. She didn't know where to begin. She had never told anyone her story. Everyone in her life, before here, already knew.

"I graduated from college a week after I turned twenty-one and got married to Jack a week after that."

Claire kept her eyes focused into the distance, but she could sense Callum's body language, next to her, and it indicated no surprise at what she'd said.

"We began dating at the beginning of my senior year, right before my dad died. We were married for a couple of years when I, unexpectedly, got pregnant with Luke. It was quite a shock. We hadn't been planning on having kids for quite a while. Four years later, we had twins. Lily and Ella. After that, it was a whirlwind of diapers and car seats and birthday parties."

Claire took a deep breath and let it out slowly.

"We were heading to my in-laws' home for the Christmas break. It was late at night. We purposely left late because I wanted the kids to sleep as we drove. They fell asleep right after we stopped for dinner. I must've dozed off, too, because all I can remember is a large crash and the car spinning out of control. A drunk teenager had gotten on the highway going the wrong direction. Jack swerved to miss him, but..."

She hadn't wanted to cry. She'd tried her best. There was just no way to tell the story of how she'd lost her family without bursting into tears. If she lived until she was a hundred and two, she knew that would always be the case. She felt the tears begin to fall and she made no effort to wipe them away.

"I was told later that none of my babies, or Jack, suffered. They were all gone in an instant."

Callum lifted his arm and placed it behind her on the swing. Gently, he began to stroke her hair. Claire was so lost in the memories, his touch barely registered with her.

"That was almost two years ago. For the first year, I did absolutely nothing. I mean *nothing*. I truly didn't know how I was going to go on. Each morning the sun would rise and I'd think, 'Why do I have to live to see another day?'"

Claire turned, ever so slightly, in her seat and looked directly at Callum.

"And then, one day, the woman at the grocery store counter told me I needed to go hear you speak. I actually listened to her, which in retrospect, is amazing in and of itself." Claire smiled softly. "Until that moment, I pretty much hadn't listened to anyone, not even my therapist, about how I should begin to reenter the world. I guess I looked at you and thought, no one understands my agony, but maybe this man, missing most of his limbs, who has clearly gone through so much of his own pain, maybe he'll have something to say that will give me a reason to live."

"And did I?" Callum's voice was barely above a whisper.

Claire shrugged, a gentle smile on her lips. "Here I am. I realized, as you spoke, my life really *was* over—that is, the life I'd led before. I could never get that back, no matter how much it ripped my heart out. But, I still had a life ahead of me and it was my decision as to what I did with it. I could lie in bed and feel sorry for myself for the next fifty or so years or I could get up and honor my family."

Callum lifted a strand of her hair and let it slip through his fingers. "Do you still blame yourself?"

"What?" Claire asked, startled by his question.

"Do you still blame yourself?" Callum asked again.

"I didn't say I did."

"I know," Callum said, picking up another strand of hair.

Claire looked back out into the night, sitting very, very still. She didn't know how to answer Callum's question. No one had ever asked it before.

"I was the one who wanted to leave late in the afternoon. I wanted us to drive while they slept so I didn't have to hear the arguing and whining during the whole drive." The tears began to fall faster down Claire's already wet cheeks. "If I'd only agreed with Jack to leave earlier in the day, or even packed us dinner so we didn't have to stop, we wouldn't have been there, in the path of that car, at that moment."

"You had no way of knowing that."

"You don't think I've told myself that a thousand times? A million times?" Claire's voice rose and she was embarrassed she couldn't seem to keep herself calm. "It doesn't change the fact I put us in the path of that drunk driver."

"Claire," Callum said calmly. "Listen to yourself. There's nothing you could've done to stop this."

"Then I should have died with them. I wanted to die with them."

"I know it feels that way. But for some reason, it wasn't your time."

Claire turned and looked directly into Callum's blue eyes. She was surprised by their shade. They weren't the sparkling blue from dinner. They were a dark blue that reminded her of a windy and cold night at the ocean. He hurt for her and it showed in the windows to his soul.

"Why *couldn't* it have been, though? Why did I have to stay here, to feel all this pain? Why couldn't God have taken me, too? You're always talking about there being a plan, Callum. What was this one? How could there possibly be a plan to *this?*"

"I can't answer that," Callum said. "But clearly, there's a different plan for you. That's not always easy to hear. Trust me. I know." His voice was deep and grave and Claire knew he did know. He understood her pain because he'd dealt with more than his own share of it.

"Can I ask a question?" Callum asked, after a moment.

"Sure."

"How's it going so far? Joining us?"

Claire lifted her right hand from where she'd been holding Callum's prosthetic one and wiped away some of the tears.

"Honestly? I knew I'd made the right decision the moment I met all of you, at that dinner. I don't know what my future looks like, and it hurts like hell to think about my past, but I'm really certain this is where I'm supposed to be."

"On this porch swing?"

Claire smiled and leaned back, into the crook of Callum's arm.

"Right here on this porch swing."

Callum leaned over and kissed the top of her head. The touch of his lips felt good on her hair. She felt safe and content, something she hadn't felt in a very, very long time.

Closing her eyes, Claire decided to forget the rest of the world. There was no more sadness. No more pain. Just Callum and Claire. Sitting alone. Swinging along in silence.

CHAPTER
EIGHTEEN

Claire couldn't fall asleep. She'd been exhausted by the time Callum had walked her to her hotel room and was certain she'd be asleep the moment her head hit the pillow. But she'd been wrong.

If she'd known, in advance, she was going to be up all night, she would've gotten out of bed and accomplished something—searched for new music online, read a book, watched a movie on Netflix, written an email to Gia.

Instead, she'd wasted all that time, tossing and turning.

Date. She'd gone on a date. It seemed too crazy to believe.

She wondered what Jack would say.

And that was the main reason she couldn't fall asleep. She couldn't stop thinking about Jack.

He'd been her best friend. Her confidant. Whenever something in her life happened, exciting or sad or crazy, he'd always been the first person she'd call. She wanted to talk everything over with him, dissect the entire event in one of their conversations.

Of course, she was generally the one doing the dissecting. But Jack had listened. Like Callum, he'd been a great listener.

She missed that camaraderie. She missed a million things about Jack. His laugh. His slow-cooked, barbecued ribs. She missed putting her hand under his shirt and resting it in the warmth of the small of his back.

She missed snuggling in bed and watching a movie together. She missed the way he sang in the shower.

For the first few months, maybe the first year, any memory of Jack had been too painful. She'd push all of them, even the happy ones, from her mind. Thinking about him, in any way at all, was excruciating.

But tonight, she wanted to call Jack. She wanted to tell him about her date. Claire knew that seemed weird. How could she possibly want to call her husband to tell him about the new man she'd met?

It was because he'd listen. He'd be happy for her.

Not once, since Jack had died, had Claire thought he'd want her to be stagnant in life. She hadn't considered dating again before these past few days, but if there'd ever been anyone who wanted her to be happy, it was Jack. She knew it then and, even though he was gone, she knew it still.

They'd talked about death at various times in their marriage. They'd never been morbid about it. Neither of them could've ever imagined the way death would invade their world and take so much, destroying the lives of all of them. But as the parents of three children, it was inevitable the topic of death would arise.

Who would raise the kids if they both died?

Gia.

Who would manage the trusts for the kids?

Gia.

Claire had no family and neither of them wanted Jack's parents to have anything to do with raising their children. It was amazing Jack had turned out as spectacularly as he had, all facets of his parents considered.

But they'd also, on occasion, discussed what would happen if only one of them died.

"You should remarry," Claire would tell him. "A.S.A.P."

"ASAP? Why so soon?"

"Our kids will need a mom."

"I can be both mom and dad to them," he'd say.

Claire would roll her eyes and sigh a deep, exaggerated sigh.

Sometimes, that would be the end of the conversation. But oftentimes, it wasn't. Once, when the two of them were sorting laundry, Claire brought up the subject again.

"You know Cathy, across the street," she'd said, more as a statement than a question.

"The single woman who lives on the corner?"

"Yes. She's very nice. We had coffee together last week."

"Okay." Jack's tone indicated he wondered where she was going with this.

"I think, if I die, you should walk across the street and ask her to be your date for my funeral."

"What???" Jack had dropped the towel he'd been folding. "You're out of your mind."

"No, seriously," Claire had said, reaching down to pick up the towel and then folding it, neatly, herself. "You need to take her as your date and then marry her. She's really, really nice. You'll like her. The kids already like her. Plus, she's a good cook. Didn't you have some of the banana bread she brought over last week?"

"You have officially lost it," Jack had said.

"I'm not kidding, Jack." Claire's voice was serious and stern. "If I die, I don't want you to sit around boohooing. Our kids need a mom. And they don't need a dad who can't get his act together. Miss me all you want, but move on."

Jack hadn't said anything after that. But later that night, in the dark, he'd rolled over and whispered in her ear, "If I die, I want you to move on, too. And not just because our kids would need a dad."

That sentence was the one Claire remembered tonight. She could still feel Jack next to her in bed. The warmth of his breath as he'd whispered those words in her ear. The way he'd kissed her cheek after them. She could still feel her touch to the side of his face in response.

Claire wished Jack were here now. She'd tell him how she hadn't once truly smiled since the accident, until she met Callum. She'd tell him how she never tired of listening to Callum's Irish accent and how, every time he opened his mouth, she felt she was in the middle of a Liam Neeson movie.

She'd tell Jack how surprised she'd been to see Callum actually walking, and how she'd realized, though it was different to see him standing, she hadn't found him one bit more attractive with a "full body" than she did when he was in his chair. She'd tell Jack how ashamed she was of herself. She'd assumed her attraction, though significant, was somehow "less" because he was disabled. But, she'd realized, when he'd stood at her door, he was a beautiful person, both inside and out. It didn't matter to her one bit if he stood or sat. She was taken with him.

Indeed she was. She'd been sad to say good night to Callum. She couldn't wait to see him in the morning. She'd had butterflies and realized she hadn't felt this way since she was a college coed, eager for Jack to call or come pick her up for a date.

Claire never thought she'd feel this way again and that had been all right. When she'd had Jack and the kids, though she'd missed the feeling of first love, she'd had something that was just as special, if not better. A love that was built on time and trust and commitment and family.

A love she no longer had and though that hurt, it didn't take away from the fact that this new feeling felt great, too.

Really, *really* great.

Without a doubt, Claire also knew she deserved this. She was going to enjoy every single second of happiness offered to her. There was no one who knew as well as Claire how precious and fleeting those moments could be.

"Hey, Claire," Mitch called out as she entered the dining room for breakfast.

She was the last one to arrive. She hadn't meant to be late. At first, she couldn't decide what to wear, and then she'd gotten nervous about how she should act around Callum when she saw him with the others. Before she knew it, she had to rush downstairs to make sure there was still food for her.

"Hey, Mitch," she said, smiling and waving to the others at the table, without looking at any of them too closely. She walked over to the buffet and grabbed a plate, which she piled high with scrambled eggs, potatoes, and bacon. Despite her nerves, it turned out being happy made a person hungry.

Pouring herself some orange juice, she listened to the conversation behind her.

"Okay, so how long will it take us to get to Texas?"

"About fifteen hours total. We'll do half today," Wyatt said. He looked at Alison. "Where are we staying again?"

"I've gotten rooms for us in Jackson, Mississippi."

"M-I-S-S-I-S-S-I-P-P-I," Wyatt sang out, his voice a sing-songy drawl.

"Wyatt's just happy because we're headed to the Lone Star State," Callum said, as way of explanation to Claire.

Claire lifted her eyes to look at him. She'd purposely avoided glancing his way, certain the inevitable blush would give away her feelings to the group.

She hadn't been mistaken. Claire's and Callum's eyes lingered on one another, just a second too long. Claire felt the flush as he smiled at her.

"Anyone need to use the potty before we go?" Alison asked.

"Whoah!" Wyatt said, glancing between Callum and Claire. "What's *that*? What is *that* I'm seeing?"

Claire looked back down at her food, intently concentrating on every bite.

She heard Callum laugh. "Don't know what you're talking about, man. Have you gotten those eyes checked lately? Maybe you should call up your eye doc while you're home. In fact, why don't you make an appointment with your regular doc, too. You can tell him how I've caught you smoking behind the back porch."

Wyatt grumbled and pushed back his chair.

"I'm gonnna start loading up the truck. Whoever is not outside and ready to go in thirty minutes is going to be left behind."

"He always says that," Mitch said.

"And one of these days, I'm gonna do it." Wyatt stomped out of the room, as Claire hurried to finish her breakfast.

Mitch, Alison and Frank rose from the table.

"I'm not packed yet," Alison said to Claire. "I need to hurry, I guess. See you in the van?"

Claire nodded, her mouth full of scrambled eggs. She wiped at her mouth with the napkin and waved at Alison as she and the men left the small dining room.

"Is that plate very interesting?"

"Huh?" Claire said, looking up.

"You've barely taken your eyes off it since you got in the room."

"Oh, I..." Claire smiled, sheepishly. "This is awkward, isn't it? I don't know how to act around you. That is, I don't know how to act around you when we're around the others."

"Worried they'll see you're falling desperately in love with me?"

"Ha ha," Claire said, humor in her eyes. "Yes. I'm very worried about that."

"You don't have to be so worried. I'm sure they already know."

"They *what?*" Claire was horrified. She was attracted to Callum, was beginning to develop feelings for him. But *love?* Who'd said anything about love? Was she coming across as desperate? Pathetic? Did the others think she was *obsessed* with Callum?

"Reel it back. Reel it back," Callum said, laughing. "I can see your mind spinning a mile a minute from across the table. I was kidding, Claire. *Kidding*. You can calm yourself down again."

"Oh." She took a deep breath and realized her heart was racing. Now she did look pathetic.

Callum wheeled his chair over to the side of hers and picked her hand up off the table, bringing it to his lips and gently kissing it.

"No one is thinking about how enthralled you are by me, because they're too busy realizing how captivated I am by you."

He laid her hand back down on the table and winked at her.

"Enjoy your breakfast. No need to shovel it in. No one's leaving without you. Come outside when you're ready."

Claire watched as Callum rolled out of the room. When she was sure he'd gone, she lifted her hand to her mouth, hoping to still feel the touch of his lips.

"I'll drive first," Callum said.

"You'll *what?*" Claire said, the words flying out of her mouth.

Wyatt and Mitch laughed.

"Don't trust your haunches to a man with none of his own?" Wyatt asked.

"I'll have you know I still have one limb. Please don't forget it," Callum said.

"Oh, yes. That thing you call an arm. I've never understood why, if you only have one of them, you'd want to cover it all up with a tattoo."

"To make sure no one misses it when they look at me, as you obviously have," Callum said, rolling his chair to the driver's side of the van. "Want to hoist me up, Mitch?"

"You're not kidding?" Claire asked, as she watched Mitch lift Callum into the driver's seat.

"Nope. Not one bit." A grin spread across his face. "Feel free to drive with Wyatt in the truck if you'd prefer. Though, I should warn you,

you'll have to listen to Merle Haggard and Willie Nelson for the next four hours until we stop."

"I like Willie," Claire admitted.

"You won't once you've heard Wyatt sing along for hours on end."

"But..." Claire looked around the group. The others seemed nonplussed at the idea of Callum behind the wheel.

"How can you drive a vehicle when you're missing...?" She gestured at his body, embarrassed to have to do so. She didn't want to seem insensitive, but she'd lost her family in a car accident.

"Some bits and pieces? Well, to risk sounding rude, I just can."

"Here you go," Mitch said, handing Callum his prosthetic right leg. "Sorry. I'd already packed it."

"I hate when that happens," Frank said, coming up behind Alison. "You want shotgun, Claire?"

"Um, none of you seem worried about this." Claire's eyes bounced from one team member to the other.

"Worried about Callum driving? He's okay. A little too slow, in my opinion. Wyatt will have drunk all the beer in the hotel bar by the time we get there, but Callum will definitely get us there in one piece."

Callum put the key in the ignition, as Frank threw his laptop bag into the van. "I'll take the whole middle row," Frank said. "We'll let the lovebirds have the whole back." He nodded in the direction of Mitch and Alison, who were looking over some paperwork, their heads bent toward each other. Claire noticed Mitch's hand was resting on the small of Alison's back.

"I guess that leaves you to ride up here with me, Claire," Callum said, pulling the sock for his prosthetic onto his knee.

"I guess."

"You have no need to worry. The van is equipped for my, um, limitations. I've never had an accident. I promise. At least, never one where I lost a limb."

"Ha. Very funny," Claire said. She walked around the van and got in on the passenger side. "Okay, I'm going to have to trust you on this one."

"You should trust me on all things." Callum attached his prosthetic and then turned his body in the seat. Claire saw him position his leg on the brake. "Would you a like a quick lesson in adaptive driving so you don't feel the need to white knuckle the armrest til Houston?"

"Yes, please." Claire was feeling a little less nervous. She did trust Callum and if the others weren't nervous, then there was no need for her to be.

She was, however, extremely curious.

"I've got quite a bit of control over my leg muscles and so, though my ankle doesn't rotate, I've no difficulty switching my foot between the gas and the brake. I can actually even drive a standard, but I need two legs for that so I can use my left for the clutch. Good thing this is an automatic, as I hear my other leg is somewhere in the trunk."

Claire couldn't help but shake her head. She enjoyed how Callum joked about his situation. He never came across as bitter and his jokes were never forced or embarrassing.

"Everyone have their seatbelts buckled?"

"Yes, sir!" Mitch called out.

"Then it's time to hit the road." Callum pressed down on the brake as he shifted the car into drive and they began their journey to Houston.

No one spoke for the first thirty or so minutes. Claire was busy marveling over how Callum handled the vehicle.

"You're awfully quiet," Callum finally said, breaking the silence. "Happy to just watch me drive? Or are your palms still sweating?"

"I'm impressed with your skills."

"As you should be. I'm looking forward to showing you some of my other skills in the future." Callum's eyes glimmered, mischievously. "What's everyone doing back there?" He glanced in the rearview mirror.

Claire turned around so she could see the group. "Frank is dead asleep."

"I figured by the snores."

"Alison and Mitch have headphones on and are watching a movie on Mitch's tablet."

"Wonderful," Callum said. "We're virtually alone."

"You're right! What should we do with that alone time?"

"How about you tell me about your kids."

"My kids?" Claire asked. She hadn't been expecting him to say that.

"Yes. I know it's difficult for you, but I'm pretty sure you have a million wonderful memories of them. If you'd like to share some, I'd love to listen."

Claire smile at Callum's thoughtfulness and gladly launched into tales of her babies—some sentimental, but most funny.

After Claire had enumerated her children's likes and dislikes, she rested her head back on the seat and quietly watched Callum as he drove. "Do you like kids?"

"Oh, yes. I love them! My brother has four, and a fifth one on the way. He and his bride seem to feel it's their responsibility to populate Ireland. I don't get to see them much, just when I go back for a visit. Fin, my brother, says there's no way he's taking his large clan on an airplane. So, I've got to settle for playing the role of Uncle Callum only on my trips home once a year."

"Does your brother look like you?"

"Nope. He's got all his parts."

Claire felt her face redden. She hadn't meant for Callum to find her comment insulting. By the way his lips were turned up, though, she realized he hadn't taken offense in the least.

"I mean, does he look like...I guess, your face."

"Oh, so that's what you meant, love? No, he's not as handsome as I."

"I imagine that wouldn't really be possible, now, would it?" Claire teased.

"I'd say not!" Callum laughed. "Actually, he looks nothing like me. He has light-blond hair."

"Really? I can't picture you having a brother who doesn't have hair as dark as yours."

"Neither could my parents, apparently. I'm not sure if they were more shocked when he popped out about his correct number of limbs or that he looked like a little German! They were going to name him something like Donavan, which means Dark Warrior, but instead decided to call him Finbar, which means fair-haired."

"Finbar?"

"Exactly. He hates it, too. That's why he goes by Fin."

"Your parents changed his name because of how he looked?" Claire asked, surprised. She and Jack had selected each of their children's names long before the delivery day. She couldn't have imagined anything that would've made her change those names once each child had been born, no matter what they looked like.

"My dad has always been very into the meaning of names."

"And what does Callum mean? I've never heard it before."

"No, it's yet to make the top ten baby names in America, but I keep hoping," Callum said, his eyes on the side mirror as he changed lanes. "It means dove."

"Dove? Like a bird?"

"Well, certainly not like the soap!" Callum joked. "My dad was a Senator when I was born. He thought if he gave me a name that had to do with peace, his constituents would somehow think he was going to be the one to bring it about."

They rode in silence for a few moments as Claire thought about that.

"Thanks," she finally said.

"For what?" he asked, briefly casting his eyes on her.

"For asking about my kids. Most people don't do that."

"Well, other than Frank, I don't think the team knows."

"No, I don't mean the team. I mean people in general, the people who knew about what happened. Everyone around me, except for my friend, Gia, stopped saying my kids' names. It was as if they'd never been born at all. No one wanted to bring them up, as if mentioning them was going to remind me they'd died. But what people don't realize is, I never, for one second, forget. They're never, ever out of my mind. When people act as if they were never here to begin with, it hurts."

Callum nodded. "I can understand that. People often like to pretend they don't notice my missing limbs. I mean, it's like this huge fluorescent polka-dotted rhinoceros. They know I'm missing parts, but they don't want to say it, in case I haven't noticed it."

"That's exactly it," Claire said, a feeling of relief that someone understood her.

"So I usually begin with a joke, something that puts them at ease with my lack of limbs. To break the ice, you know?"

"Like, *I'm standing before you, metaphorically speaking, of course?*"

"Ah! You've been paying attention to my talks!"

"I don't really have much of a choice," Claire teased.

He smiled at Claire, again, before moving his eyes back to the road. "What I'm trying to get across is that when I begin with some self-deprecating humor, everyone chuckles. They're usually nervous at first, unsure of whether I'm joking or not. Then, when they see I'm okay with making light of the situation, they seem much more relaxed about me and not as worried they'll say the wrong thing."

Claire nodded.

"Listen, Claire," Callum said, his voice getting serious again. "The timing is all up to you, but have you thought about telling the team?"

"I've thought about it."

"I don't want to pressure you. The ball's totally in your court, but as I've said, we're a family. We all have struggles and things we deal with and we've found it's best to share those things with each other. We can't help one another if we don't know what's going on. For example, Alison told you she's diabetic, right?"

"Yes."

"And Wyatt's mom has Alzheimer's. We all usually go to the nursing home to visit her and the other residents while we're in Texas. We know he'll be away from the team quite a bit while we're in the state so he can spend as much time with her as possible."

"He told me about his mom yesterday when we talked about this trip."

"Everyone's got something going on and none of it's a secret, so I'm not betraying any confidences by telling you. Frank's wife left him and his daughters when they were in elementary school. He raised them all by himself."

"And Mitch?"

"Mitch has got it *goin' on*," Callum said, with a laugh. "We haven't figured out Mitch's problem yet. But believe me, he's gotta have one!"

"Maybe being wrapped around Alison's little finger?"

"Could be. Anyway, I think you should consider telling them. You'll feel better once they know. Trust me. It's no fun to keep secrets around this group. We spend so much time together it will begin to feel like you're lying by omission if you don't get it all out."

"Okay. I'll think about it."

"Good." Callum flicked the turn signal, pulled off the highway and into an Exxon gas station. Silencing the ignition, he said, "I need to take a break. Get out and stretch my legs."

Before Claire could say a word, Callum turned to her and exclaimed, "See! That's another one I use. Stretch my legs!" And then, taking his hand off the steering wheel, he flicked his wrist, up and down, playing an air drum. "Ba dum bum. Thanks, folks. I'll be here all week."

CHAPTER
NINETEEN

"I think it's time for the lovebirds to have the back row," Mitch said, as the group returned to the van. Claire had gone inside the gas station to use the restroom. The men were already standing outside the van, except Callum, who was now in his chair, his one leg gone and assumedly safely back in the trunk.

"You and Alison already had the back row," Callum said. "It's your turn to drive now."

"Oh, I wasn't referring to me and Alison," Mitch said, his eyes dancing a mischievous jig. "Now was I, Frank?"

"I've no idea what you're talking about," Frank said.

"Sure you don't, buddy," Mitch said, patting the man on the back. His eyes then floated back to the door of the store. "Hey, babe. Ready to hit the road?"

Claire turned and saw Alison exiting the store. She was holding a bottled water and a large bag of tortilla chips.

"Okay, Callum, you and Claire in the back. Alison and I will take over the driving for now. Frank, buddy. You think you can stay awake for a bit? Your snoring will cause me to lose my mind and I might just run us into a house."

"I'll see what I can do," Frank said as he opened the side door to their vehicle. Mitch lifted Callum out of his seat and into the van. Callum quickly skirted his way into the back row and, once again, Claire was amazed by how he managed to maneuver himself, no matter what the situation.

"Gonna join me back here, Claire? Or would you prefer to sit with Frank?"

Claire looked around the group. All eyes were on her. She wanted to sit with Callum. She enjoyed his company. But she didn't want to provide any fuel for the gossip fire. Plus, she and Frank were the ones who, musically, worked together. It'd make the most sense to sit with him.

"I think I'll sit with Frank."

"Suit yourself," Callum said. If he was disappointed by her response, he didn't show it.

"You can keep me awake," Frank said, helping her up into the van. "I wouldn't want the narrowing of my airway to be the cause of our demise."

As soon as the words were out of Frank's mouth, a look of mortification crossed his face and he leaned over to Claire. "I'm sorry. That was insensitive of me."

"No, Frank. It's fine. Really," Claire said. "You can't act like car accidents don't exist in this world. People die every day in them."

Frank's pale skin beneath his dark beard showed how awful he felt about his flippant comment.

"I've already told Callum, so you don't need to worry about accidentally saying anything to him. He and I've been discussing how I should probably tell the others sooner rather than later. Maybe once we get to Houston, okay?"

Frank nodded. "I think that would be best. We don't usually keep secrets."

"So I gather. And I don't want to keep this a secret. It'd come out at some point, anyway. The truth always does. I'd much rather it be on my terms."

"Hey, Mitch," Callum called up from the back. "Put the radio louder. I can't hear it back here."

Mitch turned the knob and Bruce Springsteen's "Born in the U.S.A." blasted through the van. Callum began to sing the chorus at the top of his lungs.

"Hey, buddy, you do realize that's not true, right?" Mitch called out over the music.

"Yep!" Callum stopped singing long enough to yell back. "But as far as I know, someone is yet to write a song called "Born in Dublin." Though maybe Bono's working on one!"

With that, the others began to sing along, too, their voices filling the van as they made their way across country.

By the time they'd arrived in Houston, everyone was tired and grumpy and a little bit sick of one another.

As soon as the van pulled into the hotel parking lot and Alison had returned to hand each of them their room key, Claire was heading up to her room.

She hadn't said a word to any of the others before she left the van, not even good-bye. She felt rude about it, but she'd spent the past six or so hours thinking about how she was going to tell them about her family. She wanted them all to know. She just wasn't sure how she was going to get the words out without breaking down.

It'd been difficult enough telling Callum, but somehow, alone with him in the quiet of the night, the words had felt safe leaving her lips.

A room full of people, though, was overwhelming. Claire didn't want to appear weak. But, more than that, she didn't want them to feel sorry for her. Claire fell back on the bed as soon as the door slammed behind her. She knew that, on some trips, she and Alison would be sharing a room. They'd actually roomed together during their quick stop in Mississippi the night before and that had been fine with Claire. But, at the moment, Claire needed to be alone. Emerging back into the world of the living was proving to be exhausting.

Claire could only take being around people for so long before she needed to recharge.

She felt her cell phone vibrate in her back pocket.

"Hey," she said, the moment she heard Gia's voice. "How'd you know I was missing you?"

"I've got that psychic thing. Lights in my head flash when Claire needs a Gia-fix."

"So, what's up?" Claire asked.

"Where are you?"

"Houston."

"Cool. Make sure you eat some great barbecue while you're there."

"I hear it's on the agenda."

"How long will you be in Texas?"

"Three days here. Next, we're headed to Austin, Fort Worth and then on to Arizona."

"I'm exhausted just listening to you." Claire could hear the distinct sound of pots banging in the background.

"What are you doing? Playing the cymbals?"

"I'm making dinner."

"And, apparently, it's something that requires a pot, huh?" Cooking was definitely not Gia's forté.

"As a matter of fact, it does. Fettuccini Alfredo with shrimp."

"You have a date!"

"I do!"

"And it's date three!" Claire exclaimed with joy.

"It is!" Fettuccini Alfredo with shrimp was one of the only meals Gia knew how to make from scratch, other than spaghetti and crock-pot stew, It was her go-to meal the first time she offered to make a man dinner. Without fail, that occurred on date three.

Not many men made it past date one, let alone two. Date three was something to celebrate.

"Who is he?" Claire sat up and propped herself against a pile of pillows.

"Someone I met at yoga."

"He's a yogi?"

"Yep. We met in the midst of down dog."

"Were you sniffing each other's butts?" Claire asked, smiling.

"You think you're so funny."

"I am!" She was happy for Gia. Not many men made it to the fettuccini stage.

"He's really great, Claire." Gia's voice sounded more hopeful than Claire had heard it in a long time. She prayed this guy was worthy of Gia. Claire hadn't met many who were.

"Tell me about him." She could tell her friend was beaming.

"He sent me flowers at work. No guy has ever done that before."

"That's because you usually won't let them know where you work," Claire said.

"It makes good safety sense. I don't need a stalker showing up outside my classroom door." For the next ten minutes, Gia told Claire all about her new man and Claire was happy to listen. She wanted Gia to be happy. None of her friends deserved it more.

"Okay, I've babbled on long enough," Gia said. "Tell me more about you. How are the others in the group? Do you like them or are they a bunch of weirdos?"

"No weirdos yet. They're all really great," Claire said, rolling over on her side and propping her head up with her hand. "I'm actually glad you called. We're all meeting for dinner in a couple of hours and I've decided to tell them tonight."

"Tell them? Oh. I get it. *Tell them.*"

"Yeah. It's not a secret. Frank's known since he hired me and I already told Callum."

"You did?"

"Yeah, when we went to dinner the other night."

"You and Callum had dinner?" Gia asked.

"Yes."

"Alone?" It seemed like an innocent enough question, but Claire knew Gia and nothing got by her.

"Yes, we went out to an Italian restaurant the other night."

"Be careful, okay, sweetie? I don't want you to get hurt."

"There's nothing to get hurt over."

"Listen, I've got to go finish dinner. He'll be here in less than thirty minutes! I had to call and tell you it was date three! I knew you'd be excited for me."

"I'm thrilled!" Claire said. "Call me tomorrow so I can hear all about it."

"Of course!" Gia said. "Ta ta!"

And with that, Gia was gone, off on her date.

"How was your mom, Wyatt?" Callum asked as the group gathered for dinner. He'd selected this place when Claire had told him she'd like to talk to the team this evening.

"It's usually really quiet," Callum had said to her. "Plus, if you tell them over dinner, you can play with the food on your plate and not have to make eye contact. I know how you like to do that."

Claire had smiled at Callum. It was funny how, after such a short period of time, he already knew her. He didn't just remember the things she told him, but paid attention to nuances other people would probably never notice.

"She's doing okay," Wyatt said, his face uncharacteristically serious. "It was hard. My sister told me Mom probably wouldn't know who I was, and she was right."

"I'm sorry," Claire said. She could see the others felt such sadness for Wyatt, too.

"Yeah. It sucked. I sat and talked to her. Told her about where we've been traveling. I'm not sure how much of it she understood. She didn't say much, doesn't seem to have the words anymore. But, as I left, she spoke up. Surprised the heck out of me. She said, clear as day, 'I know I really love you. I don't know your name, but I know I love you.' Pretty much ripped my heart out."

It nearly ripped Claire's heart out, too. Losing her parents, at such a young age had been devastating. But she wasn't sure it was worse than having them live long enough to forget who you were.

"Anyway, I was glad I went," Wyatt said. "Now, I can relax over some queso and a margarita."

"I think we're all in need of some relaxation," Mitch said. "It was one heck of a long drive. No talk of work or anything depressing till dessert."

Claire and Callum exchanged nervous glances. Claire would honor Mitch's request, though he'd made it in jest, and wait until dessert. But she was definitely going to talk to the team tonight. She wasn't about to lose her nerve.

Poor Mitch had no idea how depressing dessert was going to be.

The team laughed and joked over their fajitas, chalupas and chimichangos.

"Okay, who's getting dessert?" Alison asked. "I'm stuffed, but I've been dreaming of sopapillas since we hit the Texas border."

"I'm in," Callum said, glancing at Claire.

She'd barely touched her dinner, though the bites she'd taken had proven to be delicious. The knots in her stomach left no room for food.

"I could probably take a bite or two," Claire said, but really wasn't sure she could.

"Okay, then," Callum said. "We'll get two big plates for the table. Wyatt can pack away what the rest of us can't finish."

After the sopapillas had arrived and everyone was done complaining about their sticky, honey-covered hands, Claire looked across the table at Callum. He nodded silently.

"Hey, everyone," Claire said, her voice soft. "I want to talk to all of you about something."

Slowly, the others quieted down and turned their eyes to Claire. She felt her heart speed up.

Wiping the sweat from her palms onto her thighs, she nervously looked at Callum.

"Claire and I've been talking," Callum began. "There's something about her most of you don't know. In fact, I only learned of it recently. Anyway, she and I thought it'd be best for her to discuss things with you tonight, so you're aware of the situation."

The team nodded and turned back to Claire again. Claire could see they were both anxious and concerned about what she was going to say.

She sighed and felt the tears well in her eyes before the words hit her lips. She wished Callum could tell them or that she could pass out newspaper stories about the accident for them to read. But, none of those easy-outs were an option. It was *her* story. No one else could tell it.

"I'm going to get this out as quickly as possible," she began. "Because it's not easy for me to talk about and, frankly, I don't know any way to say it other than by spitting it out. Two years ago, my family and I were in a car accident. I was married at the time, and my husband and I had three small children. We were hit by a drunk driver and everyone was killed. The other driver, my husband, our kids, everyone except me."

The gasps were audible. If not for the mariachi music playing over the intercom system, Claire would've been certain even the busboys in the back kitchen had heard them.

"I joined this team as a way of trying to get on with my life. I'm not over the loss. I'll never be over it. But I'm desperately looking for a way to move on." She could, as expected, feel the tears warm on her cheeks and she reached up to wipe them away.

"I didn't want to wait any longer to tell you. Even during this short amount of time, I've felt like I've been keeping a big secret. I really care about each of you. I want to get to know all of you better and I want you to get to know me. You couldn't do that if I didn't tell you what had happened."

The table was silent. Even Wyatt was still, the sopapilla he'd been about to devour still sticking to his hand.

Claire glanced at Callum, then to Frank, whose smile told Claire he was proud of her.

"So," Claire said. "Could someone please say something? I don't mind if you ask me questions. Truly, I don't, but I hope you still think of me as Claire and not some tragic figure. Maybe I was before, but I'm trying to recreate myself into someone my family would be proud of. I'll gladly tell you anything you want to know about the accident or my kids, but please, don't act like it's a taboo subject you can't mention. That only makes things more awkward."

For another moment, no one spoke. Claire could see Alison was quietly crying and holding Mitch's hand.

"Anyone?" Claire said nervously. "I know you must want to ask me something."

"Tell us about your family," Mitch said, gently. "We'd like to know about your family."

And, with that, Claire took a deep breath and began to share about the most important people in her life, with individuals, whom she realized, were becoming more and more important to her each and every day.

CHAPTER TWENTY

Texas was a blur. Their time in Houston flew by and, the next thing Claire knew, they were headed to Austin and then Fort Worth.

Claire had only been to Texas once in her entire life, in college to visit a childhood friend who'd married an Air Force Second Lieutenant and was stationed in San Antonio. Claire remembered she'd enjoyed her visit, though she had found the Alamo to be a bit disappointing.

"Did you know the Alamo's now across the street from a *shopping mall?*" Claire had asked Jack, once, when he'd inquired about her one and only trip to the Lone Star State.

If Claire had remembered anything about Texas, it was that it was hot. Very, *very* hot. It was late August and the summer weather was scorching. Claire was thankful for the working AC in the van. If The Weather Channel was correct, it wasn't going to cool down anytime soon.

As the team reached Austin, Mitch, who'd been driving at the time, called out, "Hey, Claire. Did Callum ever tell you he got his big ol' tattoo in Austin?"

"No," Claire said, turning her head to the back of the van where Callum was sitting with Frank. Claire was riding shotgun and Alison was sprawled out, asleep in the second row.

"He did," Mitch said. "And it's quite a story. Tell her about it, Callum."

"You make it sound so sordid, Mitch," Callum said. "I was living in

Austin for a short period of time, before I began traveling and speaking. I'd always wanted to visit Texas. I grew up in Ireland, thinking everyone in Texas rides horses and wears cowboy hats."

"And don't they?" Mitch asked.

"Well, yes." Callum laughed. "Anyway, I decided to live my dream of being in Texas by spending one semester taking some business courses at the University of Texas."

"Just for fun," Mitch added. "'Cause, that's what people do, you know. Take business courses for fun."

Claire laughed. She loved the banter between all the men in the group.

"I'd met some nice bucks in my classes and we all went out for a night on Sixth Street."

"That's where all the bars are," Mitch said.

Claire nodded. She already knew this as she'd read up on Austin before their trip. She'd been trying to learn about all the cities they'd visit, though she didn't mention this to anyone in the group. They'd tease her for being such a nerd.

"I might've had a few too many," Callum said. "I ended up in this tattoo parlor. My buddies all already had tattoos. Little ones. Their girlfriends' names, flags, skulls, those sorts of things. But, I, being Mister Tough Guy, decided to show them how it's really done. So, Mango and I picked out the most complicated tattoo in the book. Even now, I find it to be quite intriguing."

"Whoah," Mitch called out. "Back up there, buddy. *What* was the guy's name?"

Clearly, Mitch had heard this story a few times and enjoyed Callum's telling of it.

"Mango. His name was Mango."

"Whose name was Mango?" Claire asked.

Callum, Mitch and Frank all laughed. "The tattoo guy," Callum said. "That was the name of the guy who gave me my tattoo."

"Mango?" Claire squealed. "Seriously? You got a tattoo from a guy named *Mango?*"

"I did. And, apparently, at least according to him, that's his real, on-his-birth-certificate, given name."

Mitch glanced over at Claire. "You can't make this crap up."

"What'd he look like?" Claire asked, curious now.

"Oh, that's the best part," Mitch said. "Tell her what he looked like."

Callum chuckled. "He looked like a guy named Mango who would give you a tattoo."

"Meaning he was covered in them himself?" Claire asked.

"From head to toe," Callum replied. "Actually, I take that back. I didn't actually see his toes. But his head was definitely covered."

"Really?" Claire asked. "His whole head?"

"Yep. His entire head. Face. Neck. All of it. He also had a whole lot of face piercings and those earrings that make big holes in your lobes."

"Of course he did," Frank mumbled from the back.

"But let me tell you," Callum said. "Nicest guy you'd ever meet. Married. Kids. Total suburban dad."

"Or not," Mitch said, looking in the rearview mirror. "Tell Claire how you got to know him so well."

"Well, as it turns out, you can't get a big tattoo like that in one visit. I had to go back, multiple times, over the next few months. When I sobered up, I thought about not continuing, but by then, I had so much of it done, it seemed like I might as well go ahead and finish it. It turned out very nicely, in my humble opinion," Callum said. "And the ladies love it. Don't they, Claire?"

Claire felt her face blush a bit, but not as much as it would've a few weeks ago. She and Callum weren't exactly an item, but they were spending a great deal of time together. The team knew something was going on, though what it was, no one was sure. Not even Claire.

"Yes. Sexy. Very sexy," Claire said, giggling. She'd meant for the "sexy" comment to come across as sarcastic, but if she were to be honest, his tattoo *was* sexy. Mango did nice work.

"And there you have it," Mitch said. "The tale of the tattoo. Hey, Callum, you planning on seeing Mango while you're here?"

"You bet. I stop by every time I'm in town."

"You want to go see the bats?" Callum asked Claire, after they'd settled into their hotel rooms and met for coffee at the shop next door.

"The bats?"

"Yeah, didn't you read about them in your Austin tour book?"

Claire blushed. He'd caught her. So much for trying to hide that she'd been studying up on each city.

"I might have heard something about them."

Callum smiled and took a sip of his coffee. "Oh, I see. We're going to play it cool. I like it."

Claire shrugged and sipped her own drink. "Sure. What time do they come out?" It was a known-answer question.

"Right around sunset."

"Okay, sounds good to me." She'd read all about the Austin bats and was anxious to see them. It blew her mind that Austin was home to the largest urban bat colony in North America. Claire'd been planning on asking Alison to go with her one evening, but going with Callum was even better. She was growing to love their time alone, and though they were traveling together constantly, time with only him was rare.

"How about you and I meet in the lobby around a quarter to seven and walk over there?"

"Walk?" Claire asked. She knew he could, but also knew, by now, he rarely did.

"Yeah, I think so. With the crowds and trying to see over the bridge, it'd be better if I were standing."

"Okay," Claire said.

"You look great!" Callum said, as she walked into the hotel lobby.

"You don't look too shabby yourself." He was wearing lightweight khaki pants and a fitted button-down shirt that was snug enough in all the right places.

It was a bit startling to see Callum standing. She'd seen it maybe a half-dozen times since they'd met, but it still caught her by surprise each time. Usually, he was in his chair. She'd asked him why that seemed to be his preference. In her opinion, standing seemed like a better option.

He'd said to her, "The difference between me and all those soldiers you see coming back from war is this: I was born this way. I've never known what it's like to have two legs or two arms. I learned to crawl without any limbs. I learned to get around the house and the kitchen, mostly on the ground. I didn't even utilize a real wheelchair until I began school. My mam just kept me in a stroller when we went out and, if I needed to get down, I just got down and kinda scooted around."

"So, that's how you're most comfortable?" Claire had said. She'd never given much thought to how each amputee's situation was different.

"Exactly. Maybe if I'd had legs once and lost them, I'd want them back. If you grew up walking, losing that ability must be devastating. I imagine you'd want to do everything you could to regain some semblance of it."

"But you don't feel that need?" Claire had asked.

"To be honest with you," Callum had said, "I find they kinda get in the way."

"Legs do?"

"Oh, yes. And the arm. Especially the arm."

"Really?" Claire had asked, incredulous. She'd seen some prosthetic arms and they were incredible, with moving hands that could pick up the tiniest pea.

"The arm is the *worst*."

"I don't get it. Wouldn't it be easier to have two hands?"

"Sure, I guess. If you'd grown up with two hands. But I know how to do most everything with one, and pretty quickly, if I do say so myself. In the time it takes for me to figure out how to get that damn arm moving, I could be done with whatever it is that needs doing and halfway across the room. That's why I rarely wear it. The legs do prove to be practical at times. But, the arm? Oh, just shoot me now."

Claire had laughed and then realized how uncomfortable he must've been on their first date in an effort to impress her. It hadn't been necessary. She'd been impressed with him the first moment she'd heard him speak. But the fact he'd worn the arm for her touched her heart.

As expected, Callum was not wearing his other arm tonight. With his sole hand, he took hold of hers.

"Ready, my dear?" he asked, as he gently tugged.

"Lead the way."

There were already a number of people on the bridge when they got there. Despite the crowd, they were able to find a spot along the railing.

"We should have a perfect view from here," Callum said.

"I can't wait."

"I got that feeling," Callum said. "The jumping up and down kind of gave you away."

"I was not jumping up and down," Claire huffed.

"You were jumping up and down in your head when I suggested we come here. Admit it, love." Callum pushed a strand of hair away from her face.

"Maybe a little. Teeny tiny jumps," Claire said with a smile. She liked his hand so close to her face. She wished he'd let it linger a moment longer.

While they waited for the bats, Callum told her about the workout he and Mitch had snuck in that afternoon. Callum and Mitch were trying to convince Alison and Claire to work out as well.

"I can't have you collapsing on stage because you're so out of shape," he'd said to Claire, his accent as thick as potato soup. She was thankful he hadn't said something about her gaining weight. Though still thin, she knew she'd added some pounds to her frame from all the snack food and restaurant meals on the road. Eventually, she'd have to start watching her food intake, or else need to be hauled around in Wyatt's truck, but for now, she was happy to once again be enjoying food.

She'd been eating like a bird for way too long.

"Oh, look!" Claire squealed, as they gazed into the east. "I see a bat!" She was pointing to the air in front of her. "There's another."

Claire could feel Callum's eyes on her. "You'd better stop staring at me and start looking for bats," she said, keeping her eyes on the sky above the water.

"Yes, ma'am," Callum said. "I think that's one over there."

And then, as if the bat cave door had been flung open, the sky was suddenly awash with flying bats. They swooped up in front of Claire and Callum with such rapid speed, Claire took a step back out of fear one might flap into her face. The sight was spectacular. Claire turned to look behind them, to the west. The purple sunset was a magnificent background to the swarm of wings. From a distance, Claire bet it looked like a million birds gliding through the sky. The site was so beautiful. The way they hovered against the radiant sky was spectacular.

She couldn't help but think about how her kids would've loved this. The girls might have squirmed at the thought of all those rodents flying so close to their hair, but Luke would've relished every second. The grosser, the better.

Callum seemed to sense her thoughts, because he turned around and rested his back against the rail, just as she had. Wrapping his arm around her, he pulled her close. And then, with the softest of touches, he placed his lips on her hair and kissed her gently.

"I'm glad that's you and not a bat on my head," she said, smiling as she stared out over the water. "I'd heard some people get pooped on when they stand here."

She looked up at him. With his legs, he was actually taller than her. His face was soft and serious. Something about his expression told her to tilt her chin and, as she did, he bent over and kissed her, ever so tenderly, on the lips.

In that moment, as the bats rose far above their heads, Claire felt her heart climbing with them. For the rest of her life, she'd remember it was then, when the last of the bats ascended from the bridge, that she fell in love.

Again.

CHAPTER
TWENTY-ONE

Claire couldn't remember the last time she'd been this exhausted. Or happy. Or exhausted.

Did she mention exhausted?

The next few months were a whirlwind of U.S. cities and events. The stop after Austin and Fort Worth had been Arizona. Claire had finally gotten to see the Grand Canyon for the first time. She and Alison and Mitch had even hiked partway to the bottom. She'd hesitated doing the trek when she realized Callum had felt it'd be too much for him.

"I'm good on these legs, but not *that* good," he'd joked.

"You can always ride the donkey," Mitch had quipped. "Like Alice, the housekeeper, on *The Brady Bunch*."

"Nah," Callum had shot back. "I've seen enough asses in my life."

"Boys," Alison had scolded.

"I can stay back," Claire had said when the two of them were alone. She'd meant it and didn't really mind too much. She'd always wanted to hike the Grand Canyon, but Callum mattered more to her. If he couldn't do it, she was willing not to do it, either.

"Claire," Callum had said seriously. "I don't know about you, but I don't view our relationship as a sprint. I view it as a marathon. So, if this is going to be a marathon, there are a few things we need to get straight right now."

"Ground rules?" Claire had asked, one eyebrow raised.

"Sure. Ground rules. The first one being, I'm not about to hold you back in any way. If you want to do something, then do it. If I can do it, I'll be happy to join you, assuming you want me." He'd winked then. "But, if I can't—and, though I hate to admit it, there are some things I just can't do, at least not easily—I still want you to live that experience."

"But," Claire had protested.

"There is no but," Callum had said firmly. "I can't be in a relationship where I feel I'm holding the other person back. That's not fair to you and, frankly, it's not fair of you to ask me to bear that burden. I can't live in a constant state of guilt. Besides, I find great pleasure in making you happy."

He'd kissed her then. They'd been doing a whole lot of kissing since the bridge in Austin. A lot of kissing and snuggling and spending time together.

He made Claire happy. And she liked being happy. She'd been sad for way too long.

After Arizona, the team had traveled to San Diego, Los Angeles and San Francisco. By that time, the whole team knew about Claire's obsession with travel guidebooks and, though they teased her mercilessly about it, they were also happy to listen to what she thought would be the best museums, restaurants and activities to check out in each city. Sometimes Claire wondered what they'd done before she'd joined the team. Sat in their hotel rooms all day?

"You must've been a great mom," Mitch had said to her, surprising her with his compliment. "I'll bet your kids had the best time because you always planned fun things for them to do."

Claire had smiled and said she'd tried to be the best mom she could be, and hoped her kids had felt that, too. She'd always done her best to plan great activities, whether it be crafts or field trips to parks or scavenger hunts around town. Claire was a creative person and had thrown that skill into the way she mothered her children.

She was also enjoying traveling even more than she'd thought she would, back when she'd dreamt of going on tour with a Broadway show, or all the times she and Jack had discussed taking the kids on a cross-country trip when the twins were a little older.

As she visited each new state and city, Claire felt Jack's presence with her. She was certain he was happy for her. He would never have begrudged her this opportunity. Sometimes Claire had to wonder how she'd ever gotten so lucky to have found not only one man who loved her so selflessly, but two.

And love her Callum did. She'd known, that night on the bridge, she was in love, but she also knew she'd be damned if she was going to be the one to say the "L" word first.

As it turned out, there was no need to worry. When they reached San Francisco, about three weeks into their relationship, Callum surprised her with a hot air balloon ride over the Napa Valley. It was another first for Claire, one of many. The two of them had risen early to be in the balloon before the sun came up and as a result were rewarded by the most unbelievable sunrise Claire had ever seen.

He'd had his arm around her while she'd held both of their glasses, his filled with a mimosa and hers with simply orange juice. He'd nuzzled his face in her hair and she'd leaned back against him.

"It's incredible," she'd said. She hardly knew where to cast her eyes. All around her was magnificent beauty, from the sky to the scores of vineyards. Claire had found it difficult to gather it in fast enough.

"I think *you're* incredible," Callum had said. She'd smiled up at him then. He was once again taller than her in his legs. His blue eyes were even more brilliant that the sky surrounding them.

"I know I can't possibly live up to Jack, and I'm not trying to replace him, but I've never felt like this before with another woman. I can't take your pain away, but I hope you'll give me the chance to make you happy," he'd said, leaning down to kiss her. And then, right before he did, he whispered, "Because I'm falling in love with you."

"And I'm falling in love with you." The words had tumbled from Claire's mouth once his lips left hers. She did love him. She'd been drawn to him in a way she'd never experienced before, not even with Jack. Jack had been an exciting, intoxicating college love.

With Callum, they were both coming into the relationship as old souls. Both of them had experienced more pain in their relatively young lives than most people and their entire families, combined, had to come to terms with in a lifetime. Their understanding of one another went far beyond thoughtful conversations over dinner or fun date nights at the movies. They not only understood life and the nearly insurmountable hurdles that existed, they also understood each other in a way Claire had previously doubted anyone could.

Even if Claire lived another sixty years, she suspected she'd never meet another person who "got her" the way Callum did.

And, though she'd never lost a limb or had the need for a wheelchair or walked with fake legs, as Callum called them, she "got him," too, in a way he said no other woman had before.

She wondered if soulmates existed. And, if they did, could you have two in a lifetime? She wasn't sure. But, if soulmates were possible, she was fairly certain she'd found hers.

The California cities had flown by and, the next thing Claire knew, they were headed to Portland and Seattle and then back across the Midwest to Kansas City. The trip to reach the Midwest was an exceptionally long drive and, though they'd stopped to sleep a few nights, they hadn't stayed anywhere for more than twelve hours at a time and the mood in the van was dank.

"I'm sick of all of you," Alison spat out as they drove through the middle of nowhere Nebraska. "Seriously, I love you guys, and all. But, if I have to spend one more hour in this van, I'm going to scream. Whose idea was it to not have an event in Wyoming or something so we could get out of here for a few days?"

"Well," Mitch said, his voice much testier than usual. He, too, was fed up with being crammed into the van. "I guess that would be you."

"Callum had said he didn't want more than ten events scheduled during the fall stretch. Wyoming would have made eleven," Alison retorted.

"I think we're about to witness a wee lover's spat," Callum said. He was driving and, though he wasn't complaining like Mitch and Alison, Claire could tell he was tired, too, both physically and emotionally. They all needed a break, from the van and from each other.

"Maybe now would be a good time to bring up that bus idea," Mitch said.

"What bus idea?" Claire asked.

"The bus we need, but Callum won't buy," Alison shot back. She was clearly not in one of her better moods.

"Ah, yes. The bus," Callum said. "How did I know that would pop up along this drive?"

"It's going to pop up on every drive until we get one," Alison said.

"She's right, Callum," Mitch said. "We can't keep this up. We're crammed into this van like a bunch of drunk college students at a house party. If you want us to continue to work with one another and still be able to stand looking at each other, we need a bigger vehicle."

"You're always welcome to drive with Wyatt," Callum said and the harshness of his tone startled Claire. In the two months they'd been together, Claire hadn't seen anyone in the group get into an actual argument. There'd been disagreements, certainly, and good-natured teasing. But a fight? No.

She wondered if she was about to witness her first one.

"The point is," Mitch said. "I shouldn't *have* to drive with him."

"Okay, okay," Claire interrupted. "I think I'm missing something."

"What Mitch and Alison are, so heatedly, complaining about," Frank, who until this moment had been quiet for most of that day's drive, said, "Is that they, and I, for that matter, have been trying to convince Callum to invest in a bus for all of us to travel in instead of this small van. We all feel that a bus would give us more room to stretch out, work at the tables, take naps that are more restful than my head on Mitch's lap." Mitch snorted. "And, most importantly, give us some space from one another so, as was eloquently stated earlier, we can still stand looking at each other by the end of our journeys."

"So," Claire continued. "What's the issue, Callum?"

"Money!" Alison piped up from the back. "It's always about money."

"I can speak for myself, Alison," Callum said, his voice low and even and, if Claire were to describe it, a little bit menacing.

"Then do so," Alison muttered.

"Claire, Alison's correct. It's an issue of money."

"Do you not have any?" she whispered, hoping the others couldn't hear her. She didn't want to call out Callum and his finances, or the finances of his organization, in front of the others if it was a sensitive topic.

"No. That's not the problem. We make good money from our events. Of course, much of that goes to Uncle Sam and the rest goes to pay for gas, hotels, salaries, health benefits. You do all like your health benefits, don't you?" Callum called out, sarcastically, as he glanced in the rearview mirror.

"Of course, since we need them for our chiropractor visits," Mitch huffed.

"The issue isn't that we don't have the money. The issue is that I think there are more important things for us to put any excess funds towards."

"Such as?" Claire asked. She truly was curious. She didn't understand what Callum's objection to this might be.

"Such as wheelchairs and canes and Zimmer frames."

"What?" Claire asked

"That's what fancy British people call walkers," Alison piped up.

"For the record, I'm not British. I'm Irish. Southern Ireland is not a part of the United Kingdom.

"Any extra money we have is used to help other people," Callum continued. "I try to manage our money wisely. I pay everyone fair wages."

Claire couldn't argue with that. The money she was making was quite reasonable, and since she rarely spent any of it because most of the expenses on the road were covered, she was actually putting a large chunk of it away in a bank account.

Not that she needed money. Jack had made sure she'd be well taken care of if anything were to happen to him. And, she'd also received a significant insurance settlement from the accident.

Still, Claire felt a sense of pride over earning her own income. She wasn't sure yet how she was going to spend it, but she'd been toying around with the idea of creating a scholarship in her children's names.

"Okay," Frank said. "I think we've had enough arguing for a bit. If I wanted to hear bickering, I'd ask all my kids to get together for dinner."

Claire smiled at his words. She remembered how much her kids used to squabble during family meals.

"Okay, Frank," Claire said, turning around in her seat. "Since we're changing topics, tell me about your kids. I don't know much about them."

"I have four."

"Four?" Claire said. She couldn't believe Frank was the father of four children. The image of him having even one child seemed difficult for her to comprehend. He was so...what was the word she was looking

for...stuffy. Yes, that was it. Stuffy. She couldn't imagine him being "Daddy" to anyone. She especially couldn't envision him raising those children alone, as Callum had told her Frank had done.

"All of them are grown now," Frank said. "Jenny, my youngest, is a junior at K-State. I'm hoping she'll be able to make the drive to see us while we're in Kansas City."

"That'd be great," Claire said.

"Rodney, my second youngest, is in graduate school at Pepperdine."

Claire nodded. She'd remembered Frank had taken a day off in California, in between events, to go visit one of his kids, though she hadn't asked much about it at the time.

"He's studying business," Frank said. "He's the smartest of my kids, but don't tell the others I said that." Claire smiled. Ella had been her smartest. She'd known it early on in the twins' childhood. No parent wants to admit they think one child is smarter than the others, but... well...sometimes one kid just was. Ella had been the most creative and imaginative, even as a toddler. She'd picked up reading earlier than the other two had and she knew all her addition facts before she'd even begun kindergarten.

"And the twins are out of college."

"Twins?" Claire said, surprised. "I didn't know you had twins."

Frank's face reddened beneath his beard. "I didn't mention it because I thought it might hurt you a little."

Claire smiled and her heart melted over Frank's sensitivity.

"You didn't have to hide that fact," Claire said. "I know other people have twins. It doesn't sting to hear about it. At least, not anymore. Boys or girls or both?"

"Two boys. Zack and Mac."

Claire couldn't hide her chuckle.

"My ex-wife named them. I told her it was silly to have their names rhyme, but..." Frank rolled his eyes. "Anyway, those are their names.

They're both gainfully employed, thank heavens. There were some years when I doubted that would happen and feared I might be visiting them in the federal pen."

"Really?"

"Well, maybe I'm exaggerating a bit, but by no means were they easy boys to get to adulthood in one piece."

"Callum told me you raised them all by yourself," Claire said, glancing at Callum. He seemed to be calmer now.

Frank sighed. "Yep. I did. My wife left us when Jenny was three years old. At first, I thought we'd merely be divorcing and sharing joint custody. She'd never been a natural at motherhood. She'd struggled quite a bit with post-partum depression ever since we'd had the twins."

"She didn't want partial custody?"

"Nope. She wanted nothing. We signed those divorce papers and she was gone. Not just out the door, but out of the state. Maybe the country. I'm not sure."

"Really? She was *gone* gone?" Claire couldn't imagine any mother, no matter how depressed, not wanting at least some contact with her children.

"Completely. I've never seen her again. The kids have seen her since they've grown. Jenny found her mom on Facebook when she was in high school. She's always wanted a mom-figure in her life. I did my best but, you know. I'm a man."

Claire nodded. As good a dad as Jack had been, she couldn't imagine what kind of job he would have done if he'd been tasked with raising their girls on his own. Whenever Claire had gone away for even a day, she'd come back to the twins' hair being in complete tangles and them wearing mismatched, and often dirty, clothing. If Jack hadn't been able to handle simple tasks like grooming and dressing, how would he have handled the girls getting their periods and beginning to date? Claire shuddered at the thought of it.

"Jenny was young when her mom left. She hadn't been as hurt by it as the boys because she doesn't really remember it. I think Jenny still keeps in touch with her mom, though we don't discuss it much. The kids got together with her once, at Jenny's pleading. From the bits and pieces the boys told me, it didn't go well and I'm pretty sure none of them have any interest in spending time with their mom again."

"That's sad," Claire said. "But I understand why they wouldn't want to be with her. You must've been so angry with her for leaving you to deal with everything on your own." As she said it, Claire glanced to the back row. Alison and Mitch were both wearing headsets and watching a movie on the tablet. Only Callum was listening to the conversation and Claire got the impression he was zoning out as he stared at the road.

"You know, I was at first. I knew nothing about raising small kids. Not that my ex was much better at it, of course. But I'd been the breadwinner. I made the money, came home and played with the kids for an hour or two and then my wife put them to bed. I'd never gotten my hands dirty before, so to speak.

"It took me awhile to get the hang of things, but I did. As the kids grew older, my anger towards my ex-wife diminished. If anything, I felt sorry for her. She'd missed out on so much. Difficult things, of course. But so many really good things, too. And now, though I believe she'd like to have a relationship with all the kids, it's too late. Even if I were to encourage it, which I don't, my boys have minds of their own. She lost her chance with them. And, to be honest, in a way, she gave me a gift."

"A gift?" It seemed hard to believe that even Frank, as good a man as he was, could find being left alone with four kids to be any sort of gift.

"She did. If I hadn't been forced to spend that much time with my kids, I wouldn't have. I would've continued on with my two hours a night. I would've missed out on all the hours and weeks and months and years of really getting to know them as people. I wouldn't give that up for anything in the world. In the end, the memories of the time spent with your kids, as they grow up, is all you really have, isn't it?"

Claire nodded. She thought that, perhaps, Frank might catch himself and worry he'd hurt her in some way. After all, everyone knew that memories were the only thing she had left of her own children. But when she looked at him carefully, she knew he'd said those words intentionally.

Callum had said something, during one of their talks about her family, and his words had stuck with her.

"Don't let your good memories be ruined by how badly it all ended. Focus on each memory as one happy moment in time. Why would you let the day of their deaths define their entire lives?"

Claire had taken Callum's words to heart and, every day, though it was a struggle, she worked harder and harder to remind herself that the memories were singular moments in time. The end did not define the story.

And she was making sure to treasure the moments she had with Callum and with the new friends she'd made. Claire didn't look toward the future. It was too uncertain. It was not promised to any of them. She was learning to live in the moment. The past was too painful and what lay ahead was unclear. But the present? Claire found she could find contentment in that.

"I think it's time I drove," Claire said to Callum. "We all need to get out and walk around for a bit."

"You just want a Coke," Callum said, smiling, but he signaled to move into the right lane.

"Well, that's true, too," Claire said.

"I thought you were giving that crap up," Callum said.

"I am," Claire said. She'd been trying, unsuccessfully, to give up caffeine and sugar. The weight she'd been gaining since taking this new job had reached its ideal number and she didn't wish for the pounds to continue attaching to her frame. "Just not today."

Callum shook his head, but said nothing, as he maneuvered the van off the highway and into the parking lot of an Exxon station.

An Exxon station that was like the *hundreds* of others they'd visited over the past couple of months.

CHAPTER
TWENTY-TWO

"Let's talk about Christmas," Callum said. It was December and the two of them were making dinner in his kitchen.

The team had finished their fall tour at the end of October and returned to Atlanta, which was where their home base and offices were. Claire had found a small, furnished apartment to rent for the next few months. Though she and Frank still rehearsed, she found both of their roles changed when they were back "in the office." Claire had begun to help Alison with more of the logistical planning, contacting local event venues, soliciting donations, lining up speakers and filling in wherever Alison needed help.

The arrangement was working out well for both of the women. Alison had been in a continual state of treading water and Claire was afraid, if she had too much time on her hands, which seemed likely, since Frank only worked part-time when they weren't traveling, she'd go insane or become depressed.

At the start of the new year, they'd all be traveling overseas for an international tour. Until then, the work was all planning and prepping for next year's events.

A lot went into each seminar, more than Claire had even realized during her months traveling with the group. She'd seen "the shows," so to speak, but none of the rehearsals or planning that went into them since she'd joined the team so late.

"Okay, what do you want to talk about?" Claire asked. She and Callum had spent Thanksgiving with Mitch at his parents' home in Savannah. Alison had gone to spend the holiday with her family in Maryland and Mitch had told them he couldn't bear dealing with his parents and all of their stuffy friends alone. And since neither Callum nor Claire had anyone else to spend the day with, they'd happily agreed to tag along.

Christmas, though, was looming ahead of Claire like a dark cloud ready to burst open with its torrential downpour. Callum was headed back to Ireland to see his family, as he did every year. Mitch and Alison had decided to skip the family drama and escape to Fiji for the week. Frank would be spending his break with his kids in Kansas, and Wyatt was going back to Texas to be with his mom. Gia had finally found a man she could tolerate for more than a few dates, and she and her new beau were going to be spending the holiday with his family in Maine. That left Claire. Alone.

"I'd like you to spend Christmas with me," Callum said, as he chopped a carrot on a wooden cutting board.

He'd promised to buy vegetables that were pre-cut, so she wouldn't have to witness any of his choppin', which always made her nervous, but when she'd arrived, he was already hacking away. "It's so much cheaper to cut them yourself!" he'd said when she'd given him the evil eye.

"I thought you were going to Ireland," she said, in reference to his Christmas question. She'd been avoiding the topic with him, fearing she'd burst into tears the moment the holiday was mentioned.

"I am. I'd like you to come with me."

"To Ireland?" Claire asked, looking up from the onion she was cutting. "You're kidding."

"Of course not. Yes, to Ireland. I want you to come with me and meet my family."

Claire went back to her cutting. "I'd feel like I was imposing."

"Imposing? Why would you ever think that?"

"Well, you know...a woman they don't know...crashing at their house for the holiday. Christmas is for families."

"You and the whole team are part of my family," Callum said.

"It's different and you know it. We *say* that, but we're not real family or anything."

"Claire," Callum said, laying down his knife and turning his chair so he was facing her. "It's real to me."

Claire shrugged and continued to cut, not looking up at him. "You're asking me because you feel sorry for me."

"That's not true."

"Of course it's true. And that's fine," she said. "I feel sorry for me, too." She tried to smile, but instead, felt the tears well up in her eyes.

"Stop cutting."

Claire ignored him and continued to chop. The tears were fully falling now, down her cheek and onto the cutting board.

"Stop cutting," Callum said more firmly, as he grabbed her arm and silenced her hand. "And stop crying."

"It's the onions," Claire said, wiping her eyes with the back of her sleeve.

"Look at me."

Claire kept her chin down, not raising her eyes to meet him.

"Claire, look at me," he insisted.

Claire slowly lifted her head.

"I'm not asking you to come to Ireland with me for Christmas because I feel sorry for you. Though I fully recognize your situation sucks. I'm asking you to come to Ireland with me for Christmas because I want you there. I want you to meet my family. I want you to see where I grew up. I want to see what crazy tourist attraction you'll have us visit because you read about it in some tour book."

Claire smiled, a little, at that thought. She wiped at her cheeks, again, careful to keep the onion juice, which was on her hand, away from her eyes.

"And, more than that, I can't bear the thought of being away from you for two full weeks."

"You can't?"

"Of course I can't. You and I are together nearly all the time and have been for months now. How would I survive with you not around to tell me what to do?"

Claire gasped. "I do not tell you what to do."

"How's my carrot cutting going?"

"You should've bought the pre-cut ones."

"Case in point." Callum smiled and Claire couldn't help but smile along with him.

"Listen, Claire," Callum continued, taking her hand. "I love Ireland, but I wouldn't love Ireland nearly as much on this trip if you're not with me. Don't you understand?"

"Understand what?"

"Don't you understand, yet, that nothing in my life makes sense without you? Not even my beloved Ireland."

Claire sighed. She loved this man. Loved him deeply and with all she had in her. She wanted to go to Ireland with him. She hadn't considered the possibility before, but now that he'd brought it up, she clung to the idea. The holiday would be so much better, so much less lonely, if she were with Callum.

"What if your family doesn't like me?"

"What's not to like?" Callum asked.

"Well, you have a point there," Claire said. "I am pretty fabulous."

"There's my lass," Callum said, his brogue heavy as fudge.

"Can I please cut the rest of the carrots?" she asked.

Callum sighed with a deep, exaggerated breath. "If you must," he said. "But, do you think I could at least rip up the lettuce?"

"I think I could bear to watch that. As long as you use your hand and not anything sharp."

"So bossy," Callum mumbled, but Claire saw him smile as he turned and rolled to the fridge.

TWENTY-THREE

Claire had never been out of the country. Except to Mexico on her honeymoon, close to twenty years ago. She didn't really count that, though, because she and Jack had barely left the hotel room, they were so enamored with one another. So the only time Claire actually saw foreign ground was when they drove from the airport to the hotel and then back a week later. The two of them had subsisted on room service and sex for seven days straight.

It had been the best week of Claire's life.

The team was planning an overseas tour after the holidays, and Claire already had her passport. The only thing that stood between Claire and Christmas in Ireland was the purchase of a plane ticket, which Callum took care of after dinner.

"I've never been on a plane for that long," Claire said, once Callum hit the button to confirm his purchase. "Is it awful?"

"Not if you get up to stretch your legs," Callum said.

"Does that help you?" Claire asked, a teasing glint in her eyes.

"Oh, completely. The worst part, of course, is the way there's no leg room between you and the seat in front of you," he said with a laugh.

Claire tipped her head up toward his, so he could kiss her and, as he did, she slipped her hand inside the buttons of his shirt. His skin felt so smooth. His chest so hard. Claire was filled with a desire she hadn't experienced since she was a young woman.

Except, of course, for the desire she'd felt the last time they were in this position. And the time before that.

For all the kissing Callum and Claire participated in, they hadn't progressed past that point. It was beginning to bother Claire.

She wasn't worried he didn't find her attractive. She knew that wasn't the case. She also knew that, despite Callum's physical limitations, all the other "parts" he had worked perfectly fine. He'd made sure to let her know that right from the beginning of the relationship.

Callum put his hand on Claire's wrist and, though he didn't remove her hand from his chest, his grip was firm enough to discourage any wandering.

Claire sighed and closed her eyes. She wanted to be straightforward and ask Callum why he didn't seem to want to progress any further than the puppy-love stage with her. But whenever she began to open her mouth, the words became weighty on her tongue and she closed it again. She wasn't ready to ask the question.

Or maybe, she wasn't ready to hear the answer.

Claire had never been a sex fiend. She'd never been able to keep up with the amount of sex Jack had wanted. But wasn't that the case with most couples? The man always wants to have sex and the woman only wants it sometimes.

But in the case of Callum, Claire found she was the one who seemed to hold all the desire. Callum liked to hold her hand and put his arm around her. He kissed her a lot, whether it be on the lips or on the top of her head. But, he kept his hand in safe and neutral territory and, to Claire's dismay, he made sure her hands remained there, too.

Sometimes Claire wondered if the reason she wanted to hurry up and experience their first time together, intimately, was because she was anxious to get it over with. She found Callum to be incredibly sexy and was pretty certain, when he finally decided to take her, it would be amazing.

But though Claire had seen Callum every day for months now,

knew the feel and shape of his shortened legs and arm, she was yet to see all of him *at once.*

Claire had never seen Callum naked and, frankly, the thought of it frightened her a little.

She was used to his body when he had clothes on, but how would he look without them? Would it startle her? Shock her? Cause her to pause? And, in the second she took for that pause, would Callum sense her hesitation?

That was what it came down to, if Claire were to be honest with herself. It wasn't that she feared how she'd feel once she saw Callum's body; it was that she worried her reaction might be distressing to Callum.

What if her eyes lingered too long? What if they didn't linger long enough?

Would she make him uncomfortable? Cause him to feel self-conscious?

She would like to be discussing it with Callum. As he held her arm in place on his chest, she nearly brought it up. But, something stopped her. Maybe it was the look in his eyes. *Was there a subtle warning in them or was she imagining it?* Maybe it was that they'd had such a wonderful evening, she didn't want to risk ruining it.

Or maybe it was that, when she began to speak, Callum said, "What do you want to see most in Ireland when we're there?"

Whatever the reasons were, Claire quietly removed her hand from the inside of Callum's shirt and, instead, rested it on his thigh. She'd ask him about what was holding him back. She would. But not tonight.

"I'd really like to kiss the Blarney Stone," Claire said. "And I'd like to meet a leprechaun."

"Wake up, sleepy head," Callum said, shaking Claire gently by the arm. "Welcome to Dublin!"

"What?" Claire said, forcing her eyes open. She looked around her, unsure of where, exactly, she was waking up.

"You are the worst travel partner," Callum said. "You've been sleeping since we left America!"

"That's not true," Claire said, gathering her bearings and sitting up in her seat. She'd somehow slept through the whole landing and the plane was now taxiing.

"You fell asleep before we left the ground," Claire said, wiping at the side of her mouth. She'd drooled a little and hoped Callum hadn't noticed the wetness at the corner of her mouth.

"But then I woke up, and you were dead asleep next to me. I thought we were going to spend the whole flight, across the sea, chatting away. But no, I had to content myself with movies and the sound of your snores."

Claire gasped. "I do not snore!"

Callum chuckled.

"Do I snore?" she whispered to him, alarmed. She glanced around her, relieved to see no one was giving her a dirty look.

Callum looked around with her. "If they're not going to complain, then neither will I."

"I feel like something died in my mouth," Claire said, putting her hand over her lips so as to keep Callum from smelling her bad breath.

"Here you go," he said, handing her a piece of gum he already had in his grasp. "I knew you'd feel that way."

She didn't ask him how he knew. She was afraid he'd say he'd bent down to kiss her, as she slept, and smelled her morning breath.

"Once we stop taxiing, I'm going to need you to get my legs from the overhead," Callum whispered.

"And what if I don't?" she teased.

"Oh, I see. You're going to be a naughty girl on this trip," he said, smiling at her.

Callum hadn't worn his legs during the flight, but he'd brought them to make boarding easier. They'd checked his chair with the luggage and would pick it up once they were inside the Dublin airport. Callum told Claire he would likely use nothing but the chair once they were back in his homeland.

"I'm not used to walking around Ireland," he'd said.

For the flight, though, he'd told her it was just easier to have the legs. "Especially when I have to use the loo," he'd said.

As soon as they'd found their seats, though, Callum had taken off the prosthetics and handed them to Claire, who'd climbed over him to stow them up above.

She wondered, now, how he'd managed to go to the restroom if she'd been sleeping for the whole flight.

"Do you have to use the bathroom?" Claire asked, concern in her eyes. "Have you been holding it all this time?"

"Aye," Callum said, a glint in his eye. "But not very well. I have a little bit trickling down my leg right now."

Claire looked down at his legs in horror and then back up at him. A smile the size of a billboard spread across his face.

"You're awful," she said, just as the plane ceased moving and the fasten seat belt sign turned off. "Excuse me," she said, as she climbed over him, intentionally pushing into his body with her hip as she moved past.

Opening the overhead compartment, she carefully took out his legs and handed them to him. Glancing at the long line of people behind her, she cursed silently. Perhaps Callum had found a way to use the restroom while she'd been asleep, but she hadn't gone since they'd taken off. Her bladder was about to burst.

"We'll make sure our first stop is the bathroom," Callum said, reading Claire's mind as she sat down next to him. "Nervous?"

Claire assumed he didn't intend that question to be in reference to her possibly peeing herself.

She nodded. "A little."

"Ireland is going to love you," Callum said, as he adjusted the sock over one of his stumps and pulled his prosthetic on over it. It was amazing how quickly he could position the limb, in such a tight space, with only one hand at his disposal.

"I'm not worried about all of Ireland," Claire said. "Just your family."

"They're going to love you," he said. "Remember, what's not to love?"

Claire smiled meekly. She hadn't met a boy's parents in twenty years, back when she dated *boys*. Considering the last parents she met were Jack's folks, and that hadn't turned out all that well, Claire was doubly nervous.

Lightning didn't strike twice, right?

All she could think was she hoped not, as the people in front of them began to move down the aisle, and she stood with Callum to disembark.

As it turned out, Claire shouldn't have spent even a millisecond worrying about Callum's family.

"Callum!" a voice boomed the moment she and Callum cleared customs and made their way to the luggage claim area.

Before she could find the source of the voice, she and Callum were surrounded by a circus of people, all talking and laughing and hugging—Callum, her, each other. She lost sight of Callum in the crowd, but figured he was still close as she could make out his laughter, intermingled with more Irish accents than she'd ever heard in one room.

"We're so thrilled to meet you, Claire," an older woman said, once she finally let go of Claire, whom she'd held in a big bear hug for more than a quick moment. "Callum has told us so much about you."

"He has?" Claire said hesitantly. She knew she should've asked Callum, before they'd left on the trip, what he'd told his family about her. She'd thought they'd have the entire flight to discuss his family and what they knew about her situation, plus what their plans were for the time they'd be spending in Ireland. Instead, the only thing she'd learned on that flight was that flying over the ocean made her very tired.

"Yes. Yes," the woman said, nodding vigorously. By the sparkle in her eyes that mirrored the one Claire always saw in Callum's, she knew this must be his mom. Or Mam, as Callum called her.

"I'm Nora," the portly woman said to Claire. Her hair, Claire imagined, had once been jet-black, but was now more salted with gray. Her eyes were as green as a shamrock and her smile as contagious as her son's. Linking her arm in Claire's, Mrs. Fitzgerald directed her toward the exit.

"Um," Claire said, glancing over her shoulder. "My bags..."

"Oh, don't worry about that. Callum and the men will get them. It'll take a while to get Callum's chair. It always does. No matter how many times he flies in and out of here, they always somehow manage to lose his chair," Nora said. "Isn't that so, Jilleen?"

Claire suddenly noticed a very pregnant woman on the other side of her. The woman, who looked to be quite a few years younger than Claire, smiled in agreement with Nora, but Claire noticed she had her hands full with a crowd of small children. Four little ones were running around her as she hurried to keep up with Nora.

Claire slowed down her steps, causing Nora to do the same. "You're Callum's sister-in-law, aren't you?" Claire said. "I heard you were going to have your fifth baby any day now. You must be exhausted."

"You have no idea," Jilleen said. Her words were said casually enough, but it was the look of horror that flooded her face that told Claire all she needed to know. Callum had definitely told his family about her losing her children.

"These must be your other babies," Claire said, loosening her arm from Nora's and bending down so she was eye level. She'd learned from experience that if she kept talking, or changed the subject, the person who had just put his or her foot in their mouth would eventually regain their composure. "How old are you?" she said to a particularly adorable red-haired girl.

"Free," the little girl said, holding up three fingers, her voice a lisp. She answered Claire, but kept her eyes focused on the ground.

"And what about you?" Claire said to a boy who wasn't much bigger than the girl.

"I'm four," he said.

"That's Keara," Jillan said, indicating the little girl. "And this is Emmet." Her hand rested on the boy's head, red like his sister's, but not quite as vibrant. "Over there are Hugh and Riordan." She pointed to where two blond boys were wrestling each other on the airport floor. "They're five and six."

Callum wasn't kidding. His brother and his wife sure didn't waste any time between babies. Though since their youngest was already three, they'd apparently learned a little bit about spacing kids out.

"This is another boy," Jilleen said, her voice wistful as she patted her baby. "But, at least I got my Keara."

"Boys run in our family," Nora said, taking hold of Claire's arm again. "We were all so thrilled when Keara was born! I couldn't believe after two sons and three grandsons, I could finally buy some dresses!"

"Boys!" Jilleen called. "Come on. We're all going to the car to wait for Uncle Callum, Dad and Grandad."

Claire was surprised by how quickly the boys got off the floor and obeyed their mom. She wasn't sure her kids had ever done what she asked of them without her having to say it three or more times.

As they moved through the airport doors, Nora let go of Claire's arms to grab hold of the the two blond boys. Claire was surprised to feel a small hand slip into hers.

When she looked down, the greenest eyes, even greener than her grandma's, shone up at her.

"Thanks for holding my hand," she said to Keara. "I don't really know where I'm going."

Claire was rewarded by one of the prettiest smiles she'd ever seen. It hurt her heart, a bit, to have a little girl smile up at her and have her not be one of Claire's own daughters. But that feeling passed quickly, as they reached the van and all the kids piled inside.

"We stopped using this van for quite a few years, after Callum left. No need for a disability vehicle when your disabled son no longer lives with you," Nora said cheerfully. "But, once Fin and Jilleen started popping out all these young ones, Patrick and I decided we'd better give the van a good tune-up and get it back on the road again. It works out perfectly, seeing as it now seats ten people."

"Claire, you should sit up front," Nora said, as she pulled herself into the second row of the van.

"Oh, no!" Claire said. "Jilleen, you must be so uncomfortable. You take the front seat."

"And deny myself the joy of hearing Patrick interrogate the woman of another one of his sons, instead of myself? No, thank you. I look forward to sitting back here as a member of the audience."

Claire's expression must have given away her panic, as Jilleen and Nora burst into gales of laughter.

"Not to worry," Nora said. "Callum won't let him ask too tough a question."

"At least not til after dessert," Jilleen said, giggling. She had a lovely laugh, like the lilt of a harp and the ease with which she laughed made Claire smile.

"Okay," Claire said, hesitantly, turning to walk around the vehicle to reach the passenger-side door. "I'll sit shotgun," she added, wondering if that expression would make sense to them here in Ireland.

"Not that way, you won't," Nora called out after her. For a moment, Claire thought the expression must have confused her.

"But..." Claire said.

"That side is the driver's side," Nora said, a big smile on her face. "This one's the passenger's."

Claire peeked inside the window of the car and saw Nora wasn't joking this time. Despite Callum having mentioned it, more than once, Claire had forgotten the driver sits on the right side of the car in Ireland.

She sat next to Callum's dad, clenching the sides of her seat as he wove in and out of traffic. She wasn't sure what the speed limit was in Dublin, but she was fairly certain Patrick was exceeding it.

"Need a bucket yet?" Callum called up to Claire. When he, his brother and his dad had reached the van, Callum had, very happily, removed his prosthetics and Fin had stuck them in the back with the rest of their luggage. From there, Callum had been delegated to the back seat, in between Hugh and Riordan, who were using Callum's body as a road for their toy cars and his leg stumps as ramps into the wide unknown.

"Getting there," Claire said, swallowing to keep the nausea down. It wasn't just the speed that was making her dizzy, though that was extreme. Claire found herself closing her eyes, whenever they reached an intersection or they merged onto a road, certain they were moments from being struck head-on as they careened into oncoming traffic. Though that never happened, because the traffic wasn't oncoming at all. No matter how many times, per second, Claire reminded herself the turns Patrick was making were not only legal, but correct for the side of the road he was driving on, she still grimaced each time he made one.

If Patrick was aware of her uneasiness, he didn't show it. Jilleen had been correct when she'd say he'd want to interrogate Claire. The questions had begun the moment he'd slid into the seat next to her.

By the time Claire was done answering all his questions, at least the ones he was able to fit into their forty-five-minute drive home, she felt she had a clear-cut image of how he'd been as a politician. Patrick left no stone unturned, covering her education, employment, hobbies, habits ("Not to worry! I know everyone has some vexatious ones") and past travel.

He'd even managed to learn about Gia during his questioning of her college friends. The only topic he didn't probe into was family relationships, which proved to Claire she'd been correct the moment she'd seen the look on Jilleen's face. Callum had told all of them about her parents, Jack and the kids.

It was just as well. She hadn't really expected him not to tell them. If she were dating a man who'd lost his entire family, she was certain she would've told her family about it before she brought him home. That is, if she still had a family to tell.

Plus, having them all know, in advance, really made life easier for her in a number of ways. She didn't have to wait for the right moment to tell them. Didn't have to watch the awful looks on their faces when they heard her tale. Didn't have to do the telling at all.

"So, Claire, what do you want to see and do while you're in Ireland?" Fin asked her as they pulled up to Callum's parents' home.

Callum had been right. His brother didn't look a thing like him and it wasn't just because Fin had two arms and two legs. He was so blond Claire could have mistaken him for Swedish or Swiss if she hadn't heard his Irish brogue and been told he was biologically related to Callum. Despite his light hair, Fin resembled his mother more than his dad. Whereas Callum looked a lot like his dad, both men bearing chiseled features and a thin build, Fin was a bit more on the hefty side, like his mom. His belly rolled a bit over his belt, most likely a result of good home-cooked meals and a lack of time to exercise. He also wasn't as tall as Callum, though Claire knew that was a ridiculous comparison since Callum wasn't technically as tall as Callum, either.

His eyes were blue, but not the kind of blue Callum had. Whereas, Callum's eyes were a deep cobalt-blue, Fin's eyes were a lighter, powder-blue, which reminded Claire of the soft blue of Luke's old baby blanket. Fin's eyes weren't nearly as striking as his brother's, but they were kind, and they put Claire at ease.

"Well, I'm not sure," Claire said, her voice hesitant.

"Oh, don't let that innocent act fool you," Callum called out from the back seat. Claire could see the boys were now using the stump of Callum's arm as if it were a gun, taking turns moving it, shooting imaginary bullets at one another. "She has a folder as thick as your thumb, full of notes of where she wants to go."

Claire turned around in her seat and glared at Callum for calling her out.

"Go on," Callum continued. "Tell them where you want to go or I'll have to do so. Because I certainly don't want you missing out on anything you have your heart set upon."

"Truly, Claire, tell us," Nora said as she opened the side door to the van and gingerly stepped out. "We'd like to know what an American might think exciting about Ireland."

Claire opened her door and got out, too. "I'd like to see the Dublin Castle and one of the churches, either St. Patrick's Cathedral or the Christ Church Cathedral. And I'd really love to visit Kilmainham Gaol."

"Ah, the prison," Patrick said, as he walked to the back of the van to retrieve Callum's chair. "They've an excellent tour there."

"She'd also like to kiss the Blarney Stone," Callum piped up.

"But I know that's close to three hours from here," Claire said, not wanting Callum's family to feel as if she planned on imposing her plans on all of them. "I understand if we aren't able to fit that in on this trip."

"And why wouldn't you?" Patrick said. "You're here for two weeks. Plenty of time to get to Cork."

"She's worried because she's read that some of those places aren't exactly wheelchair accessible. And, despite my agility on my legs, she fears those tiny stairs and uneven halls would be rough for me."

"And she's right," Nora said matter-of-factly. "But why is that an issue? I love going to all of those places and," she leaned in to Claire and continued with a stage whisper, "Callum would be bored silly in most of them. Wherever you want to go, you let me know and I'll drive you there myself."

Claire peered into the van at Callum, who was still trapped in the back row with his nephews. Jilleen had run inside to use the loo as soon as they pulled up to the house and Fin was struggling to get a crying Keara out of her seat. No one had attended to the two blond boys, who still had their hands all over Callum as if he were one of their stuffed toys. Callum, to his credit, seemed nonplussed by the physical affection and Claire found that endearing. He nodded reassuringly at Claire as she looked at him, wide-eyed and nervous. She wasn't sure she was ready to spend that much time alone with his mother. He mouthed, "You'll have fun," and winked.

"Okay, Callum," Patrick said, finally wiggling Callum's chair from the back and gliding it up to the side of the van. "This chair used to fit in here better before we added all these extra seats for your nieces and nephews."

"It used to fit right in the middle of the van," Callum explained to Claire, as he freed himself from the boys and slid around the middle row. "I could roll right in. The vehicle used to have a ramp."

"But we removed that part when we decided to convert the van to make it more useful to our current occupation—taxi driver for our grandchildren."

"Plus, once I started driving on my own, we rarely used the van anymore."

"True," Patrick said, steadying the chair as Callum hopped down into it. "Once Callum had his license, we rarely saw him. It was if he'd found his sea legs, so to speak."

Jilleen was back at the van now, reaching inside to retrieve her boys. "Come on. Hurry now. We haven't got all day. Grandma's serving tea."

Claire had to remind herself, as they all made their way into the house, that by "tea" Jilleen did not mean a hot beverage. Instead, she meant dinner, the family's main meal for the day.

It smelled delicious in the house and Claire, who hadn't eaten since they left Atlanta sometime yesterday, was embarrassed to hear the grumble of her stomach when she walked into the dining room.

"Someone's hungry," Fin said jovially, as he strapped Keara into her highchair.

"I'm sorry," Claire said, her face reddening. "I guess it's been awhile since I had anything to eat."

"No need to apologize," Callum said, rolling up behind her. "The fact you're so ravenous will make Mam's day."

He put his hand gently on Claire's hip, and she smiled at him. It felt so odd to be in the home where Callum grew up. It was larger than she'd expected. She'd assumed most people in Europe and the UK lived in tiny homes. The kind of homes Ikea had in mind when they designed their space-savvy furniture.

As Callum explained to her after dinner, they were an unusually well-off family for that part of the world. "My dad came from family money, and then he was a solicitor and, finally, a politician. We have a smaller home in Dublin, right in the city, but as a family, we mostly spent our time here.

"It was cozier," he said. "But also, much more accessible to me and my chair. It's not easy to make a brownstone in the middle of the city wheelchair ready, no matter how hard you try."

The first thing Claire had noticed was how adaptive his home was to Callum's disability. All the doorframes were wider than average and there were ramps to both the front and back doors. Callum's bedroom was on the first floor and, when Claire peeked in there, she saw all the furniture was low to the ground. Even the dresser was long, and not tall, with two rows of three low drawers. The light switch in Callum's room reached Claire at mid-thigh. The mattress was on a pallet on the ground. The desk was designed like an architect's desk, but had the shortest legs Claire had ever seen. The poles in the closet were the height of Claire's waist.

"Well," Claire said when she first walked around his room. "This is an interesting room."

"Looks like a dwarf lives here, doesn't it?"

"Um, kind of." In Atlanta, Callum's house was wheelchair accessible, but most of the fixtures and furniture were the normal height and his bed, though Claire hadn't spent a whole lot of time in it yet, was definitely of average height, but Callum did have a stepstool next to it.

"I spent my youth on the ground," Callum said, by way of explanation. "I was rarely in my chair. I crawled on the floor, using my arm to drag me around on my bum. I use my chair a lot, now that I'm an adult. I got used to having to do so when I lived in a dorm in college. You look a little weird crawling on the floor and I was desperate to fit in as best I could once I left home. But, as a kid, I spent more time on this floor than in any wheelchair and certainly more than on my prosthetics."

"I see."

"I love my home in Atlanta. Don't get me wrong. And, I'm used to using my chair most of the time, and my legs at other times, but I am, truth be told, most comfortable bumming around on the floor."

He was in his chair now, but Claire saw something in his eyes that troubled her. Was he asking her for something? Permission? Acceptance?

"Are you saying you'd rather not use your chair while you're at home?"

Callum glanced away from her. He seemed incapable of meeting her eye. It startled Claire. It was the first time since they'd met, he'd seemed at all uneasy with her. Vulnerable. Worried she wouldn't fully embrace him as he was.

"Callum, if you don't want to use your chair here, that's fine with me. Honest," she said, turning her head toward him. "It won't bother me."

"It won't make you uncomfortable?" he asked, his eyes fixated in such a way, she wondered if he were challenging her to say she'd be bothered by it.

"No," Claire said, though that wasn't completely true. She had rarely seen Callum, up until this point, getting around on the ground. He was most always in his chair or on his legs. Still, she knew that, however he got around here in Ireland, she would get used to it. Most everything became normal once you experienced it long enough.

Callum looked like he might want to say more, but then shook his head and didn't.

Claire felt this might be the best time to change the subject.

"So, Fin and Jilleen sure do have a lot of kids."

Callum smiled then. "They sure do. Good thing all those chiselers are so damn cute."

"I'm assuming that means children."

"Aye."

Callum and Claire left his room and returned to the living room where the rest of the family had gathered after tea. The conversation was light and easygoing, with a lot of teasing and even more laughter. Claire had been so worried she'd feel uncomfortable with Callum's family and was relieved to realize she not only felt welcome, but perfectly at home.

She looked over at Callum, many times, during the evening. He would smile back at her, but she could sense an uneasiness in his eyes. She noticed, despite their conversation earlier, he never got out of his chair, even when his family asked him if he was going to ride along for the whole visit or relax a bit.

"You're home, buddy," Fin said, as he and Jilleen got up to head home. He had a sleeping Emmet in his arms, while the other three kids slept on the couch. Fin would have to carry each of them out to the car, one by one. "No need to act like you're in front of a crowd. We know the true you."

"And love you," Nora said, running her hand along Callum's back as she came to kiss Fin and the sleeping Emmet good-bye.

Callum and Claire said good-bye to Fin and Jilleen. They'd all see each other again tomorrow for the evening church service. It would be Christmas Eve and the family had plans to all go to church together. After that, Fin, Jilleen and the kids would come back to Nora and Patrick's home to spend the night, so they could all wake up together on Christmas morning and experience the children's excitement together.

Claire was a bit concerned about watching someone else's children open their presents with joy on Christmas morning, as she mourned the loss of her own, but pushed the thought from her mind. Christmas was still two days away. She couldn't think about it just yet. That was a worry for another day.

When the others were gone and Nora and Patrick had said they were heading up to bed, Claire looked at Callum and shrugged.

"Guess it's just you and me."

He'd smiled at her, but it wasn't the same vibrant smile she was used to.

"You must be exhausted," Callum said. "Jet lag isn't for sissies."

She was exhausted, but not as tired as she'd expected to be. Her long sleep on the plane had helped her avoid the crash once they'd landed in Dublin.

"Want to talk for a bit?" Claire asked.

"No. If it's okay, I'd like to head to bed," Callum said. "You might not be exhausted, but I am."

Claire did her best to hide her disappointment. She knew he wasn't lying about being tired, but she wasn't quite ready to let him go for the night. Callum wasn't acting like his usual self and Claire had hoped, if they spent a little time alone, she could jostle him back into place.

"Sure. I'll head upstairs."

Nora had shown Claire her room as soon as they'd walked in the door. Claire got the feeling she was silently laying down the ground rule that Claire would have her own room and not be sharing one with Callum.

Which, of course, was fine with Claire. She would never have expected to stay with Callum in his parents' home. It seemed inappropriate and rude. Plus, Callum and Claire weren't in the habit of spending the night together. She'd fallen asleep with him on his couch a few times and slept there until morning, but she and he had yet to fall asleep in his bed.

Most likely because they were yet to do *anything* in his bed.

She bent down and kissed him on the lips.

"I love you," she said.

He nodded and, for a moment, Claire wondered if he was going to say anything back.

"I love you, too," he finally whispered. And though Claire knew the sentiment was sincere, she felt a hesitation in his words she'd never sensed before.

CHAPTER TWENTY-FOUR

If Callum wasn't himself the night before, he showed no signs of it in the morning. Claire was relieved to see the vivid smile lighting his face when she came down to breakfast the next morning.

"Morning, sleepyhead," Callum said, as she walked into the kitchen. "We were beginning to make bets on whether you'd wake before noon."

"My money was on one o'clock," Patrick said, lowering the newspaper he was reading. "It's a good thing we hadn't finalized anything yet, as it's only...," he glanced at his watch, "eleven twenty-four."

Claire sat down at the table, which was full of bacon, sausage, eggs, baked beans and Irish soda bread. She took in the scene, startled by the amount of food.

"Are you having company for breakfast?" Claire asked, turning to Nora, who was at the stove, already preparing the evening meal, knowing everyone would walk in the door, famished, when they returned from church.

"This is how my mam cooks anytime I'm home," Callum said, sticking a piece of bacon in his mouth. "Isn't it grand?"

Claire, who was used to nothing more than raisin bran and coffee in the morning, had to smile at the smorgasbord in front of her. Her waistline couldn't afford for her to eat like this forever, but for the next couple of weeks, she felt she could make the exception.

"Baked beans for breakfast?" Claire said, startled to see them on the table.

"Callum told me, on our first trip to America, that people there only eat baked beans at barbecues. Americans don't know they're missing out on a wonderful breakfast treat."

"Apparently not," Claire said, spooning a plentiful serving onto her plate.

"So, the plan for today is that we hang around here all day," Callum said. "I have a few presents that still need to be wrapped."

"And I could use some help in the kitchen, if you don't mind, Claire," Nora said.

"Of course not," Claire said. "I love to cook." And she did, though she had a feeling Nora needed no help preparing the meal. She wanted to spend time with Callum's girlfriend and it was the worst-kept secret in Ireland.

"Enjoy your cooking with my mam," Callum said. "You'll be happy to know she doesn't let me do any of the cooking while I'm here."

"Does he scare you, too?" Claire asked his mom.

"Terrifies me," Nora said, with a wicked grin. "I taught him to be self-sufficient, but my heart couldn't take him in the kitchen."

"I'm right there with you," Claire said, putting a forkful of eggs into her mouth.

"What are you going to do, Dad?" Callum asked.

"Read my paper," Patrick said, not lowering the news this time as he spoke.

"Well, then, I guess I'll leave you to it," Callum said. He paused for a moment, glancing at Claire, before he hopped off the chair and onto the floor. "I'll be in my room if anyone needs me."

He began to scoot out of the kitchen without looking at Claire again.

"Hey," Claire said softly, touching his shoulder.

He looked up at her right away, but his face was impassive.

"I love you," she mouthed.

This time he didn't hesitate. "I love you, too," he mouthed back, as he used his arm to pull himself out of the room.

Claire watched him go. She would be lying to herself if she didn't say it was a jolting sight to see Callum on the ground like that. It made him seem so much more vulnerable. So much more *disabled*. She hated to think that way. In America, he was so sure of himself, so confident. And yet, bumming around on the floor, as Callum called it, well, it was different. It was going to take Claire some time to get used to it.

As if reading her mind, Nora broke the silence.

"You're not used to seeing him like that," she said. It was a definite statement and not a question.

Claire paused, unsure how to respond. Finally, she decided honesty was the best choice.

"No."

"We weren't used to seeing him in his chair so much, or walking, the first time we came to America. It seemed odd to us, just as I imagine seeing him get around on the ground is to you."

Claire nodded.

"You don't need to be ashamed of feeling uneasy. Callum is not your typical man, in any sense of the word. With him, you get immense strength and confidence and, dare I say it as his mam, sex appeal."

"Nora, will you, please?" Patrick bemoaned from behind his paper.

"I'm merely saying I would understand why Claire might see a dichotomy between the Callum she knows in America and the one he is here. He could, of course," Nora said, looking back at Claire as she stirred something in a giant pot, "continue to act, while he's here, as the Callum you know in America. He would do it, if it made you more comfortable. But..." Her voice trailed off for a moment and then regained its composure. "I get the sense you want to know the true Callum, with all his faults and limitations, and not just the one he portrays on his best days. Am I right?"

Claire nodded. Nora was right. She did want to know every aspect of Callum. Even the ones that might make her a little bit uncomfortable.

"My advice to you, Claire, having lived and loved Callum for all these years, is not to pretend something doesn't make you uncomfortable when it does. He'll see right through that. He's been down this road many, many times, with friends and extended family members and school mates, even employers. And not only will he see right through it, he'll start not to trust your feelings when you say what they are. That would be the beginning of the end and I get the sense you have no interest in reaching the end, do you, dear?"

"Nora," Patrick warned, from behind his paper.

"Okay, okay," Nora said, returning her attention to her pot. "I'll stop now. Enjoy the rest of your breakfast, Claire. There's no need to hurry. But, when you're done, I could really use some help preparing a salad for tonight."

Claire nodded and poured herself a cup of coffee from the pot on the table. Nora was right. She and Callum hadn't kept any secrets from each other up until this point. She had no intention of keeping them now.

If she thought about it, the whole situation was really about nothing more than geography.

Considering all she'd overcome thus far in her life, geography was something she could handle.

It turned out, handling Callum on the floor proved even easier than she'd expected. Once she got used to seeing him there, which only took a few hours, Claire barely gave it a moment's thought.

"You look beautiful," Callum said, as Claire walked into the living room in the dress she was going to wear to church. He was in a suit, which made him look even more handsome in Claire's eyes, and back in his chair.

She didn't comment on the chair, but he did.

"The floor would cause me to get lint on my suit," he said and Claire merely nodded in response.

"Everyone ready?" Patrick said, pulling on his winter coat in the hallway.

"Yes," Nora said, hurrying into the living room, already wearing her coat. "Come on. Come on. If we don't get there early, we won't get a seat."

Claire grabbed her coat off the chair and had to hurry to catch up with Nora, Patrick and Callum, who were already out the door and heading to the van.

"Um, do I need to lock the door or something?" Claire called after them.

"No, dear," Nora said, opening the passenger-side door to the van. "We don't do that here."

The church service was beautiful and Claire found herself tearing up at more than one part. Callum squeezed her hand numerous times during the program, a silent reminder he knew the holiday was going to be difficult for her, but he was by her side.

Claire wasn't just teary-eyed over her lost family. She felt her eyes fill with tears over the beauty of the Irish music in the large cathedral. It all seemed so peaceful, so sacred. It was how Christmas Eve should feel in church and Claire was very, very grateful she was getting to spend it here.

When the family returned home, they immediately convened to the dining room. The children, who were fidgety little munchkins in church, were wearing out and more than once, Claire had to gently lift Keara's head from the table, in order to keep her hair out of her soup.

"We'd better get them to bed," Fin said, once the meal was complete, but dessert had not yet been served. "They'll be up early enough tomorrow."

Claire offered to help him carry the children to bed, seeing as Jilleen was too pregnant and Callum wasn't able to help.

"Oh, you don't have to," Fin said.

"It's okay," Claire said, lifting Keara to her hip, as the girl rested her head, sleepily, on Claire's shoulder. "I'd like to."

Fin nodded in agreement as he hefted Hugh onto his shoulder. The kids were all going to be sleeping in one of the guest rooms upstairs, next to where Claire was staying. One of the nice things about Callum's parents' home was it had plenty of rooms. It fit Callum and Claire and his brother's entire family with ease. They probably could've had about three more families in here and it wouldn't have seemed snug in the least.

Claire carried Keara up the stairs, remembering, fondly, how many times she'd carried her own children to bed. None of them had ever grown too heavy for her to do that, not even Luke, as he'd been small for his age. Claire was grateful for that small blessing. She would've been so sad on the day she went to lift one of them and realized she no longer could.

Claire gently placed Keara in her bed and pulled the covers up to her chin. The girl looked so peaceful in her sleep, but then, didn't all kids? Claire used to joke to Jack, "I sure do love our kids when they're sleeping."

She bent down to kiss Keara on the forehead before she left the room. Jilleen and Fin were so blessed to have such beautiful children. She was pleased with herself that she felt no jealousy at that thought. Just joy. Joy that beautiful children still existed in this world. And, for this moment, she was given the gift of being with them.

Christmas morning came all too quickly. Claire felt she'd just closed her eyes when she heard the squeals of little children and tiny footsteps on the hardwood floors.

For the briefest of moments, right before she opened her eyes, she wanted to say, "Jack. Tell them it's too early."

But within a second, she knew there was no Jack. Those children she heard weren't hers. They were Callum's nephews and niece. They were someone else's little angels, anxious to see what Santa had brought them.

Claire didn't want to cry. Truly, she didn't. And, after carrying Keara to bed last night, she'd thought she'd be able to handle this morning with minimal agony.

But she'd been wrong. Her chest hurt. Her eyes stung. She wanted to go back to sleep and find it had all been a dream. Her children weren't gone. They were downstairs, waiting for her to descend the steps, so they could begin to open her gifts.

She put her head into her pillow and began to cry, as quietly as she could. She didn't want any of the others to hear her. She certainly didn't want to put a damper on any part of their holiday.

She wasn't sure how long she wept. She knew, by the sounds of talking and the screams of joy from the children downstairs, the present unwrapping had commenced. She wiped the tears from her face and wondered how she was going to go down there and act as if nothing were wrong.

There was a slight knock and then the door to her room opened ever so slightly.

"Claire?" The voice was Nora's. "Can I come in?"

Claire wiped at her face again and sniffled as quietly as she could. "Okay."

Nora tiptoed into the room, as if she was afraid of waking someone, though Claire didn't know who that could be. By the noise level, it seemed everyone else was up and having a wonderful time.

"Callum asked me to come check on you. He has a difficult time on our stairs. It seems he's not as spry as he was as a child."

Claire nodded. "I'm okay. I'll be down in a bit."

Nora walked the rest of the way into the room and sat on the end of Claire's bed. "You don't have to come down until you're ready. And, if you're never ready today, that's okay, too."

"Oh, no," Claire said, mustering as much strength as she could. "I'll be down. I just need to get my act together."

Nora sat silent for what, to Claire, seemed like an endless amount of time. So endless Claire began to wonder what the woman could possibly be thinking.

"You know, I don't know what it's like to lose your children," Nora finally said, breaking the silence. "In a way, I can't possibly imagine the anguish. But," she said, her eyes on the papered wall in front of her, "I think I have a better understanding of the pain you're feeling than most people.

"When Callum was born, I thought the entire world had collapsed. To me, having a child be born like that was worse than if he'd died at birth. I'm ashamed to admit it, but I did wish he'd died at birth. I couldn't function at all. I don't know if Callum has told you, but I couldn't even bear to hold him. I didn't get out of bed for months."

Claire nodded. Callum had told her.

"Of course, you know this," Nora said. "You've probably heard him tell that story a thousand times, each time he gives a speech. But, I want you to know he's not just telling some story. He's telling *my* story. And it was a long, painful, and miserable one. One that, at times, I feel I might still be living.

"The pain didn't end once I adjusted to the way Callum looked and began to interact with him. I grew to love him and, once again, I'm embarrassed to admit, loving him wasn't immediate, like it should be between a mother and her child. I had to *learn* to love him. But, even once I did that, and I loved him with a fierce and fiery passion, it still hurt. Every time I'd go to a park or see a mom in church or look at the other children in the grocery store, being pushed in the cart, all of them with four limbs, it would hurt. I'd finally gotten out of bed, but I didn't want to leave the house. I didn't want to see what other moms had. I didn't want to see other people's children. I couldn't bear the jealousy that they got to live their lives with perfect children and I didn't. I had this little boy, who was so severely disabled, and I had to find a way to not only accept that, but to raise him so that he, himself, didn't see his frailties, but instead, saw his strengths."

Claire sat up in bed, positioning the pillow behind her.

"Of course, there was no way to completely do that. Callum, more than anyone, was aware of his limitations. But I did my best to shelter him from the pain of this world or, at the very least, impart to him the tools he'd need to face that pain head-on and survive."

"You did a remarkable job," Claire said, meaning it sincerely.

"Well, that's sweet of you, dear," Nora said, patting Claire's leg, under the covers. "I didn't tell you all that so you'd feel sorry for me or praise me." She looked at Claire now, her eyes full of both sadness and understanding. "I told you this so you'd know you're in a home full of people who understand true pain and there's no judgement here. What you're going through is not easy. I imagine the hurt never truly goes away. Even now, I sometimes see handsome men on the street, in their suits, heading to their offices or I see a male model on a billboard, whose face isn't nearly as beautiful as Callum's, but his body is whole, and I can't help but think, 'Why?' Even after more than thirty years, I have to ask, 'Why?'"

"And do you get an answer?" Claire asked.

"Because," Nora said, and then shrugged. "That's the best answer I get. Because." She grinned at Claire. "It's not a good answer, but it's the only one I've been able to come up with and it's the one I hold on to. Some things just happen 'because.' And I have to learn to live with it. End of story."

Claire smiled at Callum's mom. She liked this woman. She could see why Callum loved her so much.

"Callum says there's a plan. For him. For me."

"Callum has more faith than me, always has. Where I see nothing more than 'because,' he sees a true reason. I'm not there yet, but I hope to be someday."

"Me, too," Claire said.

"I know you're missing your babies. And your husband. And, I imagine your mam and dad. But, if you'll let us, we'd love to shower you with love today. We can't take away the pain, but we can cover you in our love."

Claire's eyes filled with tears again. She almost didn't want to make the request, but then found she couldn't stop herself.

"Can I ask you something?" she said softly.

"Certainly."

"Do you think I could have a hug?"

"Of course, my dear," Nora said, her own eyes spilling over with tears. "Of course."

She wrapped her arms around a crying Claire. The embrace didn't take away the pain, but it helped. It helped to soothe some of the hurt Claire had felt as she woke on this Christmas morning.

For now, that was enough. It wasn't the way Claire would've wanted to spend Christmas morning, but it was enough.

With that realization, Claire took a deep breath and let herself fall into an embrace, an embrace that felt like the one of a mom. The one *her* mom would have given her if she'd still been alive.

CHAPTER
TWENTY-FIVE

"Now that you've spent nearly every day sightseeing with my mam, I want to take you somewhere special," Callum said as Claire came down to breakfast.

She and Callum's mom had spent the past week traveling all over Ireland, first heading into Dublin and then to areas of the country that were further away. If Claire had wanted to experience Ireland, she'd certainly done so. Not only had she and Mrs. Fitzgerald, who insisted Claire call her Nora, gone to the places Claire had mentioned she'd like to visit, but also many more. They'd seen the castles and cathedrals and prison Claire had wanted to visit and then visited the National Gallery of Ireland, numerous museums, and the remains of an old abbey, where Claire had gotten some wonderful photos amongst the ruins.

"Let's go to the Guinness Factory and the Old Jameson Distillery," Nora had said, during one of their days in Dublin.

"I don't know," Claire had said. "I don't drink, so I'm not sure how interesting I'll find them."

"Oh, nonsense," Nora had said. "You can't go to Dublin and not drink a Guinness. It's unpatriotic."

And so, because Claire found she had great difficulty in saying "no" to Nora in any way, they'd gone to both the factory and the distillery, where Claire had sampled some of both wares. The Guinness actually tasted good to her, but she quickly learned she was not an Irish whiskey fan, and one sip was more than enough.

Nora had laughed at Claire, as she herself, quickly downed her shot.

Claire had simply shaken her head. Callum's mom was quite the character and though she and Claire differed greatly, in their zest for life—Claire tended to ease into things like a turtle, slowing gliding into the water, while Nora climbed up the high dive and jumped straight out, arms waving, a scream of elation bursting forth—Claire couldn't help but adore the woman.

Nora made for an entertaining travel buddy. Never short of a tale to tell, she kept Claire amused by anecdotes from her children's childhoods to sagas about their neighbors in both Dublin and the country. According to Nora, the city ones were too uptight with "a couple of sticks up their arses" and the country ones were a bunch of "Frankies." Claire hadn't been sure what that meant until Callum later explained it was a less-than-complimentary name for people from Belfast, whom some Dubliners viewed as lacking in sophistication.

"Oh, really?" Claire said to Callum after he informed her he'd be the one in charge of today's plans. She poured herself a cup of coffee. Callum had already prepared oatmeal for her and it was steaming at her place at the table. Between his mom's cooking and Callum's always-ready breakfast and coffee for her every morning, Claire was getting spoiled.

"Oh, yes. Hurry up and eat, then go get dressed. We've a bit of a drive ahead of us."

"I can't wait," Claire said and meant it. A day alone with Callum was a gem. She'd been fully enjoying her time with Nora, and she knew Callum was getting in some much-needed bonding time with his dad and Fin, but Claire missed her time alone with the man she loved.

She was glad to see he seemed to be missing it, too.

It turned out that by a "bit of a drive," Callum meant close to four hours.

"Are we almost there?" Claire moaned, more than once.

"Nearly, love. Nearly," Callum would say. And then drive another hour.

She finally convinced him to stop for lunch in a small fishing village called Doolin, where Claire had the most amazing bowl of clam chowder she'd ever tasted, along with two slices of hot Guinness bread.

"The Irish sure do like their Guinness," Claire noted, as she took another bite of the bread. "You even put it in your bread."

"Aye. And in our stew, on our salmon, in our chocolate mousse, in our seafood cream sauce..."

Claire couldn't help but laugh. "I hate to think what you all do with your whiskey."

"Well, my mam's been known to add it to a steak marinade. And her cupcakes," Callum said.

"Her cupcakes?" Claire cried.

Callum grinned. "I should say I'm kidding. However, I'm not."

"Oh, heavens," Claire said, finishing up the last drop of soup. "That was wonderful."

"Not as wonderful as where I'm taking you. Are you ready to go, my love?" Callum stood up from the table. He was wearing his legs again which, to Claire, seemed so odd. It was funny how, a little more than a week ago, seeing him without his legs or his chair had seemed unusual to her and now seeing him standing seemed so strange.

"Lead the way."

Claire was relieved when Callum finally pulled into a parking lot and said they were at their destination. The sign in front of them read "Cliffs of Moher."

"You are the worst car tripper ever," Callum said. "How did I drive across the country with you this year and not know that?"

"I guess I hid it well," Claire said. "Or maybe I only bitched to Alison."

"Poor Alison," Callum muttered. "Okay, time to get out."

He opened the car door and went around to the trunk. Walking back over to Claire, she noticed he was holding an aluminum forearm crutch.

"What's that for?" Claire asked, surprised. In all their time together, she'd never seen Callum use a crutch.

"I think I may need this today. We'll be doing a good deal of walking and look..." He took her arm and turned her around.

At the end of the parking lot was an enormous staircase. It seemed to go on forever.

"Um, how are you going to climb those?" Claire asked, the hesitation in her voice heavy.

"Very, very slowly."

"Isn't there a ramp?"

"Not one that will take us as far up as I want to go," Callum said, adjusting the crutch.

"I don't know about this," Claire said, looking again at the staircase. There had to be a couple of hundred steps there.

"Come on," Callum said. "It'll be an adventure."

"If you say so," Claire said.

As Callum had said, they took the steps slowly. Callum was not great with steps on his best day, but with the incredible gales of wind hitting them now, each step seemed to take twice as long as normal.

Claire wanted to ask him, again if he really wanted to do this, but stopped herself. It was clear he did or he wouldn't have driven her four hours here. Whatever was at the top of these stairs was important to him.

Dozens of people hurried past them during their hike. Callum didn't seem to mind and, frankly, neither did Claire. She'd learned, over the past months, life with Callum had to be taken at a slower pace, even though he did his best to move at full steam. It was simply that his full steam ahead was slower than most.

They said few things to each other as they climbed. Claire asked him what was so special about these cliffs, but all Callum would say is, "You'll see," and then struggle to mount a couple of more steps. Claire felt a few drops on her arm and she prayed, fervently, the rain would hold off. She couldn't imagine getting all the way to the top and then have it pour on them.

Her prayers were answered when, just as they reached the last few steps, the sky cleared and the sun came out.

"I did it," Callum said, his breath rapid, a ring of sweat on his collar.

"You did it," Claire said, smiling up at him.

"Let's find a place to sit," Callum said. "Before we go any further."

"Further?" Claire said. "We're going to walk more?"

Callum winked at her. "It'll be worth it. I promise."

They found a bench and took a few minutes to let Callum rest and catch his breath. Claire was tired, too. The steps weren't easy to climb, even if you did have two legs. Claire had lost her own breath a hundred steps ago.

Claire leaned back on the bench and looked around her. There were a number of tourists, all milling around, looking over the long stone wall in front of them. Claire could see a bit of the cliffs from where they sat, but mostly she saw sky, the view obscured by the people and the wall.

They sat in silence for a bit until finally Callum said, "Okay, let's go," and got to his feet again.

Claire wanted to ask him if he was sure he didn't want to rest a bit longer, but she refrained. She knew when Callum made up his mind to do something, he planned on doing it. Now.

The two of them walked over to the stone wall and looked out. Any breath Claire had left in her from the upward trek was taken away the moment she saw the view.

Massive cliffs sprung from the water along the coast, as far as the eye could see.

"They're magnificent," Claire said, her voice reverent at their majesty.

"They span five miles," Callum said. "On a clear day, you can see the Aran Islands, Galway Bay, Aill Na Searrach and Hags Head, all in the distance."

"I'm speechless," Claire said.

"Well, that's something different. You, with no words?" Callum said, bending to kiss her head. "Come on."

His hand, which was still holding the crutch, nudged her to the right.

"I see more steps," Claire said. "We don't need to go any further. I can see all the cliffs from here."

"No, you can't," Callum said. "Trust me. Besides, these steps aren't so steep and there aren't as many."

They walked slowly, Claire taking in the view as she moved. She'd never seen anything as spectacular. Not even the Grand Canyon had left her so astounded.

"I feel like I've now seen Ireland," Claire said, gently holding onto Callum's forearm.

"Okay," Callum said. "Now for the best part." He pointed to a dirt path, off to their right. A large sign stood in the center of it.

Claire walked closer to it and read the words carefully.

The Burren Way: Cliffs of Moher Coastal Walking Trail

There was a paragraph that explained exactly where the trail would take you and how it linked the villages of Liscannor and Doolin, stating you would be able to view one of the most outstanding landscapes of Ireland.

The words that caught Claire's attention, though, were the ones that said, in bold letters, *Caution! Exposed Cliff Edges.*

"Ready?" Callum asked eagerly.

"Ready for what?" Claire asked.

"For our hike," he said.

"Our hike? Have you read the sign?"

"I certainly have, love. We should get started before it gets too windy."

"Callum," Claire said, her eyes jumping between Callum and the sign. "You're already exhausted from the stairs."

"Oh, stop worrying. We won't be walking that far. Certainly not all the way to the next village. I just want to go a ways down."

Claire looked back at the sign.

Trail features include an exposed cliff-top path, steep ascents and descents, and narrow, steep flagstone steps. The trail may be rough and uneven in places with loose gravel and stone. This walking trail requires an ability to adapt to sudden and possibly extreme changes in weather and a level of physical ability to undertake a demanding length of walk in adverse conditions.

"You're out of your mind," she said, upon reading it.

"It'll be fine. I promise."

"Callum, it says, *'Always wear strong footwear with a good grip and strong ankle support.'* You don't even have ankles!"

"You're such a worrier," Callum said, resting on his crutch. "As I said, we won't be walking far down the path. Just a little ways."

"Have you done this before?"

"I've been down this path before," Callum said, nodding.

Claire paused and looked him up and down, then back at the sign, then out at the trail.

"Okay," she finally said. "But just a little ways. And you walk in the inner part of the trail. I walk on the side closest to the edge."

"Aye. Except, of course, that the trail is so narrow, we'll have to walk one-by-one."

Claire opened her mouth to object, once again, but Callum put his lips to hers and silenced her.

Claire let him lead the way, mostly because she wanted to see him at all times, in case she needed to grab him before he fell off the cliff.

The path was narrow. The people who'd written the sign hadn't been joking there. But there were sections that were far enough away from the edge that Claire could relax for bits of the journey. In a few sections, if they climbed up a small embankment, they could actually walk away from the path and walk, instead, next to open livestock fields.

They walked in silence a bit, Claire mesmerized by the views of the cliff. She was so busy enjoying the view she didn't notice the small dip and, without warning, lost her footing.

In a fast attempt to steady herself, she reached out for the wire fence next to her and grabbed hold.

"Ouch!" Claire shrieked, yanking her hand away.

Callum whirled around. "What happened? Did you twist your ankle?"

"No. Yes. I mean, I tripped, but it's not my ankle that hurts. It's my hand," she said, shaking it. "I just got the weirdest feeling through my arm."

Callum looked at Claire's hand and then the fence next to them.

"Did you touch the fence, love?" Callum said slowly.

"Yes! I was falling."

"So you grabbed hold of an electric fence to stop your fall?" His eyes lit with humor.

Claire looked at the fence and couldn't help but smile. The tingle she'd felt through her hand and arm was subsiding.

"Oh, no!" Claire said, laughing. "I got shocked."

"I bring you to Ireland and you try to electrocute yourself? Seriously, Claire. And you were going on and on about how the trail was too dangerous for me? It seems it's you we have to worry about. I can't take you *anywhere.*" His eyes were bright and Claire could tell he was enjoying teasing her.

Claire slugged him, playfully, on the arm.

"Okay," Callum said. "I think we've gone far enough. Let's go sit over there." He pointed to a sloped patch of grass, close to the edge of the cliff, but not so close it made Claire nervous.

The two of them walked over to it and Callum asked Claire to help him get onto the ground. Slowly, the two of them sat and caught their breath.

"It's amazing," Claire said, casting her eyes out to sea. "No. Amazing doesn't cover it. Spectacular. Marvelous. Magnificent. I can see why you wanted to bring me here."

"And put up with all your moaning?"

"Hey!" Claire said. "I had reason to moan."

"And I have a reason, now that we're comfortably seated here, in the most beautiful place on earth, to say, 'I told you so.'"

"Thanks for bringing me here. I've never been somewhere so lovely."

"With someone so handsome. Don't forget the someone-so-handsome part."

"With someone so handsome," Claire said. "So, is this where you take all the ladies?"

"Only the ones I like," Callum said, a grin spreading across his face.

"I figured...since you said you've walked this path before," Claire said, sitting up on her elbows to draw in the remarkable view.

"I said I've been down this path before. I never actually said I've walked it."

Claire looked down at him in confusion.

"I came with my parents as a young boy. My dad carried me."

Claire shook her head. "If you had told me that, I would've never agreed to this walk. I thought you'd done it before!"

"I know you did. And, I knew you wouldn't agree to go if I said I hadn't."

Claire took a deep breath, a huff intended for Callum.

"And, now that we're here, aren't you glad I didn't tell you? Look at all you would have missed out on."

He pushed his hand against the ground and sat up, alongside Claire. He bent his body closer to her, nudging her with his shoulder.

She frowned at him and then looked back at the cliffs.

"Would it make you feel better if I told you that, on that day with my parents, I knew if I was ever blessed enough to meet the love of my life, I'd bring her here and, on these cliffs, declare my love for her?"

Claire said nothing for a moment. She wanted to continue to sulk, but she couldn't. Staying mad or annoyed with Callum for more than a few moments was an exercise in futility.

"Well, it does make me feel a little bit better, since I'm the one you brought here."

"You are the one I brought here," Callum said. "And, do you know why that is?"

"Because you want to declare your love for me?" Claire said, a giggle escaping her lips.

"Because I want to declare my love for you. On the most majestic cliffs in all of Ireland, the land I love most, I want to declare that never have I loved anyone more. And never will I again."

He kissed her then and Claire breathed in his essence. She didn't love him more than Jack. The thought of that would make her feel too guilty. She loved Callum in a different way. A way that was all his own, but every bit as strong as the love she'd had for Jack.

And she knew, just as Callum did, even if she lived to be a hundred and ten, she'd never love anyone more than she loved Callum at this very moment.

Not even close.

CHAPTER
TWENTY-SIX

Patrick was sitting under a tree in the front of the house, smoking his pipe, when Callum and Claire got home later that evening.

"Did Callum show you a good time today?" he asked Claire, as she and Callum got out of the car.

"It was incredible," she said, her face still flushed with the excitement of the day. "I've never before been anywhere more beautiful."

"I'm exhausted and want to get these legs off," Callum said to Claire. "Are you coming in?"

She glanced at Callum's dad and the empty chair next to him. "If your dad doesn't mind, I think I'll stay outside with him a bit."

"I'm not a man who can turn down the company of a lovely woman," Patrick said.

"Okay, have fun," Callum said, heading into the house. "Try not to scare her away; okay, Dad?"

"I'll do my best, son."

Claire sat down next to Patrick and stretched out her legs.

"I'm exhausted, too. I can see why Callum wants to get those legs off. Mine are stiff from being cramped in that small car all day."

"You wish you could take yours off, too?" He grinned.

"For a bit," she said, smiling.

"How are you enjoying Ireland?"

"I'm having a wonderful time. I've never been overseas before and I couldn't imagine a better first international trip than this one. You and your family have made me feel very welcome."

Patrick smiled. "I'm glad you feel that way. We've loved having you here. We were all very happy when Callum told us he'd met you and fallen in love. As a father, you hope and pray your child will find happiness in life. Unfortunately, we weren't always sure that'd be possible for Callum."

Claire remained silent. There was no need to ask Patrick to clarify his statement.

"I hope you'll allow me to speak my mind," he said.

"Of course."

"As I'm sure you're aware, Callum told us all about your family before we met you. I haven't mentioned it to you before now, though Nora did tell me she and you had a talk about it."

Claire nodded.

"Having a son born like Callum certainly wasn't easy. We had no idea. No warning."

Claire nodded again. She knew about their unwelcome surprise. Callum always mentioned it during his speeches.

"So, I gather Nora told you we understand a little bit about your loss, because we experienced a loss of sorts when Callum was born."

Patrick took a puff at his pipe. Claire wasn't sure if he expected her to say something or not.

"I had a little brother," Patrick continued. "He was ten years younger than me. A surprise to my parents. They thought they were done having children. I already had four older brothers."

"That's a lot of boys."

Patrick smiled. "Indeed it was. His name was Tomas and, from the moment he was born, he was my favorite person in all the world. My older brothers were gone, by then, with lives of their own, and my mam and dad, they were pretty tired of raising kids by that point. They didn't neglect Tomas, in any way. He was loved and well taken care of, but they no longer had it in them to entertain and play with a small child.

"Tomas was my little shadow. He followed me everywhere and,

despite being a pre-teenage boy, I didn't mind it one bit. He could always make me laugh. Also bring a smile to my face. My friends were all used to him always tagging along. Dare I say it, he was the light of all our lives."

Claire smiled at Patrick's memory of such a sweet child.

"When I was fifteen years old, I went away for a month to an apprentice program. I think in the States, you'd say I was working as a page in the senate. You know, where young people work on the senate floor, delivering legislative materials and correspondence in the governmental complex. It was a great opportunity for me, especially since I was already showing an interest in the law. My parents were so proud when I was selected.

"Tomas, though, was heartbroken. He couldn't bear the thought of me going away for so long. He was only five and to him, four weeks seemed like an eternity. I held him on my lap and promised him I'd be back before he knew it. And, if he was a very good boy, I'd bring him some special treat from my travels."

Claire didn't know where this story was going, but she suddenly had a feeling the ending wasn't going to be a happy one.

"One night, while I was sleeping in my dorm, I had a terrible dream. More disturbing than any one I'd ever had before. It seemed so real. I'd dreamt that Tomas was missing and no one could find him, but I could hear him. He was screaming my name. Over and over again. I heard him call to me, but no matter where I looked, or how fast I ran towards the sound, I couldn't find him. It bothered me so much that the next day, I called home and asked my mam to put him on the telephone. She said he was playing out in the barn with some of our young cousins and to call back later that night.

"I went back to work, but couldn't shake the feeling of uneasiness. As soon as we broke for tea, I ran to the phone and called my house again. There was no answer. It rang and rang and the knot in my stomach grew. I knew something was wrong.

"It took me forever to fall asleep that night, but not long after I did, I was awakened by our house mother. The police were with her. There'd been a fire at my parents' home. The barn had burned down. We later learned Tomas and our little cousins had been playing with matches. All three of them perished, along with many of our animals."

Claire gasped and put her hand to her mouth.

"That's awful. I'm so sorry."

Patrick turned and looked at Claire, a softness in his eyes, but no tears.

"My mother never recovered from the loss. She didn't live much longer after that. Not even ten years, and I believe most of those were spent in bed. The loss of a child, her baby, was more than she could bear."

Claire closed her eyes. She could feel Patrick's mother's agony. It was her own.

"I was never the same after that, either. I'd lost the person I loved most in the world. You never get over that, do you?"

Claire shook her head.

"I'm not telling you this to be morbid. I'm sorry if I've put a damper on your day. I just want you to know I saw what losing my little brother did to me and especially to my mom. It destroyed her. Completely."

"I understand that feeling."

"You are a remarkable woman, Claire. Not only do you make my son happier than I've ever seen him before, and love him for who he is in a way I've never seen him accepted by anyone else, but the fact that you're here, today, talking to me and laughing with our family, making a new life for yourself, I want you to know how much I admire you."

"That's sweet of you to say."

"I'm not just saying it to be kind. My mother couldn't do it. And before Tomas's death, she was the strongest person I knew. No nonsense. But losing him was a blow she couldn't get back up from. I wished, year after year, she would somehow find the strength to carry on, but she never did. She didn't have it in her. When he died, for all intents and purposes, she did, too. You have done what is nearly impossible, Claire. Every day you move a step forward, you honor your family. Your husband and children must be so proud of you. I'm aware you don't know me all that well, but I want you to know, I'm proud of you, too."

Claire's eyes welled with tears. She wasn't sure why knowing Callum's dad was proud of her meant so much. She barely knew him. But somehow, she was honored by his words.

"So, now that I've nearly ruined the happy mood of the day, let's try to salvage it by going inside and helping ourselves to some of Nora's biscuits. She's been baking all day."

"Because I haven't gained enough weight on this trip?"

Patrick stood and patted his belly.

"Nora shows her love through her cooking, as you can see. She's loved me in abundance all these years. She loves you a great deal, too. We all do."

With a smile, he put his arm around Claire's shoulders as together, they walked toward the house.

Claire said good-bye to Ireland much too soon. She'd never before been so sorry to leave a place as she was to leave Callum's home country.

"Oh, stop your crying," Nora had said to Claire as they hugged good-bye. "You'll be back. And we'll be in the States to visit all of you in no time. I hear Mitch has a craving for my biscuits," she said, winking at Callum over Claire's shoulder.

"He was so disappointed when you had to cancel your trip last fall 'cause Dad got the flu. He says he loves visiting with you, both, but I know he was after Ma's pastries."

"As he should be," Patrick had said, hugging Claire next. "Your ma is the best cook in Ireland."

Claire had agreed with Patrick. Nora was a spectacular cook and baker. There had not been a single biscuit or meal she'd prepared that Claire had not devoured in an instant.

Except for the black pudding.

There was no way Claire was going near that black pudding.

"So," Claire had said, when she first laid eyes on the round puck on her plate. "This is blood?"

"Aye," Callum had said, cutting into his.

"Like, real *blood?*" Claire had asked.

"Yes."

"Pig's blood?"

"Uh-huh," Callum had said, putting a forkful in his mouth. "But, you know, it's mixed with a few other things. Oatmeal, pork fat, an onion."

"But mostly it's blood," Claire had repeated.

"Yes," Callum had said, cutting off another piece.

"There is no way I can eat that," Claire had said, resisting the urge to gag.

"That's fine."

"And I need you not to eat it, too."

"What? Why can't I eat it?" Callum had asked.

"Because, if I see you take one more bite of that, I'm going to throw up all over your mom's table and that won't make any of us happy."

Callum had muttered something under his breath, but he'd put down his forkful of black pudding and not eaten it again on the visit. At least, not while Claire was around.

Other than being repulsed by the popular Irish delicacy, the trip to

Ireland had been the best journey of Claire's life and she was definitely sad to see the time there end.

As soon as they returned to the States, though, Claire was too busy preparing for their next excursion to even think about Ireland. The team would be in America for less than a month before heading over to Europe and then the northern part of Africa. They'd be gone for two full months.

There was plenty to do. Callum was busy working on the seminars, tailoring them so they were appropriate for the foreign countries and the needs of those people, in addition to lining up local speakers and leaders to conduct sessions. Wyatt occupied his time ordering wheelchairs, walkers and canes and arranging to have them shipped to their destinations so they could be dispersed to those who needed them in each country. Alison was making sure flights and hotels and transportation were in order. Mitch was working to ensure they knew, in advance, which locations were designed to be handicapped accessible and which were not. Many European, and especially African, countries were not as wheelchair-friendly as America. Claire and Frank were busy selecting and rehearsing new music, songs that would work best so that the meaning was well understood in each country. They were also tasked with lining up translators for their music and Callum's talks in numerous languages.

To say the team was working at peak capacity would have been an understatement.

They were so busy, Claire almost forgot Gia was coming for a visit the week before they left.

"Hey, love. Don't you need to leave for the airport?" Callum asked.

Claire looked at the clock on the desk. She'd been busy corresponding, via email, with a translator who spoke both French and Hungarian.

"Damn," Claire said, jumping up from her chair. "If I don't hurry, Gia will be standing at baggage claim, wondering where I am."

"Drive safely," Callum said, as she leaned down to his chair to kiss him.

"Always."

Claire was careful to maintain the speed limit as she drove, but it wasn't easy. Not only was she aware Gia's flight had landed twenty minutes earlier, but she was so incredibly excited to see her best friend. It had been close to six months since they were together and Claire couldn't believe it. On one hand, the time had flown by. Claire had been so busy and often barely had time to sleep, but on the other, she'd missed Gia terribly and couldn't believe she'd had to live without her closest friend for so long. The two had never been apart for more than a couple weeks, ever since they roomed together in college.

Claire sped through the airport's arrivals' lane and prayed no cops were hanging around, waiting to meet their speeding ticket quota for the month. Gia had texted Claire and told her she was waiting outside, having already picked up her bags.

Claire came to a hard stop in front of where Gia was standing, quickly threw the car in park and jumped out. Running, Claire practically jumped on Gia in the excitement to get her arms around her friend.

"Whoah. Whoah," Gia said, laughing. "It's not like we've been apart for years."

"Just six months," Claire said, letting go, but grabbing hold of Gia's hand. "Six long months. I've missed you so much." She felt the tears well up in her eyes. She'd known she missed Gia, but she hadn't realized she'd missed her friend this much.

"No crying. No crying," Gia said, laughing. "Or you'll make me cry, too."

"Okay," Claire said, wiping away the tears. "No crying. This is a happy day. I'm so glad you're here." She picked up Gia's small carry-on bag and swung the strap over her own shoulder.

"I can tell!" Gia said, an enormous smile on her face. "But it's not like you've been pining away for me in your hotel rooms. Rumor has it you've been busy with a certain man." Gia's voice faded, her tone teasing, her laughter light.

"I might have been a little bit preoccupied," Claire said coyly. "Come on; let's get to the car and back to my place."

"I wish you could stay longer," Claire said, when they were finally on the highway.

"I know, but I could only get one day off work. At least we have the full weekend."

"True. I'll take what I can get."

"So, when do I get to meet him?"

"Meet who?" Claire asked, though she knew.

"Callum, of course! When do I get to meet this man who seems to walk on water?"

"Actually, he doesn't do much walking at all," Claire joked.

"So what *does* he do?" Gia asked, her voice sly and knowing.

"We haven't actually done that yet," Claire admitted.

"You haven't *done* that yet?" Gia said, her shock permeating the car. "How long have you been together now?"

"Long enough," Claire moped.

"What's the deal? Is it because of...you know..." Gia waved her arm around her whole body, which Claire took to indicate her limbs, or, more likely, Callum's missing ones.

"Well, not in the sense of him not being able to complete the act. I've been reassured that all things are in working order."

"So, then, what's the deal? After he said that, did he say any more about putting those working parts to actual work?"

Claire sighed. She wanted to laugh. Gia was trying to be funny, but it was a topic that had begun to trouble her quite a bit. She and Jack hadn't had sex until their wedding night. She'd been young and viewed sex as sacred. She still viewed it that way. She'd wanted to wait to lose her virginity as a bride.

But, she really had no plans to marry Callum. She had very little desire to ever marry again. It wasn't that she didn't love Callum. She loved him deeply, with a love she hadn't known she was capable of feeling, or giving ever again. But she'd already been married and the end of that marriage had devastated her. She couldn't bear to experience such a loss, ever again.

That didn't mean, though, she didn't desire a physical relationship with Callum. She was incredibly attracted to him and though she was still nervous about seeing all of him at once, that fear was lessening over time. Claire wanted, and it was bordering on needed, something more. Something deeper. She wasn't sure, though, why Callum didn't seem to be moving in that same direction.

"Honestly, I don't know. I mean, I really, really don't understand," Claire said, glancing away from the road for a minute. "We're pretty serious about each other. We're together all the time. He's very passionate when he kisses me."

"And then?"

"And then he's not. He's not rude when he pushes me away. There's no out-and-out rejection. He just eases away when I try to do more, or he changes the subject. It's weird. A little awkward," she said. "Okay, *very* awkward."

"Have you asked him about it?"

"No."

"Why not? I thought you've said you two talk about everything."

"I guess I should have said 'almost' everything."

"Well, you need to add this to your list of things that need to be discussed pronto," Gia said. "I mean, come on, Claire. You must be horny as hell!"

Claire shook her head and glanced over at her friend. "Nice, Gia. Nice."

Gia laughed. "Okay, well, maybe I'm projecting my sexual frustration onto you."

"Are you kidding me?" Claire asked in exasperation. "You're single again? What happened to the mechanic?"

"His hands were too dirty."

"But this one didn't touch dead people. Didn't he get extra points for that?" Claire sighed loudly.

"Maybe you can introduce me to someone here," Gia said. She was clearly joking. She knew Claire was not a skilled matchmaker and Claire had given up even trying. She'd set Gia up on three dates over the course of their friendship and none of them had made it past date one. There had been no fettuccini alfredo for them. Claire had stopped trying after that.

"Yeah, okay. I'll think about that."

Claire turned the car into the parking lot of her apartment complex. "Home, sweet home."

Gia scanned the large brick building in front of them.

"Is it weird living in an apartment again?"

"No, it's fine. Easy to keep clean." She knew Gia was thinking about the large home Claire had waiting for her back in Florida. Claire thought about it, on occasion, too. Though she tried to minimize the time she spent dwelling on it. That house, though full of happy memories, was also a great source of sadness for Claire. She hadn't yet decided what to do about it. She realized she'd probably sell it, in time. She just wasn't ready for that yet.

Claire glanced at the clock on the dashboard.

"Okay," she said. "We have about an hour until we're meeting Callum for dinner. Let's go in, you can shower and get all freshened up, and we'll head out. And I wouldn't mind taking a thirty-minute nap."

The two women were dressed and ready to go exactly one hour later and a short time after that, were walking into the restaurant where they were to meet Callum. He'd texted Claire, ten minutes earlier, to say he was already at the table.

Claire spotted him the minute they walked in the door and waved.

"He's in the back," Claire said to Gia, as she led her friend to him. Callum looked exceptionally handsome tonight. The bright blue of his shirt brought out the deep sparkle in his eyes and Claire could tell he'd made an effort to try to tame down his curls, as opposed to letting them run wild. She wondered if Alison had insisted on it.

"Callum, this is Gia. Gia, Callum," Claire said, waving her hand between the two of them.

Callum put out his hand to shake Gia's.

"I hope you'll forgive me if I don't stand up," Callum said, his eyes glinting with humor.

"Oh, um," Gia faltered. "No. That's fine." She looked at Claire, uncertainly.

"Callum thinks he's funny," Claire said easily, kissing Callum on the lips before she took her place next to him.

"Thinks?" Callum said. *"Thinks?* I am quite funny, love."

"Oh, yeah," Claire said, rolling her eyes. "As Wyatt would say, you're a hoot and a howl."

Gia giggled. "Claire has been telling me a lot about Wyatt and his colorful expressions."

"Oh, Wyatt is something else," Callum said.

"I'm hoping Gia will have the chance to meet him while she's here," Claire said, lifting the menu.

"So, Gia," Callum said, turning his body to indicate she was about to have his full attention. "I hear you know Claire better than anyone else. Please tell me all about her, starting in college. And, don't leave anything out. The more embarrassing the story, the better."

"Oh, brother," Claire said, refusing to lift her eyes from her menu. She could only imagine the stories Gia would share. She certainly had enough of them, especially from their wild college days. But that was okay. Claire didn't mind Gia telling Callum anything she might want to reveal. She had no secrets from Callum, from either of them. And if bonding over her silly teenage antics would bring her two favorite people closer together, then they could laugh at her expense, all evening long.

And laugh they did. The only person who found Callum even funnier than Callum found himself seemed to be Gia. By the time the waitress brought over the dessert menus, Claire could tell Callum had won Gia over. Which, of course, came as no surprise to Claire. Callum had a way with people. He not only put them at ease, despite how awkward things might be when they first saw his body, but he brought out the best in people. They relaxed around him. They laughed.

He made them feel important.

Claire loved that about him.

Claire loved a million things about him.

"Okay, ladies," Callum said, placing his napkin on the table, at the end of the meal. "I'm going to have to take my leave now. I'm sorry."

"Oh? Already?" Claire said with disappointment. She'd been having so much fun with the two of them, she didn't want the evening to end.

"Already," Callum said sadly. "I have a stack of work that I need to get done and it's taking me longer than I thought. Besides, I'm sure you want me to leave so you can talk about me." Callum winked at Gia and she smiled.

"It's only fair," Gia said. "You made me spill the dirt on Claire. She should get to do the same on you."

"True, true." Callum rolled his chair over to Gia. "It was lovely to meet you, Gia. Claire has told me what a good friend you've been to her and for that, I could never thank you enough. A friend of Claire's will always be a friend of mine."

"Thanks," Gia said, a smile crossing her face.

"Do you think I could give you a hug?" Callum asked. "A handshake feels so formal, now that you've told me all about how Claire used to flash for beads at Mardi Gras. Who knew she was such a trollop?"

"You two think you're so funny," Claire muttered as Gia and Callum burst into laughter.

"Of course, you can have a hug!" Gia said to Callum, with enthusiasm, ignoring Claire's grumbling.

Gia bent down to give Callum his hug and they parted ways, still smiling over the delightful evening they'd had together.

Gia waited until Callum was out of the dining room before she turned to Claire.

"He's *amazing*," she gushed.

Claire beamed. "I know. He is, isn't he?"

"He's so handsome. Even more so in person than in the pictures I've seen. And those eyes..."

"Okay, down, boy. He's mine," Claire said, though she couldn't help but grin. She'd known Gia would love Callum and she was so happy to see herself proven correct.

"And he clearly adores you. He barely took his eyes off you the whole evening."

"You mean, when he wasn't staring at you, pleading for more embarrassing stories about me."

"Oh, yes. When he wasn't doing that."

"But..."

Claire looked up, startled. She hadn't expected a 'but.'"

Gia continued, "Are you sure you know what you're doing?"

Claire eyes widened. "What I'm doing?"

Gia shrugged.

"What I'm doing," Claire continued. "Is spending time with the man I love. I'm in a relationship with an incredible man. You said so yourself."

"An incredible and *incredibly disabled* man."

"Gia!" Claire's voice rose in shock. "You, of all people; never did I think you'd see his limitations first."

Gia reached across the table to grab Claire's hand, but Claire pulled it away.

"Claire, I didn't see them first. In fact, he's so amazing, it's easy not to see them at all. But because you tend to forget he's missing his limbs, doesn't mean they aren't still missing."

"Honestly, Gia." Claire couldn't believe what she was hearing. She had never, before, been so disappointed in her friend.

"Hear me out, Claire."

Claire shook her head in disgust.

"I mean it, Claire," Gia said firmly. "You've been through so much in your life...losing your parents...then losing Jack and the kids. Isn't it time for you to catch a break?"

"Catch a *break?*"

"No matter how wonderful he is, and he *is* wonderful, a relationship with Callum is going to come with a whole new set of challenges, things you can't do together. Perhaps additional health concerns. Even the way people look at the two of you."

"Do you think I care about the way people look at me?" Claire asked, her voice stone cold.

"No, I don't. But, Claire, you have to recognize you're just in the beginning stages of a romance. Everything seems great. All obstacles feel like they can be met with force. But once you and Callum get into the rut of being together for a long time, will the extra work and pressure his disability puts on you become more of a burden than a challenge?"

"You don't understand."

"Claire, I do. You're in love. No one is more thrilled to see you happy than me. I don't want to see you get hurt again and, to be honest, this looks like it could have hurt written all over it. Or, if not that, then a whole lot of struggles that might best be avoided."

"But, don't you see? That's what draws me to him. Sure, I could find a nice man to fall in love with who's never experienced tremendous pain, but how could he ever possibly understand me?

"Gia," Claire continued. "Before I met Callum, I had no idea how I'd ever move on. And then, I met him. He's full of joy, Gia. *Joy*. He deals with more challenges in one day than most people face in their entire life and yet, he's happy. Ridiculously happy, as he puts it." She reached across the table and put her hand on Gia's. "And he makes me happy, too."

"I am happy for you, Claire. Really. I am. I'm just worried," Gia said, shrugging.

The two woman sat quietly staring at one another, a chasm of shared sadness and pain between them.

Finally, Claire shook her head, as if to shake the melancholy away.

"Oh, hush," she said, patting Gia's hand before removing her own. "You know what your problem is? You worry too much."

"Oh, is that what my problem is?" Gia asked, smiling slightly. "I thought it was I couldn't meet a man who doesn't still live with his mother."

"That, too," Claire said, grinning before her face grew serious once more. "It's gonna work out, Gia. I can feel it."

Gia sighed deeply, a sigh of resignation and fear for her friend. "Okay. If this is what you really want, what will make you happy, then I'll support you one hundred percent."

"It is."

"But, sweetie," Gia said, leaning in closer to Claire, "if it's ever not what you want anymore, I'll support that, too."

"I know," Claire said, her eyes brimming with tears. What had she ever done to deserve a friend like Gia? "That's why you're my best friend."

"Really?" Gia said, leaning back in her seat again. "I thought it was because I knew all your secrets and letting me go would be a liability."

"You didn't seem to have an issue with revealing my secrets tonight," Claire mumbled, but she was smiling.

Gia lifted her water glass in the air. "To joy!"

Claire lifted hers alongside Gia's. "To joy."

CHAPTER
TWENTY-SEVEN

Claire had thought a month would have been plenty of time to get the trip in order, but found they were all still scrambling, on the last night, to make sure the final details were in place.

And then they were off. If the time in Ireland had flown by, the months overseas zoomed past like the speed of light. Many nights, Claire would drop in bed, too exhausted to remove her clothes, only to wake up and wonder what country they were in. France and Spain blended into Italy and Austria, which then blended into Romania, Bulgaria and Croatia.

Callum was, to most people, especially those in Eastern Europe, such an oddity. Living in countries that often regarded the disabled as trash to be hidden away in institutions or forced to live on the street, the people were fascinated to see such a disabled man be so independent, not only supporting himself financially, but drawing crowds of thousands of able-bodied people to hear him speak.

In each country, each village, each city, Callum spoke to those who came to hear him about pain. His pain, their pain. Different perhaps in the way it presented itself, but the same in the way it wounded and damaged souls and lives and families.

He talked to the crowds about how everyone, each and every one of them, had been born for a purpose. The greatest discovery they could ever make in their lifetime was to find out why they were born. What gift did they have? Things as visible as music or art or athletic ability or things as subtle as compassion and empathy. How would they use those gifts?

Were they stuck in the circumstances of their lives? Could they not move past their pain, their physical ailments or financial woes, even the grief of losing a loved one?

"Everywhere I go," Callum would say, "people come up to me and tell me their stories. They tell me about their pain. All of us have pain. Not just people who look like me. Or people who might look like you. The beautiful girl you see in the corner café—I'd bet you all the money in my pocket she has pain. The football player who wins the national title for his team—he has pain, too. Not everyone's pain is visible. Not everyone wears their pain on their sleeve, their only sleeve." He'd chuckle then, setting the crowd at ease about his disability. "Like me.

"The thing is," Callum would say, "as I listen to each of these stories— and some of them are too horrific to process—I'd hear and feel the pain, but I would also see a message of empowerment in every tale. I would see how each of those past hurts can be used to help others. The fact of the matter is, no situation is all good or all bad. Most circumstances are a combination of both. Sometimes, though, we get so focused on the bad parts, the sadness, the misery, the physical and emotional pain, that we miss the parts that are good. The parts that could be *exceptionally* good if we'd only spend a little bit more time focusing on those parts and not so much time being consumed by the bad ones.

"This is how you turn that pain around. You turn it into power. And the way you do that is, you give *meaning* to the pain. You find the *purpose* in it. You let go of the anger and the bitterness and you find *the plan*. There is always a plan. I promise you. There *is* a plan. You weren't just dropped on this earth for no reason. I wasn't born without limbs for no reason. I might not always *think* there's a reason.

You might believe there's no reason you're suffering right now. But we'd be wrong. There is a plan. I promise you that. And if a guy who looks like me is able to believe there's a reason he was born looking like this, I find it hard to believe there isn't a plan for your pain, too."

People loved Callum. Everywhere they went, no matter what country or language or economic level, people were drawn to him. They waited in line, sometimes for hours, to see Callum, talk to him, touch him. They came with their children and their elderly relatives, in wheelchairs, on crutches or carrying the weak on their backs.

Claire had never before seen such pain. Nor had she ever seen such hope. Callum was able to grab hold of the hurt these people brought with them and reveal how to turn it around. He'd remind them to never quit, to never give up. He'd remind them that Nelson Mandela spent twenty-seven years in prison, only to become the Prime Minister of South Africa when he was released. But more importantly than that, Nelson Mandela had found a purpose for his pain. He became an agent of change and forgiveness in a nation torn apart by apartheid.

"Nelson Mandela had every reason to be bitter," Callum would say. "I mean, I'd be really pissed, if I were him. Twenty-seven years in prison? You can never, ever get that time back. But he didn't get out of prison to lie on his bed and cry. He didn't decide he was entitled to a life of luxury and self-indulgence for all the pain he'd been through. He took his pain, his horrible, horrendous experience, and turned it into power. And, I don't mean the power he had as the Prime Minister. I mean he turned it into a power that would help millions and millions of people. He knew there was a plan for all those horrendous years in prison and he set out to find it.

"If there's a plan for a man who spent more than a quarter of a century in a dirty, nasty cell, can you see that maybe, just maybe, there might be a plan for you, too?"

Claire loved their seminars. She never tired of hearing Callum speak. Never tired of seeing the crowds and the people he touched. Never tired of meeting the leaders in each community and hearing what they had to offer during their talks. Claire loved every part of those days.

But, what she loved even more than that, were the smaller crowds, the quiet visits to hospitals and orphanages and private homes. In every place they visited, the team, or sometimes just Callum and Claire and Mitch, would seek out those who were truly in need and go to them. They'd find the ones who couldn't come to Callum and they'd bring Callum to them.

As amazing as Callum was in front of a crowd, Claire found him to be even more remarkable during the quiet time he spent with the people who seemed to need him most. He'd sit with an old woman and share a cup of tea with her at her kitchen table. He'd hold the hand of those lying in hospital beds, ripped apart by land mines or dying from AIDS. He'd get out of his chair and roll around the floor of an orphanage, while all the little children would touch his stumps in wonder and then, once they became used to him, would climb all over him or play kickball and dodgeball with him.

Callum would joke that he thought the kids were trying to knock him down like a bowling pin, but Claire knew they could relate to him in a way they'd never been able to relate to anyone before.

The first few times they visited a hospital, Claire struggled. There were so many beautiful children struggling with sadness beyond their years. It broke Claire's heart to know they had no home. She, too, wanted to get down on the ground and play with them, but something always stopped her. How would she be able to play with these children, hold them, hug them, and not wish desperately for her own? The thought of kissing the head of another little girl, who wasn't Ella or Lily, was almost too much for Claire's heart to bear.

Callum would glance at her, compassionately, across the room, as children pushed him over and giggled on the floor next to him, and smile, his eyes conveying an understanding that he recognized her aching and was proud of her that she'd been strong enough to join him today.

By the third orphanage, Claire could barely stand it, not the pain of missing her kids, but the desire to be on the ground with them, like Callum was. She couldn't resist picking up the baby who reached out to her from his crib or comforting the toddler who wouldn't stop crying.

Claire was a mom. She might not have children living in her house anymore, but the love she had for little ones still lived in her heart.

She knew Callum noticed the shift when she began to interact with the children. He'd laugh and smile at her when she'd join in on the kickball games in the courtyard.

"Hey!" he yelled once, when she kicked a particularly hard ball in his direction. "Are you trying to knock me down, too?"

Claire had laughed at him, with him. It felt so good to laugh, along with all the children who were laughing, too.

She missed her babies, every second of every day. But she also felt herself healing a little bit more, every time she pulled a child onto her lap or braided the hair of a little girl or gave a walker to a little boy who, before now, could only crawl across the floor.

They weren't her babies, but they were still special, still in need of tremendous love. And, if she could provide that for them, even for a moment in time, she'd do so with all she had in her.

Every child deserved to be loved. And Claire knew, especially now that she no longer had her own children, she had an abundance of love to give.

CHAPTER TWENTY-EIGHT

"What's wrong?" Callum said, the minute he entered Claire's hotel room and saw the expression on her face.

She shook her head, as if to say, "Nothing," but the sob that followed was a clear indication that wasn't true.

"Come on, love," Callum said, riding his chair over to her, and putting his hand on her back. "What's going on?"

Claire wiped at her tears and turned her laptop screen to Callum. He began to read the opened email.

"Wow," he said, when he had finished it. "I'd say they're not happy."

"You think?" Claire said sarcastically, though she certainly wasn't in a joking mood.

"What prompted this?"

"I sent them an email when we got back from Europe. I thought telling them about us was the right thing to do. I tried to say it as carefully as possible. I knew it would hurt them, but I tried to do it as gently as I could."

Claire had sent Jack's parents an email sharing with them her relationship with Callum. She felt she owed it to Bill and Nancy to let them know she'd met someone, that she was in love and finally finding some happiness after the tragedy. Though she never thought they'd be thrilled about it, she hadn't anticipated this angry, visceral reaction.

"Your in-laws sure don't mince words, do they?" Callum asked.

"They accused me of never loving Jack!" Claire said, a sob escaping her again. "Of finally being free of the burden of a family!"

She put her hands to her face and began to cry again.

"I thought you said your father-in-law was usually kind," Callum said.

Claire nodded, her face still covered.

"This letter doesn't sound too kind."

Claire took a deep breath and grabbed a tissue from the nearby box. She wiped her eyes again and blew her nose.

"I'm sure he wasn't the one who wrote this. To be honest, he might not even know she sent it. He might not even know about you. Knowing her, she probably never even told him."

Callum reread the email, inhaled deeply and then blew his breath out forcefully.

"Okay, then," he said. "What are we going to do about it?"

"*Do* about it?" Claire asked, blowing her nose again. "What is there to do about it?"

Callum chuckled at the fear he saw pop up in her face. "I mean, what are we going to do to calm down your mother-in-law?"

"I don't think there's any chance of calming her down. She feels I should be in mourning for the rest of my life, which, to her, means me not having a life."

"Well, that's ridiculous."

"Try telling her that."

Callum looked like he was about to speak, then paused.

"I think I will," he finally said.

"*What?* Oh, my gosh, you can't."

"Why not? Are you afraid I'll go in, guns blazing, and tell them off?" Claire paused. "I don't know."

"Oh, come on, Claire. You know me better than that," Callum scolded. "Of course I wouldn't do that. And I wouldn't do anything to hurt you, either."

"So, what are you thinking?"

"They live in West Virginia, right?"

Claire nodded.

"Where are we going to be speaking in two weeks?" Callum asked.

"Oh, no," Claire said, uneasy about where Callum was going with this train of thought.

"Oh, yes," he said. "Let's invite them to our seminar. Though I wouldn't ask your mother-in-law, if I were you. I'd go straight to your father-in-law. Can you call him when she's not around?"

"He still works part-time at his law firm."

"There you go. Call him there. Explain the situation. It would be better for him to hear your voice on the phone than for you to put it in an email. Plus, he can't forward an email to his wife if there's no email to forward. Explain the situation to him and tell him you'd really like for them to come. Tell him you miss them, would like to spend some time with them and, most importantly, don't go too much into your relationship with me. Instead, why don't you tell them how much hearing me, that first night, really helped you?"

"So, you want me to give you credit," Claire said, raising her eyebrows.

"*Of course* I want you to give me credit!" Callum said, laughing. "Who deserves more credit than me? And, don't you dare say Gia, because, though she's wonderful, she doesn't kiss you the way I do."

"I should hope not," Claire said. "Okay, so I'll call Bill and ask for them to come hear you speak."

"Yes. Tell them you've arranged for the tickets to be at the door and that, on Saturday night, after the day-long session, you'd like to take them out to dinner."

"And then I spring you on them?"

"Well, in a manner of speaking," Callum said. "But, by the time we have dinner, I'll have already won them over."

Claire raised an eyebrow. "You're very cocky."

"I prefer to say I'm confident," Callum said, with a wink.

"What if they won't come at all? To the seminar, I mean."

"They will."

"You did read this email, right?" Claire asked, gently pushing the laptop closer to Callum.

"She's in pain, Claire. She's not really angry with you. She's angry with the world. She lost her child. Her grandchildren. She doesn't know how to cope with that and so she's lashing out at you because she doesn't know where else to put her anger. She's no different than all of the people we meet every weekend. She just happens to be related to you."

"She's related to Jack," Claire said stubbornly. "She's not my relative."

"Claire," Callum said gently. "She's related to you. She's your husband's mom. She's your children's grandmother. You might not always like her, but she and Bill are really the only family you have left. You don't want to burn that bridge."

"She's the one who's burned it," Claire said, with a pout.

"And you're the one who's going to be the bigger person and mend it," Callum said, his voice stern.

Claire stared at Callum. She wasn't thrilled with him at the moment. She didn't want to mend bridges. She wanted to say, "I don't regret the bridges I've burned; I just regret certain people weren't on those bridges when I burned them." But, she didn't.

Instead, she reluctantly saw his point.

"This sucks."

"It totally sucks," Callum agreed.

"I shouldn't be the one who has to try to fix this. She's the one who's been cruel to me."

"I know."

"But I still have to try to fix it?" Claire asked.

"You do. Well, I guess you don't have to. You're not *obligated* to fix it. But I think you know it's the right thing to do. Besides, remember, love, forgiveness isn't about the other person. It's about you. You don't want to end up bitter like her. You don't want to let this anger grow in you. You're the one who'll feel the most pain."

"Sometimes I hate you."

"You do?" Callum said, surprised.

"I hate that you're so wise and forgiving and you expect me to be the same. I'm very happy to just hate her, too."

"You don't hate her or me and you know it. And she doesn't hate you," Callum said. "You can do this, Claire."

Claire shrugged. "Okay, then. I guess you should leave the room so I can call my father-in-law," she said, glancing at the clock.

"And tell him you love them and have missed them terribly."

"Now you're pushing it," Claire grumbled, as she leaned in to kiss Callum on the lips. "You'd better leave before I lose my nerve."

Callum turned his chair toward the door.

"I love you, Claire."

"I love you, too," Claire said, as Callum left the room. Taking a deep breath, she picked up her cell phone off the desk and began to dial.

Claire nervously played with her napkin on the table, as she took deep breaths.

"Will you sit still?" Callum asked. "You're going to make me nervous, too."

"Okay," Claire said, quieting her hands for a moment, before she began to, once again, play with the napkin.

"I don't know why you're so worried. They showed up for both days of the seminar. I didn't get to spend much time with them, but they didn't look miserable to be there."

"I know."

"And you spent a little bit of time with them, right?"

"Yes." Claire sighed. She'd been thankful when Bill had told her he thought coming to the seminar was a great idea and he'd do his best to convince Nancy. On the call, he'd said he missed her a great deal and, by the end of it, Claire was pretty certain he had no idea his wife had sent the angry email to Claire and Claire felt it best to not mention it.

No need to stir the pot.

To Claire's surprise, Bill called her a day later to say both of them would be happy to attend and were looking forward to spending some time with her. Claire had resisted the urge to say, "I doubt that."

Claire had been by the ticket counter when her in-laws arrived on Friday evening. She'd given both of them big hugs and, though Bill's embrace was warmer, her mother-in-law did reluctantly hug her back.

"You look great," Bill had said, holding Claire at arm's length to get a good look at her. While Nancy hadn't said the same thing, she did seem to nod when Bill said it.

It wasn't much, but Claire would take it.

She hadn't talked to them since they'd arrived, but she'd kept an eye on them from a distance. It was hard to tell, from her vantage point, what they thought about everything. Claire had noticed both of them crying at times, which was understandable. Callum was very moving to hear. Most people cried, at least a little, when he spoke.

She was curious to hear their impression of the event. But, more importantly, and what she was most nervous about, was she wanted them to meet Callum and to approve of him.

No, more than that, she wanted them to love him.

She didn't know why that was important to her, but it was.

"So silly," she said to herself, shaking her head. "They're my husband's parents. They're not going to love my new boyfriend."

But, she was wrong. Very wrong.

The moment her in-laws walked in the door, Claire could see the change in them, especially the change in her mother-in-law. She was softer. Her edges were gone. Both of her in-laws seemed more relaxed.

When they spotted Callum and Claire, they headed straight over. Before Claire was completely out of her seat, her mother-in-law's arms were around her. The older woman didn't say anything, but she didn't need to. The way she cried while holding Claire spoke volumes.

"It is an honor to meet you," Bill said to Callum, shaking his hand firmly and patting Callum on the back. "Truly. Nancy and I have never had a more moving experience than we just had at your seminar. Life changing. I can't tell you how much we needed that, what a difficult time we've had these past couple of years..." His voice trailed off.

"There's no need to tell me," Callum said, glancing at Claire. "I think I know."

"Yes, I imagine you do," Bill said, his eyes meeting Claire's.

Claire had to pull herself from Nancy's embrace. "It's okay," she said to her mother-in-law, kissing the older woman on the cheek. And it was.

Slowly, all the pain and resentment Claire held toward her mother-in-law began to fall away. In that moment, all the years of hurt, both while Jack was alive and once he was gone, no longer seemed to matter. They were a part of Claire's family. No family is perfect. Heaven knew Claire, herself, wasn't perfect. They were all coping the best they could. Who was Claire to judge the way her in-laws dealt with their grief? Thinking back to her night at the pool party, Claire wasn't always proud of the way she'd coped with hers, either.

"Why don't you all sit," Callum said. "So I'm not so lonely down here. I would like for this evening to be lighthearted and fun. I think we've had all the soul searching we can take for one weekend."

Nancy and Bill nodded, as Nancy wiped the tears from her eyes. Claire handed her a tissue from her own bag.

"But, before the festivities begin, I'd like to say something." Callum looked across the table at Claire and smiled softly, before directing his attention back to Nancy and Bill. "I'd like to say I know Claire loved your son with all her heart. She's spent hours and hours telling me about Jack and your grandchildren and, to be honest, I feel like I know them. I know that sounds silly, but I do.

"This situation can't be an easy one for you. I can't imagine how it feels to see Claire dating another man. But, I want to make sure you know, in no way am I trying to replace Jack. He will always be a part of Claire, just as he and Luke and Ella and Lily are a part of both of you. All I can say, though, is that I love Claire very much and I will do my best to always make her happy. I want you to know that. But I also want you to know, you are always welcome in our lives. Claire loves you very much. We don't want you to feel you're no longer her family. As she and I have learned, traveling with the wonderful people on our team, family isn't always about blood. It's about love. And I promise you, Claire has enough love for you that it'll never vanish."

If Claire had loved Callum before, she loved him even more now. Not only had he, clearly, won Jack's parents over, but he'd helped her heal the anger and bitterness she'd felt toward them, especially following the accident.

If it had been solely up to Claire, she would've broken all ties with Jack's parents and pushed them away forever. They were a headache she didn't need.

But Callum had been right. She didn't need the grief, but she did need her family. And, whether she always liked it or not, Nancy and Bill were a part of that family. Claire had learned the hard way that family is something you should never take for granted. You should never let a moment pass when you can tell someone what they mean to you. Never let the sun go down on your anger, because you never know what tomorrow might bring.

Tomorrow wasn't promised. But today? Today, as she sat at this table with her new love and the parents of the man she once loved, life was suddenly full of happiness and laughter and healing.

And if Claire and Nancy and Bill needed anything, it was that.

CHAPTER
TWENTY-NINE

Claire heard the curse first, followed by the crash, followed by about half-dozen more curse words.

Running into the kitchen, she surveyed the scene in front of her. The salad bowl and all its contents were strewn across the floor.

Callum, who'd left her almost an hour ago to make dinner, was fuming in his chair.

"What's going on?" she asked.

"Nothing," Callum said, his voice unusually harsh. "I'm making dinner."

"Do you want some help?"

"Does it look like I need your help?" Callum barked.

"Well, actually...yeah." Claire smiled coyly.

"I can make you dinner on my own."

"But we usually make it together," Claire said, furrowing her brow at Callum's uncharacteristic anger.

"Well, tonight I'm making it alone. Is that all right with you?"

Claire put her hands up in the air in surrender. "It's fine with me if it's fine with you," she said hesitantly. "I'm not sure it's all that fine with you."

"Have you ever tried to open cling wrap with only one hand—and then place it around the top of a bowl?" he snapped.

"Um, can't say I have," Claire said uneasily.

"Then maybe you shouldn't be mocking my frustration," Callum snarled.

"Callum! What is going on?! I'm not mocking you!" Claire said, stepping into the kitchen and walking toward him.

Callum raised his hand into the air to indicate he didn't want her to come any closer.

"Can you please go back into the living room?"

"Why don't I help you clean up the salad?"

Callum's glaze was steely. His voice was firm and low, his brogue thick. "I asked you to go back into the living room. I even said 'please.' I'll let you know when dinner is ready."

"Okay, I'll go. Let me know if you change your mind."

"I won't."

In the end, the meal had been delicious, though served close to two hours after Callum had begun cooking. Claire had noticed the kitchen was still a mess when she walked in, but didn't comment on in. She stepped over the cucumbers and tomatoes on the ground and pretended she didn't see them. If he wanted to clean it up on his own, he could clean it up, no matter how long it took him.

Callum hadn't exactly apologized to Claire for getting mad at her, but his mood was considerably improved by the time he served the steak, baked potatoes and asparagus, so Claire thought it best to pretend nothing had happened earlier. Everyone had their bad days.

She'd just never before seen Callum have one like this.

The two of them were snuggling after dinner.

"Does it ever bother you?" Callum asked, breaking the silence.

"Does what bother me?" Claire said, stifling a yawn.

Callum moved his hand away from Claire's body and motioned to his own.

"This."

"Could you be more specific?"

"Honestly, Claire," Callum said. "You're not blind. I know you love me despite the missing components, but what I'm asking you, and I promise, I won't get mad if the answer is 'yes,' does it sometimes bother you? Do you leave me at night and wonder if this is too much for you to take on? Is the burden of having a boyfriend who has to take half a day to cook you dinner, who is, *literally*, half a man, more than you can deal with at times?"

Claire sat up quickly. "You're serious, aren't you?"

"Dead."

Claire took a deep breath. She knew what she wanted to say, but was also aware she needed to be careful how she worded it. She couldn't risk Callum misunderstanding her feelings.

"I want you to listen to me very carefully," she said, her voice soft but deliberate. "Because I will not say this again. If I had the choice today of having my children back, but God said to me, 'The only way you can have them is without their arms or their legs,' do you think I'd take them?"

Callum remained silent, but took a deep breath and nodded.

"In a heartbeat," Claire continued. "I'd take all three of them at once, without any limbs, if I could just have them back. They were so much more than the 'sum of their parts.' I'd give up anything to hear their voices again, to see their smiles, to lie in bed and smell their sweet scents."

"I know you would."

Tears began to well in Claire's eyes. "So, why would you think, for one second, I'd care whether or not you have arms or legs? Lose the arm you have. It wouldn't matter to me one bit." She took her index finger and gently jabbed his chest. "I love the 'you' that's in here." She pointed her finger at his head. "You got it?"

"Got it," Callum said, but his voice remained solemn.

"I mean it, Callum. I love you. The limb issue, it's a part of you, and

I love everything that's a part of you. Besides, if you had all four limbs, chances are we'd have never met. You'd be working at the Guinness factory in Ireland and I would've remained a sad and lonely woman in Florida. I needed you to be like this," she said, waving her hand over his body. "So we could be like this." She waved her hand over the two of them.

She lay back down again and he leaned over to kiss the top of her head. Raising herself up to him, her lips met his.

"Did I make myself clear?" Claire asked.

"Crystal," Callum said, between kisses.

"Good."

"But, just for the record," Callum said, "I don't intend on losing the arm I do have just so you can prove your point."

Claire giggled and slowly moved her hand, which was resting on his chest, between his shirt buttons and onto his bare skin.

Instinctively, Callum reached his arm around her to still her hand.

"No," Claire said, kissing his neck. "Not this time. You're not going to stop me this time."

She began to kiss Callum more with more insistence and though he returned the kisses, he shifted his body slightly away from hers.

"Callum, I mean it," Claire said, sliding her body closer to his. "I want you."

She heard Callum sigh.

"Do you not want me?" she asked sadly.

"Of course I do," Callum said softly. "But..."

"But what?" Claire asked. They were the only ones in the room, but still they whispered.

"I guess this was a part of what I was getting at earlier. I am, literally, only half a man."

Claire eyed him suspiciously. "Um, does that mean you're missing another part you haven't mentioned earlier?"

"No! Of course not!" Callum said in horror. "I have all those parts, thank you very much."

"Phew," Claire said with an exaggerated gesture of relief. "I was getting worried there for a sec." She put her hand deeper into his shirt, running it along the side of his body.

"Claire, it's just..."

"It's just what?" she asked, her voice soothing and breathy.

"It's just that, well, I don't want you to be turned off."

"Trust me, Callum, it would be hard to turn me off at this point. I am completely turned on." She slid her hand back out of his shirt and began to unbutton it. "I'm very forward, aren't I?"

Callum turned his head away from her slightly.

"Claire."

"Callum."

"I don't know," Callum said.

"You don't know if you want me?" Claire asked.

"Oh, no. That's not even close to the issue. I've wanted you since the moment I first saw you in that music room, standing next to that piano."

"So then, what's the problem?"

"What if you don't want me?" he asked.

"I already said I do," Claire said, pulling his shirt out from his pants.

"But what if, when you see me, all of me, you change your mind?"

"Callum," Claire said, pausing her hand. "I have seen you. I see you ever day."

"Not all of me."

"I've seen all of you. Just not the part of you I want to see," she said, moving her hand to the button of his jeans.

"It might look a little different to you when you see my whole body, without my clothes."

"Why? Do you think you look like you have longer limbs when

you're in your clothes? 'Cause, if you think you do, let me let you in on a little secret."

"No, I mean..."

Claire removed her hand from him, once again, and lay back on the floor. She took a deep breath and then sat up, putting her hands on the bottom of her shirt and pulling it over her head. Lying back down again, she wiggled out of her jeans so that, when she was done, she lay next to him in nothing but her bra and panties.

Pushing down her panties, slightly, she ran her hand against a thin, white scar.

"See this?" she said. "This is the scar I have from giving birth to the twins. With Luke, I had a natural delivery, but with the twins, I had to have a c-section."

She moved her hand higher onto her stomach, rubbing a much larger, much redder, scar.

"This," she said. "Is from the accident. A piece of metal from the car impaled me. It somehow flew off the car and directly into my stomach. I almost bled to death."

Claire slipped off her bra straps and pulled down her bra.

"See these breasts? They don't look like they did when I was in my twenties. Oh, you would have loved them then. Small and perky. But I nursed three babies with them. They kinda lost their perk. They sag and droop and if I don't wear a bra, they hang down to my belly. Which, if you ask me, isn't all that bad of a thing, because then they hide my stomach scar. Oh, and by the way, not only is my stomach not as flat as it was before I had kids, but I have all this extra skin from how big it stretched with the twins." She lifted a patch of loose skin and then let it drop back down again. "See? No elasticity."

"Claire," Callum said.

"What I'm saying," Claire said, "is that I'm not perfect, either. My body isn't how I'd like it to be. I have scars, I weigh more than I sometimes like. I have stretch marks and, dare I say it, cellulite on my ass." She slapped her butt for emphasis.

"Claire, you're perfect. Just perfect," Callum said, running his hand down the side of her body.

"And so are you," she whispered. "Perfect for me."

She kissed him again. Intensely, with more passion than she'd ever known. She wanted him. Needed him. And, more importantly, she needed Callum to need her.

Claire hadn't been touched, intimately, since Jack. She craved Callum's touch, his hand on her body. She needed him inside of her and the desire to become one with him overwhelmed her.

"Make love to me," she whispered to him. "I need you to make love to me."

And love her he did. Claire had never felt so desired, so needed, so satisfied as she did with Callum. She'd been loved before. She'd made love before. But not like this.

Never like this.

They had sex right there on the living room floor. There was a brief discussion about moving it into Callum's bedroom, until they both realized they were too impatient to wait even one more minute for what they'd both been desiring for so long.

Claire removed Callum's shirt and his pants. The tattoo, which she'd seen in bits and pieces, was glorious. It wrapped around his muscular chest and Claire thought she'd never before seen anything so sexy.

All of Callum's concerns regarding how Claire would feel about him once she viewed his entire body were for naught. Claire loved his body. Every inch of it. And she made sure to touch every edge and angle, with her hands, her mouth and the length of her nakedness.

What she and Callum shared was so special, so unique. Claire envisioned their relationship as a delicate butterfly in her hand. There was a desire to surround it, protect it from all harm, cherish it, but mostly, watch it soar. The way she knew their love would continue to soar as their bodies rose together.

"I love you, Claire," he breathed into her ear, as he entered her.

But he hadn't needed to say the words. Claire knew. She felt it as the rhythm of their bodies became one.

And she ravenously took it.

"Well, that wasn't so bad," Callum said, resting his head back on the floor, sweat still on his brow.

"Excuse me? Wasn't *so bad?*" Claire asked in disbelief. "Have you had better?"

Callum laughed. "Not lately."

Claire huffed and started to turn away from him, but he caught her and pulled her back close.

"Come here, silly. I'm not letting you go."

"Not tonight, huh? You're not going to kick me out?" Claire asked.

"I'm *never* going to let you go."

Claire smiled and rested her head on Callum's still bare chest. Sex, with Callum, hadn't been all that different from sex with a man with all his limbs. It took them a moment or two to figure out positioning, at times, but those were mere pauses in what was one of the most amazing experiences of Claire's life.

"So, were you okay with everything?" Callum asked. There was a slight catch in his voice. "You know, with me and all?"

"Are you asking me if you're good in bed?"

"Not exactly," Callum said, his voice cocky. "I'm sure that part works *exceptionally* well. I mean, you know..." He once again gestured to his body, the unspoken way they'd both come to refer to his disability.

"You know what I learned, in the middle of our escapades tonight?"

Claire asked coyly, running her hand along the length of his tattoo once again.

"What?"

"All those extra limbs. I didn't realize it before, but they tend to get in the way," she said, a playful grin spreading across her face.

Callum laughed and pulled her closer to him. Claire laughed, too.

She didn't need a man with all those limbs. She just needed Callum. And she had the feeling he needed her, too.

CHAPTER
THIRTY

"Listen," Claire said, into the phone. "Don't worry about not seeing me tonight. I have a ton I need to do—bills, emails, phone calls I need to return. I've let a bunch go lately."

"Spending too much time with me?" Callum asked.

"Well, I wouldn't call it too *much* time, but, yes. Too much time." Claire chuckled. She was sitting, cross-legged, on the chair by her desk, scrolling through her email account. She had at least fifty emails she hadn't even opened yet. "At least, too much time to get other things done. And, though I'm not living in my house in Florida at the moment, the bank, apparently, still expects me to pay the mortgage and the lawn people want money for mowing my grass. Do you believe it?"

"The nerve," Callum said. "Okay, good then. I'm glad you'll be busy. Mitch, Frank and I really want to take Wyatt out tonight. He's been really down since, you know, his mom..."

Callum didn't complete the thought, but Claire understood. Wyatt's mom had passed away two weeks earlier. He'd flown back to Texas to plan and attend the funeral and then stayed another week to try and get some of her affairs in order. They all knew that his mom passing was a blessing in many ways. None of them would've wanted to live that way, in a constant state of confusion, but losing a parent was still never easy. Fortunately, for Callum, he hadn't had to experience that yet, but Claire had. She knew it hurt, no matter what age you were.

"No, I totally get it. Take him out. Get him drunk. It'll be good for him."

"I'll miss you."

"I know. If I were you, I'd miss me, too," Claire said.

"You think you're so funny. Why do I put up with you?"

"Because you love me."

"Well, yes. There's that," Callum said. "Okay, then. I'll call you when I get home. Or, if it's too late, I'll text you; okay?"

"Sure," Claire said, distracted. An email from Gia popped up on her screen and Claire opened it. Quickly skimming it, she grinned.

"You're not going to believe what Gia just sent me. A link to videos of you online. I think she Googled you."

Claire clicked on the link and it opened a YouTube channel.

"There must be hundreds here."

"Alison recently hired some video guy to create that page for me. She thinks it'll be good PR if there are videos available online of me speaking and being interviewed and such. I haven't even seen what's on there yet. I know a lot of videos have been filmed over the years, but I've never looked at any of them. They've kind of just gone in the can."

"Lost in the vast electronic world?"

"Exactly."

"Well, I'm going to watch them all."

"I thought you were supposed to be paying your electric bill."

"I just remembered. They automatically take their fee out of my bank account."

"Well, then. Have fun. Pop yourself some popcorn."

"Great idea!" Claire said, clicking on the first video. "I'd better go. It looks like I have hours of viewing ahead of me."

"Love you."

"Ditto," Claire said as she hung up the phone.

The first video began with a montage of Callum partaking in a variety of sporting activities. She watched as he swam, played soccer, spun a basketball on one finger, and then made a perfect shot. There were images of him riding a horse, fishing and even surfing. Even as well as Claire knew Callum, she still had to marvel at all he was able to do, despite his limitations. She didn't know many people who were adept at both downhill skiing and kayaking, even with all of their limbs. Callum was remarkable. No matter how familiar and comfortable she became with Callum, she never forgot he was unique.

The next video showed him successfully conquering tasks around his house: cooking, getting dressed, tying the laces on his sneakers, typing with lightning speed using only one hand. The images led into one of Callum's speeches. She looked at him, closely, wondering if she'd attended that particular event or if it was from before she'd joined the team. It was hard to tell. She'd heard him speak so many times by now and, unlike if he'd been a woman, there was no change in his haircut in order to help determine a timeframe.

Claire turned her attention to the papers in front of her on the desk. Her electric bill might be automatically withdrawn from her bank account, but not all of her bills were. She needed to change that and set up automatic payments for more items. It'd be slightly time-consuming for the moment, but it would save her a lot of hassle over the long run.

Claire worked for a bit, Callum's voice soothing in the background. She listened to his now-familiar talk as she answered emails on her tablet, keeping his face visible on her laptop next to her. She enjoyed glancing up at him occasionally, and smiled each time, feeling as if he were in the room with her.

When his talk ended, a new video began to play automatically. Claire glanced up when she heard the voice of a popular late-night newscaster. He was introducing Callum and the interview they were about to air. Nothing he said was news to Claire. She knew Callum's story so well by now, she could give it for him.

Claire did, however, stop her work to watch the actual interview with Callum. Though she'd heard him speak a hundred times by now, she'd never actually seen him give an interview. He looked great. He was wearing a bright-blue, button-down shirt that caused his eyes to look even more dazzling than usual. He and the reporter were sitting on a large porch of what seemed like a beach house. Callum was tan and looked incredibly relaxed, as if he was ready for any question that might be thrown his way.

The beginning questions introduced more of who Callum was, how he'd been born with this disability. She listened as Callum discussed what his childhood had been like and how he'd been teased and fallen into a deep depression during his early teen years.

"I learned, though, very early on," Callum said, "that a lot of things in life can be made better if you have a great personality. If you exude a positive attitude, smile, laugh at your own limitations and mistakes, people will be more embracing of you. You could be the most handsome man on the earth, but if your personality sucks or if you're socially awkward, people have a hard time getting past that."

"So," the reporter prodded. "Are you saying that people forget something as big as you missing an arm and two legs if you smile big enough?"

Callum laughed. "That's what the ladies tell me."

"Good to know," the reporter joked. "I'll need to remember that on my next date."

Claire smiled as she looked back down at her checkbook and signed a check for her credit card bill. Callum's response was classic Callum.

"What's the largest crowd you've ever spoken in front of?" the interviewer asked.

"So far, about twenty thousand," Callum said.

"Did you ever think, as a little boy in Ireland, you'd someday be in front of that many people?"

"Never."

"So, it was a big dream of yours?"

"No, it never even crossed my mind. I just wanted to survive the playground," Callum said.

"What, then, is your biggest dream in life?"

Callum paused before responding and Claire looked up at the screen during his silence. She was curious to hear his response. In all their discussions, the two of them had never discussed the future. They did their best to focus on the present. Some days, the present was all Claire could handle. Each day was still, often, a struggle for her. She felt blessed she had Callum to share those days with, but even with him by her side, thinking ahead was still too difficult for her.

"Honestly," Callum said, beginning to answer the question. "I sometimes dream of the day I'll walk my daughter down the aisle."

Claire froze and her hand stilled above the checkbook.

"So, having children is a possibility for you?" the reporter asked.

"Oh, absolutely," Callum said, his grin as wide as his face. "At least, the doctors say they don't see any physical reason why I can't have them. I just need to find the right woman and get started making those babies."

Claire felt the air rush out of her lungs.

"You'd like a lot of kids?" the reporter asked Callum.

"I'd love a whole houseful," Callum said. "As many as God sees fit to give us. There's no greater blessing than a child."

Claire dropped the pen and stopped the video at that point. She couldn't bear to hear any more. She put her hand to her mouth and wondered what, on earth, she was going to do.

Claire waited until she received the text from Callum that he was home from his night out with the guys before she headed over to his house. The last few hours had been agony. After watching the interview, Claire had been able to do little more than sit at her desk and do her best to remain calm.

Her mind raced with thoughts of what she was going to say to Callum when she finally saw him, how she was going to word it.

If she'd known. But she hadn't.

And, she realized, he didn't know, either. She'd never been really upfront with him. She hadn't kept anything from him, intentionally. It had simply never come up. It'd never occurred to her it might need to.

But, it did now. Claire knew that for certain. Everything needed to be discussed now. Tonight. She couldn't wait even one more day.

Callum's face registered surprise when he opened his front door and saw Claire standing there. Quickly, though, he broke into a smile.

"Hey, love. Miss me so much you couldn't stay away?" he said, his voice easy as he moved away to let her in the door.

"Did any of them come back here with you?" Claire asked, ignoring Callum's question.

"No. They just dropped me off. Wyatt was two sheets to the wind, but Mitch only had one drink, early in the evening, and he did the driving."

"Are you drunk?" Claire asked. She didn't think so, but she didn't want to have this conversation with him if he wasn't in complete control of his faculties.

"Of course not," he said, his voice becoming uneasy. "What's going on, love?"

"I wanted to make sure we have some privacy."

Callum looked around the living room. "Well, you can't get more private than this. Let's go sit on the couch."

"Honestly, I'd rather stand," Claire said, shifting her weight from one foot to the other. "I don't really know where to begin. I was working at home and I had a lot of time to think. I was watching all those videos of you and I realized..." She took a deep breath. "I need to leave."

Callum looked at her, startled.

"Leave? You just got here."

"No, I mean, I need to go home. I need to leave the team and go back to Florida."

Callum stared at Claire, clearly unsure what to say. Confusion was written all over his face.

"Wait," he said slowly. "I think I'm missing something. Did something happen tonight? Is Gia okay?"

"She's fine. No, nothing happened. I mean, something happened, but nothing terrible. And, not tonight. Well, it's terrible, but no one died."

"Okay, Claire. Please slow down. Are you sure you don't want to sit down?" Callum rolled his chair closer to her. She put up her hand to indicate she wanted him to keep his distance.

"Claire," Callum continued, nodding toward the couch. "Sit."

"Okay," Claire said, perching herself on the edge of the couch.

Callum rolled his chair over to Claire. He didn't touch her, but got as close to her knees as possible.

"Let's start this over," he began. "Last we spoke, you were going to pay some bills and watch some videos online."

"I watched the videos."

"And?"

Claire took a deep breath and exhaled slowly. "There was one of you where you were sitting on a porch and a reporter was asking questions about your life."

"Okay."

"Do you remember it?"

"Not particularly."

"Well, the reporter asked you what your biggest dream is."

"Okay."

"And you said your biggest dream is to walk your daughter down the aisle," Claire said, not meeting Callum's eyes.

"Okay," Callum said again. "I wasn't being literal, of course. Unless, you know, I decide to wear my legs. It's not like I think I'll grow some of my own by then."

"That's not the problem."

"Then what is?" Callum asked.

Claire stood up and walked across the room. She was too agitated to sit. She began to pace the room.

"I've been so caught up in the excitement of it all," she said. "I've felt so alive. After losing Jack and the kids, I never thought I'd feel this way again. I began to see I might have a future again, one that consists of more than sadness."

She stopped moving and turned toward Callum, though she still didn't look him in the eyes.

"But, I realized tonight, I haven't been truthful with you. I haven't lied to you or anything, but I never thought to bring it up." Claire began to wring her hands. "I guess I never thought it would get so serious and I was so busy thinking of all the happy stuff. I never thought to tell you."

"Okay, Claire. I think you need to sit back down again." Callum's voice was full of worry now.

"No. I can't."

"Whatever it is, Claire, it's okay."

"No, it's not okay. I'm not okay."

"Are you sick?" Callum's face was suddenly full of alarm.

"No. I mean, not really. But, I never told you about the accident," Claire said, her eyes brimming with tears.

"The accident? The car accident? Of course you have."

"No, I mean, I didn't tell you what happened to me, besides losing everyone."

"Yes, you did. You were injured. Broken ribs, collapsed lung; you said something impaled your stomach."

"It impaled my uterus," Claire said. "A piece of the car impaled my uterus."

"All right," Callum said. "What did they do about that?"

"They debated doing a complete hysterectomy, but the doctor on call decided he could just sew up the hole. So, instead, he stitched up my uterus."

"Okay," Callum said, alarm slightly evident in his voice. "Did something happen with that tonight? Are you experiencing some sort of complication? Do we need to get you to a hospital?"

"What?" Claire said, so lost in her thoughts she wasn't really focusing on Callum's concerns. "Oh. No. It's nothing like that. I'm fine."

"Good," Callum said, exhaling slightly. "So, what's going on? You've really lost me now."

"Callum," Claire said, not wanting to look at him, but knowing this was something she needed to do completely facing him. She took a deep breath before speaking. "I can't have any more children."

Callum paused, but only for a second.

"And you found this out right after you lost your babies?" Callum asked, his own eyes full of compassion.

Claire nodded, but ordered herself not to cry.

"Oh, Claire," Callum said, rolling closer to her. "I'm so sorry, love. That must've been unbelievably horrible news."

Claire nodded. "It was. At the moment, it didn't seem to matter. After all, I was mourning the children I'd already had. The thought of ones I'd never have in the future was the furthest from my mind. Imagining myself having more children would've felt like I was trying to replace them and, well, that would be impossible."

Callum took her hand and, though she knew she should pull it away, she didn't. It might be the last time he touched her.

"Honestly," Claire continued. "I've given it very little thought since then. My whole life has been about getting through each day. Surviving. Having another baby was the furthest thing from my mind. But, I was a parent. I still think of myself as a mom. I'm just a mom who no longer has any kids. And that's hard."

Callum nodded.

"And," Claire said, "The knowledge I could never have any babies again...though it wasn't something I dwelt on...it's always been in the back of my mind, hanging out there. Kind of like the final nail in the coffin. I'm no longer a mom and, in a sadistic twist of fate, not only did I lose the kids I had that night, I lost the ones I might have someday had."

Claire took her hand away from Callum, sat up straight and took a deep breath.

"That is why, Callum," Claire said. "I need to leave. We need to end this."

"End what?" Callum asked, clearly confused.

"End us."

"What?!" Callum's shock reverberated throughout the room. "What on earth are you talking about?"

"I'm talking about the fact that, before tonight, it never occurred to me you wanted children. I don't know why I didn't realize that. Of course you'd want children. You're young. You've never had them before. You'd be an amazing dad. The thing is, I can't give them to you."

"Claire, you've got to be kidding me."

"Have you not been listening to me?" Claire said, her voice rising. "I am not kidding. I cannot have any more children."

"I don't mean about that. I mean about breaking up with me."

"No. I'm not kidding about that, either." Her voice was resigned. She stood and walked across the room.

"Claire, this is ridiculous. Sit back down."

"No."

"Okay, then stand," he said, rolling closer to her. When she backed further away, he stopped moving. "This is not something to break up over."

"I think it is."

"Have I ever told you I wanted children?" Callum asked.

"No. I wish you had. I wouldn't have let this go as far as it has."

"Claire! I didn't tell you because it wasn't on my mind."

"It was during that interview."

"Sure." Callum shrugged. "I guess it was, but it hasn't been since we met. I haven't once even thought about it. I promise you that."

"Well, you would have eventually. I'm stopping this before it becomes too painful."

"Before it becomes too painful for whom?" Callum said, his voice catching. "Just the *discussion* about you leaving me is killing me."

"Callum, don't make this harder than it already is."

"It doesn't seem all that hard for you," Callum shot back. "You walk into my house and end our entire relationship, out of the blue, just like that." He snapped his fingers. "No discussion with me. Not listening to what I have to say."

"I heard what you had to say, in that interview. You were *very* clear."

"Claire, please sit down." She shook her head again.

"You deserve to have everything you dream of, Callum. Not just a great relationship. You deserve a marriage and a family. A houseful of kids, like you said. You can't have that with me."

"Claire."

"Callum, I need to leave so you're free to find the person who can give you all that."

"Oh, no you don't. Don't I get a say in this?"

"Of course, but I already heard your say. You want kids. I can't have them. End of story. People come in and out of your life for a reason. Maybe you came into mine to show me happiness is still possible for me. Maybe I came into yours to show you how completely someone can love you."

"Claire. I love you," Callum said, in his voice a hint of desperation and fear. "Please don't leave. We can work this out. It's not the end of the world if we don't have kids."

"You say that now."

"Claire," Callum said, the word a plea.

"I won't leave you in the lurch," Claire said calmly. She wouldn't let herself cry or else she knew she'd begin to sob. She was doing the right thing and knew it. It was time for her to think about someone other than herself. "I know we have one more event this week. I'll be there for Friday night. Frank can manage without me on Saturday. But after that, I have to go back to Florida."

"I don't care about that. If you don't want to sing anymore, that's one thing, but I love you. Please tell me this isn't the end of you and me. *Please*." The tears flowed freely down Callum's face now. He was not a man who shied away from his emotions. He showed no embarrassment over crying in front of Claire.

Claire's expression softened as she looked at Callum. He seemed so broken, but she knew that was only temporary. What was that saying? *If you love something, set it free.* She was letting Callum go because she loved him deeply. She knew he deserved better than her and she was going to let him be free to find that person, the woman who *could* give him everything he deserved.

He deserved the best life had to offer. Callum was the most amazing man Claire had ever met.

She knelt down next to his chair so she was eye level with him and rested her hand on his arm.

"Listen to me. I love you, Callum Fitzgerald. I love you as much as I have ever loved anyone in my entire life. You are an incredible, kind, loving, charismatic, very sexy man. I've been flattered you've wanted to be with me. I know you find that hard to believe because, despite the confidence you show in front of millions of people, *I know you.* I know your insecurities and how you second-guess yourself. I do not, *for one second,* want you to think this is about your limitations. I am doing this, not because I think less of you, but because I love you too much for you to receive less than you deserve."

"I can't do this without you," Callum said with such sadness, Claire's heart broke all over again.

"Callum, you were doing amazing things before you met me and you'll continue to thrive once I'm gone. I love you, Callum. That's all I can say. I love you."

She leaned down and kissed him on the lips. He tried to pull her closer, deeper into their kiss, but she resisted. Claire had to fight every urge in her body that was asking her to stay. She wanted to make love to him, not leave him. But, she couldn't. It would be wrong and unfair. So, instead, she pulled away from him and this time, didn't fight the tears in her eyes.

"Claire, please don't go," Callum begged. "Stay with me. Even if you still leave Friday, stay with me until then."

"I can't, Callum," Claire said. "If I spend one more minute with you, I'm likely to change my mind. And, for your sake, I need to remember why I'm breaking both our hearts."

And then, without looking back, Claire walked to the door and put her hand on the knob. Taking a deep breath, she steadied herself.

"I love you," Claire said again, opening the door and silently closing it behind her.

Claire knew she should hurry to her car and leave, but her feet wouldn't move. She could hear Callum inside, calling her name as she closed the door. And then, a few moments later, there was a large crash. If she thought he'd fallen, she would've rushed back inside, but Claire knew, instinctively, it was vase on the table that had crashed, into the wall where Callum threw it.

Claire rested her forehead against the front door and began to sob. This is not how she'd wanted their story to end. She'd never wanted their story to end at all. Callum had promised her there was a plan and, stupidly, she'd allowed herself to believe the plan was that the two of them would have a future together.

She knew, if she walked back in that door, her story could end that way, *would* end that way. But, she'd been cheating Callum of the life he ultimately deserved. He'd given her so much. It was her turn to make sure he was given a beautiful future.

Not even bothering to wipe the tears, Claire lifted her head and, with a despair she hadn't felt since she'd had to say good-bye to her family, Claire got into her car and drove away.

CHAPTER THIRTY-ONE

Since the day Claire had left her home in Florida, she'd been dreading returning to it. She'd been certain the memories of her family, which had seemed like distant dreams to her in the faraway lands she'd visited, would be waiting for her the moment she opened her front door, a tsunami of grief waiting to pummel her and knock her down. But she'd been wrong.

It wasn't grief that awaited her when she stepped into the foyer of her family's home. It was sweet memories of her babies and a man she'd loved deeply and a life which had been extremely precious. It was a life, she recognized, that was now over, but the ending no longer negated what they'd had and enjoyed as a family.

For once, the thought of her husband and kids brought a smile to her lips before it brought a tear to her eye.

Claire permitted herself one day to become lost in those memories. She went into each of her children's rooms and lay on their beds, holding their stuffed animals close. She didn't cry. Instead, she chose her favorite memories of each child and she relived those days in her mind. The day Luke had built his first Lego set all by himself and had nearly burst with pride. The moment when Ella had learned to ride a bike without training wheels and had screamed with glee as she flew down their street. The way Lily would snuggle close to Claire, hiding her face in Claire's neck, as Claire rested her own in her daughter's hair.

Those were memories no one could take away. Not even a drunk driver going the wrong way on the highway.

Claire spent hours poring over old photo albums, filled with happy days: birthday parties at the pool, family vacations to Disney World and New York City. School plays and Halloween costumes and a thousand candid shots of her children running through the sprinklers in the backyard or watching TV on the couch or building a fort in the living room.

The ones Claire cherished the most, though, were all the photos she'd taken of her children as they slept. Such sweet angels. Each of them, even before they truly were angels.

When it became dusk, Claire went into her bedroom and pulled Jack's dirty clothes out of the hamper, the ones Gia had told her would, no doubt, smell like him.

The scent was faint, but still there. Claire took those clothes to bed with her and lay with them in her arms, the way she would've held Jack if he were there. She talked to him, out loud. She told him all about her travels and the people she'd met. She told him about Alison, Wyatt, Frank and Mitch. And she told him about Callum, how she'd loved him, still loved him, but how she'd needed to let him go.

She fell asleep with Jack's clothes in her arms, her dreams a mixture of the two men she'd loved and lost.

When she awoke in the morning, she wasted no time in setting to work. She took all of Jack's dirty clothes, everything except the blue sweater she'd love him in the most, and threw them in the washing machine. While the machine was running, she drove herself to the local UPS store and bought a hundred dollars' worth of boxes.

When she returned home and put all the flattened boxes together with packing tape, she began to fill them. Jack's clothes were the first to go in, the ones from the hamper that were now clean and the ones still hanging in his closet. Next, she packed up the books from his nightstand, only keeping his Bible for herself. She emptied out his T-shirt and sock drawers. Folded all his shorts and placed them inside. When she was done with Jack's belongings, she moved into Luke's room.

This wasn't as easy as Jack's had been. She had to fight the tears that threatened to engulf her. She reminded herself there were other children who'd enjoy the boxes of Legos and the tennis racket that hung on Luke's wall. When Gia called, Claire nearly asked her friend to come and box the items up for her, but then resisted. These had been her children. Their precious toys. It was only right she, their Mommy, would hold each item in her hands, once more, before sending them off to their new homes.

She'd cried through much of Luke's belongings, but by the time she reached the girls' room, her eyes were dry. She turned on the radio, which sat on top of Lily's dresser and blasted rock music as she worked. The upbeat sounds helped soothe the ache and she found herself smiling over the clothes and items more than she cried.

At one point, she even found herself dancing, Ella's Barbie dolls in her hands, Lily's cowgirl hat on her head. She thought about how her girls would be giggling if they were here to see her.

By the time she closed the last box, having saved some of the more special items for herself, she felt a sense of accomplishment and relief.

Knowing her children's rooms remained untouched, in this house, had weighed on Claire. They were a constant reminder of the children who would never return to them.

Claire was ready to move on, with her memories and her life. She no longer wanted to trudge through the muddy waters of the past. She wanted to swim in the clean ocean of the love she'd had for her family.

But before she could do that, she needed to sell the house.

The first call she made was to a realtor, a random stranger she'd found online. Though she knew a number of parents at the kids' school were in the real estate field, Claire didn't want to use someone she knew. Selling the house needed to be a business transaction. It was the only way Claire would be able to get through it. She couldn't be distracted each time the realtor showed up with memories of her children and their friends.

The next call Claire made was to Gia.

"Let's go out to dinner."

"Absolutely!" Gia said, delight filling her voice. "Where to?"

"I hear there's a new Mexican place downtown. Let's go there."

"Oh, yippee! I've been wanting to try it out!"

"Did you just say yippee?" Claire asked, amused.

"In fact, I did. I'll pick you up in an hour."

"Sounds good. I'll go shower now." As soon as Claire hung up the phone, she ran up the stairs.

"You look incredible!" Gia said, over margaritas and shrimp quesadillas.

"Thanks," Claire said. "I feel pretty good."

"Do you?" Gia said with concern.

"I do. This margarita is probably helping a bit, though." She smiled as she took another sip. Though she was still not a drinker, per se, Claire had begun to enjoy an occasional margarita or fruity drink during her time with Callum. She never actually finished an entire one, not since the unfortunate evening at the pool party, but she'd told Gia she'd begun to find a half glass could be quite enjoyable.

"You're really going to sell the house?"

"I am," Claire said. "It's time."

Gia nodded. She wasn't about to talk Claire out of her decision. She, too, felt Claire needed to move on and it would be nearly impossible to do if she were to go back to living in that big house all by herself.

"Where will you go?"

"I thought I'd get myself a small condo, down by the water. Jack always wanted to live near the ocean." Claire took another sip. "I guess now I'm the one who wants to live by the ocean. The realtor will be by in the morning. She doesn't think it'll be difficult to sell. Apparently it's a seller's market."

"Have you talked to Callum?" Gia asked. She already knew what had happened between Claire and Callum. Claire had called her as soon as she'd gotten home from Callum's house.

At first, Gia hadn't been able to decipher any of Claire's sobbings. Once Claire had caught her breath, though, the story had flooded out.

Gia felt Claire had made the wrong decision, but didn't say so. It hadn't been the right time. She fully planned on making her opinion known, though, when the opportunity arose. It might be tonight. It might be next month. But Gia was going to make sure Claire knew she'd made a huge mistake.

"No," Claire said, shaking her head.

"Has he contacted you?"

Claire shrugged. "He's emailed me," she said vaguely.

"What did he say?" Gia asked.

"It doesn't really matter," Claire said, with a shake of her head. "There's nothing to say. He'll move on. He just needs some time."

"And you?" Gia asked. "Will you be able to move on?"

Claire took another sip of her margarita before replying. "I'll move on, too."

She smiled then, but the sorrow in her eyes betrayed her.

"Okay," Claire said. "Enough about me. Tell me about the latest man in your life. I know there's gotta be one."

Claire was exhausted by the time she got home. The packing had worn her out and, after dinner, Gia had convinced Claire to go see a movie. It had been a romantic comedy which had caused Claire to miss Callum more, though she certainly didn't tell Gia so. Her friend didn't need to feel Claire's pain. She'd done enough of that after the accident.

Claire picked up her laptop and took it to bed with her. She spent some time scrolling through her Facebook newsfeed. She'd avoided the site for the first two years after the accident, not able to bear seeing all the families together, their happy faces staring back at her hurting one. But, in the last few months, she'd been spending more time on there. She'd lost touch with so many people. It felt good to finally be reconnecting, even if she'd only corresponded with a few. Mostly, she was a voyeur into the lives of others. She enjoyed reading their posts and looking at their photos, but rarely commented or hit the "like" button. She didn't really want people to know she was on-line again, at least not yet. For now, she was comfortable merely lurking in the background.

After Facebook, she clicked on the links to CNN and *People*, her two favorite news sources, though Jack had always told her *People* did not count as news.

When she'd exhausted all interesting stories, she opened her email account.

As she'd expected, there were three new emails from Callum.

Claire had promised Callum she wouldn't just desert the team and she hadn't. She'd shown up to sing on Friday night, but had made sure to arrive at the last minute, moments before she was to walk onstage. She'd purposely gone to the side of the stage opposite the one where Callum would be waiting in the wings. He'd stared at her, pleadingly, from the distance, but she'd averted her eyes.

She didn't look over at him during her song and, when it was over, she walked off the stage in the opposite direction. He had no choice but to roll out as soon as she was done and, by the time he finished his talk, Claire was long gone, in a taxi heading to the airport.

Claire had known she couldn't go home right away. She couldn't possibly walk away from Callum, her heart broken, and walk directly into her family's home. So, instead, she'd booked herself into a resort in Arizona for two full weeks. It'd seemed such an extravagant thing for Claire to do. She'd never before splurged on herself so, but, she figured, if anyone deserved two weeks of pampering, she did.

The first few days at the resort had been difficult. Despite her luxurious surroundings, Claire's heart had ached for Callum. She'd locked her cell phone in the safe in her room to avoid the urge to call him or answer his texts. She'd only allowed herself a half hour a day online. Each time she opened her email, there'd be numerous emails from Callum waiting in her inbox.

She hadn't opened a single one.

Instead, she'd created a folder, which she called, "Him," and upon seeing there was another email from Callum, she'd immediately drag it to the folder, unopened.

She and Callum had now been apart for three weeks and she could tell, by the little number alongside the "Him" folder, he'd sent her forty-seven emails.

That didn't include the numerous texts he'd sent or calls she'd ignored.

Claire felt terrible. Not only did she miss and long for Callum, but she knew she was being rude by completely ignoring him. However, she also knew herself. She was easily swayed. It would only take one email to derail her from what she needed to do. Callum was better off without her. He'd come to realize that, in time. He'd come to understand she'd loved him enough to let him go.

Claire quickly moved each of Callum's three new emails into the "Him" folder and logged out of her email account. Just as quickly, she closed her laptop and placed it on the floor next to her bed.

The movie, tonight, had made Claire miss Callum even more. The happy banter between the couple on the screen had reminded her of the ease with which she and Callum had laughed and joked together. If the longing in her chest had caused an ache before the movie, it was creating nearly unbearable pain now.

Claire picked up her cell phone and turned off the sound. She didn't want to hear it when she got a new text or call from Callum, as she knew she would. He always called her at bedtime. It didn't matter that they were no longer together, he still called her every single night, even though she'd never once picked up since she'd left.

She pulled the covers up over her ears and closed her eyes. She knew it was unlikely she'd fall asleep. She hadn't had a good night's sleep since she'd left Callum. But that didn't mean she couldn't try.

One day, she'd eventually sleep through the night again. She couldn't go on missing Callum forever.

Or maybe she could.

As Claire snuggled up, under the covers, she remembered a conversation she'd once had with her mom. Claire had been a junior in high school, just beginning to date boys. She'd come home, positively giddy because a senior boy had asked her to the prom. Her mom had smiled at Claire, happy for her, but there'd been a note of caution in her voice.

"Don't give away your heart too quickly," she'd warned Claire. "I can promise you, there is no pain worse than a broken heart."

"Oh, Mom," Claire had moaned and rolled her eyes.

"I mean it, Claire. I would take a broken leg over a broken heart any day," her mom had said.

And she'd been right. Claire would take a dozen broken bones over her broken heart.

For she knew no matter how excruciating the pain of a broken bone might be, it wouldn't come close to the agony she felt now.

CHAPTER THIRTY-TWO

The house sold to the third family who walked through it. Claire told the realtor she didn't want to meet them. The thought of shaking hands with the people who were going to begin their life as a family in the home she'd once shared with her own was more than Claire could bear, but she was happy to hear they had small children. She liked knowing the playscape Jack had built in their backyard would be put to good use.

Once the house was under contract, Claire set out to find a new home for herself. She decided to not buy yet, but instead rent a condo on the beach. She wasn't sure what the future had in store for her. She wasn't even certain she'd remain in Florida. Traveling with the team had opened her eyes to places and worlds she never knew existed. Though she enjoyed Florida, it no longer felt like home. Nowhere felt like home, just yet. But Claire believed that, eventually, somewhere would once again feel like that safe place. She needed to give herself time to find where that might be.

In the meantime, the condo was cute and the perfect size, with only two bedrooms. Enough for Claire and a possible guest, if she ever had any. She knew Gia might spend the night occasionally and Bill and Nancy had said they'd like to come visit Claire once she was moved in. Claire's relationship had certainly improved since they'd visited with her and Callum. It was never going to be wonderful, but it was much warmer than it had been in the past.

Both Nancy and Bill had been disappointed to hear things hadn't worked out between Claire and Callum. They'd been really impressed by Callum when they'd met him and told Claire they'd loved how happy she'd seemed when they'd all had dinner.

"Just because someone is the right person for you at a certain point in your life, doesn't mean he's the right person forever," Bill had said to her over the phone when Claire had called to tell them she was back in Florida. "Take some time to breathe and relax and then see what life has in store for you."

Claire had said she would and told them both she loved them and hoped to see them soon. It made Claire happy to realize she did love Jack's parents. There were many years when she wasn't sure that was the case. And, though she realized she didn't always like them so much, especially her mother-in-law, they were a part of her family and would always hold a special place in her heart.

The weeks up until the closing on her house were a blur. There was so much Claire needed to accomplish, she often wondered how it would all get done. She had two estate sales, selling nearly all of the furniture in the house. She kept a few sentimental pieces, or items she'd always loved, such as the red side table she'd bought at a flea market when she and Jack were first married, and the soft, plush arm chair Jack had loved to relax in after a long day at work. But, for the most part, Claire decided to sell everything in the house and start afresh with new pieces in the condo. She bought a lovely bedroom set with a tan upholstered headboard, a set she was pretty sure Jack would never have agreed to if he were still alive, and a contemporary sofa she was certain he would have hated just as much.

It made Claire laugh to think of Jack looking down at her, shaking his head. "You were just waiting for me to kick the bucket so you could have full-decorating reign, weren't you?"

The items that didn't sell, from her house, were donated to charity or given to friends who expressed interest in some of the pieces. Gia had always loved the dresser in the guest room, so Claire gave her that. Their next-door neighbor had once mentioned to Claire how she admired Claire's kitchen table, so one morning Claire knocked on the woman's door and invited her to come get it.

Claire had thought she'd feel extreme sadness over seeing the pieces carried out her front door, but she found she was okay with it. Her memories were in her heart as well as in the photo albums she would never part with. They weren't attached to a couch or an ottoman or even her children's beds.

She also found such pleasure in decorating her new place. It had been years since Claire had owned new furniture and bedding and pillows and dishes, excluding the dishes she and Gia had purchased after Claire had smashed most of hers. Every time she carried a new item up to a cashier's register and handed over her credit card, Claire got a little high.

"Retail therapy," Gia said. "You've been missing out on those joys all these years."

Every once in a while, as she was buying a chair or a blanket or a set of kitchen mugs, Claire would silently wonder what Callum would think of the item. If they'd stayed together, would they be purchasing home items together? Would their relationship have gone to that level by now?

No matter how often Claire tried to push those thoughts aside, they continued to press at her mind. She wondered if Callum and she would have eventually moved in together. Would they be buying bedding for their own guest room? Would he have liked the upholstered headboard more than Jack would have hated it?

She doubted it.

It'd been four months since Claire walked out on Callum and the team. Though the texts had subsided, he still sent her at least one email every day. Claire had kept the promise she made to herself and not opened a single one. The "Him" file was quite full and she wondered, on occasion, if Yahoo had a limit to how many emails could be stored in one single file.

Eventually she'd read those emails, or at least a couple of them, but not yet. It was too fresh in Claire's mind. The pain too strong. She was still in the process of letting go and she couldn't risk anything impeding that progress.

It wasn't long before Gia tested out the new guest room. The two of them had gone out the night before, with a group of friends, and they'd all had a little bit too much to drink. Everyone except Claire, that is. A number of the women were friends who'd been at Loni's party last year and Claire had no intention of even taking a sip of alcohol while out with those who'd been there to experience her downward spiral, literally and figuratively, into the pool. Claire had been so thankful, when she reached out to Valerie and the others, to realize they weren't holding her behavior that night, against her.

"Honestly," Valerie said, with a hug when they ran into each other in Bed, Bath & Beyond one day. "There's nothing to forgive. Who are we to judge? If I'd been in your shoes, I would've gotten drunk and fallen into a pool much sooner than you did!"

Claire was so glad they were all able to laugh it off and she was beginning to enjoy spending time with these friends again. She no longer referred to them as her "mom friends." For one, she was no longer an actual mom. But, it was more than that. She was beginning to get to know these women for themselves and not merely for who they were in relation to their kids. She was learning that, in their own right, they were incredible women and she was lucky to have them in her life.

Even Loni was proving to be a little bit less superficial once she spent enough time with her. Not tremendously less shallow, but enough so that Claire found she enjoyed her company.

"What's that?" Gia said, glancing at the paper in Claire's hand as she walked over to the coffee pot and poured herself a cup. It was essential to have the coffee already brewing before Gia woke in the morning, if either of them wanted to get their day off to an agreeable start.

"The *New York Times* Best Seller List."

"Oh?" Gia said, blowing the steam off of her drink before taking a sip. "Anything good?"

"Callum's latest book," Claire said dully.

"Really?" Gia said, in surprise. "Well, that's exciting." And then, upon seeing Claire's forlorn face, she added, "For him, anyway."

Claire read the list again. *Out on a Limb*. There it was. In black and white. Number Eight.

She nodded and put the paper down on the table. "No, you're right. It's very exciting. I'm happy for him. Thrilled, actually," she said, getting up to pour herself another cup of coffee.

"Oh, yeah. You sound it."

Claire rolled her eyes at Gia. "I am happy for him. I want him to be happy. And successful. He certainly deserves it."

"You deserve to be happy, too, you know," Gia said, sitting at the table and picking up a muffin Claire had left on a plate for her.

"I am happy," Claire said, getting the milk out of the fridge for her coffee. Gia loved her coffee black. The blacker, the better, in fact. Claire needed something to tame it a bit.

"Oh, you're positively exuberant!" Gia said, licking her finger and picking up the crumbs on the table with her damp fingertip.

"Well, I'm as happy as I can be."

"Oh, woe is you," Gia said, mocking Claire's doleful tone. "And that's totally not true. But, hey, I'm not going to get into that. You know how I feel about things."

And Claire did know. Gia had made it perfectly clear to Claire, once Claire stopped sobbing over leaving Callum. Gia felt Claire should turn around, get right back on that airplane, and return to him.

"You and he were meant for each other!" she'd bemoaned.

"Apparently, not," Claire had said.

"You're being unreasonable."

"Listen, Gia. I don't want to talk about it," Claire had snapped at her friend.

They hadn't talked about it anymore that day, but periodically, Gia would bring it up. She'd press Claire on whether or not she'd heard from Callum. Claire always lied and said no. The truth was too painful to voice. She couldn't tell Gia he called every night, sent her hundreds of emails, texted her consistently. She wasn't sure why, but she couldn't tell Gia those things.

"If you're going to start in on me again, I'm going to leave."

"Where ya gonna go?" Gia asked. "It's your condo."

"I don't know. I'm going to go to the mall. I need some new shorts."

"Well, even if you're pissed at me, can I hang out here today? The exterminator is spraying my house and I don't want to breathe in all those fumes."

"Sure," Claire said. "Make yourself at home. But you might want to do something about that hair of yours. You look like Medusa."

Gia patted her mop, which had somehow gone wild while she slept. It reminded Claire of Callum's untamable hair and the thought brought a familiar ache to her chest.

"I guess I used too much hairspray last night and now it's stuck in the position of my pillow. Oh, while you're gone, can I use your laptop? I want to do some online shopping."

"Knock yourself out. Sure you don't want to come to an actual store with me?"

"Nope. I'm good. I don't plan on getting out of my pajamas today. I have a huge headache from last night. I may have had one too many margaritas."

"Only one?" Claire said, teasing her friend. "See you in a bit." And, with that, Claire grabbed her keys, and the last muffin, and walked out the door.

The air was thick with fury and Claire felt it the moment she walked back into the condo after her shopping trip.

"Gia?" Claire said hesitantly, when she spotted her friend, a huge stack of papers in front of her, sitting at the kitchen table. Gia didn't look up. "Is everything okay?"

Gia hadn't gotten changed. She was still in her pajamas. Her hair was even more of a mess than it'd been when Claire left. Claire wondered if she'd even brushed her teeth yet today. When she saw the look Gia threw her way, though, Claire decided it would be best not to ask.

Gia was pissed.

Claire had a feeling it was at her.

"What the hell is wrong with you?" Gia hurled at Claire.

"Gia!" Claire nearly fell back in shock. Gia rarely said anything worse than "dang it" and if she did, it had never before been directed at Claire.

"Oh, don't *Gia* me." She picked up the top fifty or so papers from the stack and shook them at Claire.

"What's all that?" Claire said, looking curiously between Gia and the papers.

"Well, as it turns out, this here is a stack full of emails."

"Oh?" Claire said, an uneasy feeling beginning to rise in her stomach. "What emails?" she asked, though she had a feeling she already knew.

"The emails Callum hasn't been sending to you for the past four or so months."

"Gia!" Claire cried. "You went through my *emails?*"

"I did." Gia's voice was even and unapologetic.

"You had *no* right!"

"Well, *you* had no right to archive the hundreds of emails Callum has sent you without even opening them!" Gia spat at her.

"They were my emails to ignore."

"Who *are* you?" Gia asked incredulously. "Seriously. Who *are* you? You can't possibly be Claire because the Claire I know would *never* do this to another human being."

"What are you talking about?" Claire asked, stomping over to Gia and ripping the pages from her hands. "I haven't done anything."

"If you'd have read just one of these emails you'd know exactly what you've done," Gia said, picking up another handful of papers and shaking them at Claire. "Did you read any of these? Please tell me you read one or two that just weren't in that file, the file you named *Him?* Real creative, by the way, Claire."

"Shut up," Claire said, grabbing the second stack from Gia's hand.

"Oh, no. I'm done shutting up. I have something to say and you're going to hear it."

"This is none of your business," Claire said, her voice suddenly cool and steady.

"None of my *business?*" Gia nearly shouted. "Oh, so it's my business when you can't get out of bed because you've lost your entire family and I move into your house and literally spoon-feed you and it's my business when you fall drunk into a pool and I have to leave my date to come pick up your wet sorry ass and it's my business when you've left a man you deeply love and need a shoulder to cry on, not to mention someone to help you pack up your house and *move,* but it's none of my *business* when I see you're breaking the heart of this man? When I see how unfair you're being to him? Is that what you're telling me? I should stand up for you, but not anyone else?"

"That's exactly what I'm telling you."

"I can listen to the misery in your life and be the person to pick up the pieces, but I can't call you on your crap."

"Gia!"

"You know what I think? I think you're a coward," Gia spat.

"A coward? You've *got* to be kidding me."

"Oh, no. I am *definitely* not kidding. You're a *coward*. You're scared to give yourself completely to someone again. You're scared Callum might ask more of you than you're willing to give."

"I did give myself to him. Completely," Claire said defensively.

"Oh, really?" Gia picked up another stack of papers in her other hand. "How completely would that be exactly?"

"That's different."

"Um, maybe in your little Claire world it's different, but not in the world the rest of us live in. You know what I think?"

"No, but I have a feeling you're about to tell me."

"I think it's not that you can't have any more children. I think you don't want any more children."

Claire felt like she'd been slapped.

"Gia, you know that's not true. Being a mom was the best part of my life. I'd kill to do it all over again."

"Well, last I heard, the doctor said you couldn't carry a baby inside of you. Nothing was said about adoption. It's not like you and Callum couldn't afford to adopt," Gia said, glancing over at *The New York Times* still sitting on the kitchen table.

"You didn't see the interview Callum gave. He made a point of saying physically, he's able to have children," Claire said.

"So?"

"So, I hate to say it, but there aren't a whole lot of things Callum is physically able to do—not like the average person, anyway. You should've seen him. He was so *proud,* as if he felt like a whole and complete man because he'd be able to have his own child. He wants to have his own biological baby."

"Well, we don't always get what we want, now do we?" Gia asked. "You should know that better than anyone."

Claire sighed.

"And," Gia continued, "if you'd spent even two minutes reading these emails, you'd be a little bit more clear on what it is Callum *actually* wants, instead of just *thinking* you know what it is."

"I do know what he wants," Claire said, but her voice didn't sound as certain anymore.

"No, I don't think you do," Gia said, putting down the papers she still held in her hands. "You once told me the two of you understood each other completely, but now I'm thinking he knew you, but you never had any idea who he was. You know what you want to believe, what you've let yourself believe. But I can promise you, after reading all of these, you'll realize you've never been more wrong in your life."

Claire's shoulders sagged. Gia grabbed her purse from the chair.

"I'm going to leave now and I'm going to hope you'll stop being so selfish and read his emails. Each and every one of them, Claire. He had to have spent hours writing these. No, I take that back. He must've spent *days* writing these, because the poor man can only type with one hand! You owe it to him to read them."

With that, Gia threw the strap of her bag over her shoulder and walked out the door, still in her pajamas.

Claire stood for what seemed like forever, staring at the stack of papers on her table. Seeing them, like this, piled high, she felt a sense of guilt. Callum could've written two or three more books in the amount of time it had to have taken him to write all of these letters to her.

As stubborn as she was, Claire had to admit Gia had a point. She did owe it to Callum to at least *read* them. Even if they did nothing to change her mind, even if she still felt he was better off with a woman who could bear his child, she owed it to him to read what he'd painstakingly taken the time to write.

She went over to the fridge and fixed herself a snack of cheese and crackers and fruit, sat down at the table and lifted the first page from the pile.

As she began to read, Claire felt a sense of guilt well up inside her, for not doing this sooner. But more than guilt, page after page filled her with the same growing desire she'd felt for Callum when she first realized she loved him. He hadn't changed. His feelings for her hadn't wavered after all this time. He loved her and he made it perfectly clear, over and over and over again, that if it was only the two of them, for the rest of their lives, he'd still count himself the luckiest man on the earth.

Claire realized, as she began to smile with the recognition of how great his love was for her. She couldn't keep doing this. To herself. To him. She needed no one but Callum.

And, it seemed, he needed no one but her.

CHAPTER
THIRTY-THREE

The team was in Nashville. Claire briefly debated driving there, but after realizing it would be at least a ten-hour drive, she opted to buy herself a plane ticket.

Fifteen hours later, she was in her seat, on the runway, heading to Tennessee.

She hadn't told Callum she was coming. She felt it would be best to just show up. Part of her wanted to surprise him, but most of her felt she needed the time it would take to get to Nashville to gather her thoughts and decide what she was going to say and the way in which she planned to apologize. And how she was going to beg him to take her back, despite how she'd treated him.

His emails had pleaded with her to give their relationship another chance. She knew he wanted her. But what if he'd reached the end of his rope? No one, not even Callum, could keep up that desire forever. What if, after the last email he sent her, he'd decided he was done. *Wouldn't that serve her right?*

She couldn't let herself dwell on that thought for long, though. She had too much else on her mind. She was so nervous as the plane reached its cruising altitude, she found her palms were sweating and she had to wipe them on her pants, numerous times.

The only person she'd contacted last night had been Wyatt. She hadn't even called Gia, for no other reason than she didn't need an "I told you so" at the moment. Gia would have plenty of time to gloat later and Claire would have to let her.

Wyatt had answered the phone on the first ring.

"Yello!" he'd said, his drawl as thick as molasses.

"Wyatt, listen to me. It's Claire, and if you're anywhere near Callum, don't let on it's me."

"Well, howdy there, Helen," Wyatt said, enunciating very carefully. "You missing me, baby doll? Didn't get enough of good ole' Wyatt last time I was in Tejas?"

"Oh, brother," Claire said.

"I ain't got a brother, my little lamp-chop. My mama knew she hit pay dirt the moment she gave birth to me."

"Okay, get over yourself," Claire said. "Can you please go somewhere so we can talk privately? I made a big mistake and I need your help fixing it."

The crowd was slowly making their ways to their cars when Claire reached the auditorium in Nashville. Wyatt was waiting for her at the door. She'd texted him from the taxi and told him when she'd be arriving.

"How long is the line?" she asked him, after a quick hug.

"*Long,*" Wyatt said, drawing on the word. "He's going to be busy for a bit."

"We really need to find a way to limit that," Claire said. "It takes too much out of him."

"We?" Wyatt said, raising an eyebrow.

"Yes, we," Claire said. "At least, I hope it's 'we.'"

"I do, too, darlin'," Wyatt said, putting his hand on Claire's arm and steering her in the direction that would take her away from Callum and all the people waiting to see him. Wyatt and the others hadn't been happy with her decision to leave—not just Callum, but the team. They'd become a family and they'd all deserved better. She'd hurt those she loved. She hoped that she could make it up to the rest of them, too.

"You can wait in here," Wyatt said, opening the door to a small conference area. "I'll bring him to you as soon as he's done."

"Thanks."

"I'll go get you something to eat, too, and some water."

"Oh, no. Don't bother. I'm not hungry," Claire said, waving him off.

"I *said,* I'm going to get you some food and some water," Wyatt said sternly. "As I told you, he's going to be a while. I can't have you passing out from weakness before he gets here. Plus, you're gonna be bored. Eating will give you something to do."

"I'll be fine," Claire said. "But food would be nice." She realized, she hadn't eaten much of anything since the cheese and crackers yesterday.

Was that only yesterday? It seemed like years ago since she'd read Callum's emails.

"Are you sure I can't tell Alison you're here? I know she'd love to keep you company. She's really missed you."

"No, not yet," Claire said, though she'd missed Alison terribly, too. "I don't want to see anyone until I see Callum, okay?"

"Whatever you want, darlin'," Wyatt said with a grin as he left to get her food.

When Wyatt said Callum would be a while, he hadn't been exaggerating. An hour and a half later, Claire was done with the hot dog, fries and cotton candy he'd brought her. "Auditorium food," Wyatt had said with a shrug as he put it in front of her. She was literally twiddling her thumbs, wondering what to do while she waited.

How much longer? she asked, texting Wyatt.

Not much now. About twenty more people, he wrote back.

Claire nearly moaned. *Twenty more people?* Even if they only took one minute apiece, which was unlikely, Callum wouldn't be here for almost half an hour.

She picked up her phone, which was nearly dead from all the time she'd been spending surfing the Internet and scrolled through her Facebook newsfeed again.

Forty-five minutes later, the door opened. Claire could hear Wyatt whispering to Callum, "Just one more person. This lady has been hounding me to see you. Driving me nuts, actually. Clinging to me like cellophane."

"Okay," she heard Callum say. "I get the picture."

Wyatt opened the door wide so Callum could roll inside. Claire stood as he entered.

If Claire could have bottled the expression on Callum's face when he saw her, she would have and then saved the bottle so she could open it whenever she was feeling blue.

The surprise, the joy, the love, the tremendous and overwhelming *love*, was unmistakable on his face. His beautiful, handsome, glorious face.

Claire barely noticed Wyatt closing the door behind Callum as he left.

Claire felt the tears well up in her eyes. She'd cried so often over the past few years, she was surprised to realize she had any fluid left in there. But these tears were of joy—and some sadness over how stupid she'd been.

"Is it too late to take it all back?" she asked Callum, her voice softer and meeker than she'd intended.

Claire saw the tears begin to fill Callum's eyes, too.

"No, love," he said, with a shake of his head.

That was all it took for Claire to rush to him and drop to her knees in front of his chair. He took her into his embrace, and she rested her head against his chest, as she began to sob.

"I'm so sorry. I am so sorry," she said.

"It's okay," he said, running his lips along her hair. "It's okay. I'm just so glad you came back. You are back, aren't you? I'm not dreaming?"

"I should've never left. I was so stupid. You were right. I'm so sorry."

She pulled away from him to see his face. From her knees, she had to look up at him, ever so slightly. He wasn't crying as she was. His smile was as bright as the sun.

"I love you," Claire said. "I love you so much. Nothing was right when we weren't together. I tried so hard to make it okay, but it wasn't."

"Are you kidding?" Callum asked. "How could anything be right if we aren't together? We're meant to be together."

Claire nodded. She felt exactly the same way.

"I still can't have children," she said sadly.

"And that still doesn't matter to me," Callum said. "Listen to me. When I did that interview, I hadn't met you. That was the biggest dream I could dream at the time. I didn't know you'd come into my life and bring a bigger dream than I'd ever imagined."

"No," Claire said. "You said it 'cause you meant it. I want to give you a family, but I can't do that."

"If we decide, together, we want a family, we can adopt. And, if we decide, *together*, we don't, that's okay, too," Callum said, running his hand down Claire's hair. "What is not okay...will *never* be okay...is spending one more day without you."

Callum laid his hand on Claire's cheek and gently pulled her toward him. Leaning down to her, he kissed her, ever so gently.

When Callum pulled away, much sooner than Claire would've liked, he looked into her eyes with a love she'd never before seen, not even in the eyes of Jack.

"Claire Elizabeth Matthews, will you marry me?"

"Yes!" Claire cried out, without hesitation. "Yes! Yes! *Yes!* I will most certainly marry you!"

She couldn't believe he hadn't moved on—that he'd waited for her. Still loved her. Still wanted her. Not just wanted her, but wanted to *marry* her.

What had she ever done to deserve so many blessings?

She kissed his face a dozen times, all over his cheeks and his lips and his eyes.

"Hey, hey!" Callum said, laughing. "Back away, lady. I'm not done here."

Claire sat back down on her haunches. "I love you with all my heart."

"I'm beginning to gather that," Callum said with a smile. He reached into the bag he kept on the side of his chair and then, after a little bit of digging around, he pulled out a small, black box. With his thumb, he flicked open the lid.

Inside was the most beautiful diamond ring Claire had ever seen.

"We need to make this official," Callum said.

Claire put out her left hand to Callum, her fingers slightly spread. He rested the box on the arm of his chair as he lifted the ring out and slipped it on her hand.

"You have an engagement ring with you?" Claire asked, staring down at the gorgeous stone that now adorned her ring finger. "Just rattling around in your bag? How did you know I was coming? Did Wyatt tell you?" Claire looked up at Callum with an expression that said she was going to kill Wyatt if he had.

"Wyatt didn't say a word. I promise!" Callum said, laughing. "I'd already planned to give you the ring before you left. I had it all planned out. I couldn't wait to propose. And then you dumped me."

Claire sighed. "Yeah, that was a poor decision on my part."

"That is was," Callum said with a grin. "I kept the ring in my bag all that time. Having it close to me made me feel closer to you. And, it gave me hope that someday you'd agree to be my wife."

"It's beautiful," Claire said, holding out her hand for both of them to see. "But now you won't need the ring to feel close to me."

"Good," Callum said, leaning over to kiss her once more. "Because if you ever left me again, love, I'd come find you."

"You promise?"

"I promise."

The door opened then and Wyatt and Frank and Mitch practically fell into the room. When they saw the ring on Claire's hand, which she was still holding in the air, the men all high-fived each other and Wyatt let out a whooping sound only a cowboy could make.

"I love me a good wedding," Wyatt said. "I sure do love me a good wedding."

Callum and Claire looked at each other and laughed.

"Then I guess we'd better get moving on planning that wedding," Callum said. "We can't have Wyatt disappointed, now can we? He's such a baby when he doesn't get his way."

Wyatt grumbled at Callum's teasing, but instead of punching Callum in the arm, he lifted his hand to high-five him.

"We did it, boss," Wyatt said. "We did it."

"We did," Callum said, looking at Claire. "We most certainly did."

No one even asked what *it* was, exactly, Wyatt had done. But it didn't matter. They were a team. Callum and Claire, as a couple, and the others as part of their family.

And now that Claire was back, they had no intention of letting that team fall apart, ever again.

The wedding was perfect. For Claire's first wedding, to Jack, she'd had the big extravaganza. The big venue, the big crowd, the even bigger dress.

Her parents hadn't been there—they were both gone by then—but her mom and dad had set aside money they'd been saving, ever since Claire was a little girl, for her special day. The fact that they'd scrimped and saved their hard-earned money to ensure their daughter would experience the perfect wedding touched Claire's heart and made it feel as if her parents were that much closer to her as she walked down the aisle.

There were no parents to pay for the wedding this time, but of course, that didn't matter. Both Callum and Claire were fully capable of paying for their own event. And neither of them had the desire for a large and showy wedding. They were both private people, Claire even more so since the accident. They only had a small number of friends and some family they wished to invite.

Callum's mother had begged them to have the wedding in Ireland. Callum and Claire had considered it, but briefly. They knew most of their friends wouldn't be able to take the time off work or have the money to afford such a trip. So, in the end, they settled on an ideal location just outside of Atlanta. It was a small, wooden, whitewashed church with ten simple pews on either side. The chapel was situated on fifteen acres of lush, green land and as soon as Callum and Claire saw it, they knew it was the perfect spot to begin their union. Alison served as wedding planner, at her insistence, and by the time Claire arrived at the church on her wedding day, a large white tent had been set up on the lawn to the right of the chapel where the guests would be treated to an old-fashioned Southern feast that included ham, cornbread, pecan pie and peach cobbler.

No matter how much Callum begged both Claire and Alison, black pudding did not make the menu.

Claire was certain she'd cry as she walked down the aisle toward Callum, but found she could do nothing but smile. She was so happy— deliriously happy—and everyone could see it.

"Knock it off," she whispered to Callum, whose eyes were misty, as she reached him at the front of the chapel. "Haven't you heard? Weddings are happy occasions."

That had brought a smile to Callum's face and the two of them never stopped grinning from that point forward.

"You look stunning," Callum said.

Claire was delighted he thought so. She hadn't wanted to wear an elaborate, long gown for this wedding. Instead, she selected a tea-length, ivory dress with a jeweled illusion neckline. The waist was fitted, but it flared out, ever so slightly, at her hips. The look was flattering and elegant and fit Claire perfectly.

Claire had worried she'd forget the vows she wrote and decided, as a safeguard, to write them down.

"My bride will not be reading to me from a piece of paper," Callum had said to her when she'd told him her plan.

"But what if I forget?"

"How much you love me? How handsome I am? How thankful you are that I agreed to become your husband?"

Claire had laughed. "Yes. What if I forget those things?"

"You look in my eyes, love, and you'll remember it all once again."

Callum had been right. Claire's voice shook as she began to speak her vows, but the moment she saw his sparkling baby blues, the church, with its guests and flowers, all fell away. Nothing existed except Claire and Callum.

"When I met you," Claire said softly. "I had no idea how my life was about to change. How could I possibly know? My world was full of such sadness and despair. I could see no way out of the darkness, until you came along, held my hand, and pulled me through. Because of you, I laugh and smile and dare to dream again. Thank you for being the miracle you are, the miracle I needed. Today, I give myself to you in marriage. When you lose your way, I promise to remind you where you were going. And, when you get there, I promise to have a whole lot of sightseeing planned."

There was a chuckle from the crowd, as everyone who knew Claire knew she'd never found a tourist attraction she didn't love.

"I promise to be your rock, your legs and your left arm and to remind you that, despite a few missing limbs, you were the only person on earth who was able to make me whole again.

"I love you," Claire mouthed to Callum when she finished.

"From the moment I met you," Callum began. "You surprised me, distracted me, captivated me, and challenged me in a way no one else ever has. I have fallen in love with you, over and over again, countless times, and I fall more in love with you every day. I promise to be true to you, to uplift you and support you, *to frustrate you.*"

Callum turned to the crowd and said, "I'm already really great at that one."

Turning back to Claire, he gave her his now-familiar wink. "I want to share with you all the beautiful, quirky moments of life and, maybe someday, if the stars align, I might even let you win an argument."

Claire slitted her eyes at him, giving him the dirtiest look she could muster.

"Though, of course, you're *always* right," Callum teased, before turning serious again. "No matter what trials we encounter or what hardships we endure together or how much time has passed, I know our love will never fade, that we'll always find strength in one another, that we'll continue to grow, side by side. You are my partner in crime, and I will love you, always, with every beat of my heart."

Claire leaned over to Callum as the crowd sighed at the beauty of his words. "You found that online, didn't you?" Claire whispered.

Callum winked at her again and whispered back, "I shall never tell, love."

Before Claire knew it, she and Callum had said their "I do's" and exchanged their rings. Callum had told Claire, prior to their wedding, that in countries such as Germany, Greece, Russia and Spain, it's common to wear one's wedding ring on the right hand.

"Your point being?" Claire had asked.

"Just that when we visit those countries, I'll fit in quite nicely," Callum had said with a grin.

Once Callum's ring was safely on his right ring finger and Claire's securely on her left, all that was left was the kiss. They made sure to make it a memorable one.

Callum wore his legs to the ceremony. Not his arm, because he found it to be too annoying, but he insisted on wearing his legs.

"I never turn down a chance to walk beside a beautiful woman," he reminded Claire, as they walked back up the aisle, hand in hand, as husband and wife.

Claire hadn't enjoyed dancing this much since the night at the pool party, except this time, she did it sober and knew this evening was going to have a much better ending.

Callum did his best to dance while wearing his legs. They managed one slow dance together and then he tried a couple of the faster tempo numbers, but before long, Claire was whispering in his ear, "Go get your chair," and he was grateful to oblige.

Claire found enormous delight in watching their family and friends enjoy themselves. Nearly all of those she loved were there. Nora and Patrick, Callum's brother and his family, Alison and Mitch, Frank and a middle-aged widow he'd recently begun seeing—even some of Claire's "Mom Friends" were there with their husbands. None of them had brought their kids, though. It wasn't that Claire had asked them not to, but they'd all recognized it might not be the right occasion for Claire to have to face her children's friends. The only people who didn't attend were Bill and Nancy. They had, of course, been invited and Claire had called them, personally, to tell them how much she wanted them there.

"You're my family," she'd insisted.

They'd told her they felt the same about her, and though they were truly happy for her—they loved Callum to pieces—it would be too difficult for them to watch Claire say "I do" to a man who wasn't their son.

"We promise to come visit you once you're back from your honeymoon," Nancy had said, and Claire told her she planned to hold them to it.

The most entertaining part of the whole night, though, for both Callum and Claire, was the dance that was going on between Gia and Wyatt.

"You have got to be kidding me," was all Callum said when Claire had first mentioned the idea.

But, upon further discussion, they'd both come to the conclusion that, in fact, their two good friends, Gia and Wyatt, might actually be the perfect match.

Callum and Claire had schemed, in advance, finding numerous wedding preparations, during the days leading up to the ceremony, where both Gia and Wyatt would be needed. That was all it took. By the time the reception rolled around, Wyatt was holding Gia close around the waist and she was staring up at him with eyes as big as a Texas sky.

"Perhaps now," Claire said to Callum, as they sat at their table under the reception tent, "I'll no longer have to hear about the endless parade of losers."

"Nope. Now you'll only have to hear about one loser," Callum said, taking a bite of his cobbler.

"Callum!" Claire said, swatting him in the chest. "Wyatt is not a loser."

"Of course not!" Callum asked incredulously. "Watch what you say about my best man, will you?"

Claire shook her head as Callum grinned at her. Picking up his spoon, he tapped it against his water glass a number of times. The band slowed and lowered their music and the crowd turned their attention to the groom.

"Can I have your attention, please? For just one moment." Callum reached to the armrest of his chair and raised his seat as high as it would go. "I know it's customary to stand when you give a toast, but I hope this will do. I've been looking forward to this day all my life. And, if we're to be honest here, I think we all know I wasn't always sure it would come. I might talk a good game, but there was always a part of me—the little-boy-inside part of me—that wondered if I'd ever truly find a woman who not only challenged and intrigued me, but someone who was able to look past all of this," Callum waved across his body, "to see the real me." Callum turned to Claire. "Claire Fitzgerald, you enchant me. I am moved each and every time you walk into a room. Will you all raise a glass?" Callum asked, turning back to the crowd, as he reached for his wineglass. "To Claire. My love. My life. The mate of my soul."

As the guests raised their own glasses to toast, and Callum took a sip of his wine, Claire's heart overflowed with happiness. Callum gave her more joy than she'd thought possible. She was so incredibly blessed to not only have him in her life, but to have him love her so.

Callum had called her the "mate of his soul." She smiled at the phrase. She'd never before been certain such things existed, but at this moment, on this beautiful starry night, with her groom by her side, she knew they did. She *was* the "mate of his soul." And he was the mate of hers.

CHAPTER
THIRTY-FOUR

"Morning, Mrs. Fitzgerald," Callum said, kissing Claire on the forehead as they lay in bed.

"Mmmm..." Claire moaned.

Callum kissed her again and gently brushed the hair away from her face.

"Say it again," Claire whispered, her voice groggy.

"Say what again?" Callum asked.

"Mrs. Fitzgerald."

"You have now been Mrs. Fitzgerald for three whole months. I'd think hearing it would be old hat by now."

"I could listen to you say it all day long," Claire said, her eyes still closed, as she snuggled closer to Callum.

"How about, instead of all day, you hear it for the next fifty years?" Callum asked.

"Even better," Claire said, a smile playing at her lips. "What time is it?"

"Nine-thirty."

Claire's eyes flew open.

"Damn it," she said, rolling over and throwing her legs over the side of the bed.

"What? Do you have a hot date today?"

"I forgot to take my pill last night," Claire said, walking into the bathroom. "I'm terrible about remembering it."

Removing a small yellow pill from the pack, she filled the glass she kept on the counter with water and popped the pill in her mouth.

"I haven't taken these in about fifteen years," Claire called out to Callum. "It's hard to get back in the routine again."

"You didn't take it after the twins?" Callum asked as Claire walked back into their bedroom. He was sitting up in bed now, his back propped against the headboard. Claire smiled at how handsome he was, even this early in the morning. She wished she could say she looked just as good, but she'd caught a glimpse of herself in the bathroom mirror and that definitely wasn't the case.

"Oh, no. Jack had a vasectomy right away. I should've had my tubes tied, but...well, I didn't and it seemed easier..." Claire smiled. "At least, easier for *me* if Jack was the one who got 'fixed.'"

Claire walked to her dresser and took a clean bra and panties out of the drawer.

"Remind me next week to make an appointment and I'll do the same," Callum said.

"Do the same what?" Claire asked, distracted as she dug through the bottom drawer for her favorite college T-shirt.

"Get fixed," Callum said, with a grin. "Like a dog."

"Absolutely not," Claire said, finding the shirt and yanking it from the bottom of the pile. "It's my problem. I'll take care of it."

"First of all, Claire, it's 'our' problem, not yours. And, it's not a problem. It's a situation that needs to be handled."

Holding her clothes in a bunch by her stomach, Claire sat down on the bed next to Callum.

"Callum?" she asked.

"Yes?" He reached to his nightstand to grab the remote for the TV.

"What if you marry someone else someday and want kids with her?"

Callum's arm froze, remote in hand. Slowly, he lowered it to the bed and rolled back to face Claire.

"Why would I ever marry someone else, love? Do you plan on leaving me for some hot Italian on our next tour?"

"No, it's..." Claire said wistfully. "You never know where life is gonna take you. I always thought I'd be married to Jack forever. Something could happen to me. You might want kids someday with someone else. I don't want you to limit your options."

Callum dropped the remote and pulled Claire toward him on the bed.

"Listen to me, Mrs. Fitzgerald. You are 'it' for me. There will never be anyone else. If, heaven forbid, something ever happened to you, I'd spend the rest of my life waiting to be with you again. I will not be having children with other women."

"You can't say that. I never thought I'd meet someone after Jack."

"I won't," Callum said. "I know me. So, case closed, okay?"

Claire pulled her legs back on the bed and snuggled into Callum's chest.

"You're the best, you know that?" she asked.

"So you keep telling me, love," he said, kissing the top of her head. "As I said, I'll call next week for an appointment. It's not a big deal."

Claire giggled. "Okay, let's see if you say that when you're on the couch with a pack of frozen peas between your legs."

"Ouch!" Callum yelped. "You didn't mention that part."

Claire smiled as she rolled the hair on his chest between her index finger and her thumb.

"I'll be there to bring you a frozen bag of corn when the peas defrost."

"Well, there's that," Callum said. "But, in the meantime, until I can have that lovely experience, don't forget to take your pill."

"Yes, sir," Claire said as she leaned her head up to Callum, her lips searching for his.

"You seriously are the biggest baby," Claire said, removing the ice pack from between his legs and replacing it with a new, towel-wrapped one.

"Hey, there! Watch how you drop that thing! I'm an injured man."

"You do realize I complained less after giving birth, right? And, not only that, but I had to actually get up and take care of those babies while I was busy not complaining."

"Yes. Yes. I think you've mentioned it every time you've brought me a new ice pack," Callum said, leaning his head back against the arm of the couch.

Callum added, "Want to watch a movie tonight?"

"I don't know," Claire said, walking back into the room. "I'm exhausted. I think I want to go to bed."

Callum glanced at the clock on the wall.

"It's only eight-thirty, love. Are you trying to say taking care of me has worn you out?"

"That must be it," Claire said. "Do you mind? Raincheck on the movie?"

"Sure, that's fine."

"Do you want me to help you into bed?"

"No, I'm not ready to fall asleep and I'll keep you up if I watch TV."

"How will you get into our room when you're ready?" she asked him. She normally didn't have to help Callum get into bed at night, but she knew he'd struggle, tonight. Any man would struggle, but moving around would be even more difficult for Callum.

"I'll sleep here on the couch, love."

"Really?" Claire said, her voice full of disappointment. They'd been married for close to five months and had yet to spend a night apart, even a room apart.

"Don't look at me like that!" Callum said. "Enough of those weepy eyes. I'm just sleeping on the couch, not filing for divorce. You'll survive one night. If you really miss me, you can always come out here and join me."

"I doubt I'll miss you that much," Claire teased, heading into the bedroom.

"You're still sleeping?"

Claire pulled the pillow over her head and moaned.

"Hey, sleepyhead, come on. Time to get up. I made you breakfast."

Claire could hear the hum of Callum's chair as he rolled closer to the bed.

"You've been doing an awful lot of sleeping this past week. Taking care of me for a few days last week wasn't all that exhausting, was it?"

Claire nodded that it was.

"Now, Claire, you know if I move that pillow off your head, I'm going to drop this breakfast onto the bed. I'm not an octopus, you know. I don't have eight arms."

Claire pulled the pillow further around her head.

"That was supposed to be funny, love," Callum said. "Get it? I don't have eight arms? You're supposed to say, 'You don't even have two.'"

When Claire didn't stir, Callum said, "Okay, then. I'll leave the food here on the nightstand and when you're hungry, you can eat. But, you'd better hurry up. It'll get cold quickly."

Claire didn't say a word, but she heard him roll out of the room.

She continued to lie in bed, without moving, for a few more minutes and then decided Callum was right. She needed to eat something. She hadn't had much of an appetite for at least a week now. She'd still been preparing meals for Callum—things that sounded good to her before she began to cook them—but then found, once the food was on the table, all she was able to do was pick at it.

She hoped she wasn't coming down with something. They were due to go back on tour in a little more than a week and she had a ton to do before then. Not only did she and Callum have to prepare for their trip, but she also needed to get busy putting their home and lives on hold until they got back two months later.

Lowering the covers from over her head, she slowly sat up and lifted the plate, which Callum had left beside her, and placed it on her lap.

Scrambled eggs, toast and strawberries, usually one of her favorites. She took a spoonful and raised it to her mouth.

The smell was overwhelming. The odor nauseating. Quickly shoving the plate to the side of her, Claire threw off the covers and ran to the bathroom. She barely reached the toilet before she began to retch.

She wanted to believe she had a stomach bug. But she knew that wasn't the case.

She'd been here before, clutching the porcelain god as she prayed the heaving would stop before her entire insides spewed from her body. She knew what this meant.

It meant she and Callum had one big problem on their hands.

CHAPTER
THIRTY-FIVE

Claire sat on the blue tile floor of their bathroom as the plus sign slowly darkened on the stick.

She was expecting it. Just like she'd been expecting it with the four other tests she'd taken this morning.

How was she going to tell Callum?

She couldn't believe this was happening. They'd been so careful. Until Callum got his vasectomy a couple of weeks earlier, she'd taken the pill religiously. Well, *semi*-religiously. She'd only forgotten it a couple of nights, but she'd always remembered it as soon as she woke and would take it immediately after that. She hadn't thought it was such a big deal to be late by twelve or so hours.

Apparently it was.

Claire stared at the stick and thought about what this meant, for her, for Callum, for them.

The foremost thought was that this was dangerous, for her and for the baby. A pregnancy after what she'd been through, physically, could put them both in danger. She wasn't exactly sure what kind of danger or what the ramifications could be if she carried this baby to term. She hadn't asked those kinds of questions after her surgery. She hadn't really cared at that moment and avoiding any future pregnancy hadn't mattered to her. She'd just wanted her babies back. It never crossed her mind to worry about future children.

Callum was going to flip out. That was the second issue. She had to present this to him in such a way that he'd see it as a blessing and not a curse.

A blessing. The longer Claire sat on the cold floor, her back propped up against the cabinet of the sink, the more she began to believe it. They hadn't been trying for this. They hadn't wanted it. In fact, if they'd been trying for anything, it was to keep this exact thing from happening.

This hadn't been the plan. Not *their* plan, at least. Didn't the saying go, though, the easiest way to make God laugh was to tell Him your plans?

She and Callum had created a baby. A life. The two of them were together, forever, inside this incredible new creation. Claire couldn't think of anything more beautiful than that.

And she'd be a mom again. She'd hold her own child in her arms. This baby could never replace the ones she'd lost, but maybe he or she would be able to fill some of the void that still remained inside Claire.

Callum and the doctors were not going to see this as positive news. But, if she were able to defy the odds and give birth to a healthy baby, wouldn't it all be worth it? Wouldn't the possibly difficult pregnancy be worth the prize at the end?

She certainly thought so. Now she needed to convince Callum.

The thought of that, and how he was going to react, almost made her want to begin vomiting again.

"Whoah, love," Callum said as he came home after work. "What's all this?" He was eyeing the dining room table, which Claire had set with the china they'd received as a wedding gift from Callum's parents—the same china they hadn't really wanted but received graciously. There were flowers in the center, candles flanking either side, and a feast of seafood and steak near their plates.

"Just a little romance," Claire said, smiling. "We need to eat more home-cooked meals. With all our time on the road, we've become too reliant on restaurants and takeout. It's time to begin eating healthier."

"And steak and shrimp are now considered healthy?"

"Well," Claire said, smiling. "They're a start. At least they're home-cooked."

"It looks delicious."

"Before we eat, though, let's go into the living room and relax for a moment. I'll cover the food so it doesn't get cold."

She went to the kitchen and came back with a couple of large bowls. She placed them over the food and then indicated to Callum he should go into the other room. She picked up the glass of wine she'd poured him and followed behind him into the living room. Callum rolled his chair to the couch and then climbed onto it. Claire sat next to him and handed him the glass.

"I could get used to this," Callum said, taking a sip of the wine.

"What's that?"

"Coming home to a hot meal and a glass of wine waiting for me."

"What about the beautiful wife?" Claire asked.

"I'm already used to that part. I come home to her every night."

He leaned over and kissed Claire.

"Well, actually, I have a confession to make," Claire said, doing her best to steady her voice. "We're actually celebrating."

"We are? What's that, love?"

Claire paused.

"How would you like to come home every night to a hot meal, a glass of wine, a beautiful wife and a family?"

Callum didn't speak for a moment.

"Are you saying you'd like to adopt?"

They hadn't discussed the idea since they got back together. Claire knew Callum didn't want to pressure her and if and when she was ready to consider that option, he knew she'd mention it on her own. She hadn't felt the desire to bring it up and so she hadn't.

"Not exactly." She'd practiced, all day long, how she was going to tell him and yet, here they were, and she had no idea what to say.

She might as well spit it out.

"I'm pregnant."

The words weren't out of her mouth a half a second before Callum dropped his glass of wine, splattering the red liquid all over himself, Claire and the couch.

"Geez, Callum!" Claire cried, jumping up off the couch. "What a mess!"

"Is this a joke?" Callum asked, his voice cool. "If it is, it's not a very funny one."

"No, it's not a joke," Claire said as she walked into the kitchen to grab a rag and some club soda. Walking back into the room, she said, again, "It's not a joke. I'm pregnant."

"How?" Callum asked, his voice more shaky than Claire had ever heard it before. "You were on the pill."

Claire knelt down next to the couch, poured some soda onto the towel and began to dab at the wine on the cushion.

"Well, I guess it didn't work as planned."

"Did you do this on purpose?"

Claire stopped what she was doing and stared up at Callum. His question nearly took her breath away.

"Callum! How could you even ask that?"

"Well, I don't know. How could I? Hmm, let's see." His tone was cool and Claire could sense the anger lying just beneath the calm.

"You're accusing me of not only putting my life at risk, but deceiving you, too?" She scrubbed harder than she knew she should. She didn't want the wine to set deeper into the fabric. "I don't know how it happened," Claire continued truthfully. "Maybe because I didn't always take the pill at the same time every day. Or, I had that sinus infection two months ago. I was given a prescription for it and, it turns out, antibiotics can mess up the effectiveness of the pill. I don't know. Really, I don't."

"Stop cleaning," Callum ordered, moving from the couch to his chair.

"I can't," Claire said. "In fact, why don't you give me your shirt? It's a mess." He had dark red stains all down the front of his polo shirt and his jeans.

"Oh, you're right about that. It's a mess," Callum barked at her. "But the wine has nothing to do with it."

He rolled across the room, away from Claire. She could practically see the steam rising from his ears. He was furious. She half wondered if he was going to pick up something breakable and throw it into the fireplace.

"Callum," Claire pleaded, resting back on her feet. "Please stop. You're scaring me. I wanted you to be happy."

"Happy?" Callum practically screamed the word at her, spinning his chair around to face her. *"Happy?* Are you out of your mind? How could you have *ever* thought this might make me happy?"

"You've always wanted a baby."

"I have always made it perfectly clear to you that what I wanted was you! A baby could kill you. *Do you get that?* You could die."

He said the last three words as if each one was its own sentence.

"I won't," Claire said softly.

"You don't know that." His voice was softer, but still full of the same anger or was it...fear? Yes, beneath the anger, Claire heard the fear.

"Callum," Claire said, laying down the rag and resting her hands on her thighs. "I know it's scary. I'm scared, too. But, I also didn't want tonight to go like this."

"I don't know how it could have gone any other way, Claire."

Claire put her hands on the ground and crawled the four or so feet over to him. When she reached him, she got back on her knees and reached up to him, resting her hands on his legs.

"I really feel this is going to be okay," she said.

"Well, I'm glad one of us does," Callum said, his voice dripping with sarcasm.

"Please don't be upset. I made a doctor's appointment for tomorrow. Let's wait and see what he says. Please. Let's not be upset for the rest of tonight."

Callum sighed loudly. He put his hand on top of Claire's.

"Okay, but let me make something very clear. I will not lose you. Do you hear me? I will not lose you."

"You won't," Claire said. "I promise. Everything is going to be okay. I know it."

Callum looked at her, clearly not convinced.

But Claire *was* convinced this would, somehow, all work out. She wasn't sure how, but she must have gotten pregnant for a reason. Even with the issues with the pill, she wasn't a young twenty-something woman. Getting pregnant at her age couldn't be as easy as it had been when she was newly married to Jack. If she was pregnant now, with her age and the precautions they'd taken, especially in the short amount of time there was before Callum got his vasectomy, there had to be a reason for it.

A plan. Callum was always talking about there being a plan.

She just needed to convince him this was somehow a part of it.

"I'm going to be perfectly honest, Mr. and Mrs. Fitzgerald," the doctor said as Callum and Claire sat, nervously, in his office. Claire had gone in for an exam an hour earlier and she'd had her medical records sent over from her doctor in Florida. "This will be an extremely high-risk pregnancy. I can't lie. If you insist on carrying this pregnancy..."

"We do," Claire said, interrupting.

Callum sat perfectly still next to Claire. Claire forced herself to look at the doctor and not at Callum. She knew the expression she'd find on his face if she turned her head. Misery, anger and fear. Claire couldn't bear it.

Claire saw the doctor glance at Callum and sensed the two of them were exchanging a look that said they weren't sure Claire was being realistic here.

"As I was saying," the doctor continued, looking back at Claire. "If you insist on carrying this pregnancy to term, you'll need to follow my instructions to a tee. No exceptions. Is that understood?"

"Yes," Claire said.

"No physical exercise. Minimal exertion. At some point, during your second trimester, you'll be put on full bedrest. Do you understand?"

"Yes," Claire replied again.

"Most importantly," the doctor said. "I don't want you to go into labor. We'll schedule a c-section prior to your due date."

"Why would going into labor be so dangerous?" Callum asked. It was the first thing he'd said during their meeting.

"It would put a big strain on Claire's body. And we can't risk the uterus rupturing. We want to get this baby out on our terms—not his."

Claire glanced over at Callum. His face had a greenish tint, as if he might be ill at any moment.

"Do I have your support in this, Mr. Fitzgerald?" the doctor asked.

Callum swallowed hard. "I'll do anything to make sure Claire comes out of this alive."

"Me and the baby," Claire said.

Callum remained silent and didn't look at Claire.

"Okay, then," the doctor said, rising from his chair. "Come back and see me in two weeks. I'll be monitoring your progress very closely, Mrs. Fitzgerald."

"Please call me, Claire," she said as she stood.

"Claire, then," the doctor said.

"I need to go schedule my next appointment." Claire turned to Callum. "Meet me by the elevator, okay?"

Callum nodded.

"Thank you, Doctor," Claire said, putting out her hand. The doctor took her hand in his and shook it.

"Don't thank me, yet," he said.

Claire gave Callum a little wave as she left the office.

Callum rolled his chair back, but as he began to turn it toward the door, he stopped.

"Dr. Lindberg?"

"Yes?"

"Please promise me if you have to decide between saving Claire or the baby, you'll save Claire. I know that sounds terrible. I shouldn't be asking you such a thing, but you have to understand. I can't lose my wife."

Callum's eyes were brimming with tears. The doctor came around the desk and gently rested his hand on Callum's shoulder.

"I'll do my best to make sure you don't lose your wife *or* your child."

"Thank you," Callum said, rolling out the door in search of Claire.

CHAPTER
THIRTY-SIX

Claire leaned against the door of Callum's home office. He was at his desk, staring at the screen of his laptop. If he knew Claire was there, he didn't acknowledge it. Yet, in the five minutes Claire had been standing there, he also hadn't typed a single word, so she knew he wasn't concentrating on work.

"I never thought I'd say this, Callum," Claire said, breaking the silence. "But you're a hypocrite."

Callum lifted his head and met her eyes. He remained silent.

"You go around the world, telling people how God has a plan for their lives. You write books about it. Best sellers. People buy into what you're selling. I've seen you tell disabled *orphans* to believe there's a plan for them, too."

Callum's eyes were steady on Claire, but he didn't move.

"And then, when something happens in your own life—something you don't like, something you weren't planning on—you decide God must've made a mistake," Claire continued. "I can't live like that, Callum. I can't trust some things happen for a reason and others are happenstance. And the Callum I married couldn't live like that, either."

Claire started to leave, but then stopped in the doorframe and turned back to him.

"The way I see it," she said. "You either believe what you preach or you don't. If you can't accept this pregnancy is meant to be—for *whatever* reason, no matter *what* the outcome—then maybe it's time for you to look for a new profession."

Without glancing back at Callum, Claire turned and walked away.

Claire's hands glided over the ivory keys. She rarely played the piano these days. Hadn't really played it in years. Callum had bought her a beautiful baby grand as a wedding gift and though she loved to look at it, to sit at it and gently touch the keys, she'd barely played a single song since he'd given her the gift. Playing the piano had been something she did years ago, first when she dreamed of a music career and then, later, as entertainment for her children. They'd sit on her lap, their hands on top of hers, as she'd play lullabies to soothe them and rock songs that would make them squeal with glee.

She hadn't played, just for herself, in a very long time.

But tonight, her heart was heavy. She could think of no better way to express her melancholy than through music.

She played the first song that came to mind. "Too Ra Loo Ra Loo Ra." The song she used to sing to her children before they went to bed.

"My mam used to sing this song to me when I was a tiny lad in Ireland," Callum said, startling Claire. She hadn't heard him come in behind her.

"Really?" Claire quietly asked. "I used to sing it to my kids every night before bed."

She continued to play the tune, soft and sweet.

"I'm a jerk," Callum said.

Claire smiled as she continued to play but said nothing.

"I guess you agree."

"You're not a jerk, Callum." Claire sighed. "You're scared. I get that. You have a right to feel that way."

"And you don't?"

"Have a right? Sure," she said, though she knew that wasn't what he'd meant. "And it's not that I'm not frightened. It's just I'm more excited than scared."

Callum ran his fingers up and down her arm as she played.

"How do you do that?" he asked her.

"What? Play the piano and talk at the same time?"

"No. Trust everything will be okay?"

"Maybe because I've already lost everything. In a way, so have you. How much bad luck can two people have in a lifetime?"

"I'm scared to find out." Callum's voice was so very small.

"I never thought I'd be given this chance, I mean, to be a mom again, to carry a baby inside of me. I refuse to see it as anything but a blessing."

"It's not a blessing if I lose you."

"You won't."

Callum moved closer and rested his forehead on her shoulder.

"Promise?" he begged.

"I promise," Claire said, leaning her head so it touched his.

"I want to be excited."

"I know."

"Be patient, okay? I'll come around."

"I'll be right here waiting for you when you do," Claire said.

"I love you, Claire Fitzgerald." He put his hand on her belly. "And I love her, too."

"Her, huh?" Claire said, softly playing the upper keys.

"Yep. Her. A little girl as precious as her mam."

"Too La Loo Ra Loo Ra. Too La Loo Ra Li. To La Loo Ra Loo Ra. Hush now, don't you cry."

Claire's voice filled the room—beautiful and sweet—as she sang, gently, to the baby she was beginning to love, and the man she loved even more.

"Look who I found at the airport," Callum said, rolling into their bedroom, a very excited Gia behind him.

"Gia!" Claire exclaimed upon seeing her friend. "I'm so glad you're here! You have no idea. I was afraid your flight might be cancelled because of the snow."

Gia headed straight to the bed and climbed in next to Claire before giving her best friend a hug.

"You think a little snow would keep me away?" Gia said.

"I'm going to leave you ladies alone now. I'm sure you don't want me around for all your girl talk. You don't mind if I go into the office for a bit, do you?"

"No, that's fine," Claire said.

Callum leaned down to kiss Claire.

"Have fun catching up."

"I love you," Claire said.

"Ditto, love. Glad you're here, Gia. Claire is sick of me hovering over her like a mama bear."

"Now I'll get to do the hovering," Gia said, patting Claire's ample belly. "And take care of my goddaughter."

"You're in good hands," Callum said to Claire as he left the room.

"Sweetie," Gia said, turning to Claire once Callum was gone. "That is one *huge* belly."

"I know," Claire said, grinning. "She's going to be a big girl."

"What does the doctor say?"

"Everything's going smoothly. I'm supposed to stay in bed until my c-section next week, but thank heavens this bedrest thing is almost over."

Claire had been on bedrest for one hundred and thirty-three days, not that she was counting. At her insistence, she and Callum had both completed the first six-week tour they'd already planned. Callum had wanted to cancel it, but Claire insisted she wasn't even showing yet.

"The baby is the size of half a pea, right now," she told him. "It's hardly going to rip me apart."

Still, Callum was always around to drive Claire insane.

You shouldn't be carrying that.

You shouldn't be standing for so long.

You shouldn't be lying in that position for the entire night.

Claire usually appeased him and gave in to whatever it was he was concerned over, but when he asked her whether it was healthy for her to be gaining so much weight—he'd read a woman should gain about one pound per week during the second and third trimester and Claire was gaining closer to a pound and a half—she nearly slugged him.

"If you ever comment on my weight again," she said, her eyes blazing. "I'm going to rip off the one arm you have left; you got it?!"

She was fuming and there was no mistaking her furor. He backed down and never mentioned it again.

She'd argued when the doctor put her on bedrest during the fourth month.

"Already?" she'd asked during her regular appointment. "It seems so early."

"She'll be in her bed in an hour," Callum had said to the doctor, ignoring Claire. "And I won't let her up again."

The doctor had said she was allowed to get out of bed to use the restroom and to shower, but that was it.

"We can't take any chances," he'd said and Callum had wholeheartedly agreed.

Claire knew Callum and the doctor, whom she'd come to really like during all her visits, were only doing what was best for her and the baby, yet that didn't help ease her boredom.

In the past hundred-plus days, Claire had watched nearly every movie and TV series on Netflix. When Nora came to visit for a nearly two-month stay, she'd taught Claire to knit and by the time Gia arrived, Claire had completed three blankets, two pairs of booties and four little caps.

"Are you going to start a business?" Gia asked, looking through Claire's completed projects as she and Claire rested on the bed.

"You never know. I'm getting quite good at this knitting thing."

Claire had also read a whole stack of books, which were now piled high on her nightstand. Callum had offered to take them away and put them on the bookshelf, but she'd told him she liked to see the pile. It made her feel as if she'd accomplished something during the past few months.

"You have accomplished something," Callum had insisted. "You've grown our baby."

Claire had rolled her eyes at Callum. Keeping this baby inside her was no small feat, but it wasn't like she'd been kneading their child together. She was the oven, not the baker.

"I can't wait to get up and go for a long walk," Claire told Gia. "I've been stuck in this bed for way too long."

"You won't feel like doing any walking after that c-section," Gia said. "Remember how you felt after the twins were born? You couldn't ingest that hydrocodone fast enough."

"Yeah," Claire said, remembering how miserable she'd been after that delivery. "That sucked."

"Soon you'll be begging to get back into this bed."

"Hard to imagine," Claire said. "I feel like the mattress is permanently attached to my rear end."

"No, that mass you feel back there is your actual rear end. How much weight have you gained anyway?"

Claire glared, but Gia laughed.

"You look great. I'm just giving you a hard time. Callum said you're very touchy about your weight."

"As you'll be, someday, when you're pregnant," Claire said. "Wait and see."

"If you say so."

"Speaking of which," Claire said. "How are things with you and Wyatt?"

"Well, that was quite the transition there," Gia said. "It's not to the point where I'm pregnant, I can assure you."

"I wasn't insinuating that. I'm just curious."

"All's good. Great, actually," Gia said. "I really like him."

"Like?" Claire asked, digging for more.

"Okay, love. I love him."

If Claire had been able to, she would've leaped off the bed and jumped up and down.

"I knew it! I knew it! I could tell by the way the two of you were staring at each other the last time we were all together. I am the best matchmaker ever."

Ever since the wedding, a year earlier, Wyatt and Gia had been an item. Because Claire was on bedrest, she'd missed out on spending a great deal of time with the new couple when Gia had flown out to see Wyatt in the various cities he, Callum and the team had visited.

Claire had insisted Callum continue with his scheduled appearances, even after she was put on bedrest and could no longer join them. Callum had argued, but Claire promised she was fine and he'd be disappointing a whole lot of people.

"Not to mention the financial mess it would be to cancel all of those venues," she'd said.

"I am not going to leave you alone," he'd said.

"I won't be alone," she'd protested. "Your mom said she'd come. And Nancy said she could visit and help me out, also."

"You really want to be alone with Nancy for that long?" Callum had asked, raising an eyebrow.

Claire had laughed. No, she didn't. She and her former in-laws had a really great relationship now, much better than when Jack was alive, but Claire didn't want to push her luck. A dinner with Nancy was probably her limit.

"Okay, not really, but I also don't want to hold you back."

"Hold me back?" Callum had asked. "You are my back!"

"That doesn't make sense."

"It doesn't have to. The point is, I'm spending every moment I can with you before this baby comes."

"Because you still think something will go wrong?"

"No, love. Because once this baby comes, we'll be so busy, we won't have much alone time anymore."

"Oh, you have *no* idea," Claire had said, laughing. And he really didn't. But then, what first-time parent could possibly comprehend the way his or her life was about to be turned upside down? She hadn't understood it. Neither had Jack.

Callum had agreed to finish his last few speaking engagements while Claire stayed at home, as long as his mother came to stay with Claire for the weeks he was gone. After that, he'd insisted Alison put an indefinite hold on any future speaking engagements until the baby was born. He told the team, from that point on, they'd concentrate more on the charity portion of their organization, the fundraising and donation of walkers and wheelchairs. Callum also wanted the team to increase their focus on making sure more amputees could afford the prosthetics they needed.

"So, what's the plan?" Claire asked Gia.

"The plan? What plan?"

"The plan for you and Wyatt." She cupped her hand to her ear. "What? Is that wedding bells I hear?"

"Ha ha," Gia said sarcastically. "Very funny."

"I am funny," Claire said, picking up the remote for the TV. "Tell me your plans and then let's watch a chick flick."

"I thought you've already seen every movie on Netflix."

"Oh, I have. But there's a new one out on On Demand I've been dying to see."

"I don't know where things are going to go with Wyatt. We've talked about marriage."

Claire clapped her hands like a little girl.

"Oh, calm yourself down now," Gia said, gently hitting Claire with a small decorative pillow. "It's not like he's proposed."

"But he will," Claire said. "And I can't wait to be the matron of honor!"

"Oh? You think you're a shoo-in for the role, huh?"

"Uh, of course. Duh," Claire said.

"Okay, Ms. Cocky. Turn on the movie. I'm in need of some mindless romance."

CHAPTER
THIRTY-SEVEN

"Are you crying?" Claire said, peeking over at Gia, who was lying on the bed next to her.

"No."

"You are *too* crying!"

"So what if I am?" Gia said defensively. "It's a sad movie!"

Claire shifted her weight in the bed. She was getting stiff. "Yikes!"

"What?" Gia said, sitting up so quickly she knocked her popcorn bowl on the floor.

"Oh, nothing. Sorry. Didn't mean to frighten you. Maggie just gave me quite the kick."

"Maggie?" Gia said, reaching down to pick up her bowl and the few bits of popcorn that had spilled out onto the floor.

"Yeah. Do you like it?"

"Love it. Sounds very Irish," Gia said.

"Callum insisted on an Irish name, but I was the one who chose Maggie."

"Maggie doesn't know it yet, but she's going to be the most loved baby ever born."

"That she is," Claire said, rubbing her belly and glancing at the clock on the table next to her. "It's getting late. I wonder where Callum is."

Claire sat up in bed and slowly lowered her feet onto the floor.

"Whoah! Where are you going?" Gia asked, sounding alarmed.

"To the bathroom. I have to pee. Unless, of course, you want to stick a bedpan under my butt."

"Well, not exactly."

"That's what I thought. It's only five feet away. I'm allowed to get up to use it every once in a while as long as I don't stand too long. I'll be fast."

She stood up, gingerly, and stretched her arms and legs as soon as she was in an upright position.

"You have no idea how good it feels to get out of that bed."

As she headed into the bathroom, Gia picked up the remote and flipped through the channels.

"Hey!" she called out to Claire. "You'll never guess what's on! *The Bridges of Madison County*. Remember how we watched that movie over and over again in college? Clint Eastwood is still so sexy."

The bathroom door opened and Claire stood in the doorframe. Gia's eyes remained on the screen.

"Oh, I love this scene," she said. "You know, where they slow dance in the kitchen and she's wearing the new dress she bought."

"Gia."

Gia turned her head and noticed Claire standing there.

"My water broke," Claire said.

"You're kidding, right?" Gia asked. Seeing the ashen look on Claire's face, she knew the answer before Claire shook her head.

Gia jumped off the bed and rushed to Claire.

"And I'm bleeding," she said, both her voice and her body shaking.

Gia took her by the arm and led her to the bed. She helped Claire lie down, putting a pillow under her legs.

"Don't move," Gia ordered. "I'll call the doctor. Where is your damn phone?"

"Callum probably left it in the kitchen. Or on the couch? He was playing a game with it when his phone wasn't charged."

Gia could kill Callum at this moment. Sure, she had her own phone, but Claire's doctor's number wasn't in there.

"I'll be right back. Don't move. You hear me? Don't move!"

"I won't. And call Callum."

"I will. Don't move!" Gia called over her shoulder as she ran out of the room.

"I'm here, love. I'm here."

Claire turned her head to see Callum rolling into the operating room. He was wearing scrubs and, despite the situation, seeing him brought her some small relief. If she wasn't so scared, she would've made a comment about how they could save the outfit to play doctor and nurse one night at home.

"I didn't think you'd make it," she said, instead.

"Did you honestly think I'd miss Maggie's grand entrance into this world?"

"No."

"There was a lot of snow on the roads. I'm so sorry. I shouldn't have left you."

"It's okay. Gia took care of me," Claire said.

"Thank God for Gia."

Claire nodded. She'd said that to herself a million times over the past few years.

Gia had finally called an ambulance after reaching Claire's doctor and, upon looking out the window, realizing there was a near-blizzard going on out there. Gia could've driven them to the hospital in Claire's car, but considering the falling snow, and the fact she didn't know where she was going, it seemed better to dial 9-1-1.

As soon as Claire and Gia arrived at the hospital, Claire was rushed up to the O.R. Gia had called Callum and he'd reassured both of them he'd be there shortly and wouldn't miss a thing. Nonetheless, when the nurses asked Gia if she wanted to put on a pair of scrubs, just in case the father didn't arrive on time, she did so to ensure Claire wouldn't be alone during the delivery.

She stayed with Claire until Callum rolled into the O.R. Gia was sure she'd never before been so happy to see anyone as she was to see Callum at that moment.

"Okay," Dr. Lindberg said, from his place behind the curtain dividing Claire's neck and head from the lower half of her body. "You shouldn't feel any pain, but you will feel some pushing and then some tugging when I go to get her out."

Claire nodded. "Okay."

"Take a deep breath. It won't be long until she's here," the doctor said.

"Do you want to look?" Claire asked Callum.

"No thanks, love. I'm not so good with blood and all that. I'll just keep my eyes on you. We can see Maggie together."

Claire nodded again, as Callum squeezed her hand.

"Listen, Claire," Dr. Lindberg said, his voice suddenly very grave. "Once she's out, things are going to move very quickly. I'm going to cut her cord and hand her to the nurse and then I'll need to do some repair in here."

"What kind of repair?" Callum asked. The fear in his voice did nothing to calm the panic rising in Claire's chest.

"It's what we thought might happen. The placenta has grown outside the uterus."

The doctor stopped speaking as he continued to work on Claire. The room was very still. No one spoke, not Claire or Callum or any of the members of the medical team.

Claire held her breath. She'd been here before. In an operating room that looked just like this. With a sheet in front of her face. With a husband holding her hand. Only, this was a different O.R. in a different state with a different doctor—not the one who'd delivered her first three babies—and a different husband. But one who was as loving as Jack, and just as anxious and excited to become a dad as Jack had been.

Everything was the same, yet everything was also so different. She'd never before been so scared to give birth as she was now.

What if something happened to her baby? She couldn't bear it. She wouldn't be able to live if she lost another child. She hadn't told Callum this, but it would be the end of her if they lost Maggie.

Just then, a baby's scream broke through Claire's fear. Claire hadn't realized she'd been holding her breath until that moment, when she released it. The cry was pure and clear and the most beautiful sound Claire had ever heard.

"You have a daughter!" Dr. Lindberg announced. "And what a set of lungs on her!"

Claire couldn't see anything, but could sense the medical staff moving quickly from behind the curtain.

"Can I see her?" Claire asked.

Dr. Lindberg didn't say another word and Claire assumed he was busy "fixing" whatever it was he needed to fix. She wasn't too worried. The baby seemed to be fine and Claire had full confidence in her doctor. Now that Maggie was safe, she knew Dr. Lindberg would make sure she was, too.

"Sure, sweetie," a nurse said, reminding Claire of Gia and the term of endearment Gia often used when speaking to Claire. "Let us clean her up and weigh her and then we'll bring her to you."

"Seven pounds, four ounces," a nurse announced from one side of the room.

"I can kind of see her," Callum said, squeezing Claire's hand tighter. "She's really here."

A moment later, the nurse walked over to Callum and Claire, their baby girl in her arms.

"I can't hand her to you just yet," she said. "But you can see her. Look at how beautiful she is."

She held the baby close to Callum and Claire so they could gaze at their daughter's face.

"She has all her arms and legs, right?" Callum asked nervously. The thought she might not be born with all of her limbs had actually never occurred to Claire. For a moment, she felt ashamed. Of course it would have been something Callum would fear the entire pregnancy, no matter what the ultrasounds seemed to reveal. She couldn't believe he'd never mentioned his worries to her. But, of course, they'd both been worrying about so much already.

"Two arms, two legs, ten fingers, ten toes."

Their baby had all her parts.

"She's beautiful," Callum said, his voice full of relief. He couldn't take his eyes off his daughter. *His daughter.* He couldn't believe it. He and Claire had made a child, together. She was here and healthy. Claire was right. He'd worried all those months for nothing.

"Look at her eyes, Claire. She's looking at us like she already knows who we are. Isn't she just gorgeous, love?"

When Claire didn't respond, Callum turned toward his wife.

"Claire?" Callum's voice cracked. "Claire!"

Claire's eyes were closed and her face suddenly had a sickly gray pallor Callum had never seen before.

In less than a half a second, everything in the room began to spin and move at lightning speed.

"Mr. Fitzgerald, we need you to leave."

"But Claire..." He held tightly to her hand.

"Mr. Fitzgerald," a nurse said firmly. "I need you to move your chair and get out of the way. Please go wait outside the door."

"I can't leave her. Claire, love," Callum said, looking back at Claire's ashen face. "Wake up. Come on, love. Wake up."

"You need to go and let the doctor do his job." The nurse's voice was decisive and absolute.

Callum nodded and mechanically reached down for the knob on the arm of this chair. He put it in reverse and then forward again as he rolled out the door and into the hallway where Gia was waiting for him.

He wasn't sure how much she'd heard, but when Callum saw the fear in Gia's eyes, he knew she'd heard enough.

Gia was terrified.

He wanted to reassure her. He wanted to tell Gia about their beautiful daughter, Maggie, who was as lovely as Claire and as healthy as they could ever pray she'd be. He wanted to tell her how great Claire had done during the delivery.

But he could say none of those things. All he could think about was how the color had left Claire's face. How she'd been there with him one second and then the next, it was if she was gone.

Gia grabbed Callum's hand. Her palm was clammy with fear.

"Pray, Gia," he said. "Pray. Pray harder than you have ever prayed before."

And then he bowed his head and did just that.

CHAPTER
THIRTY-EIGHT

"Mornin', love," Callum said, as he stroked Claire's hair. She struggled to open her eyes and, once she did, had difficulty focusing on Callum.

"The baby?" Panic rose in Claire's voice.

"Beautiful. Just perfect. Has all her bits and pieces, just like her mam," Callum replied proudly.

"Good," Claire said as she remembered, a sigh of relief relaxing her chest. She closed her eyes again. "I'm so tired."

"I know. You've lost a lot of blood. You began to hemorrhage on the operating table. They said you broke the record for the number of units of blood used during one operation."

Callum smiled, but that definitely wasn't a reason to smile. He'd been terrified. Petrified. They'd almost lost her and they certainly weren't out of the woods yet.

The doctors had worked on Claire for close to two hours. Later, Dr. Lindberg told Callum it had been nearly impossible to stop the bleeding. Every time they thought they had it under control, the bleeding would begin again.

"We've done everything we can," the doctor had told Callum when Claire was in recovery. "All we can do now is hope and pray. She's lost an enormous amount of blood. And there's a chance she'll begin to hemorrhage again. We'll have to wait and see."

That hadn't been the response Callum wanted to hear when he'd asked Dr. Lindberg for an update. He'd wanted the doctor to say she was fine—she'd *be* fine.

No one truly knew if she would be fine, but Claire was here, now. And that's what mattered to Callum.

Claire slowly opened her eyes again and looked directly at Callum. "I need to tell you some things."

"Nothing that can't wait, love," Callum said, stroking her face.

"It can't."

"Claire, you need to rest..." Callum said, trying to hush her.

"I love you."

"I know you do," he replied. "You don't have to waste your strength telling me that. I love you, too."

"You need to promise me you'll take good care of Maggie."

"*We* will take good care of Maggie—together, love," Callum said softly.

"I know you don't think you can do this alone, but you can. You're going to be the best dad. Just don't give into her every whim." Claire smiled weakly at him. "You're not tough enough."

Tears filled Callum's eyes. He'd cried copious amounts of tears while she'd been in surgery and had promised himself he wouldn't cry in front of Claire, but he was failing miserably.

"I'm plenty tough!" he said, forcing a smile.

"You're a big softy," Claire countered, her voice so tiny that Callum had to lean in to hear it.

"Then *you* have to stick around to play bad cop, love!" Callum joked nervously.

If Claire heard Callum, she gave no indication of it.

"It's okay if you need to ask for help," she said. "It's hard to be a parent. I know. Gia will help you. I'm sure Alison and the team will, too. Maybe your parents can come stay for a while."

"You're talking nonsense," Callum said, desperately, continuing to stroke her hair, her face, her arms. "You'll be home in no time and *you* can take care of Maggie with me."

"Make sure you tell her every day how much I loved and wanted her," Claire said, with more strength than she'd had all day.

"You tell her," Callum replied, no longer holding back his tears.

"Promise you'll tell her," Claire said, her eyes steady on his.

Callum sighed. "I promise. I'll tell her."

"She's a part of you and me...the best part," Claire said. And then, in the strongest whisper he'd ever heard, as if she were conveying the most important revelation of her life, the only thing she ever wanted him to hear, she said, "She was *the plan*."

"What do you mean, love?" Callum leaned closer, not willing or able to absorb the meaning of what she was saying.

"You always tell people how God has a plan for their life. *Maggie* was the plan for ours." The soft gleam in Claire's eyes was unmistakable.

"*We* were the plan, Claire. You and me. *That* was God's plan." Callum no longer tried to hide the desperation in his voice.

"Now He has a new plan."

"Don't say that, love. In a few days, we'll all be going home together—you, me, our little girl." He reached for her hand and held it in his.

"Callum, do you know how amazing you are?" Claire asked. "I wish that, for one moment, you could see yourself the way I see you. Strong and beautiful."

"Claire..."

"You remember that," Claire said, every word demanding more of an effort for her. "When you're sad and lonely...when you feel overwhelmed...when you miss me... remember I knew every inch of you... of your heart...of your body...and I found them perfect."

Callum had to choke back a sob. The tears cascaded down his face and onto Claire's arm and chest.

"Claire, please don't say things like that. You're going to be fine. You're going to stay with me."

"Kiss me," Claire said, so quietly Callum had to lean in to hear her.

He bent down and kissed Claire on the lips. He stroked her face. She smiled with her eyes closed.

Callum sat up and, hearing a deep gasp from Claire, scanned her entire body. Bright red was slowly easing its way across the bleached-white sheet down near her legs—rolling along like water spilled across a kitchen counter.

Before Callum could register what was happening, he heard Claire gasp again.

"I see my kids. I see my babies!"

Callum screamed out for someone to come, for someone to help him. Her. Them.

He barely heard the commotion that began in the hallway behind him.

His sobs were loud and, for once, he didn't care if Claire heard them.

"Claire...I need you. Don't go. Please, don't go," he begged. He pleaded.

"I love you," Claire said, casting her eyes on him, but already they were missing their shine. "I'll be waiting for you."

And then she closed them one last time.

"Claire!" Callum screamed, grabbing tight to her hand, willing her to stay. "Claire!"

Callum would later remember nothing from that moment, as if it were just a blur, and yet somehow every single detail would be burned into his subconscious. The long dull sound of the heart monitor, screeching loudly in his ears. The doctors and nurses who rushed to Claire and pushed him out of the way. The way the screams echoed in his ears, knowing they were his and yet, causing him to wonder where they were coming from. The noise and the yelling and the commotion, all simultaneously in slow-motion and muffled. The way Gia was suddenly there and the two of them held on to each other more tightly than they'd ever held on to anyone before.

The movement of Claire being rushed to the operating room again. The silence that followed in the hallway, as they cried, and begged and prayed.

The way it was over so quickly. Much too quickly.

The noise. The praying. The begging.

Claire. Their life together.

All of it. Over.

In the literal last beat of one very selfless, loving—and loved—heart.

CHAPTER
THIRTY-NINE

"For years, I've spoken of how, though I never received the miracle I was looking for—specifically two legs and a spare arm—I knew there was still a purpose for my life."

Callum looked out to the crowd in front of him—a crowd of thousands—all in this auditorium to hear a message about hope. He prayed he was still capable of providing that.

"What I may not have mentioned, though, was that I did, in fact, receive a miracle." His voice was loud and clear. Firm and truthful. He spoke from his heart.

"No, it wasn't the one I'd spent my whole childhood praying for. As you can see, I'm still missing my limbs. But it was one that meant more to me than fingers or toes ever could.

"Her name was Claire."

The sound of Claire's name on his lips triggered the tears in his eyes. Even now, he couldn't say her name without feeling the familiar sting behind his eyelids. He wondered if that would ever go away. If the day would come, for him, too, when the thought of her brought a smile to his lips before it brought a tear to his eye.

"I've met millions of people in my years traveling the world," Callum continued. "I'm thankful to say most of them have been able to, eventually, move past my disability to see and get to know the real 'me'—not the me who's in this chair, but the me I am inside. With Claire, though, she was the first person I ever met who didn't see the disability first. She saw just *me*."

Callum smiled at the memory. A sweet one in the midst of great sadness.

"And, because I'm not a stupid man, I recognized the rarity of that and jumped at it—metaphorically speaking, of course."

The crowd laughed as Callum knew they would.

"I asked Claire to be my wife and, to my amazement, she agreed."

The crowd oohed and aahed. Callum knew many of them knew what was coming, but some of them would not.

"I've claimed, over the years, to understand what the deepest pain felt like, because I'd been born like this, different. I have to apologize, now, though, to many of you out there. I thought I knew excruciating pain. I spoke to you as if I understood your pain, but what I felt before was only a scratch. I didn't understand the depth of true pain."

Callum took a deep breath, forcing back the tears.

"Until I lost Claire."

He choked back the sob. Those words were still so new to him, so raw. Saying them aloud brought a whole new sense of emotion. He reached down to the table beneath him and lifted the glass of water Mitch had left there, to his lips.

After his sip, he gently placed the glass back down again.

"Because I would give anything—my one arm, my nose, my lips— all of it to have her here with me. For the chance to have one more day with her, I'd give everything I had left.

"I thought having limbs was so important until I lost my heart. And what I learned when I lost that was what matters most are the people in your life and how you love them. How you value every single second you get, never knowing if it might be your last."

Callum looked off to the side of the stage and nodded to Alison. She nodded and took her cue to walk toward him, carrying six-month- old Maggie in her arms.

The baby reached out for Callum when she saw him and Callum took her in his arm, as Alison walked off stage again.

"I would like to introduce you to Margaret Claire—my little Maggie. She's the best bits of me and her mam, all rolled into one."

This time the crowd oohed and ahhed louder and longer, and Callum smiled at their obvious delight in his little girl.

"And I'm happy to say, she has all of the parts!"

The crowd burst into spontaneous applause as Callum beamed.

"I will raise her, loving her and doting on her, just like Claire would've done." Callum adjusted Maggie against him as she wiggled. Even now, he was still getting used to holding on to a squirming baby when he had only one arm with which to do so. Taking care of her, with his limitations, was definitely proving to be a challenge, but it was one he relished and would never, ever give up. As Claire had reassured him, he had more than enough people around him—ones who loved him and Maggie and had loved Claire with all their hearts—willing to help.

"I've spent my whole life, years and years and years—because I'm getting up there, you know." Callum winked at the crowd as Maggie put her chubby little hands on Callum's face and began to explore every inch of it. He smiled at her and kissed her nose. "Telling people that there was a plan for their lives. I didn't just say it. I believed it. That is, until something went drastically wrong in my own life and I needed Claire to remind me that the plan we have for ourselves may not be the plan God has in store for us.

"I may not always like every component of the greater plan. Though I love Maggie, I would've much preferred it if Claire was here with us today. Just like I would've preferred if, perhaps, I could have an extra limb or two or three—but then, if I had a few extra limbs, I also wouldn't be able to do this for a living. See? Sometimes the parts of the plan we hate the most are the ones that are most essential."

Maggie began to twist her body, trying to break free, and Callum held on a bit tighter. He made a funny face at her and she smiled back at him, distracted for the moment.

"I can't say to you I understand the plan here. I can't say I understand why I lost my Claire. But, I do know I've reached a point in my life, thanks to Claire and my little girl, where I'm willing to do more than just say there's a greater plan for my life, but also truly trust there is. That's what I'm going to hold on to.

"And, I beg and beseech all of you, no matter what your struggles, you come alongside me, and you hold on to that truth, too."

As the crowd stood and began to applaud, Maggie picked up her chubby hands and began to clap along with them.

Callum laughed as he looked at the crowd and then back at Maggie.

She looked just like Claire. Beautiful. Innocent. Pure.

She was a miracle, just like her mam.

He would never forget that—no matter what dark days lay ahead.

Claire had begged him to love Maggie, to take care of her, to tell her, over and over again, how much she'd been loved by her mother.

He would do that, every day for the rest of his life. He'd never forget the gift Claire had given him and the sacrifice she'd made.

He'd make sure Maggie knew all about it and Claire and the love they'd shared.

He still wasn't sure how he was going to do it, raise Maggie all on his own. But he would. And, he'd continue to ask for help, just as Claire had told him to do. He wouldn't let his pride get in the way of making Claire proud.

He and Maggie would make it.

Together.

He knew nothing would make Claire happier.

And he wanted nothing more than to do just that.

EPILOGUE

Thirty-Five Years Later

"Hey, Sergeant Rodriguez. All ready for the big day?"

The man sitting on the treatment table was young. Too young, in Maggie's opinion, to be dealing with such weighty issues. But then, weren't all of the patients she worked with too young, even if they were in their sixties?

"Okay, then," Maggie said. "Why don't you stand and let's see how much weight you can put on that foot?"

The young man stood, gingerly, as if taking his very first step, which he was. His first step since the IED had detonated in front of his vehicle.

His first step on *this foot*.

He reached for the parallel bars in front of him, which were set at hip height, and held on as if gripping for dear life. His knuckles whitened.

"Relax, Sergeant Rodriguez," Maggie said easily. "It's going to be fine. I promise."

The man took a deep breath and hoisted himself from the table, all his weight on his left foot.

He was tall. Maggie had forgotten his records had said he was six feet three. He'd nearly always been in a sitting position when they'd spent time together.

"Great, now why don't you try to put some weight on the other foot?"

The man grimaced, but Maggie didn't think it was from pain as much as from fear. How would it feel? Would it hurt him? Would the foot hold? Would it feel like, well...*a foot?*

Only he could tell her. He and the others in her study.

The man, who in every aspect of his being was a soldier, leaned into his right foot.

"Here goes nothing," he said as he released his weight.

Maggie held her breath.

"How is it?" his young wife—really not more than a girl—asked eagerly. "How does it feel?"

Maggie wasn't sure what came first, the man's grin or his tears.

"It feels amazing," he said, nearly gasping. "It feels like *my foot.*"

The girl started to sob as she rushed to hug him. The man didn't let go of the bars, still uneasy in the standing position, but put his head down to hers as she cried.

Maggie turned to the doctor next to her and smiled.

"Are those tears in your eyes, Dr. Lewis?" Maggie asked.

"Nope. Are those tears in your eyes, Dr. Fitzgerald?" he asked her.

"Of course not," Maggie said. "I'm a professional."

"Me, too," Dr. Lewis said, nodding.

Maggie sometimes wondered if certain aspects of her chosen career would ever get old. Certainly the paperwork would. Definitely the bureaucracy. Without a doubt, the hoops she had to go through to raise enough funding would someday do her in.

But this part? She knew, with all her being, *this part* would never, ever get old.

It would be as fresh and exciting and exhilarating each and every time.

Because, each and every time, the person standing across from her would be experiencing their miracle for the very first time.

Maggie didn't hear the team of residents come up behind her until one of them spoke.

"Is that a new type of prosthetic?" a young doctor asked Maggie.

"No," Maggie said, watching Sergeant Rodriguez carefully. She'd need to examine him. They'd be spending most of the day together as she asked him a thousand questions and did a hundred more tests. She knew he wouldn't mind. Neither would his family, who were all—his parents, his brothers, his two little children—now running into the room.

This was the happiest day of their life, better than any wedding day.

And they all knew it.

"I'm sorry," she said, turning back to the resident. She'd gotten distracted by the scene of joy taking place right in front of her. "Sergeant Rodriguez came to us two years ago, having lost his right foot in combat."

"Were you able to reattach it?" another resident asked.

"No," Maggie said. "That limb was never recovered. And, even if it had been, I'm fairly certain it would've been too damaged to reattach."

"Then what did you do for him?" a third resident asked. Clearly, they were all confused.

"We enrolled Sergeant Rodriguez in a clinical study we've been conducting for the past six years."

She turned to look at the group, purposely making eye contact with each one of them. She was about to blow their minds.

"We helped him grow a new foot."

"What?!" The cry escaped from each resident's mouth at the same, precise moment with the exact high pitch.

Maggie chuckled, as did Dr. Lewis next to her. *The reactions from people?* That part would *definitely* never get old.

"Dr. Lewis is going to take all of you into a conference room and explain the entire study in great detail. But, to give you a quick understanding, so you can comprehend what you're seeing as you look at Sergeant Rodriguez, we discovered a human gene which is active early in a human's life, but remains silent in mature tissue. It can reprogram human non-reproductive cells, rewinding them back to an embryonic-like state. We realized, when this gene is reactivated, it can enhance the healing power, and grow new tissue."

"Dr. Fitzgerald keeps using the pronoun 'we,' but that is *not* accurate," Dr. Lewis interrupted.

"Yes. It *is* accurate," Maggie said.

"No, it's not," Dr. Lewis said. "On top of being a genius, she's obsessively modest. It's true we are all part of a team, but it is led by Dr. Fitzgerald and she is the genius behind our findings."

Maggie waved off her colleague and friend as if she were swatting away a fly.

"The point is," she said, smiling at Dr. Lewis. "This protein can boost the metabolism, fooling the body into thinking it's younger than it is, thus stimulating a complex cascade of chemical reactions. Those reactions generate energy."

"Energy that becomes *a foot?*" a stupefied resident stuttered.

"Well, it's a bit more complicated than the brief explanation I've just given you," Maggie said, smiling. "As I said, Dr. Lewis will explain it all in more detail. I hear he's got a fancy PowerPoint presentation and everything." She winked at her colleague, teasing him good-naturedly.

"How many people have re-grown limbs so far?" another resident asked.

Maggie looked at Dr. Lewis as the two of them counted in their heads.

"Six feet, nine hands, numerous individual fingers and toes, fourteen ears, eleven noses," Dr. Lewis said, looking at Maggie. "Did I miss anything?"

She shook her head. "Sounds good to me, or close enough. Now, some of those limbs were on the same person. We never work on more than one limb at a time, per person, in case the individual has an adverse reaction to something. But, once we see they had success with one foot, if they'd lost both, we would then begin working on the second limb."

"What about entire legs? Arms?"

"So far, we've only been able to regenerate smaller limbs, but we're working on the process of larger ones."

"How old were all of your participants?"

"That's a good question," Maggie said. "They've all been quite young. In their twenties or younger."

"Why is that?" a resident in the back piped up.

"Well, first of all, we had to start somewhere. Since we're rewinding the cells back to an embryonic-like state, it seemed most practical to begin at an age where the cells didn't have to travel back so far."

"Have you tried it on older amputees?"

"Not yet," Maggie said, her voice softer than before. "But we will."

She turned away from the group. The last couple of questions had hit a nerve, though of course, none of the young doctors would know that. *How could they?*

None of them knew the reason she'd set out on this path. The one person she'd hoped to help—to heal.

The years had gone by so quickly. Maggie was constantly praised, by colleagues and medical journals, alike, for her magnificent forward-thinking. She'd advanced medicine light-years in her own, so far short, life. And yet, none of it had come fast enough—not the knowledge, not the ideas, not the studies, not the results.

None of it had come in time to help her dad.

She loved her patients—all the participants she worked with. Each new limb was a blessing. Each one symbolized a new life, for the amputee and those he or she loved. But she'd wanted that blessing in her own life—in her dad's life.

Each time she saw a patient wrap his new fingers around his child's hand, she felt a pang of jealousy. Every time she saw an amputee stand on his own regenerated feet, she wished she could've given her dad that same gift.

She'd come to recognize, though, some things were not in the cards. He was too old. His missing limbs were longer than they could yet regenerate.

Someday they'd get there—science and Maggie. But they weren't there yet. And, Maggie wondered if Callum would still be alive to see it when they did.

"No dad has ever been prouder of his daughter than I am of you," Callum had told Maggie, thousands and thousands of times, as she grew up, but never more emphatically than when she'd brought him to their lab and shown him what the team—what *she*—had accomplished.

"He grew a new *hand?*" Callum had said, completely floored after meeting one of Maggie's very first patients. "An actual, real *hand?*"

Maggie had laughed, half wondering if her dad was about to fall out of his chair from shock.

"Yes, Papa, he grew a hand. With some help from us, of course."

"You mean, from *you*," Callum said. "*You* helped that man grow a brand-new hand."

"Yes, Papa." Maggie giggled. "I, your little Maggie Claire, helped that man grow a brand-new hand."

Callum had just shook his head in amazement. His eyes shone brightly with pride for his little girl and all she'd accomplished.

"But it's not enough," Maggie had said to him, when they were alone that night.

"What do you mean it's not enough?" Callum said in disbelief. "How could growing a whole new appendage possibly be *not enough?*"

Maggie hadn't said anything then. Just stared at where her dad's legs, had he been born with any, should've been.

"Oh, my Maggie girl. You wanted me to get some of those new limbs, too."

Maggie had nodded. If words escaped her, so would the tears.

"Come here," he said to her, calling her over to the couch where he sat. She cuddled up next to him as he wrapped his arm around her and pulled her close.

"I've never believed, for one second, the plan for my life included getting a new set of legs and one extra arm. Never."

"But," Maggie said. "Science has come so far. I've come so far."

"And you'll go further yet, love. Someday, they'll name an entire solar system after you, that's as far as you'll have come. But we both know, you won't get there while I'm still here."

"But, Papa."

"Maggie Claire, you have discovered how to help human beings— people like me, who've lost or been born without limbs—regrow them! What could there possibly be to cry about?"

"But I wanted you to grow them," Maggie said, knowing she sounded like a little girl not getting her way. "I wanted you to be the one to get the legs."

"It wasn't a part of the plan," Callum said.

"You and your *plan*," Maggie replied, in frustrated exasperation.

"Oh, no, my sweet girl. You're not about to roll your eyes at me. We are all a part of a much larger plan. You know that. We *both* know it."

Maggie nodded her head, but wouldn't look up at Callum.

"But, just because I won't be the one jumping around on my own legs, doesn't mean that I'm any less thrilled for the men and women who will someday be doing that for the very first time. And all because of you. *You*. To me, knowing you've helped all those people is so much better than you being able to help just me."

"If I could have only helped one person, it would've been you."

"I know, love," Callum said, holding her closer. "I know."

"You would have looked great in a new set of legs," Maggie said.

"You think? I'm not so sure. I don't think I would've known what to do with them. All those extra limbs? I think they would've gotten in the way."

Maggie laughed as Callum had kissed her. No one was ever more proud of their child than Callum was of her.

"I don't know how to thank you, Dr. Fitzgerald."

Maggie looked up quickly. She'd been so lost in her thoughts she'd nearly forgotten where she was.

"Oh, Sergeant Rodriguez. There's no need for thanks," Maggie said hurriedly.

"How can you say such a thing? Do you understand what you've done? How you've changed my life forever?"

"I think I do," Maggie said, smiling at him. "My dad is a congenital trilateral amputee. There's no telling what a break-through like this would have done for his life if it had happened when he was younger."

"I'm a scientist," one of the residents said, "and I don't tend to believe in miracles, but this...if this isn't one, I don't know what is."

"But isn't that what science is?" Maggie turned, posing the question. "One miracle after another?"

"And you're the miracle maker," Sergeant Rodriguez's wife said, as she held on to her husband.

"Oh, no," Maggie said, shaking her head. "I'm just a part of a much larger picture."

"Part of a bigger plan?" Sergeant Rodriguze asked with a knowing grin.

Maggie paused and looked at this tall young man in front of her, so full of hope and dreams. Dreams he'd now reach because of Maggie.

She smiled as she reached out to grasp his hand.

"Exactly," she said. And then, because she knew it was true, she said it again. "Part of a much bigger plan."

Callum knocked at the door. He was nervous. His palm was sweating. He wiped it on his pants' leg. He couldn't remember the last time he was this anxious and yet, also excited, all at once.

Gia opened the door and smiled at him, broadly.

"Ready for the big day?" she asked him.

He nodded, not trusting his voice. He felt like a teenaged boy, worrying it might crack.

Gia looked beautiful. Her hair was pulled back into a chignon. She wore a long, slate-gray, one-shoulder gown with applique along the neck. Covering her shoulders was a sheer, mid-length-sleeve bolero jacket.

She looked ever the role of mother-of-the bride.

Except, of course, she wasn't.

"Close your eyes, Papa," Maggie said, from behind Gia. "I want you to be surprised."

Callum did as he was told and sensed Gia stepping out of the way so he'd have a clear view of his little girl.

"Okay, you can open them!" Maggie said.

Callum had never seen a more beautiful woman in his life. Not even Claire, and he wasn't ashamed to say that. He knew Claire, as stunning as she was, would have taken such pride in knowing their daughter was even more striking. Callum had never thought that possible until he saw the beauty Maggie became as she grew.

She had the best parts of both of them. Callum's dark, curly hair, though she'd never let hers become the wild mess his often was. She'd always taken great care in her appearance, fixing and braiding her own hair at an early age, perhaps sensing her dad had difficulty doing it for her, not only because he was lacking an arm, but also because he was a man.

She was tall and thin, but curvy in all the right places. Callum had often wanted to hit the boys with his prosthetic leg when he'd seen the way they'd admired her. Didn't they know they were ogling his *baby?*

She'd inherited her mother's musical ability, too, though she much preferred playing the guitar with a group of friends to performing on the stage. She had both Callum's and Claire's love of travel and the world. But then, how could she not? Ever since she was a little baby, she'd visited all corners of the world with Callum and the team. She was raised on Wyatt's shoulders, in Alison's arms, and on Frank's lap as he let her bang along on the keyboard. They'd all loved her and raised her together.

Callum had hired a nanny to travel with them, too, so the team could get their work done. Polly had been a widow who'd retired and had loved the opportunity to have a second career, her first one being an elementary school teacher. It had been great fun to have Polly with them. She passed away a few years back and Maggie had mourned her as she did her own grandparents. Both Nora and Patrick had died when Maggie was in her late twenties. Losing them had been difficult on both Maggie and Callum. Maggie had spent many a summer and Christmas break in Ireland with her grandparents, sometimes with Callum and sometimes on her own. Callum's entire Irish clan had doted on Maggie and she'd lapped up all the attention like a puppy does his milk.

Maggie was smart. Wicked smart. Callum had realized that when she was able to read full books at the age of four, before even beginning kindergarten. He wasn't sure where her genius mind had come from. Neither he nor Claire had been dummies, but they were no prodigies, either. Their daughter, however, was.

She'd finished high school by the age of sixteen and college by the age of twenty. Maggie had breezed through medical school as if she was doing nothing more than taking a summer poetry class. Callum had almost felt sorry for all of her classmates who, certainly, must have hated her and the ease with which she ingested knowledge.

But, of course, no one could hate Maggie. She was as kind as she was smart. Her level of empathy astounded Callum. Though, how could she not be empathetic when she'd been raised by a man with only one limb? She'd grown up understanding what is inside a person is much more important than any outward appearance.

He'd hoped, from the moment she was born, she wouldn't be teased because of him. That, sadly, could not be avoided. Kids were mean. Always had been, always would be. Maggie had come home one day in first grade, in tears, running straight to her room. Callum had had to bang on her locked door for close to an hour before she'd open it for him. And, when she finally did, it'd taken him another hour to pry out of her what had happened.

A boy had made fun of Callum while the class was on the playground, saying mean and hurtful things. Maggie had taken them to heart. Not before she'd punched the boy in the mouth, though, knocking out one of his front teeth.

Thank heavens it hadn't been a permanent one!

Once the crying was over, Maggie had handed Callum the letter from the principal, saying he was required to show up in the office, with Maggie, the next morning.

He'd scolded Maggie, properly, and punished her at home, as was expected. And hand in hand they'd walked—well, he'd rolled—into the office where she took her school punishment with her chin raised high. She'd have to eat in the classroom, away from the other kids, for two weeks and write an apology letter to the boy and his parents.

Though Callum did not condone violence, he'd been secretly proud of Maggie. Not because she stood up for him, but because she'd stood up for herself.

Maggie never lost that feisty nature. She was fearless and stubborn, both traits she got from her mam. She knew what she wanted and would do anything to get it. She let nothing stand in her way. And, thus far, nothing had.

He hoped the man she was about to marry was ready for Hurricane Maggie. She'd certainly turned Callum's world upside down with her arrival, but looking back, even with all the struggles and challenges raising her had brought, he wouldn't have changed a thing.

Other than wishing Claire had been there to experience it, too.

Now, here Maggie stood before him, a bride. How could that be? Where had the years gone? It seemed just yesterday she was clapping with glee as the two of them sped around parking lots in his chair.

"Faster, Papa. Faster!"

She took his breath away. All little girl and grown woman rolled into one.

"How do I look?" she asked.

How did one answer such a question?

"You look like your mother," was all Callum could say. "And she'd be so very proud of you."

Maggie smiled that gentle smile, the one that reminded him of Claire and the one Maggie had always given him whenever he mentioned Claire's name.

"You didn't have to wear your legs," she said, eyeing him in his dark-blue linen suit.

"I never miss a chance to walk beside a beautiful woman."

Callum rarely used his legs these days, even less than he did in his youth. They'd become more uncomfortable over the years, though he'd gotten new ones whenever the other ones became worn. His body, now in its seventies, didn't adjust to changes the way it used to. He was much more comfortable in his chair. Yet, on special occasions—and there had never been any more special than this— he dusted the legs off and put them on again. He used a cane now when he walked. He was no longer quite as steady on his feet. But there was no way he was going to miss actually *walking* his daughter down the aisle.

"I'm going to go take my seat," Gia said. Callum had nearly forgotten she was still in the room. He only had eyes for his daughter.

He turned as Gia kissed him on the cheek and then did the same to Maggie.

"You look incredible," she said to her goddaughter.

"Thanks, Aunt Gia...for everything."

Gia nodded and turned before Maggie could notice the tears.

Gia had been a godsend all these years. Her pain over losing Claire had been as raw as Callum's, nearly ripping her apart. But the two of them had held tight to each other for support, and onto Maggie, whom they both loved fiercely.

Three years after Claire died, Gia and Wyatt married. Maggie had been their flower girl. Callum was sorry Claire had missed the special day. She would've been so excited for her best friend, seeing how happy she was, finally with a "real man," as Claire had called Wyatt. And not a "loser," as both Claire and Gia had referred to the other men Gia had dated.

Wyatt and Gia had gone on to have three children of their own. Two boys, Cole and Preston, and a girl they named Clarissa, a variation on Claire's name.

The three adults had raised all the kids as cousins and Maggie and Callum had always viewed them as family, spending most of their holidays, birthdays, and special events together—the ones that weren't spent in Ireland. Clarissa was the little sister Maggie never had and was serving as her maid-of-honor.

"Are you ready?" Callum asked Maggie.

"Not yet," she said. "I have something to show you first."

Claire went over to her laptop and inserted a flash drive into the USB port. Flash drives were a thing of the past, of course. Technology had progressed faster than Callum could keep up with it. However, when Claire was alive, flash drives were what one used to save documents and pictures and videos. Callum knew, if Maggie was holding one now, what she was about to show him had to do with Claire.

"This was in my wedding letter," Maggie said simply.

My wedding letter. Callum needed no more explanation than that.

Callum had thought Claire had spent all those hundred-plus days on bedrest doing nothing more than watching movies, reading and knitting. But he'd been wrong.

Unbeknownst to him, she'd been making preparations.

Claire never thought she'd die. Callum believed that with all his heart. It wasn't that she'd put on a brave face for him. She truly didn't think something was going to go wrong.

However, she'd also never thought she'd lose her whole family one December night.

So she was prepared. Just in case.

Callum had found the box about six months after Claire's death—and Maggie's birth. He'd been missing Claire terribly that day. Maggie had just cut her first tooth and the fact that Callum couldn't share that news with his wife had nearly broken his heart. He missed her so much. Missed her touch. Her voice. Her smell.

He went into her closet to try to find that smell. He'd pulled her dresses close to his face, trying to breathe her in. And that's when he saw it. A box, on the floor behind her clothes.

Callum was all it said.

He'd pulled it onto his lap and rolled back into their bedroom. He found the letter she'd written him. The sight of her perfect, flowy handwriting had nearly made him sob.

My Dearest Callum,

I don't expect you'll ever read this. I plan on destroying it once the baby and I are home from the hospital and we are finally alone as a family—the three of us.

But, just in case...

I have loved you with a love more fierce than a mama lion protecting her cub. You put me back together when I was nothing but pieces of grief. You fought for us when I was too cowardly to fight alongside you. You believed in me when I could no longer believe in myself.

If I'm no longer here, but Maggie is, I know—in the deepest part of my soul—you will raise her to be an amazing woman. She is blessed to have you as her father. As I was blessed to be your wife.

I'm not gone. I will never be gone. I'm in the smile of our daughter and her laughter and the way she looks up at you with complete trust. I'm in the music you hear and the cool breeze of the spring. I'll never truly leave you. And you will never leave me.

These letters are for Maggie. I plan to be there, in the flesh, for all her special days.

But, just in case...

You'll know what to do with them.

Until we're together again...

Claire

It had taken Callum the rest of the day, and most of that night, to stop crying. When he finally did, he took out the envelopes in the box and held them close.

Claire had left a letter for Maggie for each of her special days. One letter for every birthday until she turned eighteen. A letter for her fifth grade, eighth grade, high school and college graduations. And one more, just in case she went to graduate school. A letter for her first date. A letter to be opened when she got her period. A letter for when she started wearing makeup—with photos of how to apply it. A letter for her first broken heart. A letter for when Daddy seemed to be mean and not understanding. A letter for the first time she was bullied. A letter for the day she lost her first tooth.

There was a letter for everything of significance in Maggie's life. Claire hadn't missed a thing.

There was even a letter for the day Daddy someday remarried.

That letter had never been opened. And never would be.

Callum would never remarry. He knew it from the moment Claire had died. He knew it before then.

She was his whole world. The mate of his soul. There would be no other.

In her hand, Maggie was holding the letter Claire had written for her wedding day. Inside it had been the flash drive.

"Watch this," Maggie said, pushing "Play."

An image of a young Callum popped up on the screen. It was a video Callum hadn't seen in years. *Decades.* Definitely not since Claire had been gone.

It was the interview he'd done. The one where the reporter had asked his greatest dream. The one that had nearly cost him Claire.

Callum watched with tears in his eyes.

"Did you ever think, as a little boy in Ireland," the reporter asked. "You'd someday be in front of that many people?"

"Never."

"So, it was a big dream of yours?"

"No, it never even crossed my mind. I just wanted to survive the playground," Callum said.

"What, then, is your biggest dream in life?"

Callum watched as his young self paused before responding.

"Honestly, I sometimes dream of the day I'll walk my daughter down the aisle."

"So, having children is a possibility for you?" the reporter asked.

"Oh, absolutely." Out of the corner of his eye, the current Callum could see Maggie smiling. "At least, the doctors say they don't see any physical reason why I can't have them. I just need to find the right woman and get started making those babies."

"You'd like a lot of kids?" the reporter asked.

"I'd love a whole houseful. As many as God sees fit to give us. There's no greater blessing than a child."

Callum put his arm around Maggie and kissed her hair, as Maggie stopped the video, just the way he'd kissed her mother's a thousand times many years ago.

She picked up a small, folded sheet of ivory paper and held it up to Callum.

"This was in the envelope for you," she said.

He removed his arm from around Maggie and opened the paper.

Here's to making that dream come true.

It wasn't signed. Callum knew who had written it.

He tucked the note inside his jacket pocket and held out his elbow to his daughter.

"Shall we?" he asked.

The church was filled with a hundred people—all the ones they loved, some new friends, some dear, old ones. Alison and Mitch were seated on the bride's side, their children and grandchildren by their sides. Frank was there, too. He was getting up there in age and had problems seeing these days, but he was there. He'd married the widow he'd begun to date around the time of Claire's death. Between his children and hers, they'd been blessed with fourteen grandchildren. And one great-grandson.

Nancy and Bill had passed away many years ago, but not before becoming an integral part of Maggie's life. Maggie grew up knowing all about the brother and sisters she'd had who'd lived, and died, before her—Luke and Ella and Lily. She knew Nancy and Bill had been their grandparents and, because of a great love, they were hers in a way now, too.

Maggie and Callum walked down the aisle, very slowly, as that was the only way Callum could walk these days. His mind was suddenly flooded with precious memories. To the side of the altar, there was a small photo of Claire, but he didn't need a photo to remember her. The memories were as clear and vivid as the day she left them—the day she'd given him the greatest gift by making the ultimate sacrifice.

Along with the memories, Callum couldn't help but reminisce over the plan that had been laid out for his life. It hadn't always been the one he'd have wanted. Oftentimes, it'd had more valleys than mountains. But, in the end, it had come to a beautiful conclusion.

He'd been given the most amazing daughter a man could desire. She, in turn, was literally changing the world, giving hope and life and mobility to millions who, without her, would be left dealing with the greatest nightmare of their lives.

If there hadn't been Claire, there would never have been Maggie. If there hadn't been a Callum with nothing but one arm, there wouldn't have been a little girl, growing up in his care, seeing his struggles, traveling the world, understanding the needs of so many.

His little girl had taken the best, and worst, parts of him and Claire and turned them into something that shined.

He could have never seen that coming.

Never seen that part of the plan.

All he'd been able to do was trust.

As Callum and Maggie reached the end of the aisle, and he lifted Maggie's veil to kiss her cheek, Callum suddenly remembered the rest of that interview, the part that came later.

"And what about walking your daughter down the aisle would be so special?" the reporter had asked him.

"Well, walking her anywhere on my own two legs would be, in and of itself, a sort of miracle." Callum had laughed at that point. "A miracle, by the way, I expect to see possible in my lifetime. You mark my words. Someday, some genius doctor or scientist will come along and find a way for amputees to walk, again, on their own two feet, or drive a car with their own two hands.

"But, what will be so uniquely special about someday walking my own daughter down the aisle is that it will signify the completion of a journey. Sending my daughter into the world to learn what plan God has in store for her life. The plan he had before she was even conceived."

Callum placed Maggie's hand in her groom's outstretched one and stepped back to take his own seat. He was alone in his row. There was no mother-of-the bride by his side. But she was there. Claire had been right. She'd always been there. Today, she was in the smile of their beautiful bride, the sparkle in their little girl's eyes and in the hand he and Claire were, together, offering to one very lucky man.

As he gazed at the photo of his lovely wife, the end of the interview continued to play through his mind.

"It's the discovery of that plan that makes life worth living, you know?" he'd said to the reporter. "It may not always be an easy path, but the way I see it, it's the only one worth taking. They say the way to make God laugh is to tell him your plans. I'd choose God's plan, over mine, any day, no matter how difficult certain parts may be. Because, in the end, His plan is perfect. I know all things, even if you can't see it at the time, work together for the good."

Callum remembered the smile he'd given the reporter at that moment, just as he was smiling now.

And then he'd said, "It's that, not my wheelchair, which keeps me moving forward."

The End

ABOUT THE AUTHOR

Kelly Bennett Seiler is the best-selling author of *Shifting Time* (2015) and *The Plan*. A former high school English teacher and school counselor, Kelly has written articles for such websites as *The Daily Muse, eHow* and *Livestrong*. She's been featured by *Woman's Day* magazine, NPR and PBS and was on the cover of *Military Spouse* magazine. Kelly has edited numerous books, including a *New York Times* Best Seller. In addition to creating test questions for nationally standardized exams, she has scored over 200,000 standardized test essays. She received both her undergraduate and graduate degrees from Bucknell University in Pennsylvania, where she majored in English. A native of New Jersey, Kelly can be found on Facebook and Twitter and, in real life, Austin, TX, where she lives with her husband and three young children.

If you enjoyed "The Plan," please be sure to check out

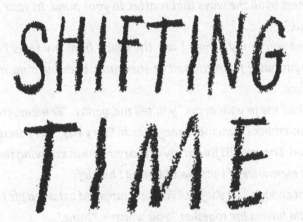

SHIFTING TIME

By Kelly Bennett Seiler
Available from Infinite Words

PROLOGUE

S ometimes, when the sun begins to peek over the horizon, the seagulls circle the water in search of their first meal of the day, and the tide rushes up and then slows down so as to tickle my toes, I can hear your voice. As I close my eyes and feel the salt breeze across my face, as gentle as one of your kisses, and bury my fingers deep in the sand, just the way I used to do into your thick, black curls, I feel you next to me.

"What are you doing?" you ask me.

"Missing you," I reply.

"But I'm right here," you say.

"You're not here for me to touch. You're not here for me to hold."

"I'm here in all the ways that matter. In your mind. In your heart. In your soul."

"I want you in my arms," I say, the saline from my tears becoming indistinguishable from the salt of the water, both burning my wind-blown face.

"You had me in your arms," you tell me, gently. "Remember?"

I do remember. I remember every touch. Every kiss. Every secret glance we shared. The ones I'd forced myself to remember, knowing that some-day, the memories of them would be all I had left.

"It's not enough." I cry softly. "We were supposed to have a life together."

"We did have a life together," you whisper. "Mine."

"It was too short."

"It was all I had to give you," you remind me gently.

"I wanted more," I say, the words barely passing my lips.

"So, did I, my love. So did I."

I lie back, my head resting on the soft, damp sand. I hear a foghorn in the distance and momentarily wonder if the captain of that boat has ever felt such pain. Did he plan a future with someone, only to realize his future would be spent alone? Did he wonder, as I do now, how things could go so wrong when, for a brief moment, they seemed so perfect?

"There's so much I want to talk to you about. So much I want to ask," I tell you.

"You can ask me one question. That's all. I can't answer any more," you say.

"Just one? What if that question leads to more?" I ask.

"Only one, so make it a good one," you say and then chuckle. "I know this is hard for you. You never were good at making decisions."

"I chose you," I tease. "I made a good one there."

"Touché," you say.

I hear you lie down next to me, feel the heat of your body on my side.

"One question," you remind me. "Are you ready?"

"Yes," I tell you. "I know what it is."

And, I do know. It's the one question I've held on the edge of my tongue for what seemed like forever. It wasn't if I'd been loved. I knew I had been. Completely and utterly. It wasn't "Why?" Some questions would never produce a satisfying answer, so there was no point in asking.

Delicately and carefully, I form the words. The ones I've wanted to say aloud, but never had the courage. The question I have craved an answer for and never thought I'd get.

I make my request, very softly, my question lingering in the air. I hear your deep sigh. Was it one of regret? Was it sadness?

This time, I say it more clearly. More certain than ever this is the one question I need answered.

"What if?" I ask again. "What if?"

"When a guy says, 'I'm pretty much single,' he really means, A. I'm completely single..."

Daniel moaned and rested his head back on his pillow. "You know I hate these quizzes."

"I know," Meade replied, holding the copy of *Cosmopolitan* in front of her face so he couldn't see her smile. "B. I'm not really interested in dating you."

"Then why do you keep giving them to me?" Daniel asked.

"They're fun." Meade giggled. "Or C. I have a girlfriend, but I think you're hot."

"C. I have a girlfriend, but I think you're hot," he instantly replied, picking up the TV remote and flicking on the set.

"C?" Meade asked, marking in his answer with a pencil. "Really? That's what a guy means?"

"Yep," Daniel answered, changing the channel. "Want to watch *Judge Judy?*"

"No, she scares me." Meade picked up her feet and rested them on the bed next to Daniel's knees, slumping deeper into her chair. "Why doesn't he just say that then? Isn't honesty the best policy?"

"Not if he wants to get in your pants," Daniel said matter-of-factly.

"Daniel!"

"What?" He asked, grinning, eyes still focused on the TV. "It's true."

Meade threw the magazine at his head as he dodged to miss it. It landed, with a loud thud, on the cold linoleum floor next to the bed.

"Ow!"

"Oh, come on," Meade said defensively. "It barely touched you!"

"No, not that. The way I moved. It hurt a little." Daniel grimaced as he shifted to get more comfortable in the bed.

Meade jumped up, suddenly concerned. "Where? How much? Should I get the nurse?"

"No, silly girl," he said, reaching for her arm and gently pulling her down next to him. "It's fine. It hurt for a second. I'm okay now."

He tugged on her sleeve. "Kiss me," he said softly.

"Again?" she moaned playfully. "Didn't I just kiss you about an hour ago?"

She giggled and leaned closer, gently touching her lips to his. They tasted slightly medicinal. She would, of course, never tell him that. She did her best to make sure, while she was with him, everything seemed normal—the way it had always been. It was why she had brought *Cosmo* and *Glamour* and *Teen* magazine with her to the hospital and grilled him with the questions he despised. It's what she'd always done—since they had first fallen in love. She'd sit at their lunch table, peppering him with the silly questions as he ate his lunch, and often much of hers, complaining as he answered.

"Is there room for me in the bed?" Meade breathed into his ear.

"I think I can find some in here," he whispered, seductively, scooting over. "If you promise not to take advantage of the many slits in my hospital gown."

"I ain't promisin' nothin'." Meade giggled. "Easy access is easy access."

She lay down in the crook of his arm, resting her head on his shoulder and her hand on his chest. She could feel the beat of his heart through the thin fabric of the gown. It felt so steady. So strong. *Keep beating*, she wanted to whisper. *Please keep beating*.

"Why are you in this gown, anyway?" she asked him. "I thought your mom brought you some of your regular pj's to wear instead."

"Yeah, she did," Daniel replied, touching his lips to her hair. "But I'm supposed to have some tests done this afternoon and I have to have a gown on for that."

"Well, I find it sexy."

"Yeah?" he asked, his eyes twinkling. "If I'd known that, I would have started wearing them years ago."

Meade laughed, even though she didn't think it was funny. She couldn't bear the thought of him in these gowns years ago. She could barely stomach the thought of him in them now.

She hadn't said anything to Daniel about his attire when she'd entered his hospital room that day after school. She'd never want him to feel self-conscious. But she'd been taken aback by the sight of him in it. Usually, when she showed up, he was in sweats and an old T-shirt, like he always was when she'd go to his house to hang out on the weekends. Somehow, seeing him dressed in regular clothes made it easier to pretend everything was okay. She could tune out the medical equipment and the hospital bed and the buzz of the nurses as they made their way up and down the hallway and into his room every twenty or so minutes. She could ignore the wires he often had on him and the tubes that were taped to various parts of his body. If she set her mind to it, she could even pretend they were just hanging out, after school, catching up on their homework, as she filled him in on the latest gossip she'd heard from all her girlfriends.

But the hospital gown—that had thrown her for a loop. She'd paused at the door before entering. Fortunately, he'd been deep in discussion with one of his nurses so he hadn't seen her arrive, and never saw the expression of shock she was sure must have been on her face.

He looked so frail. So thin. So...she hated to say the word...*sick*.

There was that word again. *Sick*. It was never far from her mind and it made her stomach do somersaults. As a child, she'd kind of liked the word. When she was eight, it meant staying home from school and watching TV in her mom's bed and drinking ginger ale while munching on saltines. But now, the word had a whole new connotation. It was scary and full of uncertainty and sadness. It meant watching Daniel be pricked and prodded while he did his best to keep a smile on his face for her sake. It meant no longer being able to make plans to go to a movie together because they never knew if Daniel would feel well enough to sit in the theater without running to the bathroom to throw up. It meant watching Daniel's olive skin turn a pale color she couldn't name because it had never been in any of her crayon boxes as a child.

"What are you thinking about?" Daniel asked her, running his fingers through her long, brown hair.

"What?" Meade said quickly, embarrassed to be caught daydreaming. She shouldn't let that happen. She needed to stay present when she was with Daniel. There was plenty of time to worry about the future when she lay in bed, alone, at night. She needed to focus on only him when they were together. Their time was precious. Not because she thought they wouldn't have much more of it. No, she wouldn't let herself go there. She *couldn't* let herself go there. Daniel spent his whole day waiting for her to get out of school and show up at his hospital room door. He deserved her undivided attention for the few hours she could give him each day.